PRAISE FOR DEATHLY WATERS

"With DEATHLY WATERS, Shoshana Edwards takes us deep into the darkness of American folklore while created genuine contemporary thrills. Absolutely terrific!"

> —Jonathan Maberry, NY *Times* bestselling author
> of INK and V-WARS.

A cozy dark fantasy, it's like The X-Files *meets the Hallmark Channel.*

> —Michelle Cori, Author of The Kind Mosaic &
> The Forgotten Ones series

DEATHLY WATERS

OCCULT AMERICA: HARPER'S LANDING

To Lee Ann

SHOSHANA EDWARDS

Shoshana Edwards

Prince
of
Cats

Literary
Productions

Trade Paperback ISBN: 978-1-952825-20-0
Ebook ISBN: 978-1-952825-21-7

Cover Art by Jake @ J Caleb Design copyright © 2021
Interior layout and design by Kind Composition

Prince of Cats Trade Paperback Edition 2021

Published by Shoshana Edwards in Association with
Prince of Cats Literary Productions
New Jersey, USA 2021

DEDICATION

*To Chris Brkich, who inspires me and keeps
me going when everything seems impossible.
To Rough Acres RL McGee, who kept
me on track throughout.
And most of all to my beloved Husbeast,
Rex Jemison, who keeps me fueled, watered,
and reminds me to sleep.
Thank you all. If there were a real Harper's Landing, I would want
to live there with all of you.*

CHAPTER ONE

G et a barrel of the water," they said. "We need water from our beloved Ukraine, for the new world. It will ensure good crops."

Yuri Harasemchuk was nineteen years old, powerfully muscled, and supremely unhappy. He loved Ukraine and Maria Molovna. Both were being taken away. And now he was tasked with this superstitious nonsense by his demanding and uneducated parents.

Yuri snorted. He had been to the great university in Moskva, where he learned modern agricultural practices. He had returned home, sullen and angry at being denied further education when the new government ruled that only Russian citizens could attend the state university. He soon found that his parents were resistant to all the things he had learned about crops and irrigation, certain that the old ways were the best. And now, they were leaving. Going to America because his parents had heard that anyone could lay claim to property if they got there first.

He didn't believe it. What he did believe was that they were going to lose their farm here to the ethnic Russians who now were at the top of the social and legal ladder, both in Russia and in Ukraine.

It was no use. Yuri had to go to America with them. Perhaps Maria's family would come, too. He hoped so. There was no arguing with his parents over the water. The barrel must be filled, sealed, and brought along. He stood at the small pond at the edge of their property. Yuri had come here rather than the large pond further down in the meadow that his parents used to water their crops and the animals. This small one was never used. He didn't know why, but today he didn't care. It would be harder to go down the slope and then back up again with a full barrel. They would never know where he got the water, and it didn't matter as far as he was concerned.

He lowered the barrel into the water, using ropes attached to the iron staves. Although it only held ten gallons, once filled it felt much heavier. He made sure the lid was on tight and hoisted it on his muscular back, slipping his arms into the ropes he had used to lower it into the pond. He slowly walked back to his waiting parents, trying to memorize every tree and shrub he knew he would never see again. It was summer, and the meadow was filled with sunflowers, blue bonnets, and clover.

Yuri arrived home to find a pile of steamer trunks and boxes waiting. He helped load everything onto the back of the wagon and glanced longingly at the only home he had ever known as he swung himself onto the packed wagon. He memorized the thatch roof rising to a center point, the small waterwheel attached to the barn, the rustic wood fence that enclosed their property. In his mind, he saw the new family that would occupy the house. Russians! Even though they looked exactly like his family, he hated them.

His father chucked at the horses, and they started the long trek to Odessa. Yuri was overjoyed to see that Maria's family had joined the procession of wagons headed for the docks. He would do his best to make sure they were on the same boat, bound for the same destination.

✳

The sailing was smooth, at first, as the ship glided slowly across the Black Sea, through the passage of the Dardanelles and Constantinople, and then across the Mediterranean Sea toward the Atlantic. It was summer; the spring storms were over, and the autumnal squalls would not arise until after they had reached their destination, or so the captain assured them. Maria's family was on the same ship, and Yuri and Maria spent many a happy day sitting on the edge of the deck, chatting, and planning their new lives. Yuri was less resentful, happy that the love of his life would be in America, too. He thought about proposing now but decided to wait until he had claimed some of that homestead land and spoken for her with her father. It was the old way, but it nevertheless appealed to him.

Neither Yuri nor Maria were plagued with the seasickness that struck most of the immigrants. Men, women, and children alike were either puking over the side of the ship or sleeping in their hammocks. A few of the children also remained unaffected, and it fell upon Yuri and Maria to keep an eye on them. No one wanted to have to stop and try to fish out a child gone overboard. Yuri solved the problem by telling the little ones stories of great sea monsters with glowing teeth and a taste for tender meat. Though Maria told him more than once he should not frighten them, secretly she approved since it kept them far away from the edges of the decks.

Late one night several weeks into the trip, and well into the Atlantic, a surprise squall came out of nowhere and tossed the ship about. This caused great distress among the seasick crowd since they had just become accustomed to the rocking motion of the boat, and now found themselves once again sick and wretched. This time, Maria felt queasy and was unable to manage moving about. Yuri stayed below deck, tending to both of their families, unconcerned about the young ones since it was night-time, and they would be asleep.

In the morning, Yuri and one of the sailors went to the hold to make sure everything in the ship's hold had stayed attached and secure. The suitcases, trunks, and bags were still firmly tied down. Yuri saw that the lid on his barrel had come loose. He found a hammer and refit the lid, pounding it firmly in place and testing it to make sure it was tight. A small black boot, which must have fallen out of one of the boxes or trunks, lay on the floor near the barrel. Yuri picked it up and stuffed it in his pocket. He would ask the others later whose child it belonged to. As he turned away, he thought he heard a sloshing noise. He touched the barrel and could swear he heard something like a grunt, or perhaps a crunch. He and the sailor with him heard pounding feet headed for the deck and cries of "Man Overboard." They ran up the stairs to the main deck.

Mikhail Sloven's parents stood on the deck, his mother screaming and his father looking frantically this way and that. When they awoke that morning, they discovered that Mikhail wasn't in his bunk. His red jacket, which he had removed before going to sleep, was missing. The parents were sure he must have wandered up on deck to look at the storm and been swept overboard. The passengers and crew searched the entire ship and found nothing. It seemed the boy had fallen overboard during the night.

His parents begged the captain to turn back and look for him, but after a while even they had to agree he could not have survived the stormy waters and finding him would be impossible. His mother took to her bed for the rest of the journey, refusing to eat or drink, and died of dehydration shortly before they reached the shores of America.

Her tiny body was placed in a hastily constructed coffin, made from food barrels that had been emptied during their long voyage. Mischka Sloven and Yuri carried it on deck, where a small service was conducted, and she was sent to rest in the sea where it was presumed Mikhail had also met his demise. During the ceremony, Yuri stuck his hands in his pockets and found the boot he had put there. Now wasn't the time to ask. Instead, after they were done, he went to the hold and placed the boot on top of a stack of trunks. Surely someone would claim it.

When they finally disembarked in New Orleans, they found a wainwright and Yuri's father purchased a wagon and team of horses for the journey north to Missouri. A young man at the local bank who spoke Ukrainian and English helped them complete the transaction. These Americans seemed obsessed with paperwork, requiring something called a *bill of sale*. They obligingly filled out the paperwork, but the wainwright was confused by the name Harasemchuk. After several failed attempts to pronounce it, he asked the interpreter, "What does the name mean in English?"

"Musician; or perhaps, Harper," replied the translator.

"Then Harper it will be," he said, and completed the bill of sale and handed over the wagon and team of horses. Yuri and his father drove the team back to the docks, where they hauled their goods and the barrel of water off the ship and onto the wagon.

Oleg, Yuri's father, called to his friend, Maksym, to come sit on the front seat of the wagon with him.

"It seems our children are fond of each other," said Yuri.

"Yes. Katerina and I noticed. It would be a good match. Don't you agree?"

"His mother and I both do. We like Maria, and Yuri will be a good husband and father someday."

They travelled north, alongside the Mississippi River. At farms along the way, Yuri purchased two pairs of young sheep, five brood hens and a rooster, and seeds for rye, using the money he had gotten from the sale of his farm in Ukraine. The countryside here was similar to the home they had left, with meadows in bloom, birch, hemlock, and oak trees. It was late summer, and Maksym and Katerina were able to purchase a large barrel of apples, along with apple seeds. Yuri's mother also purchased a small bag of cherry seeds. The women hoped to plant an orchard that would last for generations.

Yuri and Maria were married a year after the families arrived in Missouri and claimed their land. The wedding took place under a tree near the small pond that was part of the land his parents had claimed. Their parents built them a small, two-bedroom house on the hill above the pond. As part of the ceremony, Yuri and Oleg emptied the barrel of water they brought from their homeland into the pond. For a moment, Maria thought she heard an extra splash and a menacing chuckle as the old-world water mingled with the new. But she shrugged and wrote it off to marriage jitters.

A year later, Maria gave birth to their first child, Jennie.

CHAPTER TWO

Harper's Landing sat at the juncture of Deer Pass Highway and County Road 22. The Martin's Way River was on the west, and the Mississippi was about fifteen miles east. The town had once been a thriving mill town, but with the end of the Civil War and the abolition of slavery the Harrison Textile Mill was shuttered, its great looms gathering glistening cobwebs. The giant waterwheel that once powered the mill sat silent as the Martin's Way flowed around and through it. Several of the freed slaves and their families had remained in the area, taking up residence in the houses deserted when the owners and shop supervisors fled after manumission was granted to their laborers. Old man Harrison and his wife and seven children had packed up all their belongings, closed up their huge mansion, and moved to Chicago, where it was rumored he had invested his considerable fortune in an adventure called the Pullman Palace Car.

The *Harper's Landing Gazette* offices were on First Avenue across from the courthouse. At one time, the paper had flourished along with the town, publishing daily and featuring colored comics on Sundays. Now, it published once a week with an occasional special edition if something of note happened.

The sheriff's office occupied the entire ground floor of the

County Courthouse. It was a large open space with ancient black-and-white shots of the Harrison Textile Mill and its large water-wheel decorating pale green walls.

Jim Burch sat at his desk, not even pretending to look busy. Instead, he fixed his gaze on the window of the *Harper's Landing Gazette*. Linda, the publisher and editor, was no longer a young woman, but she was still easy on the eyes. Jim wondered, not for the first time, why she had never remarried after Joey died in that mill accident. He also wondered why he hadn't asked her out to dinner yet.

Jim was six feet two inches tall, strong as an ox, with a head of dark curly hair and steel blue eyes. While not exactly handsome, there was something in his bearing that naturally caught the eye of every woman who met him. Even Linda Collier, the current subject of his gaze, had cast a few flirtatious looks his way. He was in his mid-forties, settled, and sexy as hell. Jim was impervious to the come-ons, believing that he would remain a widower forever. He was content to do his job and leave well enough alone. Nevertheless, he did feel a bit of a pull where Linda was concerned.

Maybe I'll ask her to join me for a drink at Happy Time, he thought. *That should be safe enough. Be nice to have some female conversation for once.*

Jim wasn't a native of Harper's Landing. In fact, he might be the only sheriff they'd ever had who wasn't. He had been seeking the peace and quiet of a small town after being passed over for promotion again in the big city police department he had called home for nearly twenty years. He wasn't a politician or glad-hander. That, coupled with his penchant for speaking truth to power, had kept him at Detective Third Grade long after friends, partners, and even trainees had gone on to lieutenant and captain. The Chief was only too happy to grant his request for early retire-ment, and had even suggested to the Police Commissioner, who was equally happy to say yes, that Burch be retired at full pay although he wouldn't qualify for it by the rules for another year and a half.

"Let's call it an early disability retirement," said Chief Halsey. "That way you get your full retirement pay and medical until you hit sixty-five and can get Medicare. If anyone inquires, we'll say severe depression as a result of the loss of your wife."

Jim shook hands on the deal, signed the necessary paperwork, and put his house up for sale. It was a Craftsman, built at the turn of the century with all the features typical of that style. Jim had spent hours restoring the floors, ceiling beams, and woodwork. The original leaded glass had been encased in double panes for insulation. It would undoubtedly sell quickly and at a good price.

Beth, his wife of twenty years, had died two years earlier after a short battle with pancreatic cancer. They had no children, and his only sibling, Sylvia, lived in Malaysia, where she worked with an international refugee organization providing legal assistance to those wanting to seek asylum in the US. Jim considered it gut-wrenching work, but she seemed to thrive under the challenge. Her husband was equally happy working for Doctors Without Borders. They, too, had no children.

He called Sylvia late one night, shortly after retiring, knowing that it was early morning there, and told her of his decision. They chatted briefly about what she and Brandon were doing—apparently, there was no shortage of need for doctors at the refugee camps—and about his own plans. He had none—except to leave the city and move somewhere quieter.

"Are you sure you will be happy in a small town? You've lived in the city for so long." Doubt tinged Sylvia's voice.

"I'm long past loving the city," he replied. "Perhaps after I've gotten my fill of fishing and local diner conversation I'll move on, perhaps not. But for now, I'm ready for a simpler life."

The house sold the day of the open house. Jim accepted the first offer since it was fair and the couple who made it seemed to have genuinely fallen in love with the place. Their three-year-old daughter immediately claimed for herself the room Jim and Beth had intended to use as a nursery. After touring the rest of the house, her parents found her sitting on the window bench, entranced with the view of the backyard. Escrow closed swiftly. Jim put everything in storage except his clothing, personal items, and the box of books he hadn't yet read. He packed up his Explorer, handed the house keys to the new owners after the interminable document signing was done, and headed south on I-35 toward Missouri.

That was three years ago.

Jim arrived in Harper's Landing quite by accident and liked it immediately. He had intended to head straight down I-35 to New Orleans before searching for his new home. But the sign announcing Deer Pass Highway had intrigued him, and he pulled off the freeway and went exploring. The downtown was neat and clean, and although there were several empty storefronts, nothing seemed neglected or shabby. It was as if the town had suffered some middling calamity and was now holding its breath, waiting to come alive again. He pulled to a stop in front of Morey's Diner.

Best Hamburgers in Missouri! The sign was inviting, as were the bright blue awnings and the large windows facing the street. Through his dusty car window, Jim could make out red checkered tablecloths, and suddenly his stomach growled massively.

He entered the diner and looked for a place to sit. A tall, lean man with a head of snow-white hair and an equally white beard motioned to Jim to join him at his booth. His skin was sun-dried and brown as shoe leather. His eyes were a striking shade of blue, and Jim immediately recognized *cop* although the man wore no uniform. He approached the man, stuck out his hand, and grinned.

"You must be the chief of police here," he said.

"Nope. Sheriff. No money left for local police, so the county pays me to sit and glare at folks. And you have the look, too. Care to sit? I'm gonna be here a spell."

Jim gratefully lowered his large frame onto the well-padded

booth bench. The Explorer was great for backroad travel, but it wasn't designed for comfort, especially on a long trip. Before he could reach for a menu, someone sat a cup of coffee and a tall glass of ice water in front of him. The waitress was tiny, muscular, and exuded an earthy sensuality she wore as naturally as her long auburn hair. The ring on her left hand gave him a momentary twinge of envy. His Beth had this same earthy appeal, and he knew that whoever this woman was married to was among the lucky ones.

"What can I get for you?" she asked.

"I know I'll want more, but for now can I have some apple pie?" Jim asked, surprising himself. He hardly ever ate sweets, yet he suddenly felt an intense craving for apple pie.

"And with a wedge of cheddar if you have it," he said, again feeling a strange compulsion for something he never ate. He knew people ate apple pie with cheddar, but he had never tried it.

"Happens every time," the sheriff chuckled as the waitress left to get his order.

"What does?"

"Jen decides what will be best for you, and you find yourself ordering it. Dunno how she does it, but I guarantee you will love that pie."

Jim took a bite and nearly choked. It was pure ambrosia. The apples were soft with just a bit of crunch; the crust was flaky yet moist. And the sharp cheddar cut right through the sweetness. He let the forkful lay on his tongue, savoring the myriad flavors, until he realized that he was about to start drooling. He quickly swallowed and looked up to see the laughter in his dining partner's eyes.

"John Hartley," said the long, lanky man. "Sheriff Hartley to some; John to most. Been in Harper's Landing since I was born, sheriff for the last fifteen years. Reckon I'll die here, too."

"Jim Burch. Former detective third grade from a big city I'd rather not remember."

"You planning to be here long?"

"I don't have any plans. But this town feels right for some reason. Like I'm supposed to stop here. I suppose I might stay for a while. Is there something like a boarding house? I hate hotels."

"Not a boarding house. But let me call over to Mary and Bull Harper. They have a spare room in their house, and they're good people."

"But you don't even know me," protested Jim.

"Not really. But I know you're a fellow cop and that's good enough for me."

"How do you know I wasn't kicked out for something horrible, like police brutality?" asked Jim.

"Folks who do such things aren't likely to confess to it," said the sheriff. "And this town has a way of bringing folks to it that it needs."

Jim's eyebrows climbed toward his hairline.

John laughed heartily, and pulled out his cell, punching in a number. After a brief conversation, during which Jim ordered a cheeseburger, fries, and a strawberry shake, John hung up and said, "Gotcha a room for as long as you want it."

Jim's head swam a bit. He had known the minute he drove into Harper's Landing that he wanted to stay, at least for a while. But things seemed to be happening that were out of his control, and Big Jim Burch liked to be in control. He liked John Hartley the moment he sat down, and he wasn't one to warm up to people quickly. And then there was the puzzle of Jen, the waitress. How had she known that pie was just what he needed? And that burger! It was cooked just the way he liked it, with a nice thick slice of sweet red onion, sharp cheddar, a bit of catsup, and a bun slathered in mayo. The fries were his favorite, thick cut and double-fried. This was notable only because one table over he saw a family happily downing a large plate of the standard thin, single-cooked fries, salted within an inch of their lives. His were lightly salted with a hint of paprika, the way Beth used to do it. He glanced over at the waitress, and she grinned and gave him a large wink.

A tiny bald man came out of the kitchen, waving a towel to fan himself, and looking around to make sure there were no other customers waiting to be fed. He turned the sign on the door to *Closed* and set the clock face beneath it to read *Will open again at* 6:00 PM *for dinner*. John yelled, "Morey, come over here and meet your newest regular."

Jim raised an eyebrow.

"Trust me, you will love Mary Harper, and Bull, her husband, is a great guy. But you really do want to eat here. And Morey's got a meal plan thing that makes it as cheap as cooking for yourself."

Morey sat next to Jim, breathing more slowly now, and in almost one swallow downed the glass of ice water Jen set in front of him.

"John's right," said Jen. "Mom couldn't cook her way out of a grocery sack with the bottom ripped out."

"If you're staying at Mary and Bull's," continued Morey, "you'll be wanting the three-a-day plan. That's seventy-five dollars a week, seven days, three meals. We aren't open on Sunday, so people pick up their Sunday meals at the Saturday night buffet and heat them at home on Sunday."

Without hesitation Jim said, "Sign me up."

CHAPTER THREE

Three days later, John Hartley died of a massive heart attack. The coroner's report showed he had three severely clogged arteries and a massive chunk of plaque had broken loose and blocked blood flow to his heart. Death came instantly and without warning.

The funeral was held on Saturday, and the whole town was in attendance. John was loved by just about everyone, except Gary Miller and his gang of ne'er-do-wells. But even those boys attended and behaved with proper solemnity throughout the service. Jim stood at the back, wondering at the strange melancholy he felt for a man he barely knew.

Harper's Landing was hardly a hotbed of crime or incivility. But the position of sheriff could not remain vacant for long, not the least reason being there was only one deputy. Jim sat on the back "patio" of Morey's, which was a flat area of ground with a little garden surrounding it. Jen and Maggie, Morey's wife, had set up all the folding tables and chairs they could find, and "Morey's Regulars"—Jim had no idea how he had become one of them so quickly—were sitting quietly, drinking beer or sweet tea, gobbling up Maggie's giant chocolate chip cookies, and reminiscing about John.

"Remember that strange night at the fireworks show?" asked Harve Sanders. "Now that was never settled, was it? John never said, one way or the other."

"You mean the pond that appeared over by Jenkins Farm?" Bull Harper took a long pull at his beer and eyed Harve.

"Yup. That thing must have been at least thirty feet wide and ten feet deep."

"Came right up out of the ground after the grand finale of the fireworks show," said Linda Collier. "I wonder if all that ground shaking had anything to do with it?"

"I think it's more likely someone was doing something up at the mill," replied Bull. "Remember, it was around that time that they closed operations after the failed start-up."

"Wasn't that the same time that Will Jenkins lost his prized bull?" asked Linda.

"Yup. He was certain Horatio had run off because of all the noise," replied Bull Harper, chuckling. "More likely someone took advantage of everyone being away from home and hauled him off. That was one damn fine animal. As for the mill having anything to do with that flood, it's more likely the shaking from the explosions jarred something loose in the underground waterways."

"I don't think it was the fireworks that caused it," said Jen quietly.

They all stared at her. She looked down, twisting her fingers, and then looked up at all of them, rather defiantly.

"I know you all think I'm a bit touched. But John and I went over to check out that pond, seeing as how we were watching the show together."

She blushed a bit, causing several members of the group to wonder if there had been more than friendship between the two. Her eyes were quite red from crying over John's death.

"We arrived after the fireworks had ended. The pond was growing smaller, but we both saw a strange *something* in the ground where the water was coming from. It might have been an animal, or a trick of the eyes in the dim light. But the water was swirling."

Jim sat in the back, listening intently, convinced by the sincerity of her tone, and persuaded that there had been much more to her and the sheriff's relationship than anyone in the town knew. He resolved to ask her later to show him where the pond had been, and then wondered why it seemed so important. He was just passing through, wasn't he? He stretched and got up to walk around a bit, admiring Maggie's thriving garden. He had only been here three days, but already he was considered a regular at the local diner, and had seen a small, tidy house for sale that he liked.

Something else was niggling at the back of his mind.

They needed a lawman. That was it! And at his core, Jim Burch was a lawman. He sensed that the need for political wrangling and butt kissing would not be required here, that he might find his niche in this delightful town, and that being sheriff of the county would mean there would be more to the job than catching stray dogs or teenagers playing hooky. It also meant that there would not be a lot of stress, since John had intimated as much before his untimely death. He admitted he rarely even carried his gun, leaving it locked in a cabinet in his office. Jim could never bring himself to be that casual, but that was the big city still in him.

Suddenly he wanted the job more than anything.

"I'd like to be your new sheriff," he blurted out, much to his own astonishment. "I was a detective up north, in the city. I know law enforcement, and I've got good references. I want to stay, and I want to be your sheriff."

To his surprise, his announcement was met with cheers and applause.

"Tell you what," said Morey. "Guess you didn't know that I'm also the mayor of this burg, for whatever that means. Haven't had a town meeting since forever. But you and I will go talk to Judge Cramer at the County Building Monday, after breakfast. If he says yes, well, you got the job. Pays twenty-five hundred dollars a month plus a fifteen hundred a year stipend for uniforms and travel. Everything else like gas, office supplies, and ammo is paid for by budget requisitions to Mary here. She's our county auditor. Come November, you'll have to run for election, like all the other county officials, but if the judge agrees, you can have the job as acting sheriff."

The judge said yes.

CHAPTER FOUR

Three years later, Jim sat in his office, pretending to go through papers and otherwise look busy. He was about to return his attention to Linda Collier, who had come outside and was watering the planter in front of the newspaper office, when he heard moans, groans, and retching from the back room, signaling the return to consciousness of his smelly and unhappy guest.

"Ben," he yelled, "don't you be puking on my floor, now, you hear? You got a bucket in there for that."

He heard the bucket scraping across the floor and settled back into his chair.

A car full of teenagers drove slowly past, daring him to come out and say something. Harper's Landing School was over on Second Street. The grade school was next to the high school, and the students shared recreation areas and ball fields. Occasionally, Jim had to go over there and remind some of the older kids that the little ones weren't their personal punching bags.

He peered closely at the car. It was that Miller kid and his cronies, always skipping school. He wondered if they had any inkling of what kind of life awaited them without a high school diploma. Sometimes he thought he should arrest them and put them into a cell with Ben. But he was too fond of Ben, loser that he was, to do that to him.

His thoughts turned to Ben Jenkins.

Loser isn't exactly fair, he thought.

He remembered the night a year ago when he had picked up Ben, crying and puking, out near the farm that still bore his name. The farmhouse was on fire, and though Jim called the volunteer FD immediately, there was nothing they could do to save it. Ben was shaking with fear and cold and would only say that he had run from the pump house to the farmhouse, where he accidentally knocked over an oil lantern he was using to save on electricity.

Jim sighed deeply and got up to make a pot of strong black coffee. Ben was going to need lots of it, as well as some food.

Me too, he thought.

Food and coffee sound rather good right now.

Once he got the pot going, he left, not bothering to lock the front door, and headed for Morey's Diner to get takeout.

Morey's was usually empty this time of day. Today, it was buzzing with townspeople gossiping over pie and coffee as Jen hurried about trying to keep up with the unexpected flow of orders. Morey was sweating over the grill, out of sorts at having so many customers at an unfamiliar time. He waved a spatula at Jim as he entered, and Jen muttered a quick greeting as she hurried by.

Jim chose an empty seat at the large communal table and ordered a double of his usual breakfast: two breakfast burritos, mild hot sauce, two cinnamon rolls, and an extra side of bacon. To go. He leaned back in his chair, sipping gingerly at the strong, hot, bitter coffee, and listened to the gossip.

The gossip, it turned out, was about a man named Grossman, who had purchased the mill and its surrounding property and was preparing to restore it as an historical site. Harper's Landing was already a summer tourist destination because of the great bass fishing on the Martin's Way River. Additionally, Mary Harper's national reputation as a master quilter brought many fellow quilters to her workshops and to browse her shop. Having a working museum would bring even more visitors who would bring money with them.

"Jim," said one of the regulars, "you gotta talk Ben into selling the rest of his land. They need a better road to the mill if this project's going to be successful, and the only good place for a road runs right through his property."

"I'm not going to talk Ben into anything. He lost his brother Will last month; give him time," replied Jim.

The bell over the diner door jingled, and in stumbled the subject of everyone's conversation.

"Jim," yelled Ben, "you gotta come back to your office. Mary Harper is there, and it's bad. Worse than you know, even worse than she thinks."

Silence fell over the diner. It was obvious Ben was completely sober now, and terrified. Everyone was ready to rush to the sheriff's office at once. Jim rose.

"You all stay here. You'll know what's going on soon. Let's not upset Mary, or Ben, for that matter, any more. And for heaven's sake, stop gossiping. You'll know soon enough what Ben will do with the property and if there's going to be a mill again."

He wrapped a long arm around Ben and gently steered him down the steps and back around toward his office. Jen, the waitress, ran after carrying a bag with their forgotten breakfast and pressed it into Jim's hand.

"Don't forget to eat. He needs it, even if you don't."

The door shut behind her, but she stood in the window watching their slow progress down the street, a worried frown creasing her brow. After a few moments, the conversation again picked up regarding Ben's competence, this time tinged with concern about what had got him so riled up.

Jim made sure Ben was settled into a chair at the side of the office, and carefully put his breakfast and a cup of strong black coffee on the table in front of him. Throughout this process Mary Harper sat on the straight chair by the door, clutching her purse, alternately glaring at him and wiping her eyes. Eventually, having settled into his own desk and placed his breakfast before him, Jim turned his attention on her.

"Mary, you look upset. Now take it easy and tell me what's going on. Would you like a cup of coffee or some water?"

Mary shook her head.

"Go ahead and eat your breakfast, Jim. I can talk while you chew."

Jim picked up a burrito and took a huge bite. The food hit him like a warm sauna on aching muscles. He hadn't realized how hungry he was. He tried to focus on the terrified woman before him.

Mary O'Connor Harper was forty-two, tiny but determined, and an internationally acclaimed quilter. She owned Quilt Heaven, where she held classes and sold quality quilting fabric and supplies. Her classes for kids and adults were always full. During the summer, she would hold quilters' retreats at The Rectory, a bed and breakfast owned and operated by the town preacher. She was married to Bull Harper, formerly the mill foreman and now the town carpenter and handyman.

Mary had raised her kid brother, Rory, after their parents were killed in a car accident out on Miller Road one winter. Everyone in Harper's Landing knew how strong the bond was between brother and sister. When Rory returned from Iraq, wounded in both body and spirit, Mary and Bull had taken him in and nursed him back to good health. But Rory never again worked. Even the slightest noise could send him, trembling, to a corner. The shrapnel in his leg bothered him whenever the weather changed. Mary and Bull built him an apartment over the garage. He made do with his VA pension and medical care from the new VA clinic and hospital over in Wilton. Sometimes he would go to Mary's shop and run the big longarm quilting machine. He had a real talent for quilting the creations of her students, and he loved the quiet hum of the stitching and the soothing back and forth motion of the process.

Rory bought himself an older car and would regularly go

fishing for crappie and bass at Big Bass Pool where the Martin's Way curved and formed a deep pool. Sometimes in the early fall, he would find wild blackberries and bring home buckets of them for Mary to make into jams and pies. Occasionally, he would attempt to borrow Bull's rifle for deer hunting, but he would invariably start to tremble and shake and have to put the long gun back. He contented himself with the occasional rabbit trap and the berry foraging, as well as his success as a fisherman, as his contribution to the family larder.

And now, according to Mary, he had disappeared.

"Harve Sanders called him up yesterday morning," she said. "Asked if he would drive out to the old pump house on the Jenkins farm in Harve's landscape truck to pick up some fertilizer bags. Haven't heard from him since."

She drew a shaky breath and made a feeble attempt to sit up taller.

"Has anyone been out to the farm?" asked Jim.

"Harve went out there this morning. The truck was there, all loaded up with the fertilizer bags, just waiting to be brought back to town."

"What's got you so spooked, Mary?" asked Jim.

She was trembling and near tears, not a normal reaction for this practical, tough woman.

"He saw scuff marks, Jim. Harve said he saw scuff marks when he opened the pump house doors."

"Scuff marks?"

"Harve said he saw marks, like heels of boots would make if someone was being dragged across the ground. Not long, two to three feet, going toward the center where the pump used to be. The opening to the pump is covered up now, or it's supposed to be."

Her voice raised and the words came faster. Jim got up, put a hand on her shoulder and squeezed.

"You just sit here for a moment," he said gently.

He walked back to his private office, dialed the phone, and waited.

"Yup," grumbled Bull's deep voice.

"This is Jim Burch. You'd better come to my office. Mary's here, and something's got her in a state."

"Be right there, Jim."

Jim turned to the cabinet behind him and poured a small amount of bourbon into a clean glass. He topped it off with water from the cooler and carried the drink back to his office.

"Here," he said, in his best sheriff voice. "Drink this. You'll feel better."

Mary grabbed the glass and tossed back the whole thing. She was seized with a small choking fit, but then sat back and said, "Can I have another, please?"

Jim went to his office and returned with a somewhat stiffer version of the first glass.

Mary sipped at it cautiously, and slowly began to relax. As she did, the tears began to roll down her cheeks. Jim handed her a box of tissues and waited for her to gather herself and for Bull to arrive.

Bull Harper lived up to his name. He was short, wide, muscular, and stubborn as a mule. What he lacked in stature he made up in swagger, and no one in their right mind would have ever allowed him in a china shop. After the mill closed a few years ago, he had contented himself with handyman jobs around town. He had loved his mill job. He liked people well enough, but in small doses. He had been a great supervisor at the Harper's Landing Textile Mill because he knew how to stay out of other people's business unless it was necessary to intervene. He was excited at the news that this Grossman fella was planning to reopen the mill.

Bull was known for his steadfast loyalty as a friend and his fanatical devotion to Mary. He quite literally worshipped the ground she walked on and defended her with every fiber of his being. The door banged open with a force that would have jolted a lesser building as he stormed into the sheriff's office.

"Jim, where is she?" he yelled, sweat beading on his red face. He had obviously run much of the way from the only available parking behind the building.

"Calm down, Bull. She's right here with me and Ben, having a drink. You want one too?"

"Sure. What the hell, gotta be past noon somewhere."

Bull plopped into the chair next to Mary and took her tiny hand in his. His frown of concern turned into a slight smile when he saw that she seemed calm. However, the moment she felt his hand she burst into tears and leaned into his arms, sobbing and shaking.

Jim returned with a drink for Bull, which he sat carefully on a nearby table, and waited patiently for the two of them to get composed. He leaned back and regarded his three guests with curiosity. Ben was still utterly and completely sober and seemed terrified. Mary was gathering her calm. And Bull was moving from concerned to pissed and back again.

"All right," said Jim, leaning back in his chair. "Let's see if I've got the facts straight. Mary, you said you never heard from Rory after Harve sent him out to the old pump house on Ben's farm to pick up the fertilizer bags."

Mary nodded, picking at the embroidery on her sweater. She tried to control her emotions and not look at Ben.

"And Harve said he found the truck with the sacks loaded, but no sign of Rory?"

Mary nodded again.

"And he said there were marks, like something or someone was dragged toward the well where the pump used to sit?"

Ben whimpered and started to shake uncontrollably. To Jim's shock, a puddle of yellow liquid started to pool at his feet.

"Good God, Ben! You're peeing yourself."

Ben continued to whimper and shake uncontrollably, while Bull and Mary looked away. Jim led him back to his usual cell, handed him a pair of clean white prisoner pants, and gingerly took away the soiled jeans. He then got the mop and bucket and cleaned up the puddle. Mary and Bull sat watching, distracted and appalled all at the same time.

After seeing Ben safely into the shower, Jim sat and took a long pull at his cup of now cold coffee. He poured himself a fresh cup and thought longingly of the bottle in his back office. But he was still on duty.

"Sorry about that. I don't know what got into him. I'll find out later. But for now, has Rory ever gone off like this before?"

"Nope," said Bull. "He doesn't like to be alone, 'cept when he goes fishing up at Big Bass Pool. Not that he's particularly social; he mostly sticks close to home."

Bull wiped his face. He was less red now, and Jim's initial alarm faded as the big man got control of himself.

"Let me make some phone calls, investigate this. I'll probably go up to the pump house myself, to see what Harve thinks he saw. You two go home. Bull, can you get the rest of the day off? I don't think Mary should be alone."

"Nope," said Bull. "But I can get someone to come to the shop with her. Mary, will you be okay at the shop?"

Mary nodded. She gathered her things, looking forward to the familiar smells of textile and wool, the gentle clack of the sewing machines, and tried not to cry again when she realized that Rory would not be there to run the quilting machine.

"Where is he? she wailed silently, trying not to let her imagination run wild.

CHAPTER FIVE

He sat in the warm, well-lit studio of his small house, leaning over his work desk, contemplating the specimen on the board. He carefully placed the eyes in the head, turning them this way and that. Finally, he sat back, satisfied. It was perfect. Fischer Supplies made the best eyes. It was the eyes that made the work perfect. If you didn't get them exactly right, then the specimen looked wrong.

He sat back, contemplating where this one would go. It was quite large. He had sent a tooth to the lab, along with his usual fee. Their discretion came at a high price, but their work was impeccable. It was a bear. A young black bear. As usual, the head had been intact although messily removed from the rest of the animal.

Yes, it was perfect. The eyes turned slightly to one side, as if hearing a noise to one side. The mouth slightly open. The tongue had been difficult, but weren't they all? Some taxidermists used jaw sets, but that was cheating. Molding and shaping the tongue right was an art. And using silica gel to create the suggestion of saliva was imperative.

Now he had to decide where to mount it. He couldn't just leave it sitting, even though mounting it would be displeasing to the eye until ... how long would it take him to find another animal to fit between this large head and that perfectly matched pair of weasels? Perhaps a fox? Yes, that would do. He would ask for a fox.

He carefully set the completed head on the back of his workbench. Then he cleaned the bench thoroughly, waxing the wood until it shone. He lined up all his tools, smallest to largest, using a straightedge to make sure the tips were all perfectly aligned. Good work requires good work habits. Mother always told him that.

CHAPTER SIX

Time to get to work, Jim thought. First, I'd better get Ben
settled back at home.

Not for the first time, he wondered if he should try to get Ben
some help. Jim knew Ben might not accept his help, so he'd never
tried. He was fairly sure Ben knew that he could confide in him if
he so desired. But the man could hardly bring himself to look at
Jim, let alone bare his soul. Jim wondered if Ben was religious.
Perhaps Arthur could talk to him.

Arthur Willingham III, DD, was a cheerful, pudgy man with
a penchant for loud ties and comfortable shoes. Harvard educated,
he, like Jim, had stumbled onto Harper's Landing shortly before
the demise of one John Buford Harper in a boating accident on
the Martin's Way River. Reverend JB had been the preacher for
thirty-two years. Everyone agreed that only a damn fool would go
out fishing during the spring floods at age seventy-two; a damn
fool or someone like Reverend JB, who always seemed certain that
he and the Almighty had a special friendship that bestowed extra
protection upon him. It was too bad no one knew what Reverend
JB thought of that protection now. Arthur had no such pretenses
regarding his relationship with the Divine Being. He had left the
large Congregational Church in Boston after the horrible bombing

at the Marathon had taken the life of two of his dearest friends and driven west, not knowing where he would end up.

Like Jim, Arthur had fallen prey to the charms of apple pie with cheese and the three-a-day plan. He, too, had stayed at Mary and Bull Harper's place. And when Reverend JB met his watery demise, Arthur had blurted out, "I would like to be your preacher."

Five years later, he still did not regret his choice. The towns-folk loved his gentle approach to the gospels. They had grown quite weary of the fire and brimstone sermons of Reverend JB, which seemed to have become more fear laden in the final months of his life. Arthur was educated, well spoken, and given to compassion and caring. He was also a master woodcarver and delighted in holding classes in the church social room. He persuaded Linda Collier to start a reading group, and Harve Sanders to start a large community garden on the empty land behind the stone building.

His newest project involved restoring The Rectory, a large wood structure behind the church that Arthur purchased two years ago. It had formerly been a hotel, so all that was required was new carpets, paint, and modernization of the bathrooms. He and Bull Harper had managed to get the two large rooms into shape, where Mary held her summer quilters' retreats. The goal this year was to complete all twenty bedrooms, four more bath-rooms, a larger dormitory, and a cheerful kitchen.

Jim pulled to a stop in front of the church. He could hear the sounds of carpentry going on from the building out back.

The church in Harper's Landing had been there since 1854, according to the date carved in the cornerstone. The building was made of carefully carved granite stones, laid smooth and level. Every twenty years or so, the church members held a grouting party and repaired or replaced any damaged areas. The roof was made of timbers, carefully laid on top of the solid rock walls. No one was sure when the roof had last been replaced, but Jim knew it was due for it soon.

"Why we stopping here?" muttered Ben.

"I want you to see something," said Jim. "Come on."

The two men walked to the back of the building, where they found Arthur diligently weeding one of the plots in the garden. There were four raised beds and eight large ground plots. Jim could see beans, peas, carrots, tomatoes, young corn plants, and onions. These were just the plants he could identify. There were two smaller plots of what he guessed were herbs.

"Hello," called Arthur. "Are you here to help? This is the garden for The Rectory."

"Finally decided to call it that?" asked Jim. *So much for originality*, he thought to himself.

"Yup. The Rectory. Seemed appropriate."

Jim introduced the two men. Arthur exuded his usual good cheer and that special something he had that seemed to charm everyone. Even Ben was captivated with the man.

"You look like a fellow who could grow anything," said Arthur, taking Ben's hands in his. "You're a farmer, aren't you?"

"Used to be. But my land won't grow anything anymore. It got all salty or something."

"Well, maybe you can help me solve the bug problem with these carrots."

The two men became engrossed in examining the carrots and digging around in the soil looking for the culprits.

"All right then," said Jim. "I'm going to check out a situation. Will you be okay here, Ben?"

"Sure. Maybe Arthur here can take me home later?"

Jim was elated, though careful not to show it. This was the most involved he had seen Ben since the incident last year that seemed to propel him into the bottle and rob him of all dignity and social connection. Arthur had indeed been the right person to take custody of Ben.

The road out to Jenkins Farm had once been a poorly maintained county road. The state had obtained funds for rural infrastructure improvements, and the road was one of their first projects. It was now blacktop and allowed him to make good time. He arrived at the dirt road to the Jenkins' pump house in about fifteen minutes. To his surprise, Harve Sanders' truck was still parked beside the structure. Jim pulled out his cell phone. Harve answered on the second ring.

"Hi, Jim. Been expecting you to call."

"How come your truck's still out here?"

"Well, it's my old one, and I don't use it much anymore. And considering what I saw inside the pump house I thought you might appreciate my leaving things alone until you got there."

"Can you come down here and join me? Tell me what I'm looking for?" asked Jim.

"Sure," said Harve. "We were about to take lunch break anyway. You want me to bring you something?"

"Nope. Had a late breakfast."

"I'll be there in fifteen minutes or so."

Jim walked around the truck, examining the ground. He was looking for footprints, tire tracks, anything that might suggest someone else other than Rory had been there. He found prints that looked like combat boots and another set of prints leading from the dirt track to the truck that looked like the rubber boots Harve wore when he was working. Both prints led to the building, where the door stood open, and back out again, several times. He knew that the door was usually padlocked shut, but he found the padlock hanging from the hasp, key still in it. He opened his cell and took multiple pictures of the boot prints and the lock. He re-examined the prints and determined that the wearer of the combat boots had made one more trip into the pump house than the rubber boot wearer. He made note of the patterns in the small notebook he carried in his breast pocket.

Harve's work truck came rattling up the hill, tools and lunch buckets banging around in the back. He came to a stop, hopped out, and handed Jim a bottle of water.

"Didn't know if you had any. It's warm for springtime; too warm if you ask me."

The two men walked toward the pump house.

"Was the door open yesterday when you came up here?" asked Jim.

"Yah. I left everything just like I found it, even the thermos and half a peanut butter and jelly sandwich next to the bucket I'm betting he was sitting on."

"Peanut butter and jelly? Did you pick it up?"

"Nope. That's all Rory ever ate for lunch. Sometimes I wonder if he ate anything else. But since he's healthy, he probably eats dinner. Though Mary's cooking ..." He shook his head.

They walked inside, careful not to step on the footprints. The interior was dim, lit only by the light from the open door and what little shone through the grimy windows at roof level. Cobwebs festooned the abandoned cabinet that stood half-open, and any tools that might have once been stored there had long since been removed. Once his eyes adjusted to the dimmer light, Jim saw the scuff marks. They started halfway between an overturned bucket and the capped well, and ended about a foot from the edge of the metal cap. Jim noted the sandwich and thermos. He decided to wait to package them until he was done looking over the entire scene. He examined the scores in the dirt floor closely. They appeared to be made by something rounded, such as the toes of boots. They were approximately two feet apart and they appeared to be deeper in a couple of places. He took out his high-power Maglite. Additional scuff marks could be seen under the bright light. In Jim's experience, marks like these were made by people being pulled or dragged against their will. He took multiple pictures, having Harve angle the light to outline the different marks in the dusty ground. Jim noticed footprints leading up to and then away from the well that he had not seen before. He also noted that the metal cap that normally sat flush on the top of the well was off-center just a bit.

There still wasn't enough for Jim to justify bringing a state crime scene team out here. Rory had been known to go off on his own, sometimes for days at a time. However, he took as many pictures as he could, carefully bagged up the sandwich and the thermos, and sealed off the pumphouse with yellow caution tape.

"Who else has a key to this place?" he asked.

"Besides me, I would guess the Jenkins' lawyer. He's the one who gave me this key when I told him I needed to get stuff out. He took possession of the family papers, deeds, keys, and all when William died last month. He's hoping to catch Ben sober and discuss things with him."

"Give me his name and number," said Jim. "I'll give him a call. In the meantime, would you please lock up and seal the key in this envelope?"

"I reckon. You should ask the lawyer about you taking the key. I don't want it. Why don't you call him now? He's that new guy in town, the one who took over the tax accountant's office at the Pro Building couple months ago. He's probably there chewing on a cup of coffee and praying for clients."

Jim called the attorney, Martin Rutledge, and asked if he could keep the key. He also asked for a meeting, right away if the lawyer was available. He was. And he consented to Jim taking possession of the key. Jim locked the pump house doors, and Harve got in his truck and headed off to his work site for an afternoon of hard labor. Jim sat on the edge of his car, feet on the ground, head bent, assembling the events of the day in his mind to transfer to paper later.

I need to talk to Ben when he's sober, he thought, *and find out what the hell spooked him so badly out here to throw him into a bottle. And make him piss the floor a year later.* He climbed into the Ford and headed for Martin Rutledge's office. As an afterthought, he pulled over and called Arthur.

"Is Ben still with you?"

"Yes, he is. We are having a wonderful afternoon planting and weeding and talking. I've hired him to work on The Rectory with me."

"Could you do me a favor and bring him on over to Martin

Rutledge's law office in the Pro Building? I should be there in fifteen minutes or so."

"Of course. I think I should come and stay with him if he'll have me. He's still fragile. We are talking about him coming and living with me. I could use the company, and he can definitely use the help."

CHAPTER SEVEN

Martin Rutledge was quite young, only twenty-six years old and two years out of law school. He came to Harper's Landing looking for a fishing vacation. He spent a few days staying at Mary and Bull Harper's home, eating hamburgers and apple pie at Morey's, and catching the finest bass he had ever wrangled ashore on his daily fishing expeditions in the company of Rory, Mary's brother. On the fifth day of his vacation, as he polished off his excellent breakfast at Morey's and started on his third cup of coffee, a middle-aged man in a sheriff's uniform, wearing a badge that said Deputy, rushed in calling for Morey.

"George Paper died," blurted Deputy Randle. "Had a heart attack in his office. The cleaning lady found him this morning."

Martin wondered who George Paper was and why his death prompted such concern for Morey and his wife Maggie.

"Well," said Morey, "there goes my lawsuit against that damned supply company. Can't go sixty miles to St. Louis just to see a new attorney over a piddling matter."

Martin was hit with the same compulsion that had taken over Jim Burch and Arthur Willingham—namely, a sudden and overwhelming desire to be the town's attorney.

"I'll take your case," he blurted out.

That was a year ago. At the time, he was one year out of law school, clerking for a judge in St. Louis and hating every minute of it. He had managed to save enough money to move to Harper's Landing, though he knew he had to get clients soon if he were to survive on his own. But the rightness of the situation was strong. He wanted to stay and knew it would work.

His office was currently full. Jim Burch sat in the large, comfortable wooden chair at the right front corner of his desk. Directly across from him sat Ben Jenkins, and Arthur Willingham sat on the couch behind Ben. Arthur was reading the various diplomas and honorariums on the wall. He noted that the young man had attended both Harvard undergrad. and Harvard Law. They would have to share their experiences over a fine scotch sometime soon, he decided. He took in the familiar scents of leather furniture, old books, and polished wood.

Jim was providing Martin with a short version of the events as they knew them at the Jenkins' Farm pump house. He stressed that no one knew what had happened to Rory. He told Rutledge that Rory was given to wandering from time to time, something Martin already knew. Jim also emphasized that he did not yet want the pump house declared a crime scene. It would not do anyone any good to have CSIs crawling all over the place and have Rory show up in the middle of things. Martin agreed.

"Ben?" he asked. "Is it okay with you if we leave the pump house locked and marked with caution tape?"

"It might work," said Ben. "I guess so. Don't think it will keep it in if it wants out, though."

The other three men stared at him; his words were incomprehensible to all of them.

"What do you mean?" asked Arthur. "Ben, what are you talking about?"

Ben began to shake, asked for a drink of whiskey, and then changed his mind and asked for water instead. Although it would take longer than one day of sobriety for the man to regain his former robust physical status, he was already looking better and had more color. He drew a deep breath.

"Jim, I gotta tell you. I know that now. And Arthur here says he's going to help me stay sober. I don't want to drink no more. But you ..."

"I what?" asked Jim.

"All of you, none of you, you won't believe me. But I gotta tell you."

"Take your time," said Martin. "We don't have anywhere else to be, do we?"

Jim and Arthur shook their heads. They both wanted to hear this.

Ben took a deep breath and then paused. He gave Martin a long look. "William hired you?"

"Yes, just before he died. He knew he was dying and planned to tell you. But the cancer got him before he could. He didn't tell you sooner because he ..."

Martin blushed deeply.

"He thought I was too pickled to understand," finished Ben.

Martin nodded.

"Fear, big fear, does things to you," said Ben. "It makes you do things like drink yourself half to death, or gamble, or run. At least that's my experience. Me, I fell into a bottle. William was right. But I'm fine now. You tell those mill folks I'll sell the land to them. After what I'm about to tell you, you'll understand why I don't ever want to set foot on there again."

He paused for a moment, pulled a candy bar out of a pocket, and took a long drink of water.

"You mind if I eat this? I'm powerful hungry."

"Go ahead," said Martin.

"Start whenever you want, Ben. We can all wait, yes?" said Arthur.

Jim and Martin both nodded.

"It was what, Jim? A year ago?"

Jim nodded.

"I went out to the pump house to see if the doors were locked. I wanted to be sure the cover over the well was secure, in case some kids broke in. Used to be a favorite smooch spot after the farm shut down. Anyway, I didn't want to be responsible for any kids getting hurt. I was living in the farmhouse by myself. William didn't want to ever come back.

"I found the door to the pump house open and without a lock. I went to the house, came back, and attached the hasp lock to the door. But before I locked up, I decided to check inside. There are no lights in the pump house. Come to think of it, that place is almost big enough to call a small barn. There were windows high up that gave a little light, and with the doors wide open I could see well enough.

"The pump was gone, sure enough, and in its place was a large circular metal plate. It had grooves in the top, presumably for fitting handles to turn and lift it if the need ever came to go into the well."

Ben was now sweating profusely and shaking more than a bit. He had another drink of water, took a bite of the candy, and sat quietly, chewing and visibly attempting to calm himself.

"Jim, you remember what I told you when you picked me up on the road? About the eyes?"

Jim nodded.

"I figured you thought I was always a drunk, but up until that day the most I'd ever had was a beer or two at the Happy Time or an occasional glass of wine at a family dinner."

He took a deep breath and resumed his narrative.

"You remember my dog?"

Jim and Arthur nodded.

"He was a big fella, part Berner, part coonhound. I had him with me that day. He jumped out of my truck and ran into the pump house with me. I was busy looking around, checking the shelves, counting Harve's fertilizer bags. When I was done, I went over to check out the well, replace the cover that had been moved. When I looked down, I heard quacking, like a duck had got stuck down there somehow. Then I heard singing. Clear, beautiful singing. I found the metal hooks meant for lifting the well cover hanging beside the door and started pulling the cover off. I had it halfway off, when ..."

He suddenly bolted for the bathroom door at the back of Martin's office, where he was violently ill. After a few minutes he returned, shaking and white, and again sat, although this time on the couch next to Arthur. The other men waited silently, and finally Ben continued his story.

"I had the cover half off when I saw them eyes. Big, bulging eyes, and a mouth that seemed to take up half the face. It was huge, green, and evil. And it was reaching out of that well, for me. My dog leaped up, pushed me back, and that thing grabbed him by the hind leg. He couldn't get away. I grabbed hold of his collar, and the two of us—monster and me—pulled and pulled. But it was too strong for me, and the dog went straight down into that well. His screams ... well, they still haunt me. And that sound, that godawful crunch, crunch, crunch.

"I slammed that lid down and ran back to the house; didn't know where else to go. Didn't have a cell, so I grabbed the phone in the house and called you. But as I hung up, I knocked over the oil lantern I'd been using as light. And, well, you know the rest. It was gone by the time you got there. Me too, come to think of it. Gone, that is."

The silence in Martin's office was palpable. Jim was impassive, his cop's brain refusing to believe what he had just heard, searching for a more plausible explanation. Martin was chilled, not knowing what to think, and wondering if Ben was sane enough to be signing the sale papers to the farm. Arthur was wracking his memory for any legends or folktales he might have encountered about such a creature, at the same time saying a small prayer for his new friend's soul, and for an ease to the pain he felt radiating from him. Ben sat bent forward, elbows on his thighs, his face buried in his hands.

Finally, Jim spoke, gently but forcefully. "Ben, I'm damn sure there's a reasonable explanation for all of this."

"I knew you wouldn't believe me."

"Oh, I believe that something happened out there. I'm just not sure about monsters. There's something going on, and we are going to get to the bottom of it. First your dog, and now Rory, both missing and both last known to be at the pump house. Could be they're related, or maybe not. We are going to find out. I promise you that."

Jim sat quietly, deep in thought for a few moments. Then he spoke up again.

"As for what you saw, you said it was dark in that pump house, so maybe you did see something, just not what your mind interpreted it to be. If there's something down there, we'll find it. Meantime, I think you should stay with Arthur here, if he'll have you."

Arthur nodded enthusiastically. "If you're willing, we will go to your place together, gather up your stuff, and move you in now. I agree with Jim. I don't think you should be alone."

Jim sat quietly for a few minutes, and then looked directly at Arthur. "I want to deputize you," he said.

Arthur looked puzzled. "Don't you already have a deputy?"

"Yes," replied Jim. "And Harry's a good guy, dependable and smart. I don't want you full-time, but I want to be able to call you into action when needed. Given what we've all heard here today, I think you need to be what the legal eagles call *an officer of the court*."

Arthur agreed, and the oath of office was delivered immediately with Ben and Martin as witnesses.

"You'll be paid for the time you are on the clock, when I call you into action," said Ben.

"I don't need pay."

"Maybe not, but we need to keep this as legal and straightforward as possible. You're on the payroll when I say so, and I want records of your time turned in regularly."

Arthur reluctantly agreed.

"Before you leave, Ben," said Martin, "here's the paper you need to sign, if you're sure you want to do this. They are offering you $75,000. That will last you a long time. I could manage the money for you if you like, until you feel more on your feet."

"I like that idea," said Ben, and hastily scribbled his signature on the bottom of the deed of sale and again on the paper allowing Martin Rutledge, Esq., to handle the sale and the money transfer to his client account.

CHAPTER EIGHT

He was more than a bit horrified. It was a head, for sure, and he had asked for a head. But it was human, and the eyes and much of the skin were gone. A boot lay beside it, with a foot in it. He looked beyond the door, peering into the woods behind his house. There was nothing to be seen, no trace of his "benefactor" could be spotted.

This he had not asked for. He had been clear when he presented his last gift, a lovely new lamb still warm and luscious, like all the others. Every time, every single time, he said exactly what he wanted. He had asked for a fox, and he had held the picture in his mind, waiting for the assent that always was given when the message was received.

Yet here it was, human, and a boot, with a foot. The horror of it nearly overwhelmed him.

Hastily he put on his taxidermy gloves, gathered up the offending items, and threw them in the back of the red pickup truck that was parked behind his brother's house. He drove down to the river where it gathered strength for the rapids and threw the head and foot in. With any luck the fish would take them, or the current would carry them all the way to the Mississippi. He needed to be home. He had a schedule to keep. In his haste, he cut his arm on the tailgate as he closed it.

He parked the truck behind his house, and by the light of the moon got the hose out of the toolshed between the two houses. With care, he washed his arm with strong disinfectant soap. The gash was deep; he would stitch it himself once the truck was cleaned. Once he bandaged his arm, he washed the bed of the truck until it gleamed. Then he parked the truck precisely where it had been earlier. Finally, he washed the back stoop, careful to remove all the blood, including his own. His arm was bleeding again through the bandages, and he wrapped it in his shirt. He rolled up the hose when everything was clean and hung it on the peg in the shed. Done, he went inside and immediately attended his wound, washing it, applying disinfectant, and stitching it carefully and precisely. Tomorrow he would ask his brother to drive him to the clinic in Harwood for a tetanus shot. Good work requires good work habits. Mother always told him that.

CHAPTER NINE

J im sat in his office, ruminating on the incidents of the previous day. Ben's story had been harrowing. He was sure that Rory had wandered off and was betting he would show up in the next few days. He imagined that Ben's increased drinking had given him a retreat from the memory of the sound and of his failure to save his dog. Guilt is a hard thing to endure.

He remembered that Ben had been badly shaken—incoherent, in fact—when he picked him up on the road near the pump house that night, and Jim knew he was sober at the time. Although he had little prior contact with the man, the few times he chatted with him at Morey's he had not considered him as someone easily shaken. He was fairly sure that the loss of the house to fire, on the heels of his brother's cancer diagnosis, had compounded Ben's fears and left him in desperate straits.

Jim turned his thoughts to serious consideration of the events of the day. He would have to decide soon if he should call in Blake Meadows from the State Police in Jefferson City. There was little to go on other than the disappearance of Rory. Jim did not want to be the one who tried to explain Ben's encounter in the pump-house. Meanwhile, it was time for lunch, and he was more than ready. The loud growl from his stomach reminded him that he hadn't eaten anything since breakfast. He closed the office and headed for Morey's.

The usual customers were nearly finished wolfing down today's lunch offering: meatloaf smothered in browned-butter gravy, mashed potatoes, and fresh-roasted carrots. Jim asked for a salad to go with it, knowing that while one serving of lunch would not be enough to quell his hunger, he needed to be aware of calories and carbs these days. The meatloaf was nearly as legendary as the apple pie, and Tuesdays were always busy at the diner.

Jim took his customary place at the communal table and listened to the gossip. He wasn't surprised to hear that someone had learned that Ben had sobered up and signed the sale deed. Martin had probably hurried to the courthouse to register it before the end of the business day. One of the young clerks working there had most likely been unable to resist the desire to share the news, even though it was a breach of policy. He was genuinely pleased to hear that Ben's newly discovered sobriety was being celebrated.

The main topic of conversation was the restoration of the mill and the former slave quarters. Several of the customers wondered if they would put the mill back into operation, and, if so, would they hire back some of the former workers. Skilled craftsmen would be needed not only to restore the mill but for the restoration of the quarters. The building had been closed for years, and everything inside and out needed repair. Despite its tainted history, the building was well constructed of native wood, and the restoration would enhance the mill's operation as an authentic historical site. The new owner hinted that someday there would be a museum and tours for school kids and visitors. Anything that brought tourists to the town was welcome.

Halfway through his meal, the bell tinkled above the door as a young, lanky man wearing fishing boots and a mill cap came rushing in calling for the sheriff. Jim rose, took him by the arm, and went outside, aware of all eyes on him and his unexpected guest.

"What's up?" asked Jim.

"Oh god, it's awful. I've got it in the back of my truck."

He looked a bit green around the gills, like he was about to throw up. Which he did just before they arrived at his truck.

While Jim waited for him to regain his composure, he glanced in the back of the truck. There was a bucket that held a bit of water and what appeared to be three or four bass, a fishing tackle box, and a pole, still rigged for fishing. It had obviously been tossed in the truck bed by someone in a hurry. But what caught his eye the most was a large burlap tarp, covering something and held in place by a couple of large rocks and a tree limb.

"What's your name, son?"

"Zak. Zak Millbank. I live up on the hill, work at the mill as project manager for the restoration."

"Okay. What did you want to show me?"

"Oh, god, I can't. It's under the burlap. Please, go ahead, look."

Jim lifted the burlap and recoiled. Two items lay on the truck bed: a foot, or, more precisely, a left boot with a foot in it, and next to it, Rory O'Connor's eyeless head.

The customers in Morey's could see Jim's reaction, and they poured out onto the street like cats to a fishmonger. Jim quickly replaced the burlap, but not quickly enough to keep Jen Harper and one of the diners from seeing the grisly cargo. Jen blanched while the customer hurried around the corner behind the diner, holding his hand over his mouth.

Everyone began talking at once, while Zak Millbank sat on the curb, crying, and refusing to respond to their questions. Jim turned and yelled at them.

"Leave him alone, you hear?"

There was sudden, open-mouthed silence. In the three years Jim Burch had been sheriff of Harper's Landing, no one had ever heard him raise his voice. But there was no doubting now that he was, at the very least, pissed off.

"You folks, either go back and finish your dinner, or go home. This is now a police matter, and I won't have you bothering Zak here or getting all up in what might end up being evidence."

Jen gave him a hard look, and he rested his hand briefly on her shoulder and gave it a small squeeze. She nodded, turned, and went back into the diner, herding her customers like first graders coming in from recess. Some chose to button up their dinners in to go boxes and head home, but most chose to stay, hoping for a glimpse of something more interesting than some fishing gear and a burlap cloth.

Jim pulled out his cell phone and hit speed dial for the Missouri State Police headquarters. After identifying himself, he requested to be put through to either Meadows or Murdoch. He was connected to Clay Murdoch.

"Clay, Jim Burch here. I need you and Blake up here in Harper's Landing as soon as you can, along with some CSI folks."

Quickly he gave him a brief description of the contents of the truck and then mentioned there was more to the story that they would both want to hear.

"We'll be there. Blake's wife wanted to get him to some church social, so he'll be grateful for the excuse to leave. Do you want us to drive, or should we take a chopper up?"

"How long to drive, do you think?"

"Oh, about two hours this time of day."

"Then chopper up if you don't mind. I have a feeling about this, an itch I can't quite scratch. But I do know the sooner we have people working on it, the sooner I can keep this town under control. Something strange is going on up here. Can the CSI folks fit in the chopper, too?"

"Oh yeah, those babies will carry six to eight people."

"You got one of those snake cameras? You know, the ones you can stick under doors or down into dark places?"

"Yeah, sure," replied Clay. "But seriously? You need one of those?"

"I'm thinking so, with fifty foot of cable if they can manage it. And equipment for water analysis. And you'd better be prepared to get evidence to the lab as quickly as possible, because ... Oh, hell, I don't want to speculate. I'm just going with my gut."

Jim tucked away his cell and told Zak to go to his office and stay there.

He called Mary and Bull Harper.

"I need you to come to the office," he said.

"You found Rory?" asked Bull.

"Come on down with Mary. If you don't mind, I'm going to get Arthur Willingham to come too."

Bull sighed deeply. Bringing Arthur along could only mean one thing. He helped Mary into her jacket and held her close as they walked to their car. She held his hand the entire way to town and let go only to get out once they were parked in front of the sheriff's office.

Arthur immediately agreed to come but asked if perhaps Deputy Randle could be called to stay with Ben. Jim agreed and called Harry, who was only too happy to get out of bingo night at the church. *Tuesday seems to be church stuff everywhere,* Jim thought. *No church here, though. This is going to be hell.* He mentally went over what he was going to tell Arthur and decided he might as well tell him the whole thing.

Jim drove Zak's truck and put it behind the building in a locked garage. Jim bagged the head and shoe, zip-tied the bag, and filled out the necessary forms, signing as both sheriff and coroner. He then placed the bag in a freezer in the back of the garage. He went to his office, where he found Arthur already there, waiting for the others. Mary and Bull arrived next and sat on the couch. Jim pulled out a chain of evidence form and filled in the details, except for the name of the forensic tech who would take possession. He waited to sign it in the presence of official witnesses. Zak sat across from Jim, on the end of the couch, trying to control his nerves.

Jim got himself a large mug of coffee. The rest declined anything to drink. He told them all they would have to wait until the state folks arrived. He pulled Arthur aside under the pretense of needing him to look at a broken door. Once they were in the hall, Jim quietly filled him in on what had been found in Zak's truck. Arthur sighed deeply as they both returned to the main room. Bull was beginning to get antsy when the state chopper set down on the lawn behind the courthouse. Of course, this immediately attracted a small crowd from Morey's, but Jen hurriedly shooed them back inside with the promise of free apple pie for everyone.

Blake Meadows was first out, followed by Clay Murdoch. Behind them came a woman carrying a large CSI bag and two men, each carrying similar bags and wearing cameras around their necks. Jim met them out back, where he filled them in on what he knew about the body parts discovery, and watched as the CSIs photographed and then bagged the head and boot and stored them in the refrigeration unit in the back of the helicopter. Since the CSIs were remaining in Harper's Landing, planning to examine the location where the parts had been found, Jim had the pilot sign the chain of evidence form, and Jim signed off, both in the presence of Blake Meadows as witness. The pilot then took off with specific instructions to get the body bag to the lab as soon as he landed. The woman called ahead, and Jim overheard her telling them to move as quickly as possible to determine if they had one or two potential vics. Somehow, he didn't think there was a second potential vic. But he knew that even if the boot was the same as Rory wore, it was necessary to verify that the foot and the head were indeed from the same person.

"We have a van on the way up here, too," said one of the two men. He made a quick call on his cell, providing directions to Harper's Landing and stressing the need for at least two divers, body bags, and a van with refrigeration.

The other man approached Jim, holding out his hand.

"I'm Bill Whiteman," he said. "The spitfire there is Helen Green. And that other fella is, believe it or not, Michael Moriarty."

Jim called Arthur and asked him to tell Zak to come out back. When Zak arrived, Jim asked him to tell everyone what he had found. Meadows and Murdoch both took notes while Zak talked, even though Jim had, with permission, turned on the recorder on his cell.

Zak was the project manager for the restoration project at the mill. He had moved to Harper's Landing six months ago and was renting one of the newer houses that had sprung up on Jackson Hill. He loved fishing, a passion his wife did not share, and got out to Big Bass Pool, where he had gone today, as often as he could. He preferred bank fishing to river fishing.

Meadows consulted his notes and started to ask a question when Zak blurted out, "We've had a lot of pets go missing up on Jackson Hill since they hooked up the waterwheel again. Do the missing pets have anything to do with what happened to Rory?"

"We don't know, son," said Blake. "We'll discuss that later. For now, let's get you and these CSI folks out to where you found the head."

The CSI team had wanted to take Zak and go immediately to the location where he found the body parts. Jim asked if they needed to process his truck first. They were eager to get to the site and protect it. They told Jim to keep the truck locked up and they would process it when they returned. Jim promised to send Harry Randle out to secure the scene at Big Bass Pool and keep any prying eyes away, as soon as Arthur could return to The Rectory and stay with Ben. Jim handed them the keys to the Explorer, and Green and Moriarty left immediately, with Zak in tow.

Jim decided to ease into things gradually. He hoped Mary hadn't noticed the blood spots on Zak's arms and chest. He suspected it was Rory's blood, since Zak had picked up the head and boot and put them in his truck. He slowly walked back to his office.

"What happened to Rory?" Mary demanded.

Jim cursed under his breath. There went his plans to make this easy, as if it ever could be easy. He nodded at Bull, who gently pulled Mary back down on the couch.

"Mary," he said. "Zak? The young man who was here, well, there's no easy way to say it. Zak found Rory's head and a boot with a foot in it that looks to be Rory's also. We will start a search as soon as these folks say, for, you know, the rest of his ..."

His voice trailed off.

Mary let out a small scream and collapsed into Bull's arms, muttering "No, no, no," as she sobbed and shuddered. Arthur moved into place next to her, while Jim sank into his desk chair. Everyone sat still, looking helpless and uncomfortable as Mary continued to sob uncontrollably. Finally, Bull and Arthur took Mary out of the office and gently put her in the car. Bull drove home with Arthur following, after Bull assured Jim and the state men that they would be available for questioning the following day.

The remaining group sat silently. No one liked giving news like that. No matter how often he had to do it, Jim never got used to it. This was his first since moving to Harper's Landing, and it was his worst, because he knew these people well. They were friends, close friends.

CHAPTER TEN

The Martin's Way River was thirty-five miles long. It started ten miles above the mill as a tributary of the Mississippi. As it flowed toward the mill, it gathered strength and expanded to twenty feet wide and approximately eight feet deep. There were places here and there along the river where water swirled, and the undercurrents were powerful. It was in one of these places that the Reverend John Buford Harper had gone missing, presumed drowned while fishing. His boat was found, full of bass and crappie and various tackle, but JB and his fishing pole were never located.

The children of Harper's Landing were forbidden to swim in the Martin's Way, and after Gary Miller's younger brother Mattie drowned while on a family picnic, they needed no further warning to stay away.

The river had several twists and turns, and at many of these turns, pools had formed and been dug out larger by the town's residents to create attractive bank fishing spots. Big Bass Pool was the most popular because it was large, deep, and quiet. Those who used this pool regularly had created a packed dirt path from the parking area off the county road. Harry Randle sat in his F-150 blocking access to the parking area, as Jim had requested. He moved his truck before the other vehicles pulled in. Helen Green jumped out, camera in hand, and started photographing all tire tracks going in and out of the area. She also took multiple pictures of Zak's tire tracks. She continued to photograph both sides of the access road for several minutes and then waved them all in. Once she was finished, Harry repositioned his truck to block the path.

Zak showed them where the path led to the pool. On the steeper parts, railings had been installed, and at the bottom near the pool someone had placed a couple of picnic tables and a fire pit. There was a fish-cleaning station built close to the edge of the pool, with a small grassy area around it where fishermen threw entrails and heads for the scavenging birds and forest critters. It was there, next to the gut bucket, as the guys called it, that Zak made his grisly find. Helen doubted that any useful fingerprints could be obtained from the railings, but she nevertheless attempted to lift some starting at the top on one side while Mike Moriarty worked the other.

"I was about to clean the bass I caught. They're still in the bucket back there," he said, pointing at his truck. "I saw the boot first, caught in the branches there, and got curious. Then when I went over to look at it, I saw the head."

"I'm sorry," he said, addressing Helen, "but I couldn't help myself. I'm afraid my lunch is over there, too."

"Why did you move them?" asked Whiteman.

Helen and Michael were already busy roping off the area and setting up the spotlights.

They discovered the generator in Jim's truck and started it up.

"I don't know," said Zak. "I didn't want some animal coming along and chewing on them, or maybe the head and boot coming loose and floating on downriver. I don't have a cell when I come out here. I lost one worth near a grand once, and Mollie, my wife, makes me leave it at home now. Otherwise, I would have called the sheriff to come out."

Helen was quite obviously pissed.

"Now we gotta deal with puke, with two- and three-day-old

fish guts, and footprints. And hunt for the rest of that poor bastard. Is this place always so clean? There's no trash, and I don't see any kind of trash barrel or burn barrel."

"We like to keep things clean here," said Zak. "Most of us take our trash out with us. Sometimes we'll find a beer can or two, but mostly it's always this clean."

Meadows and Murdoch had their large flashlights out and were carefully examining the area between the gut bucket and the pool, looking for footprints. Whiteman was photographing everything, while Moriarty and Green began walking the grid, mapping everything. Green took multiple pictures with her cell and the digital camera, of everything from leaves to raccoon prints. At one point, Whiteman was bent down near the water, taking photo after photo of what he later called strange footprints.

Jim and Arthur arrived in Arthur's old Chevy and parked up on the road. They walked in and stood next to Zak, watching the others at work. Helen Green walked over.

"Is the bank like this all the way downstream? Come to think of it, how far is downstream?"

Jim was unfamiliar with this part of the Martin's Way, but Zak appeared to know it well.

"I fish a lot," he said. "Gives me time to think. The bank gets steep in between the picnic and fishing spots. It's not a walk beside it river. We're getting close to the end of the Martin's Way here. It's only about two miles to the Mississippi."

Helen let out an oath.

"If a body were to be carried on downriver, are there places before it hits the big river where it might get washed ashore?" asked Green.

"No," said Zak. "From here on down there's no bank access. The river gets narrow and fast as it flows into the Mississippi. If there's more of poor Rory, we probably aren't going to find it here."

Jim had been wandering downstream a bit, avoiding the steeper parts, and continuing to look for footprints. As he probed bushes close to the river's edge, he heard a duck quacking.

Because he rarely came to the river, he couldn't say that there were no ducks, but this one sounded strange even to his untutored ear. He listened for other ducks to respond, but there were no further quacks.

He returned to the crime scene to find everyone still busy photographing and documenting the entire area. He recommended taping off the head of the path at the park area, but Meadows wanted the entire parking area taped off and guarded.

"Can you keep your deputy down here overnight?"

"Yeah. Don't know who will be unhappier, him or his wife. But the promise of overtime pay should do it."

Harry agreed to stay, though Jim noted he didn't promise to be alone or to stay awake. He figured if someone were here, with all the police tape and all, things would be okay. Folks in Harper's Landing tended not to be lawbreakers, even at their most curious. He would make sure, however, that no one in their present company mentioned Big Bass Pool where anyone else could hear it.

Jim walked over to Zak, who was sitting on the back end of the Explorer looking weary and shocked.

"Heard a duck quacking down there. I thought they swam in flocks."

"They do. And it's the wrong time of year for ducks this far up on the river. They shouldn't be up here until early to midsummer. And generally, they prefer places like Harve's pond to the river. Current is too strong for them."

"Maybe it was a frog and I misheard," said Jim. "Could have sworn it was quacking and thought it was strange."

He shrugged and turned to helping the CSIs pack up the evidence they'd gathered so far.

"We're going to need to send the divers," said Helen, "to see if anything caught on any snags or other possible protrusions between here and the Mississippi."

Harry Randle had taped off the parking lot for Big Bass Pool. Meadows and Murdoch both were stressing the importance of preventing anyone from entering the area. They also told Randle he needed to stay awake until someone arrived in the morning. He held up a six-pack of Red Bull.

"Reckon I can make it," he chuckled.

"I'll have someone bring you food from Morey's," said Jim. "And don't you be going down there snooping at the river. One person missing is enough for me."

The divers arrived in the big CSI van that held all the equipment they would need for analyzing any evidence. They assessed the scene and said that though they agreed that checking the river for any snagged body parts should happen soon, it was too dangerous to do it at night. The light was swiftly fading. The divers would sleep in the CSI van, which was equipped with cots and blankets.

"I'll arrange to have food brought to you," said Jim. "Do you like meatloaf?"

Both divers agreed, and one said, "I was up here couple of years ago and had fantastic pie. If they still have it, be sure to have them send some."

Jim grinned wolfishly. More pie fanatics.

Meadows yawned hugely.

"Where can we stay for the night? I didn't see anything that looked like a hotel."

"Arthur here has a bed and breakfast," said Jim. "Used to be the town hotel. He bought it and called it The Rectory. There's plenty of rooms for all of you if you want to stay in one place."

"I think we'll do that," said Meadows. "That way we can get an early start. You reckon you could get Morey and Maggie to send us over breakfast there? Would help avoid a lot of gossip. The fewer people who know we are here, the better."

Jim heartily agreed with that sentiment. He called Morey, who was quite happy to provide breakfast for all of them, including Jim and young Zak, at The Rectory early in the morning. He also agreed to send someone to Big Bass with breakfast for the divers.

"How's 6:30 AM?" he asked. "That'll get you out of there before most folks get into town to get their breakfast."

Jim agreed. He reluctantly allowed Zak to go home to his wife and kids. First, the young man had to remove his boots and surrender them to the CSIs for examination and print comparison. Jim extracted a promise that Zak would join them for breakfast at The Rectory at 6:30 AM the following morning and promised to square things for him with the mill. He dropped him at home and headed to The Rectory.

It was going on 7:00 PM when they arrived. The state folks were tired, dirty, and hungry. Arthur showed them to their rooms, each with its own attached bath, and happily provided soap and towels. He offered to let Jim stay also, but the big man wanted nothing more than to be in the peace and quiet of his own home, surrounded by his and Beth's things. His stomach, however, had other ideas. He started for the door to walk over to Morey's when it flew open and in marched Maggie, Jen, and two of the high school football team members, loaded down with baskets emitting glorious smells. Jim went back to the dining room. Home could wait.

Helen Green was the first of the state officers to arrive in the dining room after her shower, freshly dressed, hair damp and curling.

"My god, if that tastes even half as good as it smells, I may never leave this town."

"Wait until you taste the pie," said Jim. "You'll be buying land tomorrow."

Meadows and Murdoch arrived next, agreeing with Jim. They had eaten Maggie Farmington's pie on more than one occasion, and Murdoch, a lifelong bachelor, had promised Morey that if anything ever happened to him it would be Clay Murdoch's pleasure to care for Maggie until her dying days.

Moriarty and Whiteman were last to arrive and were treated with the sight of everyone, including Arthur and Ben, chowing down on ribs, mashed potatoes, buttered corn on the cob, fresh rolls, and hot coffee. Ben kept eyeing the last basket, which he knew held at least two apple pies. He had seen Jen put vanilla ice cream in the freezer but was hoping for cheese with his slice of pie. When the basket was opened, there lay a large slab of cheddar cheese for those who preferred it.

When dinner was over, Jim rose to leave but Ben stopped him.

"Jim, I reckon it's time I told these folks what I told you'n Arthur and the lawyer yesterday. Especially if they're going to go out to the pump house tomorrow after whatever else they're doing."

Jim sighed. He had hoped to get home soon, turn on some jazz, and relax. But Ben was right. They all needed the rest of the story.

"You'd best not make me lose my supper," growled Helen. "Or there'll be hell to pay."

"Oh, it's me who gets upset," said Ben. "And not so much now that I'm seeing things clearer. But I doubt you're gonna be more inclined to believe me than this one was," nodding his head toward Jim.

They all helped clean up the dishes, put away the ample left-overs, which did not, of course, include pie, and packed up the baskets for Morey to pick up in the morning when he arrived with breakfast. A couple of them eyed the clock over the mantel in the spacious sitting room, knowing that 6:30 AM was going to get there all too soon.

Ben was brief but thorough in his retelling. He told them the exact same story he had related in Martin Rutledge's office, though it took less time because he didn't need to leave or to pause. When he finished, the state police folk looked bemused and incredulous. Jim could hardly blame them, what with eyes, and teeth, and giant mouths.

After a moment of quiet, Murdoch said, "I think we have to treat this all of a piece. But like Helen or one of you said, let's deal with people stuff first. That means a more thorough daylight look at where Rory's head and foot were found, then on to the rest of the Martin's Way River. The divers can do that. We'll leave Helen and Moriarty to assist the divers. The rest of us can take the camera and equipment out to that pump house. We had the chopper take the head and foot to the State Medical Examiner in Jefferson City. We should know by afternoon tomorrow if we are dealing with just one body. Jim, are you willing to make a formal identification of the head as that of Rory O'Connor?"

He set his cell phone to record.

Jim nodded and then remembered to say yes for the official recording. Although the neck was badly torn, or chewed, from where it had once joined the body, the face was almost untouched, and decomposition had not yet set in. Even without the eyes, which were always the first thing to go, it was obvious to Jim that the head was Rory O'Connor's. Jim wiped away a tear. He had been in cop mode since Zak first rushed into the diner, but now that he had eaten and had a chance to relax a bit, the loss of his friends' brother was hitting him hard. He stood up without speaking, strode out the door, and got into his vehicle. He needed to be home, now!

CHAPTER ELEVEN

E arly morning is the best time of day. Everything is fresh and dewy and ready to go. Even though coffee is the primary morning fuel for most humans, for morning people dawn is the kindling and anticipation is the match. Those who stay up late and sleep through the awakening of the day never get to know the splendid promise that each dawn holds, whether blue-skied or cloudy. This is why night owls hate morning people; they are so perky, excited, and ready to go.

Jim Burch was one of those morning people. He was a hard, deep sleeper, rarely remembered his dreams, and always woke promptly at 5:00 AM, clearheaded and refreshed. This wasn't one of those mornings. He had gone home the night before, tossed back a shot of quality bourbon, neat, and fallen into bed at ten. He dreamed on and off all night, with Rory chasing dogs, rabbits, and cats with frogs nipping at his heels. He remembered his nightmares vividly and wanted nothing more than to knock back some bourbon, enough to send him deep into slumber, and stay in bed until it all went away. He also knew this was nonsense. And there was work to do.

"Dammit, Beth," he said out loud as he showered. "This was supposed to be my quiet place, my solace. It's mornings like these, ones I thought I'd never have again, that I miss you the most."

He leaned against the shower wall, letting the hot water wash the ache from his joints, and cried until there were no tears to shed. He hadn't cried like this for Beth in two years, but today he ached from the absence of her.

"Are you happy where you are?" he asked, as he put on his work clothes and slid his feet into his heavy boots. "Are you anywhere? Or did you just stop?"

This was a conversation he had nearly every morning. He thoroughly expected someday to get an answer, though by what means he wasn't certain. But he couldn't bring himself to accept that Beth wasn't somewhere waiting for him. He knew it was wishful thinking, but it kept him going each day. He wasn't sure why it felt so real that day nor why he had completely lost it in the shower.

He finished dressing and locked the door on his way out. He walked the two blocks to The Rectory, since he figured he would have a lot of standing and sitting to do today. This might be his only chance to stretch out. Breakfast arrived as he got through the front door. Arthur had set the long table in the front dining room with china plates, cloth napkins, large mugs for coffee, and pitchers of orange juice. Morey and Jen had brought enough food to feed a small army, and Deputy Randle was helping set things up, while constantly sipping from his mug of coffee. His eyes were drooping.

"Who's watching the crime scene?" demanded Jim.

"A couple of state fellas woke up an hour ago," said Harry. "They had IDs and all the diving equipment. I was glad to get out of there. Damn quacking like to drove me nuts, but at least it kept me awake. Can I go now and get some sleep?"

"Sure," said Jim. "But before you go, where was the quacking coming from?"

"Not entirely sure. Sometimes it sounded like out in the middle of the pool, but when I shone my flashlight there wasn't anything there. Other times, it sounded like it was on the other side of the river. Of course, that wouldn't be possible to hear, seeing how it's forty, maybe fifty yards across. And once, scared the life out of me, damn thing sounded like it was right behind me in the parking area. And then there was the singing."

"Singing?" asked Jim, incredulously.

"Yah. I figured I was hallucinating by then; I was so damn tired. Might have been young'uns at the turnout downriver. Beautiful voice though. Just heard it once."

"You'd better get some sleep. You're going soft in the head," said Jim.

Harry left, but not before snagging one of the giant warm cinnamon rolls Maggie had set out on the table.

The others straggled in, taking a seat at the long table.

"Holy cow, those must be the biggest cinnamon rolls I've ever seen," said Helen, grabbing one for herself. She also dug into the fluffy scrambled eggs and heaped her plate with bacon.

Meadows eyeballed Zak, who had arrived promptly at 6:30 AM. The CSIs had taken possession of his boots before he left the night before, and he now wore running shoes. He looked like he hadn't gotten much sleep.

"Now," said Meadows, "what's this I heard about missing pets?"

Zak took a long sip of coffee and snared one of the cinnamon rolls. He shook his head at Arthur's offer of eggs. He sighed deeply, and then began to speak.

"A week after the mill started the restored waterwheel, people started losing pets up on Jackson Hill. The Millers lost both their cats. Like to break their kids' hearts. They had signs up and everything. Gene Herbst and his partner, Lloyd, had two of those big German shepherd dogs—Malinois, I think they're called. They disappeared one day, right out of their backyard. And Elsie Mix lost her four pet rabbits from her back yard. This was about a month ago."

Zak paused, staring at them all.

"What I'm about to tell you, I don't want it to get back to Grossman and his pals that it was me who told you. I need that job. I have two young ones and another on the way."

"Don't you worry, son," said Jim. "Unless it's needed in a court of law, what you say for now stays right here."

"All those people—the Millers, Gene and Lloyd, and Elsie—they had wells, old wells in their backyards that had pumps on them. They used the pumps to water their yards, their flower gardens, and such. The mill owns the properties. We pay rent to them. It's quite reasonable and part of our pay package. Anyway, they came in and closed those wells—put metal caps over them and told folks they would have to use city water for their gardens. There are lots of other people up there with pets, but only the ones with those closed up wells lost theirs."

He stared at his feet for a few moments.

"I'm scared," he said softly. "We have one of those wells in our backyard, and Mollie—that's my wife—thinks I'm being silly. But I won't let my boys play back there anymore. I have Mollie take them to the park over by the library."

He paused and looked as if he might cry.

"I worry every day that Mollie will decide I'm being a nervous Nellie and let the kids out back. Or the kids will wake up during the night and wander out there. You know how kids are."

"I take it you haven't been sleeping much," said Arthur.

Jim realized this explained the young man's apparently ill appearance.

"No, sir, and neither would you if you'd heard what I did," he blurted out.

Everyone in the room was paying full attention now.

"What did you hear?" asked Meadows.

"It was shortly after the waterwheel started up. I was out one night, looking at the stars. Suddenly I heard what sounded like a tapping or knocking. It was coming from the well. I let out a holler, thinking maybe someone got stuck down there, but there was no answer. I figured I was wrong about where it came from.

But then the knocking got louder, almost like banging. I went over to see if I could spot anything. As I got closer, I heard a—don't know—like a chuckle. Only there wasn't anything funny about it. Made my hair stand on end."

Zak was pale and shaking, and Jim shoved the plate with his cinnamon roll in front of him.

"Eat!" he instructed, and Zak took a bite or two. He swallowed, then resumed his story.

"I got Mollie out of bed and brought her out there. And, of course, by then there was no noise at all. She accused me of drinking one too many beers and went back to bed. I stayed and listened for a while longer. When I didn't hear anything more, I went to bed too."

He took another bite of roll.

He put his face in his hands for a moment, and then sat up straight. "What the hell is going on?"

"That's what we're here to find out," responded Meadows. "First, let's get a good breakfast under our belts. I know you don't feel much like eating, son, but it's going to be a long day for all of us. Try to eat as much as you can."

Zak accepted a plate with hash browns, scrambled eggs, and two slices of bacon. Surprised, he discovered that he was quite hungry and managed to eat it all. He took a cinnamon roll, wrapped it in a paper napkin, and tucked it away in his jacket pocket for later.

Everyone was silent, wolfing down the wonderful spread prepared by Morey and Maggie. Too soon, it was time to saddle up and get to work.

Their first destination would be Big Bass Pool, to be certain they hadn't missed anything yesterday. There they planned to meet up with the state divers. Jim called over to Morey's to see if there were any more cinnamon rolls. Jen appeared soon thereafter with three large thermoses of coffee and Styrofoam cups, along with three large containers full of cinnamon rolls. Immediately after her came Morey carrying a big metal box which, when he opened it, revealed a large quantity of fried chicken. He loaded it into the back of the Explorer, along with paper plates, silverware, and a tub of potato salad, all carried over by Jen's daughter, Bridgette. Jim had learned by now never to question how this family seemed to know exactly what was needed without asking. Apparently, Meadows and Murdoch were of the same opinion. The three CSIs looked startled but didn't comment.

It was a long day. Three divers had arrived early that morning. They were ready to go in and insisted on starting at Big Bass Pool. When they slipped into the river, they were startled by the force of the current once they got out beyond the pool. One of them swam back and grabbed an underwater scooter from the back of the van. He once again slipped into the swift-flowing river and turned on the bright lights on the scooter. The other two divers took either side of the river, and the three worked their way downstream, searching for clothing, body parts or anything else of interest. While the current was swift, Martin's Way was only about fifteen feet deep from Big Bass to where it rejoined the Mississippi, approximately two-and-a-half miles south. At its widest, it was ten yards, narrowing to twenty feet as it turned east toward the Mississippi.

The divers made two passes, one down and a more difficult one back up to Big Bass Pool but found nothing of interest. They did note at least four different points along their way that appeared to be underground channels leading westward from the river. However, a test of the currents showed little if any movement of the water in these channels.

When the three emerged from the river, they engaged in a long and heated discussion with Meadows and Murdoch. The latter two wanted the divers to go back with the fiber optic camera, but the divers were insistent that a search downward from the wells would be more productive. One of them, Jerry Barton, had grown up in this area and was familiar with the underground waterways that crisscrossed the region. He was certain that examination of the wells and the river north of Big Bass Pool would be by far the best use of their time and resources.

The divers won the argument. With Jerry at the wheel, they drove out in the van, searching for wells. They started at the textile mill, north of town, and carefully examined the waterwheel. Nothing had caught on the paddles or on the shore. After a quick examination of the river at that point, Jerry decided they should do a pass down the river to Big Bass Pool and back up to the mill, just to be thorough. They called Meadows and informed him of their plans. It was Meadows who suggested that the others search for wells in the area and mark their locations for the divers to search with their fiber optic camera.

Meadows planned to stop at Jenkins Farm and run the camera down that well first. He quickly filled in Jerry about Rory having last been known to be at the pump house and told him if they found anything, they would call the divers immediately. Jerry asked him to call either way.

Jim, Zak, Meadows, and Murdoch all drove up to the Jenkins Farm. Helen Green and her two partners were at Big Bass Pool, searching in full daylight in case anything had been missed the night before.

The pump house was locked, as Jim had left it. He fished the key out of his pocket and opened the doors. In the dim light inside they could barely make out the metal disk lying beside the open well. Jim could have sworn he left that disk mostly covering the opening. He began searching through the photos on his phone. He found the barn pictures and sure enough, he had left the disk on the opening. Helen stopped them from entering the barn while she and Bill took multiple pictures of Rory's half-eaten lunch and the scuff marks that led toward the well opening.

Once they were satisfied that they had photographed and mapped the area, they let the others in. Jim and Meadows began feeding the fiber optic camera down into the water. After an hour of searching, watching, and retracing the well area and into the waterway below, they all agreed there was nothing to be found.

Jim told them how he had left the cover over the well and showed them the pictures on his cell phone. They were all perplexed. Helen compared his pictures to the present state of the dirt leading up to and around the opening, and there was no apparent change beyond the tracks the two men left on the far side when they fed in the camera.

"Guess it's time to start searching the other wells," said Helen. "How many do you suppose there are?"

Zak piped up. "The mill has records. They mapped all the underground waterways and marked all the wells. It is being transferred to a large map that will be at the front when you first enter the mill, once it is opened to the public."

"Then let's get up there and get those maps," said Whiteman. "The sooner we get on this, the sooner we'll have answers."

"Can you send me copies of those pictures, Jim?" asked Helen. He got her cell number and sent them immediately.

The senior manager of the mill restoration project was reluctant to provide the maps and well locations without a warrant. However, when the situation was explained, and he was assured by both Meadows and Murdoch that the mill had no culpability in Rory's unfortunate demise, he agreed to call Saul Grossman and ask for permission to give them access to the mill's records, both online and hard copy.

Jim looked around while they waited. He had never been to the mill before, and his first impression was how big it was. The portion they were in was a one-story lobby of sorts. Men were constructing display cabinets, while others replaced worn or damaged woodwork. Jim could see through the windows to the main floor where the now silent looms stood waiting to be powered once again. The loom area was at least two and half stories high, with catwalks over the looms, barely above their tops. He promised himself to return later when operations had resumed and have Bull show him around.

Grossman finally called and gave permission for the group to examine the maps and geologic surveys. Zak promised to keep tabs on the materials and make sure they were returned in good condition. The team spent the rest of the day mapping out the wells, designating which team would go where. They had three fiber optic cameras and thus were able to designate three teams. They all decided it would be best to get some rest, organize what little evidence they had found, and get an early start the next day.

After a full day of thorough investigation of every well in the area surrounding Harper's Landing, the divers again entered the Martin's Way, this time starting at the waterwheel that would soon power the textile mill and moving south to Big Bass Pool. However, ten feet from the waterwheel they encountered a steel mesh grating across the entire river. There they found a torso, mutilated and missing arms, legs, and head. Tattered remnants of clothing clung to the body, including ripped and torn jeans. After taking multiple pictures, the divers brought the remains to the shore, where the CSI team took over.

In one of the back pockets of the jeans they found a wallet with a picture ID for Rory O'Connor. They bagged the torso, got Jim as coroner to sign the forms, and the remains were sent with the CSI van to the State Medical Examiner's office in Jefferson City. Examination might reveal the cause of death. Two days later the Medical Examiner's report was faxed to Jim. Autopsy revealed that he had died of drowning. The mutilation had occurred postmortem. Comparison of DNA from all of the various body parts with the Army DNA database confirmed that they were the remains of Rory O'Connor.

CHAPTER TWELVE

What remained of Rory O'Connor was buried in the family plot above the mill, along the Martin's Way River. At Mary's request, there was no formal church service, just a gathering at the gravesite for his entombment. Like all the O'Connors and Harpers before him, Rory was wrapped in linen and lowered into the ground in a plain pine box. Out of compassion for both the family and the populace of Harper's Landing, Rory's remains had been laid to rest in the grave before the service. Most of them knew that not all of Rory rested in that grave. Nevertheless, they had dug a full-sized grave, and built a regular pine casket. Then Arthur Willingham started to deliver Rory's eulogy.

"How do you speak for a man you barely knew?" he began. "Rory was a friend to many of you, a beloved brother to Mary and Bull, and a hero to everyone. He served his country with honor and returned to the comfort of family and friends when the horrors of war overtook him. He will live on in our memories, in our love, and in our compassion for his family."

The Army had provided an honor guard, as was his due, though at Mary's request they refrained from the usual rifle salute. The head of the guard handed Mary the carefully folded American flag, Rory's purple heart placed on top. She clutched it to her chest as silent tears rolled down her cheeks.

Arthur then invited others to speak if they wished. They spoke of Rory's humor, of his skill as a fisherman, of his love of family. No one spoke of his terrors, his retreat when the Fourth of July came around, his inability to find love or companionship after war had left him emotionally and spiritually shattered. Instead, they talked of the Rory they wanted to remember, the man they would entomb in their memories as well as the grave.

When "Taps" was played, Mary collapsed into Bull's arms. The grief of everyone involved was palpable. Life cut short is never easy, no matter the cause. But life cut short without cause or explanation is unbearable and soul bending.

Jim Burch stood next to Linda Collier, and although both had strong feelings and rich memories about Rory, neither spoke. They shared a silent grief for a friend taken too soon. Nor did they attend the wake afterward at Morey's. Instead, without being asked, Linda followed Jim to his office where they shared the better part of a bottle of well-aged scotch in silence.

The Missouri State Police lab had been unable to identify any DNA other than Rory's after swabbing both the neck and ankle. Reluctantly, they had released the remains for burial and marked the file *unsolved; no further investigation requested*. It wasn't the usual means for handling what appeared to be a homicide, but without other evidence they had no choice.

Things in Harper's Landing slipped back to normal, with only an occasional discussion about what had happened to Rory. One of the more popular stories was that someone had released baby alligators into the Martin's Way, and they had found their way into the underground waterways. Despite the lack of alligator or any predator DNA, the story gained popularity. Some wanted to introduce poison into the wells, to do away with the critters, while others favored placing traps or blocking side passages in the hope of catching or starving them to death. Jim had to warn folks off the poison route, which never gained popularity anyway. He didn't have to worry about people trying to close off the passages from the waterways to the Martin's Way. People were honestly too frightened to be willing to go into the river to place traps or other means of blocking things off.

Gradually, fishermen returned to Big Bass Pool, and by the time tourist season was in full swing the stories had died down. This was a great relief to the few townsfolk who made a significant portion of their living off the tourist trade. Even Mary was able to set aside her grief enough to deal with the influx of customers seeking local yarns and unusual cottons from her well-stocked shop.

Summer was just around the corner, and things in Harper's Landing appeared to be back to normal.

CHAPTER THIRTEEN

Gary Miller sat rigidly behind the steering wheel of his Mustang, trying not to grip it so tightly that the others would notice. It was the first day of summer vacation, and Gary, Billy Martin, Steve Blinder, and Mike Stoneman were on their way to mischief. The other boys wanted to go skinny dipping at Harve Sanders' pond. Harve would be gone, working on the big landscaping project at the Jackson Hill Library and Community Center. It was barely warm enough for swimming, and Gary had much preferred the idea of stealing beer from his dad's cooler and going down by the river to fish and skip stones.

Gary was mortally afraid of water, afraid in the way a child fears the dark or old people fear death when they have not spent a life well lived. He remembered his brother's drowning vividly, although he was only five at the time. In fact, it was his most vivid memory. That and his father beating his mother near to death for having been drunk when it happened. Never mind that the old bastard was six sheets to the wind himself. It was her job to watch the kids, and Mattie had wandered unnoticed down to the river's edge while his parents and younger brother picnicked on deviled eggs and peanuts. And the parents on vodka-laced iced tea.

Mattie's screams of terror still haunted Gary's eighteen-year-old nightmares.

He drove slowly down the back road toward the pond, praying for Harve to come home early or for Big Jim Burch to decide to come looking for them. No such luck. They arrived at the pond unseen and parked under a large beech tree which hid the car from view.

Missouri in the late spring is a wondrous place. Green grasses mix with wildflowers, and trees spout pollen in all directions. It was getting on toward summer, and the wind was pleasant with a slight edge of brisk. The cottonwoods were nearly ready to unleash their allergy inducing fluff balls on the world, and the bulrushes were already poking up in the pond. They all knew that the pond was deep in the middle, though how deep no one was quite sure. But the edges were shallow, and bullfrogs perched on lily pads among the rushes, fat, and content on a heavy diet of late spring mosquitoes and water walkers. The cicadas were out in full voice, and a family of rabbits were playing and eating on the far side of the pond.

Billy Martin pulled a fat joint from his shirt pocket and lit it with a wooden match. After taking a long pull, he passed it on, and the boys shared it one after another, waiting for the blissful hit that would provide the courage required to strip and jump into the water. Gary also took a hit but made no move toward undressing. When prodded by the others he demurred, claiming an infection from a barn accident. He pulled up his pant leg to reveal the bandaging.

"Yeah," said Billy. "You don't know what's in that pond. Might make the infection spread to your balls."

They all fell on the ground with laughter, overreacting as the pot hit their juvenile brains.

"Maybe his dick will fall off, too," snorted Mike.

And again, they all collapsed in raucous laughter.

The other boys, now filled with cannabis-fueled courage, peeled off their jeans and shirts, and one by one leaped, shrieking, into the still, cold water. Gary sat on the hood of his restored muscle car, keeping a wary eye out for the sheriff or, more likely, the owner of the pond. He allowed his mind to wander, musing over the considerable charms of one Miss Bridgette Stevens. Bridgette was the daughter of Jen Stevens (now Harper), who worked at Morey's Diner, and Will Stevens, who had gone off to war in Afghanistan and come home in a plain pine box.

Jen and Bridgette struggled through that first year of grief and shock, moving back in with Jen's parents. Jen worked full time at the diner, and Bridgette sometimes filled in on busy tourist weekends.

While puberty sneaked up on most of the girls he knew, it hit Bridgette like a wrecking ball. One day she was flat, freckled, and gangly; the next, she had two glorious mounds of fleshy wonderfulness on her chest, and her hips swelled just enough in all the right places.

Gary knew that Bridgette wasn't going to be an easy conquest. She was a good girl. Bridgette was genuinely good. She tutored the little kids, protected them from bullying, helped her neighbors, and was unfailingly cheerful. And he wanted her. Not just in a fleshly way. He wanted her to like him, to want to be with him. The other guys would tease him unmercifully if they knew how he felt. They all lusted after her with a verbal vulgarity that nearly broke his temper. They referred to her as Miss Goody-Two-Shoes, which also infuriated him, though he was careful never to show it.

Gary wondered if having the admiration and loyalty of these boys was worth the role he had to play. He knew he would have to give it up if he were to have any chance with Bridgette. He had so far refused her pleas to join in the tutoring sessions or the food deliveries for the older residents of Harper's Landing. But he felt himself weakening, and not for the first time he wondered why. Certainly, her physical charms were breathtaking, but she was most definitely not his type. Or at least he had thought so. Now he found himself longing to find some purpose, some goodness that would stand him in good stead with her. He needed some kindness in his life, something to soothe the rage he felt toward his drunken and abusive father. And his mother, who refused to stand up for him or to bring a complaint against his dad when he beat or shook her.

He brought his attention back to the three boys splashing and swimming in the pond. He felt ashamed of his fear, of being unable to let it go and jump in with the others. He doubted he would ever be able or willing to go swimming anywhere. As he watched, he saw a strange swirl forming in the middle of the pond. He stood up on the hood to get a better look. It looked like a whirlpool, and he began to shout to the others.

The three boys felt the pull of the current and started toward shore. Their laughter quickly turned to screams of terror as the vortex grew larger and stronger. Gary jumped to the ground and grabbed a fallen limb beside the car. He ran to the edge of pond, and extended the branch out to Billy Martin, who was closest to him. Billy caught hold, and Gary pulled. The strength of the growing whirlpool was too strong, and he watched in horror as Billy, Steve, and Mike were sucked into a large, gaping hole. Gary jumped into his Mustang as the whirlpool grew larger and the pond started lapping at the tires. Before he could start the engine, the raging current pulled the car with him in it into the pond, where it slowly sank under the surface. Gary struggled and finally got the door open, but when he started swimming upward, something grabbed his leg and pulled him deeper into the pond. The water continued to swirl for a few more minutes, slowing, until the surface of the pond was once again still. The Mustang was completely submerged. The bullfrogs began their spring song once again.

CHAPTER FOURTEEN

H e stared in horror, again. What was it thinking? Four heads? Four. Human. Heads. Was it taunting him? Was it angry? Hadn't he managed to steer the deer into the pond, where it quickly disappeared? Was that not enough?

Four heads, all human. He dared not think upon it, dared not look closely at the faces. If he did, he might know who they were, as he had known the first one. He did not want to know. He would have to drop these into the river, like the first one. After dark.

Were these a gift? Perhaps he had not been clear enough with the Provider. He only wanted animal heads.

Does it see us as animals? He shuddered at the thought. He could just as easily be next. It was inhuman; it did not speak, it only radiated hunger and evil.

Jeremy put on his taxidermy gloves. Gingerly, he picked up the heads and put them into a burlap bag.

The Provider seemed to read his mind, so it was obvious he had not been precise in his thoughts. No more human heads. He would be precise. As he had with the fox.

He put the bag in the back of the truck and drove to the southernmost end of the river. He forced himself to go slower, not to panic. He opened the bag and emptied its horrible contents into the river. The current of the Martin's Way was strong here as it flowed into the mighty Mississippi. Jeremy watched as the heads bobbed and then sank. This time he was sure they would not be found.

At home, he washed the truck bed as before, and burned the burlap bag in his fireplace, making sure that nothing was left. He got the small shovel and bucket he kept beside the fireplace, scooped up the ashes from burning the bag, and carried them out deep into the woods.

He then returned to the house and carefully placed the bucket and shovel back in their place on the hearth. Before he went to bed, he checked everything: his tools, the house, how he had parked the truck. Everything was in its proper place. Good work requires good work habits. Mother always told him that.

CHAPTER FIFTEEN

S unday lunch at The Rectory dining room had become
something of a ritual. Jim and Arthur both picked up their
Sunday meals at Morey's on Saturday evening after dinner, and it
seemed natural to put the food into Arthur's big refrigerator and
warm it up after Sunday services. Mary and Bull Harper started
coming sometime midsummer, and their daughter Jen and granddaughter Bridgette joined them. Arthur extended an invitation to
Martin Rutledge, the town's only attorney. He was a lively dining
companion and a welcome addition to the group. Linda Collier
also became a regular and brought with her a wealth of interesting
stories and a slightly risqué sense of humor.

It was early summer. School had let out the previous Friday,
and the tourists were beginning to show up. This might well be
one of the last meals they would all attend until tourist season was
over. The group had just sat down to eat when Jim's cell rang.

"Jim?" It was Linda Collier, who had begged off from lunch
that day because of what she referred to as pressing business at the
paper. "You'd better get to your office, unless you want me to send
them up to you there at Arthur's place."

"Who's them?"

"Beth and Dan Miller, Tina and George Martin, Michael and

Nancy Blinder, and Suzie Stoneman. I wrote all the names down for you. They're waiting outside your office. They all claim their kids are missing, four of their boys, teenagers."

"I suppose Beth and Dan would be Gary Miller's parents," replied Jim.

"Yeah. I know you think Gary's a troublemaker, and maybe he is sometimes, but that father of his is a mean bastard, and Beth's sporting a good big bruise on her arm. I would handle him with kid gloves. If you don't know him, he's the tall one in the red plaid shirt with the military-grade haircut."

"Send them up here. Arthur can help keep anyone in a good mood."

"Will do, Jim," she said and hung up.

"Got a crowd of folks coming up here," said Jim. "Arthur, I know you can sit more people around this table. Can you rustle up more coffee mugs?"

By the time the seven parents arrived, chairs had been found and placed at the long table. More coffee was made, mugs were set out, and a stack of plates sat on a side table in case any of the parents were hungry. There was more than enough food to go around.

The parents arrived as a group, Dan Miller leading the way. They were exhibiting varying degrees of worry, anger, and confusion. As they entered, Dan Miller and Suzie Stoneman started talking at once.

"My son Mike is missing, and it's his kid's fault," she said, pointing at Dan.

"Gary and his friends have gone missing," said Dan at the same time, glaring at Suzie.

"Okay," said Jim, raising his voice slightly. "Everyone, calm down and talk one at a time. First, I know you, Suzie, and I've met you once, Dan. The rest of you, I don't think I've had the pleasure."

At Arthur's urging, the seven parents sat down and accepted

coffee. Dan reached out and snagged a roll, as did Mike Blinder. The others declined any food.

Mike Blinder introduced himself and his wife, Nancy. Their son Steve was a junior at Harper's Landing High School. George and Tina Martin were the parents of Billy Martin, a senior. Suzie Stoneman was a single mother to Mike, who was fourteen and a sophomore. They all seemed somewhat embarrassed to admit that they did not attend Sunday services, but Arthur waved off their apologies.

"I'm not your usual minister," he said. "We sing a bit, read, discuss, sometimes hold silent prayer. Harper's Landing is an anomaly in the Midwest when it comes to religion. We are more a fellowship than a congregation."

They all relaxed a bit, though Dan Miller was still defensive and on edge.

"How long have the boys been missing?" Jim asked.

The parents all started to talk at once. Jim held up his hand.

"Mike, is it?" he asked Mike Blinder. The man nodded. "You first."

"Steve, my son, left yesterday morning along with Gary Miller, Billy Martin, and Mike Stoneman. They were going to go for a drive, maybe do some fishing at Big Bass Pool. At least, that's what they said."

Jim turned to Suzie Stoneman.

"Mike's your son?"

She nodded.

"Did he take anything with him? Anything unusual that you've noticed?"

"No. He said he was going to spend the day with the other guys. I work the swing shift at Wally World. Most nights I get home and Mike's asleep. I didn't know he was gone until this morning, when I went to get him up for breakfast. I thought maybe he'd stayed at one of the guys' houses, so I started calling them at around 10:00 AM or so."

Tina Martin spoke up.

"Billy didn't come home either. We were out at a fundraising party for the mill restoration, along with Mike and Nancy." She pointed to the Blinders.

"I guess we all thought that they'd stayed the night at Gary's house," said Mike Blinder. "They've done it before, but never without asking first."

"What about you?" asked Jim, looking at Dan and Beth Miller. "When did you realize Gary wasn't home?"

Both parents blushed deeply. Finally, Beth blurted out, "We didn't get home until this morning." Dan gave her a vicious glare.

"We went to St. Louis, to the new Budweiser expansion opening," he said. "Gary knew we wouldn't be home until this morning. He's graduated high school, old enough to be alone," he declared defiantly.

Jim finished his lunch, letting the parents calm down, deliberately taking his time under the glare of Dan Miller. The man was obviously a bully and, from Beth's reaction to his glare, most likely a wife beater.

Finally, he put down his fork, took a sip of coffee, and said, "None of you have seen your children since yesterday morning?"

They all nodded, beginning to look worried as the gravity of his question sank into them.

"And none of them said anything about a road trip, mentioned a concert in the city, anything like that?"

They all shook their heads no.

"What about family troubles? Issues with school? Detention, grounding, anything?"

Again, they all responded no, though Jim noticed Beth's glance at her husband.

Suzie Stoneman sat up a little taller in her chair.

"Mike ... he's too young to be running with the others. He's only fourteen; they're all seniors or graduated. But he likes them. He's lonely since his dad died. I let him go with them."

"Don't you go blaming my son," interrupted Dan. "He didn't force your son to go with them."

Jim leaned closer to Arthur.

"Would you mind taking Dan outside? I'm not sure what excuse you can come up with but please think of something," he said softly.

"Sure," whispered Arthur. "Dan, would you and your lovely wife mind joining me for a moment? I'd like your opinion on a project I'm contemplating, and I'm told that you are handy with building things."

"Right now?" asked Dan. "Can't you see we're involved in something important?"

"Oh, I'm sure Jim will want to talk with each of you." Arthur smiled. "I'm just sure I'll forget and then want to call you down here again. It'll be a good break from the anxiety, anyway."

Reluctantly, they followed him out to the back, where he pulled out the plans he had drawn up for redoing The Rectory into a bed and breakfast. Despite his mood, Dan found himself drawn in by the plans and Arthur's enthusiasm, and soon Beth joined in with suggestions about interior design and a new kitchen.

Meanwhile, Jim sat with the other parents, who seemed far more relaxed now that Dan and his mercurial temper were removed.

"How likely do you think it is that the boys might have headed south on a lark?" asked Jim. "Maybe a post-graduation trip for Gary and Billy."

"I think it would have been more like an escape," said Tina. "Dan's got a temper. I don't think Beth got that bruise from banging into something. Billy would have gone along with him. He likes Gary and sees something in him, something maybe the rest of us miss."

Mike Blinder spoke up. "Steve has commented more than once that Gary would give anything to get away from his dad. But I don't see Steve going off without telling us first, even if he did just graduate. We have a good relationship, no problems. Right, Nancy?"

She nodded. "He talks to us both, about things many boys wouldn't discuss with their parents. But if things got bad between Dan and Beth, well, maybe the boys went with Gary instead of coming to us, or even you, Sheriff. Kids stick together."

Jim nodded, and beckoned to Arthur to come back in with Gary Miller's parents.

"I'm not going to open an official investigation yet," he said, holding up his hand against their protests. "I will notify the State Patrol to be on the lookout for Gary's Mustang. You folks"—he turned to Gary's parents—"write down his license number. That's the blue number he likes to drive around town, right?"

They nodded.

"If the state boys spot them, I'll ask them to pull them over to make sure they're okay and insist that they call you folks. If they resist, then we'll have them taken in for you to go and pick them up."

The parents all reluctantly agreed.

"Now, if we haven't heard anything by tomorrow, then I'll open a missing persons report. We usually wait forty-eight hours anyway unless there's evidence of foul play. If it were just Mike, given his age, I'd do it now. But since he was last seen with the other boys, and two of them are old enough to be regarded as adults, we'll wait. You be ready to come in and file a report if I call, and then we'll get more people on this. Until then, all we can do is wait."

There was grumbling among the parents, but, ultimately, they agreed that it was best to wait. Two days later Suzie Stoneman, Mike and Nancy Blinder, and Tina and George Martin all filed missing persons reports on their sons. Dan and Beth Miller did not come in, nor did they respond to messages from Jim. He went ahead and took the reports on the other three boys and sent a private message along with copies of the reports to Clay Murdoch. In it, he voiced his concerns that Gary may have had something to do with the disappearance of the other boys. While he had no reason to believe the parents knew anything, he also wrote of his opinion that Dan Miller was a violent and potentially abusive father and husband. There certainly was more than enough circumstantial evidence leading to that conclusion.

Around town the majority opinion, voiced loudly and often by old Ethan White at Morey's Diner, was that Gary Miller had talked the other three boys into leaving with him, and that they were larking about somewhere in or near St. Louis. Jim kept silent during these discussions. It was his duty as a lawman, and as a responsible citizen. Privately, he told Arthur that none of the boys had taken any money out of their bank accounts (he left out how he knew that since his conversation with Jim Ledlow up at the new Harper's Landing Citizens Credit Union was somewhat extra-legal).

The days stretched into weeks, and by mid to late summer the search for the boys stalled. Although the parents were still upset, they stopped badgering Jim to call the state police headquarters daily. Mike and Nancy Blinder drove to St. Louis to demand that the search be stepped up. After a long and heated conversation with Clay Murdoch and Blake Meadows, they returned to Harper's Landing, disheartened, and anguished, believing their boy to be cold and lonely, wandering the streets of St. Louis.

CHAPTER SIXTEEN

It was August in Harper's Landing. As in the rest of the Midwest, the sunlight seemed saturated, dripping wet and making everything humid and unbearable. Charity Farmington sat on her porch, chasing away mosquitoes with her large fan and listening to the faraway whoosh of the Grossman Textile Mill waterwheel. Her stone cottage, built by her great-great-grandfather Stephan in 1792, was cool and comfortable. It was square, with a pointed, thatched roof. Inside were two rooms, one for sleeping and the other for cooking, eating, and any other family activities. The stone walls were lined inside with hand-planed lumber, and sheep fleece was layered between the stone and the planks to hold back the winter cold and the summer heat. Charity loved sitting in the rocking chair made by her great-great-uncle Mikhail. The heat did not bother her; in fact, it felt good to her old bones. The cottage was sturdy and had required refurbishing only once since she inherited it from her aunt.

Charity rarely went into Harper's Landing except to visit her nephew, Morey, and his delightful wife, Maggie. On these trips, she would bring bushels of apples for Maggie, who had inherited the family pie recipe when she married Morey. Charity's trees were ancient and gnarled, with great, thick trunks and twisted roots coming up to the surface. From early spring, after the flowering, until the first frosts of late fall, her trees drooped with abundant fruits: heirloom apples, they now called them, and three kinds of cherries. Morey and Maggie's helper, Jen, would come up regularly with her daughter Bridgette, and they would fill Charity's ancient yet sturdy wagon with apples. Charity would then harness her sturdy little Icelandic pony, Birgit, and take the apples to the diner where they were stored in the cold cellar out back.

Today, Charity was especially aware of the creak of the waterwheel. She sensed a strangeness in the air, a feeling of *not rightness*. She wasn't surprised to see Jen ride into her yard, leaning her sturdy red bicycle next to the well out front.

"You feel it, too," said the old woman.

"Yes," replied Jen. "And Bridgette, too, though I did not know she had the sense."

"What about Maggie? Is she baking up a storm?"

"Now that you mention it, I would guess she's made forty pies in the last three days. My hands certainly feel it from all the peeling and cutting."

"I think part of it's the mill," said Charity, taking a puff on the old, long-handled pipe she kept by her side.

Jen smelled the sweet heady scent of hemp but said nothing. She had long ago realized that Charity wasn't ordinary and could only hope that Jim Burch would never take it into his head to come up here. She liked Jim, but she also knew that he was a cop through and through and not likely to look the other way.

She sat next to the old woman and listened to the waterwheel.

"You're right," she said finally. "It sounds different. Not the wheel, but the way the water flows."

"No deer came through this spring," said Charity.

"Something's up," replied Jen. "Like you said, not right."

※

The mill was operating again, powered by the giant waterwheel in the Martin's Way River. It had been easy enough to reattach the waterwheel, and with the combined force of the wheel and the smaller wheels placed underwater, the mill was turning out a large amount of well-spun cotton and wool, as well as bolts of cotton and wool cloth.

Grossman Textiles, the company that had purchased the mill, intended to have a fully operating mill and a museum dedicated to the history of cotton and textile mills in the Midwest. They had begun importing raw cotton and wool from throughout the Midwest. Charity and Jen both approved of all of the company's plans. It would bring work back to the town, and anything that preserved history was something they both deeply appreciated.

Grossman built a new road across the land that used to be the Jenkins Farm, connecting the mill complex to the county road, which in turn intersected with Interstate 35 fifteen miles west. All that was left of the old farm was the pump house, which was now being used to store building materials and equipment for new operations.

New buildings began appearing along the road leading to the main mill, and power lines were put up. One of the larger structures was a hydroelectric power plant built upstream from the waterwheel, a mile from where the Martin's Way River began its departure from the Mississippi River and made its way south. The current was strong enough to operate the plant, which in turn provided the power to operate the new thread making operation. And as the water was released from the newly built dam, it gathered strength enough to turn the waterwheel two miles downstream.

One of the new buildings next to the power plant contained sixty spinning mules. These machines were a hybrid of a water frame and a spinning jenny. They were partly powered by a smaller version of the main mill waterwheel and partly by hydroelectric power. Each mule held thirteen hundred bobbins, and when finally in operation, the mules would provide all the cotton and wool yarn needed for the main mill operations. The mule was the most common spinning machine from 1790 until about 1900 but was still used for fine yarns until the 1960s. The new thread making operation meant jobs once again, and many townsfolk who had moved away were returning as they accepted job offers made first to former workers. Additional jobs were available at the power plant and the museum complex. Grossman had offered every former millworker their original position and at a higher wage.

A second building was reserved for dyeing the yarns once they were spun. Grossman hired twenty workers for this operation and sent them all to a two-week training seminar held in historic Williamsburg, where they learned traditional dyeing techniques using plant colors and natural mordants.

The Harper's Landing Textile Mill wasn't the only mill operation that had flourished in the region. In the early years of the twentieth century, Gerhard Frohm built a lumber mill in a large clearing near the stone cottages where the first immigrants had settled. The lumber mill was close to the apple and cherry orchards, and the woodworkers who used the mill became well known for their quality birch and oak blanks, prized by wood turners and carvers.

Charity had no plans to rebuild her grandfather's lumber mill, which had burned to the ground during a freak attack in the early 1900s. She still had nightmares about the night the mill burned down. Her father had died in the fire, attempting to rescue her aunt. The burned-out shell of the mill was now overgrown with hemlock and blackberries. Charity had other pressing concerns. She worried about the continuation of the apple and cherry orchards, which supplied all the fruit for Harper's Landing and the surrounding farms. The cottages that had once housed her great-great-grandfather's siblings were in as good shape as hers, and she decided to approach Mary and Bull about their daughter and granddaughter. These were no ordinary fruit trees, and caring for them required training in arts more occult than horticulture and farming. Both mother and daughter had shown great promise. At one time, Charity had thought Maggie Farmington might take on the job. But though she had great talent with the spells that went into the crafting of the various pies, her magical skills ended there.

"Why don't you ask Arthur to bring you and Bridgette tomorrow night and come up for dinner?" she said to Jen. "I've got a spring lamb that broke its leg, poor thing. Had to put it down swiftly, and it's hanging in the cool house waiting to be turned into a nice roast with new potatoes and fresh carrots."

"We'll be there," replied Arthur when Jen called. "I presume this is for more than just lamb and company."

"You'd presume correctly," said Jen. "Charity says she has things to show you." Jen departed, heading for the diner and the lunch crowd that would soon arrive.

Charity wondered if she could persuade Jen and Bridgette to move up here. It was a short distance to the town, the road was in good condition, and there was enough power of all kinds in this area to fulfill their needs. Surely, they must be ready to leave Jen's parents' house and live on their own. It had been five years since Jen's husband had died. It was time for them to be independent.

This land had been in her family since the late 1700s when her great-great-grandfather and his siblings arrived. When Charity left town and moved back to her family's original land-holding, she searched through the old trunks stored in one of the cottages. She found an old deed. It provided enough information to establish her claim to the land if it ever became necessary.

Charity also found a diary belonging to Stephan in the same chest where she found the deed. It was written in English, and she had been reading it before Jen arrived. She picked it up and continued to read.

We arrived in America in 1792 at Baltimore, where we managed to purchase a wagon and team, large enough to carry us, salt, cloth, and our tools. We have passed other small communities on our way west, some Ukrainian like ourselves; others were from western Europe. And some were freed slaves, strong, black-skinned men and women whose eyes bore the pain and sorrow of lives uprooted and families torn apart. In all these places we have found kindness, generosity, and curiosity. The few Ukrainian communities we have encountered are a joy but have made us even more homesick.

We have not found anyone possessed of the power we have kept secret from others, the powers of the old ways that forced us to leave and come to this strange land. We found something similar in one place. We stumbled upon a native village. The people are tall, sharp-boned, thick-skinned, and proud. They live in strange shelters built of animal hides and shaped like a cone, large and stable at the bottom rising to a small hole in the top where the smoke from the cooking and heating fire escaped. The tribe was at first resistant to having anything to do with us, but when we offered to share our freshly killed deer they relented and let us sit by the great open fire.

It was among these people that Katya first detected power not unlike her own. She told me that I was being carefully observed by a wrinkled old man who sat in a seat higher than the others. When their meal was finished, and I was about to fill our water jugs and continue our journey, the man rose and lifted the stick he carried. It was covered in feathers and symbols, and I saw Katya gasp as she felt the power of it. He then motioned to the child next to him, who ran into a nearby structure and returned with a smaller version of the stick. The old man carefully walked through the gathered tribe to me and held out the smaller stick. Katya, sensing what was about to happen, had already reached into her pack and pulled out a bundle of herbs she had brought with her from Ukraine. Once I had accepted the stick, she pressed the bundle into my hand, and I held it out to the old man.

She knew that the bundle would be saved for as long as it could be, just as she and her siblings would treasure and protect the stick.

The following morning, as we set out again seeking land that would call to us, I handed the stick to Katya. She gasped again at the power of it and carefully wrapped it in a soft sheepskin and placed it in the trunk that held her ritual clothing, books, and candles. She felt it would be necessary to incorporate the stick in any workings in this new world.

We came upon the fertile and forested land on which we settled, just south of where a small but swift river broke off from the Mississippi. There was a narrow portion at the headwaters where the river had not yet gathered strength as it tumbled south down to where it curved east back to the Mississippi.

There was a cotton mill two miles downriver from the first rapids, but no one lived north of the mill. We built our cottages from stones Mikhail and I carried from the riverbank, while Jane and Katya built temporary shelters with tree branches they cut from the birches in the nearby woods. It was midsummer, and we would be warm enough, if exposed to possible predators, until at least one of the cottages could be built. My sisters also busied themselves planting the precious apple and cherry seeds they had brought with them, as well as vegetables, in a small garden area they prepared using the team of horses and the small plow I purchased in Baltimore.

Charity wondered again at the hardships they must have faced, both in their journey from Baltimore to this remote area and in building a place to live before the winter storms set in. She also marveled at the construction of the cottages. The exterior was carefully placed stone, but the inside walls were hand-cut slabs, carefully fitted together with mortise and tenon joints. The bark was left on one side of the slabs facing outward, sheep wool was stuffed into the openings, and then the stone walls were built over the bark and wool.

This couldn't have been accomplished in the few months they had before winter arrived. Did they all stay in one cottage at first and then build the next? Did they find shelter elsewhere while they built? Did they have help? These were questions for which she had no answers. She decided to ask Arthur and Jen to look through the other three cottages for trunks she hoped would hold more journals or diaries.

Dinner the following afternoon was a lovely affair. Arthur brought a full-bodied deep red wine to go with the lamb, and Bridgette brought a pear tart she had made under the watchful eye of Maggie. While Morey was the one who was part of the family tree going back to Stephan, it seemed that Maggie was the one possessed of the talent that brought the fruit from the orchard to life. In fact, all of her talent showed itself in her baking and cooking. Charity was delighted to learn that the skill was being passed on to Bridgette. When Maggie was included in the discussions around Charity's table regarding traditions and spells, her only comment was that it explained why her baking was so sought after. She also mentioned that after once deviating from the old recipes, she never did it again. She refused to go into detail, and it was universally assumed among the others that the resultant product had been a disaster.

After dinner, Charity tentatively put forth the idea of Jen and Bridgette moving up there into one of the cottages, or perhaps even each having her own cottage. To her surprise, both thought the idea was wonderful and agreed to come up the following day and throughout the summer to select cottages and do what needed to be done to make them comfortable and inviting. Jen was certain her father, Bull, would help in the restoration. She was equally certain that her parents, even though they loved her and her daughter dearly, would be happy to have their home to themselves once again.

Arthur, too, was delighted, and suggested that perhaps the fourth cottage could be renovated at some point as living quarters for students who might happen to pass through. Arthur Willingham may have been ordained by the Congregational Church, but few people knew that he was also highly skilled in the arcane arts and a gifted seer.

The conversation soon took a serious turn. Arthur had also sensed something was wrong, and they all compared notes. Arthur was concerned about the missing boys, who had disappeared so soon after Rory's demise. He filled the women in on the details of

Ben's encounter in the pump house. Charity was equally concerned about the disappearance of the boys, plus the decrease in wildlife traveling through her woods.

They all knew someone had put a protection spell of some kind on the village so it would always attract the people it needed. It had brought them Jim Burch, and Arthur himself had felt pulled to come. He also believed Martin Rutledge had been called and the reason would be revealed in due time.

But some other protection, unknown to them all, had been broken. Arthur felt the need to know exactly what it was, and soon. He urged Charity, Jen, and Bridgette to go through the trunks stored in the three unoccupied cottages, while he would seek out the assistance of Linda Collier in exploring the newspaper morgue files. He wasn't sure what he would tell her they sought, but missing animals or people was high on his list. How he would explain it was a different matter.

They settled on a loose schedule of sorts. As Jen had predicted, her father was willing to help with the renovation and restoration of the cottages, especially since The Rectory project was nearly done. Mary had a full schedule of quilt retreats, so money, at least for the summer, wasn't a problem. They would start renovating the cottages the following Monday, just three days away. And Arthur would start serious research immediately. Charity promised to spend the next few days going through the various trunks and boxes in the vacant cottages, and after much begging she agreed to have Bridgette come and help. Jen also relayed the happy news that as soon as the mill resumed operations, her father would have his old job back as foreman.

As Arthur rose to leave, his phone rang. It was Jim Burch. Arthur sighed to himself.

These days it was never good when Jim called midday or unexpectedly.

"I need you at Harve Sanders' place. You're official now, on the clock. Harry's in St. Louis for a couple of days."

"Be right there."

CHAPTER SEVENTEEN

Harve Sanders was a muscular man, thirty-four years old, single, and a gifted landscaper. His home was his showroom, resplendent with iris, coneflower, butterfly weed, bluebells, geraniums, goldenrod, hydrangeas, and asters. His vegetable garden was equally marvelous, though this early in the season the plants were only beginning to climb up the trellises, ladders, and tipis he had constructed in the numerous raised beds around the east side of his house.

Harve did all the landscaping in Harper's Landing, and he had a crew of five young men and two young women to help him. Currently, they were finishing the landscaping for the new Harper's Landing Library and Recreation Center, which was part of the historical complex Saul Grossman was building around the renovated textile mill.

He stood near the pond that lay in the lower portion of his ten-acre property, cell phone in hand, lunch pail forgotten. He had come home at 1:00 PM to pick up the lunch he had left at home when he noticed that the pond level was unusually low, even for midsummer. He walked down to the well, intending to get the pump going to fill the pond when he saw blue just under the surface. It was the roof of a car, a blue muscle car by the looks of it.

He hadn't noticed anything when he drove in earlier, even though his driveway ran from the county road past the pond and up to his house.

No way was he going closer, not even when Jim arrived. They could deal with this without him. The pump house had been bad enough; now this, and in his own backyard. He wanted to run, to get in his truck and go back to the worksite, return to planting boxwoods and laying sod. Instead, he stood obediently, staring at the pond.

Jim was nursing an extremely sour stomach on the ride out to Harve's. He liked the man, awkward and reclusive as he was. But he couldn't ignore the fact that Harve had been the one to send Rory to the pump house, the last place he was known to have been alive. And it was his pond where what was probably Gary Miller's blue Mustang was now resting. He'd asked Arthur to drive, so he could call Meadows and Murdoch and get things rolling. His gut was telling him there wasn't going to be a happy resolution. He'd let Blake and Clay decide when to call the parents.

The Missouri State Police helicopter arrived as Arthur and Jim pulled into Harve's driveway. Blake explained they had arrived so quickly because they'd been finishing up with a nasty accident on the nearby interstate. Blake Meadows took one look at the pond and called in a CSI van and instructed Clay Murdoch and the chopper pilot to tape off the driveway.

"No one in or out."

"Get back to headquarters," he said to the pilot once they finished. "I'm thinking we'll need a couple of divers up here. How deep is this pond?" he asked Harve.

Harve shrugged. He had no idea, had never explored it.

"Jim," said Clay, "I know this is your jurisdiction, but I'm going to ask you to officially hand over this investigation to me. Things are getting out of hand, and if I'm in charge it makes it easier to call in the resources I think we're going to need to deal with all of these events."

Jim knew he was right. Nevertheless, his acceptance was

given somewhat grudgingly. He did ask for and got the right to be the first to interview any locals they might take an interest in.

Jim and Arthur led Harve back to the Explorer. Jim pulled out two canvas folding chairs from the back and sat Harve in one. He sat in the other.

"Arthur, would you help me? I want you to take your cell and walk around the outer perimeter of the pond, fifteen feet or so from the water's edge. Take lots of pictures, even if nothing's there. If you spot anything of interest, get Meadows or Murdoch over to look. And be careful not to step in any footprints or animal tracks."

"Sure thing."

In fact, Arthur was delighted to have some alone time around the pond. He sensed something *wrong*, in a way quite alien to him. There was a subtle attraction pulling him toward it, nothing strong enough he couldn't resist; but it could be quite difficult for someone untrained in the detection of and resistance to such things to resist. He dared not tell Jim, since he was certain he would immediately lose his badge, and perhaps his freedom, for seventy-two hours. Though probably not the latter. He needed to introduce Jim to this arcane side of what appeared to be happening with finesse. Carefully, he sent out a *go away* command, repeating it as he walked around. Finally, he felt the attraction fade and ultimately disappear.

Meadows and Murdoch stood back and watched as the CSI who had accompanied them from the accident scene carefully photographed everything as he, too, walked around the pond. No one noticed Arthur, who was doing the same but from a much farther distance.

Arthur was the one who found the clothing. He yelled for everyone to come look. There was a pile of discarded clothes: shoes, socks, blue jeans, T-shirts, even underpants. Once the pile had been thoroughly photographed, Jim and Clay Murdoch donned gloves and began searching the clothes. In one pair of pants Jim found a wallet containing a school ID picture with the name Michael Dean Stoneman. He also found a few dollars, a picture of a pretty young girl, and an emergency contact card with his mother's name and phone number. He found a cell phone in the pocket of the jeans, completely uncharged.

The second pair of pants produced another wallet, this time with the picture and ID of William Blake Martin. There was a twenty-dollar bill and two condoms in the wallet as well as some nude pictures of twenty-something blondes. The third and final wallet was that of Steven James Blinder. His wallet held condoms, three ten-dollar bills, and a ticket stub from the drive-in outside of town. Neither Steve nor Billy's jeans held cell phones, but Jim would have wagered they would be found at the bottom of the pond.

Nothing belonging to Gary Miller was found on the banks of the pond, either in the pile of clothing or near it. Jim had no doubt that the car was his, but this would have to be established officially once Mick's Garage arrived with their tow truck. It turned out that Mick Harris was finishing towing away one of the totaled cars from the same accident scene that Blake Meadows had been at. He told Jim it would be at least twenty minutes before he could get to the pond.

Reluctantly, Jim decided it was time to question Harve. He pulled Meadows and Murdoch aside, leaving Arthur to sit and chat with Harve. Jim explained why he felt it was time to question the landscaper. There were, in his mind, too many coincidences to leave them unexplored. First, there was the disappearance of Rory, who was working for Harve. Then, a bit of questioning on his part had revealed that Harve had done all the landscaping and had a maintenance contract for the houses where the pets went missing. And now this car, submerged in his pond, was, in his opinion, too much to be ignored. Meadows and Murdoch agreed.

"You want to do it here? Or take him to your office?"

Clay Murdoch wasn't going to question a possible murder suspect out in the open if he could avoid it.

"What about at his house," said Jim. "If he's willing, it's right there. That way we can keep an eye on his reactions if the divers find stuff."

"If he agrees willingly, then I see no problem with that," said Meadows. "I want to Mirandize him, though. Because you never know what is going to come out of discussions like these."

"How about I let him know that he can and probably should have Martin over here with him, even though he's not being charged with a crime?" asked Jim. "That way we may not put him quite so much on edge."

Meadows agreed. He wasn't sure what was going on here. Although there was plenty of interesting stuff connecting Sanders to the missing animals and the locations, there wasn't anything even circumstantial connecting him to the deaths. Hell, they didn't know if they were dealing with a homicide or a horrible accident in the case of Rory O'Connor. And who knew where these boys were or what had happened to them?

Jim called Arthur over to the Explorer, and together they spoke with Harve.

"Harve," said Jim, "we"—pointing to the state guys—"want to ask you some questions about the pump house, the wells up on Jackson Hill, and, of course, about this business here."

"I figured as much," replied Harve.

He sighed deeply and started toward the house. Jim reached out and stopped him.

"Hold on a moment. We don't know what is going on. But in case this whole thing turns nasty, I think maybe you might want to have Martin Rutledge with you while we talk. Your choice, but that's what I would suggest."

Arthur chimed in with his agreement.

"Can Arthur stay, too?" asked Harve.

"Yeah, I'll clear it with them," said Jim. "You call Martin; get him to come down here."

CHAPTER EIGHTEEN

Charity was disturbed. Arthur's abrupt departure was unsettling. He only said that Jim needed him at Harve's pond. Charity needed no further details. She knew it would be about the missing boys. Jen and Bridgette knew, also. Bridgette wanted to go there immediately. The boys were friends, school-mates. But Jen and Charity were having none of that.

"Once people start going down there, everyone in town will be over there. And then they'll start talking about Harve. And getting in the way of Jim and the state police."

Mom was right; Bridgette knew that. But they were her friends. She desperately wanted them to be okay. She looked at Charity's face, then at her mother, and knew that nothing about this was going to be okay. Jen pulled her close.

"I'll call Jim, ask him if he can let us know when or if they know anything. Okay?"

The girl nodded, deliberately slowing her breath. This was the kind of thing she was training for. All her family had trained for it. She felt the *wrongness* as strongly as the other two women, perhaps more. Was it because it was her friends? No, that couldn't be. She had felt this *wrongness* long before she learned that Arthur had been called to Harve's pond about the boys.

Jen dialed her cell. It went directly to voicemail. She frowned. That wasn't like Jim, not like him at all. She tried Arthur instead, and again got voicemail. This time she left a message, asking Arthur to call them the minute he learned anything that might be of interest.

"Come on, then," said Charity. "Let's get this lamb put away and the dishes washed. They aren't going to do themselves."

CHAPTER NINETEEN

Harve led Jim, Arthur, and Blake Meadows into his tidy sitting room. There was a large window where they could sit and observe the pond in the distance. Clay Murdoch stayed behind, watching for the divers and the tow truck to arrive.

Jim was struck with the construction of Harve's home. He noted that the walls were planks put together with mortise and tenon joints. The floor was the same, and the planks gleamed in the afternoon sun. The furniture was all wood, handmade by the looks of it, and polished to a high sheen.

He could see the kitchen from the comfortable chair he had chosen near the front door, and it appeared to be an add-on.

"How old is this house?" he asked Harve.

"I think it was built in 1809 or so," said Harve. "My great-great-grandfather, Yuri Harasemchuk, built it along with his father-in-law, Maksym Molovna."

"That's a mouthful of a name," said Blake.

"Yeah, he changed it to Harper when he arrived here from Ukraine. But the family papers, diaries, journals, and such all refer to the old name."

"You're another Harper?" asked Arthur.

"I guess. There seems to be a lot of us. My great-great-grand-parents had two kids: Jennie and Levi. Levi died young, of the flu. Jennie, my great-grandmother, married Louis Collier. They had a passel of kids, couldn't begin to tell you all the names. But my grandfather, Henry Collier, married a local girl, Melissa Farmington. They had a son named Willard. He married some foreign gal, think her name was Ariel. She died in childbirth. The daughter, Linda, grew up here and stayed here. That's Linda Collier, the newspaper lady. Took her maiden name after her husband died in the mill accident. Guess that means she and me are related somehow."

Harve suddenly stopped, realizing he had been babbling on about family and probably bored everyone to death. It was nerves; he knew it, and it probably wasn't doing him any good.

And if he talked much longer, he might forget and tell them about his family, too.

Arthur, however, had been taking copious notes which he now stuffed into his inside pocket. It would be interesting to construct a timeline later, and perhaps Charity and Jen could fill in more details after they found their family journals. Once this was settled, he would ask if he could borrow Harve's diaries, or at least read them. He was beginning to think that most, if not all, the longtime residents of Harper's Landing were related or had strong family connections. And he was damn sure Harve was hiding something.

Blake Meadows had ignored Harve's nerve-related narrative. Instead, he was focused on the connections between this mild-mannered man and the various locations where animals or people had gone missing. He was jumping to conclusions, and he knew it. But it was hard not to assume that they were not going to like what they found in the bottom of that pond.

Just as the wait for Martin Rutledge to arrive was becoming interminable, a large tow truck rattled up to the pond. The driver hopped out, and after a brief conversation with Murdoch and the CSI, backed his truck up in line with the car in the pond and turned on the winch. The CSI technician and Clay took the large hook at the end of the cable and slowly walked into the pond. They reached the car without incident, and Clay, taking a deep breath, ducked under the surface and wrapped the chain around the back axle. He secured the hook and then resurfaced. The two men walked back to the edge of the pond and signaled to Mick to pull it out. Mick put the winch in reverse and set the motor for slow. At first, nothing happened, and then Mick turned off the winch motor with a shout. His truck had begun sliding toward the pond. Jim, Arthur, and the others came bounding out of the house and toward the pond. Martin Rutledge arrived at the outer gate and headed down Harve's long driveway.

The group stood staring alternately at the pond and at the deep ruts where Mick's truck had slid toward the pond until he turned off the winch. All three of the state police—Meadows, Murdoch, and Jim Cleveland, the CSI—agreed nothing further would happen until the divers arrived. Clay hadn't seen an obstruction when he was under the water placing the winch chain and hook, but he hadn't been looking for anything special. Mick's truck was much larger and heavier than that Mustang; it should have pulled the car out easily. They would wait.

No one was in a mood to talk, let alone ask questions. And none of them wanted to leave the pond in case something was to happen. They stood around, each lost in his own thoughts, waiting for the divers.

Except for Harve Sanders and Martin Rutledge. The two men were sitting on handmade Adirondack chairs on Harve's front porch, deep in conversation. Martin wanted every detail about any connection Harve had to the location where Rory was last known to be, the place Rory's head had been found, and where the pets went missing. The pond connection was obvious.

At long last the divers arrived, pulling up in a large van and accompanied by two additional CSIs from the state headquarters in Jefferson City. The divers stood at the pond's edge, assessing the situation. They asked who the landowner was, and Harve was hailed down from the porch. He loped over, trailed by Martin.

"Have you ever drained this pond?" asked one of the divers.

"Nope. Never had cause."

"How low does it get during the summer?"

"I've never seen it much lower than this."

"Have you ever been in?"

"No. I don't swim. I did try to fish once, but nothing there."

"Where does the water come from?"

"Well, I reckon from somewhere down in the center. Great-great-grandpa Yuri owned this cabin, and his in-laws owned the other one back there. The pond was here when they claimed the land."

Harve stopped himself from launching into still another Harper family genealogy lesson.

"Why didn't you call this in sooner? Looks like the car's been visible for at least a couple of days."

"I didn't notice. I've been working long hours; leave at 6:00 AM and stop at Morey's for breakfast. Stop back there at 6:00 PM for dinner, and then home after dark. The only reason I noticed it today was I saw a deer down there drinking when I came back to get the lunch I forgot. Don't see that much lately."

"Okay," said Meadows. "The divers want to drain the pond. They have the hoses and the pumps to do it, and they would send the water toward the road and that depression on the other side. Will you allow it? I should warn you that if you say no, we will get a warrant. I'm sure Mr. Rutledge here will have questions about it all, too."

"Oh, you bet," said Martin. "I think you should give permission, Harve, but first I want it understood that he hasn't been charged with a crime. And the minute you see anything that sends you in that direction, I want him Mirandized."

"Of course," replied Meadows.

"I will do it," said Jim. "But I don't think we are talking arrest yet."

He wondered why Harve kept looking back at his house. Or was he looking farther, toward the old log cabin by the woods?

The big police van contained a large pump and two equally large hoses. They attached one to the input valve and the other to the output. The output hose was stretched across the road and into the tree-filled area beyond. Then the input hose was put into the pond and the motor started.

At first nothing seemed to happen, but rather quickly they all noticed the pond level going down. Bullfrogs hopped about complaining loudly. Arthur grabbed a large bucket which he filled with water and started dropping bullfrogs in. Harve joined him, and once the bucket was full Arthur emptied it into a small depression he had located near the pond. They continued the process until they had captured and relocated all the frogs they could find.

By then the pond had been almost completely drained. The blue Mustang was nose down, apparently stuck in the mud. Before they attempted to remove it again, the divers and the CSIs slogged in the muck and mud of the now empty pond, looking for anything that seemed of interest or out of place.

As they drew close to the front of the car, one of the CSIs called a halt. While the others remained in place, he bent and retrieved what appeared to be a shoe. It was a red Nike Jordan. Jim's heart sank. He knew from experience that Gary Miller wore red Nike Jordans. The CSI called for Jim to retrieve a body bag from the van, and once he reached the shore, he put the shoe in the bag. Jim could see what appeared to be the remnants of a foot. The smell of decomp was slight but detectable. His heart sank further.

"I'll call the parents," he said. "I guess we should have them out here."

The lab tech sighed. He knew it was necessary, but it was a part of the job he hated. He returned to continue the search.

As the waters receded, they could see that the driver's door was open. They searched diligently in the muck around the car. Nothing was found.

"Let's get this car out of there so we can process it," said one of the CSIs.

When Mick showed the CSIs what had happened when he tried to pull it out, the state guys decided to add the winch on their lab van.

While all this was going on, Jim retreated slowly to Harve's porch. He grabbed a soda out of the Explorer on his way and sat, sipping it slowly. He didn't want to make the call. When a child dies you lose a piece of your future. How could he tell these parents that their hopes and dreams were buried somewhere under a Mustang in a pool of mud and muck? He knew, in his gut, that those boys were gone. What haunted him now, and would haunt him for some time, was the real prospect that they would not find their bodies. They might find pieces, if they were lucky, but it seemed apparent to him that the boys, all but Gary, had gone skinny dipping and were somewhere under that Mustang. How the Mustang got there, however, was a complete mystery. There were tracks. He had seen them. But why had Gary driven into the pond? The crime lab boys were going to have their hands full.

He, in the meantime, had his hands empty, except for the cell phone. He still hadn't dialed anyone. The red shoe haunted him. He hadn't liked that boy, hadn't given him a chance. The kid never did anything wrong, other than occasionally skipping school. He was just a smart-mouthed kid who rubbed him the wrong way. And now, apparently, he was dead. Or at the least missing a foot. He was fooling himself. The kid was dead, as were the other three. And he got the grand prize: to call the parents and tell them to come down here.

CHAPTER TWENTY

Charity let out a whoop. She raised the journal high, waving it at the two women who were digging through chests on the other side of the cottage.

"Jackpot!" she exclaimed. "1812, written in English, by Stephan Farmington. It refers to his sisters, Katya and Jane. And his brother Mikhail. It's the first one in English I've found."

Jen and Bridgette sat next to her, peering over her shoulder at the tight, crabbed hand. The diary was bound in soft leather, probably goat or sheep hide, and knotted together with rawhide. The paper was obviously handmade and quite fragile. They handled it with care. Charity laid it open on the table, the small oil lamp illuminating it. She read aloud:

The great earthquake has done serious damage. People and animals have disappeared into the earth where fissures suddenly opened. The Mississippi ran backward for a while, which caused the waters here, both in the river and underground, to suffer changes and disturbances. Some of the wells have overflowed, and the pond on Yuri's property has risen several feet.

Last week Katerina told us that the herd of deer that regularly drinks from the pond has disappeared. She also said that several sheep have gone missing and that the bullfrogs no longer sing along the edges.

Although it is early, and he should have slept for another month at least, we all agree that the bolotnik has awoken, probably disturbed by the great quaking of the land.

The three women stared at the diary. *Bolotnik?*

"What in the three hells is a *bolotnik?*" asked Bridgette.

"I have no idea," replied Charity. "We will have to look it up later."

But Bridgette already had her phone out and was Googling *bolotnik*. She gasped, and then snorted in derision.

"This can't be for real," she said, even though she knew it was this for which she had been training the last three years.

From folklorepedia.com/bolotnik: A Slavic myth, bolotnik (Russian: болотник) "swampman," Belarusian balotnik (Belarusian: балотнік), Ukrainian bolotyanik (Ukrainian: болотяник), a male swamp creature or spirit. Bolotnik is often portrayed as a man (sometimes elderly) who has large, amphibian-like eyes and a beard and long hair the color of algae. His body is covered in scales, algae, and dirt.

Other tales describe him as a large, eyeless creature that can be found sitting still at the bottom of a swamp. Yet other times he has a tail and long arms. The tales claim he lures his prey into the water and to their death.

In some legends, they are portrayed as a lone creature, yet other tales say he is married to a bolotnitsa (or bolotnica), a female swamp spirit.

The most common behavior described in legends is the ability to lure people or animals to the swamp by quacking like a duck, mooing like a cow, or screaming. Once his prey is near the water's edge, the bolotnik grabs it by the feet and drags them to their death.

. . .

"Well, that would explain a lot," Charity broke the silence.

Jen sat silent and then said, "Jim told me he heard quacking, on the river, when they were hunting for Rory."

"Does it eat them?" asked Bridgette, her voice quivering.

"I don't know. You have the phone. Is there more information anywhere?"

Jen immediately regretted her sharp tone, even though she knew it was prompted by fear. She leaned over and hugged her now tearful daughter.

"No, nothing else. Doesn't say anything about their eating habits. Just that they drown people they catch."

Charity picked up the diary.

"Let's see if Stephan tells us more."

This bolotnik *has grown if it is eating this much. My other fear, one I dare not voice to the others yet, is that he has found a mate. We must face that possibility, but not yet. For now, we know that he is not like the* bolotnik *we encountered outside of Kiev. That one was easily disposed of and, as far as we know, never ate anyone. This* bolotnik, *taken by accident from his home, was transported here where he was dumped into the pond. We believe he may have been responsible for the death of little Mishka Sloven on the boat trip here, and, if so, he has developed a taste for both animal and human flesh.*

Yuri and his family have been warned, and we believe they are staying away from the pond. Yuri is difficult, for he prides himself on being an educated man. But his wife, Maria, and her mother, Katerina, are strong, willful women who will protect their families. We must assemble soon, before the bolotnik *comes out of the pond seeking sustenance.*

I fear for the future. Will the spell be forgotten? We have not yet found a way to keep him silenced for more than a year. But we are working on it. And this year we will try the vials of yarrow root, rosemary, and elderberry, all steeped into a liquid that should induce hibernation. We will also cover the sacrificial lambs with anise and elderberry juice. This plus the spells for sleeping and silence should keep him for another year.

"Well, isn't that just terrific," said Charity. "No spells here that I can see. I wonder if we will have to plow through more diaries and hope to find something in English."

"I could take the ones in Ukrainian down to St. Louis," said Jen. "There's a young man at Washington University in St. Louis who has been studying folk history. He's from Ukraine."

She blushed unexpectedly.

"You've been following his studies?" asked Charity, with a sly grin.

Bridgette just stared. Mom had shown no interest in anyone since Dad was killed in Afghanistan, other than Sheriff John. Was Mom looking for someone?

"No," replied Jen. "I saw him mentioned on the evening news a while back and was interested in his work. I wrote to him to ask if he knew anything about our Ukrainian relatives who moved to this area. He was quite interested, though he didn't have any information. He mentioned he would like to come up here. Maybe now is the time to invite him."

"He could stay here in Stephan's cabin, now that it is restored," said Charity. "Unless you were planning to move in right away."

"We could stay together in Jane's," blurted Bridgette. "And if he stays longer, we will probably have Mikhail's cabin done soon."

"Then I think I will call him," said Jen, as she rose and walked to the bench by the well. Charity stopped Bridgette from following her.

"Your mother's been alone long enough," she said. "Let her talk to him. Maybe we will all like him, you included."

"I never really knew my father," replied Bridgette. "It's just that it has always been me and Mom. And what if he doesn't like what we do? Who we are? I don't want her to be hurt."

"Your mother has the strongest gift I've ever known,"

responded Charity. "Except for you. If he were predisposed to judgment, she would know by now. See how she is talking to him? It's obvious she's been communicating with him for a while."

Jen pocketed her cell and returned to the cottage.

"Dan will be here this coming Saturday," she said, sitting at the table. "Three days should be enough time to finish Stephan's cottage."

"What?" she said in response to the stares from the other two.

"Dan?" said Bridgette. "I thought you didn't follow his studies."

"He answered my letter. I couldn't be rude, now could I?" Jen responded belligerently. She suddenly blushed a deep red and sighed deeply. "Okay. His name is Danylo Balanchuk. He is from Ukraine, here on a permanent resident visa after claiming asylum as a religious refugee. He practices the old religion. He is my age. And yes, we have been talking to each other as well as writing. I'm lonely. I will never, ever, stop loving Will. But I am young, and I want to move on. Is that okay with you?"

"Of course it's okay," said Charity. "We all want you to be happy."

Charity's cell phone rang. It was Arthur Willingham.

"I think maybe you should come on down here and bring Jen and Bridgette."

CHAPTER TWENTY-ONE

D<i>eath—even now I cannot write about it.</i>
        Jim tossed his pen onto the desk. How could he do justice to the horror of four headless, mutilated corpses, tossed into the air as they pulled the Mustang out. Apparently, when the Mustang had slid nose first into the opening at the center of the pond, mud and muck had poured in around it, sealing the opening. Gary Miller's foot had been severed at the juncture of the frame and the partially open driver's door. Tissue samples found in the hinges told a gruesome story of the amputation.

They had assumed that the car—and the boys—had for some unknown reason been sucked into the hole in the center of the pond. Once the car was pulled loose, they expected the remaining water and muck around the vehicle to be likewise sucked into the hole. However, quite the opposite had happened. A sudden, violent spout of water shot out of the hole as soon as the car was free, raining all kinds of debris in all directions. As the spout slowed down, the pond continued to fill with water until it reached its normal level.

The bodies floated on the surface, bloated and stinking, all four headless and mutilated in various ways. Only one, presumably that of Gary Miller, still had some clothes on what remained of the corpse: a belt, tattered jeans, a fragment of white T-shirt, and—the most gruesome of all—the other red Nike Jordan, its laces caught in the tongue of the belt buckle.

Harve had fainted dead away. Arthur quietly withdrew behind some bushes where he could be heard vomiting copiously. Jim wanted to run, to be anywhere but here, especially knowing that at any minute cars were going to drive up with parents inside who must at all costs be kept from seeing this.

Blessedly, Harry Randle arrived first, and while he blocked the entrance to Harve's land up at the county road, Jim persuaded the divers and forensic lab boys to move their two vans to mostly block the view of the pond from the driveway. They had begun to retrieve the first body when Gary Miller's parents drove up, closely followed by George and Tina Martin. A few minutes later, the Blinders drove up with Suzie Stoneman in the back seat. Jim hurried up to the end of the drive before they managed to storm past Deputy Randle.

As Jim arrived at the gate, a car pulled up with Charity Farmington at the wheel and Jen Harper beside her. Bridgette Stevens sat in the back seat, tight-lipped and red-eyed. Jim quickly sought the help of the two women in calming the parents and persuading them to follow Bridgette's car to Harve's front yard. Jim returned to the pond where he told Meadows and Murdoch he was going to go up to Harve's and try to break the news. Arthur had recovered enough to be of assistance. Harve had been revived by a pale and shaky Martin Rutledge and was now being led inside his house, presumably to a safe distance from Dan Miller or any other parent who might start drawing conclusions.

Harve, however, insisted that they all come inside and sit at his large dining table. It was round, handmade, and the chairs were comfortable. He and Martin busied themselves bringing glasses and pitchers of ice water and finding boxes of tissues. Arthur, having found mouthwash in Harve's bathroom, now sat at what passed for the head of the table. Bridgette, Charity, and Jen sat in another part of the room, next to the huge stone fireplace.

Shortly after they were settled, and before Jim could begin, Clay Murdoch came in carrying a pile of carefully folded clothing. The parents saw them, and all but Gary's parents cried out in shock, recognizing their child's clothing.

"What did your boy do to our kids?" yelled Michael Blinder, jumping up and grabbing Dan Miller's shirt front.

Before a fight could break out, Meadows and Jim had the men apart. Jim ordered Blinder to his seat and glared at both of them.

"Sit! And stay seated!" he commanded. "None of your kids did anything to the others that we know of, yet. This is going to be hard enough. Don't you two assholes make it any harder!"

Jim realized he was losing control. Jen magically appeared with a glass of water, and he drank it all.

"Okay," said Meadows. "First things first. I want you to look at these clothes, piece by piece, and the cell phones, wallets, etc. If you recognize them, you tell me, one at a time. I need to keep a record of this."

"Is it okay if I turn on my cell phone to record?" asked Martin Rutledge. "I'll be happy to allow a transcript to be made of it."

"That's an excellent idea," said Meadows. "Two records are always better than one."

Slowly, they went through the pile of clothing, one or another parent identifying them one piece at a time. The mothers were crying, and finally poor Suzie Stoneman collapsed. Charity helped her up and led her to the couch where she lay with her head in Charity's ample lap, sobbing deeply but softly.

Meadows then asked Dan Miller what his son was wearing the day he went missing.

"I don't know. Jeans, I guess, and those damn red tennis shoes. Damn things cost a fortune."

"Red Nike Jordans," said Dan's mother quietly. "And a white T-shirt with a picture of the earth on the front."

"Do any of your boys have birthmarks or scars on their bodies?" asked Meadows. Finally, Tina Martin spoke up. "Billy has a strawberry birthmark on his right shoulder."

"Steve has a scar on his right knee from football," said Mike Blinder.

"What about Mike or Gary?" asked Jim.

"Mike has a burn scar on his left hand, back of it," said Beth Miller. "He and Gary tried making candles in boy scouts once, and he poured hot wax on his hand."

"And Gary?"

"No. Not really. At least none that I know of."

Bridgette spoke up from the far corner.

"He had a crescent cut on the bottom of his foot. He didn't want you to know about it because he stepped on a piece of glass. It probably left a scar."

Dan Miller looked up at Meadows, considerably subdued.

"Enough questions, please. Tell us. What did you find?"

Blake Meadows started to speak, but Arthur held up his hand.

"If I may," he said, and Blake nodded.

Arthur delivered the news, carefully and gently. The parents sat in stunned silence, unable to process the news. Arthur enlisted the help of Bridgette and Charity in driving them home, and then had the two women join him at the library in The Rectory, where he comforted them both. Jim had gone to The Rectory when he left Harve's place. He and Arthur needed to share a drink and their impressions of the day. He would write his report later.

CHAPTER TWENTY-TWO

J im sat at his desk, trying to write a report, the kind he had written dozens of times before during his career as a police detective. But this one, this was the hardest, because he had become attached to these people in a way he had never allowed himself before. He had prided himself on his reserve, his distance, and now he was paying the price of failure. Strangely, this deep caring and sorrow was a price he was happy to pay.

He remembered long ago reading a book on Buddhism, one which had impressed him greatly. He recalled it now, how it had told him that there is little joy in providing solace for the pains of others when your own soul needs surcease. Time passes slowly. You hear their cries; you comfort their sorrow. If you are truly compassionate, you avoid trite phrases of empty pity and instead employ the deep work of empathy. You do not profess to understand their pain, for everyone's sorrow is different; everyone's grief is unique. Instead, you share your pain with them, as they are sharing with you.

These were not the words he could put into a report, but they guided him in avoiding conclusions, in keeping his personal demons at bay.

After a couple of hours, when all the rage and sorrow and fear and grief and denial had been pasted onto the walls of Harve's main sitting and dining room, tearing through his rooms like a tornado of emotions, after the parents had gone, after the lab techs had stopped for a drink and a sandwich and then continued their painstaking work; after nothing more could be said or should be said, Jim decided to leave. He drove slowly to The Rectory and entered the library.

He and Clay agreed that although they would need to interview Harve in depth at some point, there was neither sufficient evidence nor the will on either of their parts to do so at this time. They also agreed that Harve wasn't a flight risk. They would summon him and Martin to the sheriff's office sometime in the next couple of days. Clay left for Jefferson City, leaving Blake Meadows behind to continue the investigation.

Arthur sank into the couch in front of the fireplace and gave in to his own deep agony. Charity held him close. Jen built a fire, even though it was warm outside, for she could feel the deep, piercing cold in his bones. Only those with the gift knew the intensity of his pain. He cried until there were no more tears. And then together they quietly chanted the song for the dead, for the passing of souls into the hands of the eternal. It wasn't a Christian prayer; none of Arthur's small congregation would have recognized it. Jim did not. And yet he felt the presence of Beth, a sense of her spirit, unlike anything he had felt since her death years ago. And he also sensed the despair and fear that tinged those ancient, foreign words.

Harve and Martin arrived soon after, both dealing with a different worry. Harve was keenly aware, as was Martin Rutledge, who sat silent at the table, that he was a person of more than a little interest. He had sent Rory to the pump house. He was known to fish Big Bass Pool. He had done the landscaping on Jackson Hill and now maintained it. And it was his pond where the bodies of what he presumed were the four missing boys were found. And he was terrified at what might happen if they ever entered the cabin out back under the trees. He had not told even

Martin Rutledge about that. As they sat, each in his own puddle of misery, Harve's cell phone rang.

"Harve?" said Blake. "We need to look in your tool shed."

Blake had remained behind at the pond with the CSIs while Clay took the bodies to the State Medical Examiner in Jefferson City. Harve put the call on speaker. Martin Rutledge sat up straighter, put his hands on the table, and drew a deep breath.

"I'm going to advise my client against allowing that without a warrant," he said. "Unless you're planning to charge him with something right now."

Blake asked them to stay put. He would be there in ten minutes. When he arrived, Blake sat at the table, motioning Harve to sit, which he did, but next to Martin. The rest sat up, listening to what was going on.

"Here's the current situation," said Blake. "The forensic guys have retrieved the bodies, or what remains of them, from your pond. They sent them to Jefferson City for DNA identification and to see if cause of death can be determined. Next, they are going to dredge the pond with large nets to see if there is anything else they can find. The divers are getting underwater lights prepared so they can examine that hole in the middle of the pond. It's ten feet down or so; they want to get a good look. Gary's Mustang is being taken by flatbed to Jefferson City for a thorough examination at the state lab.

"Right now, all the evidence pointing to you is circumstantial. I don't want to have to charge you just so I can get a closer look at your premises, but if I have to I will. And I can have a warrant faxed up here within the hour. Thing is, a warrant will let me search everything on your property. You think about that, talk with Rutledge here, and let me know what you want to do. You can cooperate, you can get arrested, or you can wait for a warrant and have me and a ton of other guys snooping all over your property. Don't take long to decide."

"What should I do?" Harve asked. "What should I do?"

The door opened, and a forensic tech came in. He held a

whispered conversation with Blake after which Blake walked over to the table.

"Mr. Sanders," he said. "I'm afraid I'm going to have to ask you to stand up and put your hands behind your back."

Harve stared at him open-mouthed, while Martin Rutledge got to his feet and stood next to Harve.

"What's going on, Trooper Meadows?" asked Martin.

"I'm placing your client under arrest for suspicion of murder, five counts. You have the right to remain silent." He continued with the entire Miranda reading. "Now, please, sir, stand up and put your hands behind your back."

"On what grounds, Blake?" asked Jim.

The forensics tech held out a tablet for Jim, Harve, and Martin to see.

"This is the result of tissue samples we took from the bed of your truck."

Before Martin could object, Clay produced the warrant that had been sent to the lab van's fax machine, allowing them to search the truck.

"We're in the process of getting one for the entire premises," said Clay.

"Can I sit?" asked Harve.

Clay nodded.

"Please continue," said Martin to the forensics tech. "And what is your name, sir?"

"Walter Corbin. That's C O R B I N. Anyway, we found some tissue in the hinge of the blue truck's tailgate. The rest of the back was washed clean, clean as I've ever seen a truck. But whoever did that cleaning missed this tissue. We've bagged it, as Sheriff Burch here instructed, along with all the other body parts. But first we ran a quick test and determined that it is human tissue. Once Sheriff Burch has signed the release papers, we are going to fly all the evidence down to the state lab in Jefferson City to see what we find. But it was and still is our recommendation, based on the evidence found so far, that warrants be obtained for

Mr. Sander's Econoline that he uses in his business, and his house and outbuildings."

Jen stood and quietly signaled Arthur, Charity, and Bridgette to join her out on the porch. She went as far to the side as she could away from the door and perched on the wide top railing.

"Do we tell them?"

"Not unless you want a quick trip to the nearest psych ward for seventy-two hours," replied Arthur. "Let's wait until Dan gets here. I did some background on him, and he's solid. We'll tell him everything and go from there. In the meantime, our job is to keep them away from the back cabin for as long as we can."

"And how do you propose to pull off that miracle?" asked Charity.

"I don't know."

"Well, you'd better come up with something soon, because they can hold Harve for twenty-four hours without taking him in front of a judge for arraignment if Martin talks them into taking that route instead of insisting on filing an arrest warrant. Either way, the best we can hope for is a few hours, maybe overnight if we're real lucky."

Jen and a confused Bridgette sat silently. Charity wandered as close to the pond as the cops would allow her and stood watching the activities. Arthur returned to Harve's living room, where he surreptitiously slipped Martin Rutledge a note.

Need to talk was all it said.

CHAPTER TWENTY-THREE

M eals at Morey's for the next many days were a trying affair for Jim, Harry, any of the state troopers who might need sustenance, and poor Martin Rutledge. Most of the population of Harper's Landing managed to drop in for at least one meal a day, and after being berated by nearly all of them, Jim and Harry took to eating their meals at the jail when Jen brought over Harve's food. Jen was her usual cheerful self, dispensing food and conversation equally between prisoner and captors, deftly avoiding the elephant in the room.

Harve Sanders sat in his cell, a pile of misery clothed in jeans and plaid, trying desperately to maintain silence as Martin had instructed him. He wanted to talk to Jim, to Jen when she brought him his meals, to Charity when she brought a change of clothing. At least Jim had allowed him to wear his own clothes, and Linda Collier brought him copies of the *Harper's Landing Gazette*. Ever since the bodies had been found and Harve had been tossed in a cell, she had been publishing daily updates.

Harve's trucks and his Econoline van with all his tools had been gone over thoroughly. The red truck, coincidentally the one Rory had taken to the pump house, was loaded onto a flatbed and towed to Jefferson City where the lab was going over it microscopically since finding what had proven to be human tissue caught in the tailgate hinge. The tissue did not match any they had on file: not Rory nor any of the boys. All four boys' mutilated corpses had been identified by comparison to DNA samples provided by their parents: combs, toothbrushes, and mouthguards from their gym lockers.

The boys' parents vacillated between wanting Harve strung up and doubting that the nice man who did such beautiful landscaping could have had anything to do with all this horror. Dan Miller was drinking more, often spending entire days at Happy Time Tavern, and Beth Miller hadn't been seen since Gary was identified. Rumors abounded, the most common being that Dan, in a drunken rage, had beaten her badly enough to keep her from being seen in public.

Martin Rutledge was on his way to The Rectory to speak with Arthur Willingham about his strange note. The judge had driven down that morning for a preliminary hearing and bail hearing on Harve Sanders. Martin had tried his best to get Harve released on his own recognizance. He spoke of Harve's strong ties to the community. He pointed out that the State had failed to provide anything other than circumstantial evidence that would connect Harve to the murders. He lost. Due to the seriousness of the charges, the judge also refused to set bail. Harve would have to remain in jail until the arraignment. Martin, after consulting with Harve, asked for a continuance until August first. The request was denied, and the arraignment was set for July fifth. Martin wanted all the evidence to have been processed by the state crime lab and to have time to speak in depth with Harve and all his relatives, employees, and customers. Now he had to hurry and hope that in his haste mistakes were not made. Arthur was first on his list.

There were at least ten cars parked in The Rectory parking lot. Arthur had finished all the restorations, and the notoriety of five gruesome murders had drawn tourists like fleas to a random dog. Martin found no one in the dining room and assumed they were all at Morey's, hoping to hear juicy gossip. He shook his head at the morbid nature of so many people. He, for one, preferred the peace and quiet of pre-murder Harper's Landing.

He found Arthur in the library, sitting at an ornate desk near the fireplace. It was early June, the temperature outside was in the mid-seventies, and the flowers in the beds around The Rectory were in full bloom. Harve had done an amazing job of landscaping. The windows in the library were open, and the sweet smell of roses drifted in on the soft spring breeze, mixed with the tangy spice of petunia and the succulent richness of mock orange. Calming music floated through the room. It might have been Deuter or Enigma, perhaps Kitaro or Bliss. It was exactly the music Martin expected to hear.

Arthur rose, leaving the cover open on his laptop. He had been writing, probably Sunday's sermon or perhaps an op-ed for the *Gazette*. Martin walked in, shook his hand, and sank into the overstuffed wing chair Arthur indicated. Arthur took the matching chair on the opposite side of an exquisitely carved side table. He poured Martin a small glass of scotch in a crystal glass and the same for himself.

"I've asked Jen to bring us lunch. I'm sure this morning's court proceedings have left you hungry as well as dismayed."

"As long as she brings some of that apple pie, too, I am grateful. The judge was fair, but I am still disappointed in his ruling. Harve is not handling his incarceration well."

"Give him freedom to talk," said Arthur. "He needs to talk. Just remind him not to talk about the case."

"But that's the whole point," replied Martin. "The case is all he wants to talk about. He keeps saying that he needs to explain, but then he won't explain to me. And I'm afraid if he starts talking to Jim, or to Jen or Charity when Jim's in earshot, he'll say something horribly incriminating."

"Tell you what," said Arthur. "I'm going to invoke something I rarely do. We clergy also have some client privilege; not as much as if I were a Catholic priest, but some. I can ask Jim to allow us some private conversation. He knows that if I ask a judge, I'll get permission. He will let me. That will help. Also, I need to stress with Jim, and the state police, that Harve's property line stops at the far edge of the back garden. It doesn't go all the way to the woods, and I wouldn't want to see anything useful tossed because they went onto someone else's property."

"That would be a good thing for us," replied Martin. "But it probably wouldn't have any negative affect on whatever was found on Harve's property. The arraignment is on July fifth. I had originally got an extension to August, but then the state attorney's office intervened. The judge reversed his opinion, so now I have less than a month to prepare motions to dismiss and the like. The state is sending some hotshot from the state attorney general's office to represent them. They want to get this over with as fast as possible, but I'm not going to let them ramrod this through. Right now, all they have is circumstantial evidence. Not that such evidence isn't enough to convict in many cases, but I'm not going to allow for any pressure for plea agreements or the like until all the evidence is in. Lab work takes time. I want to know how the limbs were removed from those bodies, whose tissue that is that was found in his truck, everything. They haven't met stubborn like me before."

He stopped and sat back.

"Why don't you want them going back to the woods? Is it that cabin back there? Is there something I should know about?"

"Later," said Arthur. "I promise, we will talk about that."

Arthur grinned. Internally he sighed in relief. He hoped the rest of their conversation was going to go as well as this first part. He knew Martin had come to pick his brain about Harve. Unfortunately, he had little to tell. Harve had done the landscaping when The Rectory renovation was complete. He was a steady, reliable worker. His prices were fair. He was kind to his helpers and never gave Arthur a single reason to worry or be unhappy.

As they finished talking, Jen arrived with lunch. She had brought enough for four, and shortly after she emptied all her baskets and started setting up, Charity Farmington appeared at the door. Martin was delighted to see that Jen had indeed brought apple pie and cheddar cheese wedges. He was confused as to why the women were there but welcomed their presence at the table.

Lunch was an enjoyable affair, with fruit salad, large ham slices, potato salad, and pickled asparagus and green beans. Arthur produced an exceptionally fine vintage of rich red wine, and the pie, as usual, was ambrosia. They chattered on about the crops, the influx of tourists, the restoration of the mill, and the opening of the adjoining museum. Not once did they bring up the alleged murders or the impending trial. It was a welcome mental vacation for Martin.

After lunch they all cleaned up, packing dishes, plates, serving bowls, and glasses back into the baskets. Jen refused Arthur's offer to wash them at The Rectory kitchen, murmuring something about state rules regarding dishwashers. The four then returned to the comfortable wing chairs that looked out on the blooming gardens. They sat in a semicircle of sorts, comfortably warm in the afternoon sun. Jen spoke first.

"Martin, did you know that Harve is related to me and Charity?"

"No, I did not. Is everyone in this town related to each other?"

"It does seem that way sometimes, doesn't it?" Jen laughed.

"I'm not sure exactly what the relationship is," she continued. "But I do know that he and I and Linda Collier and all the Harpers and Farmingtons in the area are all the descendants of Yuri and Maria Harper. And indirectly of Maria's parents, Maksym and Katerina Molovna. Charity here is the descendant of four siblings who first came here from Ukraine around 1802 and built the cottages where we now live. And at least one of those siblings married into the Harper/Molovna line."

It was Charity's turn to speak. "Martin, we need to tell you some things. Things that probably don't sit comfortably in your logically trained mind."

Martin laughed uncomfortably. "First, you tell me you're all related. What's next? You're all witches?"

"Something like that," said Arthur. "Except I'm not related to any of them. At least not that I know of."

Martin sat, staring, his mouth half-open.

CHAPTER TWENTY-FOUR

They were gone. All of them were gone. Would they be back? He didn't know. But they were gone, and the Provider was happier now that he was back in his home. He could hear the Provider's voice at night, echoing in his head.

"Food. Need food. Send food."

He looked out again. The yellow tape was gone. The trucks were gone. Once, he had been afraid they were going to come back here. But they didn't. It was getting dark out. It was safe to feed the Provider, he thought.

The barn was dark after sunset, so he took a flashlight. The sheep bleated, as much in hunger as fear, when he opened the door to the stall. He tied a small rope around its neck and led it out and down the slope toward the pond. He would have liked to stop at the well and throw the hapless animal down there, but he knew from experience that would not suffice. The Provider didn't like going into the deep waters unless it had to. He took the sheep to the pond. He untied it, let it root in the grass for a while, and then gave it a mighty shove into the pond. The ram paddled frantically toward the shore but was suddenly pulled under and did not surface again.

That should do, he thought. *That should do. That sheep was huge.*

Once safely inside, he picked up the shoes he had removed at the door and placed them on a plastic sheet. He sat on a stool next to the plastic, his workbench at his side. He picked up a scraper and carefully removed all the mud. He next took a dental tool from his bench and carefully removed any remaining detritus from the soles. He lifted a brush next and brushed the work boots vigorously until they shone. But still he wasn't done. He opened a small drawer and removed a flat tin of black shoe polish and a rag. After removing the shoelaces, he carefully applied the polish and once again polished the boots with the brush until they shone a brilliant black.

He set the boots on his bench. He returned the polish to the drawer and threw the rag into the fire in the small fireplace. Then he lifted the plastic sheet carefully and took it, along with the scraper, the dental tool, and the brush, to a large sink in the back of his workroom. He washed everything, including the sink, after he had thoroughly soaped and rinsed the plastic sheet and his tools. He hung the sheet on the rack that stood next to the sink, over a drain. The cut on his hand stung from the strong soap. It had been a deep wound, requiring many stitches, which he had inserted himself. He would be more careful if the truck was ever returned. He went back to his workbench and carefully lined up the scraper, the pick, and the brush. Everything was as it should be.

He picked up the fox body he had found in the woods before all the noisy ones came. He began to carefully trim the fur around its neck. He had prepared the body for his treatment, for his skill. He would do his best work on this prize. It would calm him. Everything would go back to normal.

He picked up a magnifying glass and began meticulously cleaning and polishing the black claws. His work was precise, born of long habit and patience. Good work requires good work habits. Mother always told him that.

CHAPTER TWENTY-FIVE

B y unspoken consent they had left the explanations to
Arthur. He pulled his chair closer to the stunned and silent
Martin Rutledge.

"Witch might not be quite the right terminology," he said with
a chuckle. "We follow the ancient ways, the Path set out by the
old ones long ago."

"Do you cast spells, stir cauldrons, stuff like that?" asked
Martin.

"Spells, yes. But spells are nothing more than concentrating
one's connection with the earth, with the unseen powers. Think of
them as a way to focus and channel the many electric currents
that surround us constantly, and the sound and light waves."

"Okay," said Martin. "But seriously, why not use scientific
equipment? I mean, they have stuff that can focus all those things,
so why spells?"

"Think of them as a prayer," replied Arthur. "You wouldn't
try to use your cell phone to talk to God. Spells are as much about
focusing and centering ourselves as they are about manipulating
the physical world. But we do try to do that. Mostly we use physical tools to deal with physical things: tinctures, scents, flowers,
stuff like that."

Martin sat silently. Then he leaned forward, looking at all three intently.

"Why are you telling me this? Is Harve a wi ... erm, *practitioner*, too?"

"No," said Charity. "But he is family, which means that to some extent he has the gift. But no. Not because of that."

"Then why?"

"Because," said Jen, "we need you to be willing to at least consider an alternative reason for these deaths. We are quite aware that an occult explanation would be laughed out of court. But, if we could establish by proof that there is a creature in that pond, or in the waters underneath it, then you could use that, yes?"

Martin sat for a moment, thinking, a deep frown on his face.

"Yes," he finally said. "I suppose there is a way. But it would have to be physical, provable evidence. Not some theory or myth."

"That is why Dan is driving up this coming Sunday," said Jen. "He's a professor at Washington University in St. Louis. And he's Ukrainian. He is coming to translate the diaries for us."

"The diaries?"

"Our relatives kept diaries from the time they arrived here until they died," answered Charity. "Most of them are in Ukrainian, a few in English. We are guessing that they wrote in detail about what they think might have been brought here and how they dealt with it. If it is what we fear it might be, then there is an explanation for the murders that will clear Harve."

Martin was intrigued. The idea that a creature had been accidentally transported here, set free, and allowed to breed with similar creatures in this new alien environment? That seemed likely to him. And it certainly made more sense than labeling the quiet, humble Harve Sanders a mass murderer.

"Can I be here for the translations?" he asked.

"We were hoping you would want to be," said Arthur. "Your input would be invaluable, and we think it would be important for you to have the information."

"Oh, you betcha. Stuff like that is gold with juries, especially if you can get an impressionable one. If it comes to trial, and I hope it doesn't, it won't be here, though. Couldn't find anyone who didn't know and love Harve, 'cept maybe the parents of those poor boys."

CHAPTER TWENTY-SIX

Sunday afternoon was usually quiet at The Rectory. Ben would putter out back in the vegetable garden or sit in an overstuffed chair in the library, reading a book or magazine. Arthur greatly enjoyed puffing on his Meerschaum pipe, while reading Sherlock Holmes or Miss Marple, and sometimes a new Harlan Coben.

Today was different. All the available chairs had been pulled up to the large library table. Martin Rutledge sat with a legal pad and several sharpened pencils, ready to take notes. Dan Balanchuk had arrived in time for the luncheon in the dining room and was now eagerly eyeing the pile of journals, papers, and diaries which Charity had stacked up on the table. Charity Farmington sat next to Dan, ready to hand him the volumes. Mary and Bull Harper had come, along with Jen Harper and her daughter Bridgette. Morey and Maggie Farmington rounded out the group, happy to have something interesting to do on their day off. Arthur came into the room bearing a large stack of writing tablets and several pens and pencils. Behind him came Ben, with an easel and a whiteboard. He set up the easel and lined up erasers and dry-erase markers in various colors.

"I'm going to stay," said Ben. "I'm not sure what this is about, though I can guess a bit, but my hobby before I nearly drank myself to death was genealogy. I probably know more about drawing family trees than most of you."

He blushed deeply, realizing how that sounded.

"Anyway, I want to help, if you'll let me."

They all agreed at once, and Ben snagged a stool to perch on beside the whiteboard.

Before sitting, he drew out the top of the tree and branches below, with places for names.

Charity knew from the few English diaries she had found that Yuri and Maria Harper, along with her parents, Maksym and Katerina Molovna, were the first to arrive in the area from Ukraine. Yuri's parents remained in St. Louis, where his father became assistant to the brewmaster of a large beer brewery. They kept begging Yuri to move down and live with them and get a job managing the horses the brewery kept for pulling the delivery wagons. But Yuri declined in favor of a more rural life.

Ben entered those names and waited for more names to emerge, either from memory or from the diaries. He sat waiting, until Charity looked up and said, "You're going to need a second tree."

Ben looked puzzled.

"There were four brothers and sisters, not related to Maksym and Katerina, who lived in the cottages that Jen and I now live in. Three of them married, and they have progeny in the town, too."

Ben redid the tree, putting the two branches side by side.

"Any chance any of them married into the Molovna line?"

"I'm almost certain of it," replied Charity. "But I guess we will find out."

"All this talk of family trees and relations might be interesting to some of you," said Jen. "But I'm much more interested in what, if anything, they wrote about something evil living in that pond. Can we please make that the primary target of our research?"

Bull Harper spoke up. "Why did you want me and Mary here?"

"Because you're a Harper. And you likely have the gift. And Mary is likely a Farmington, which means she has it, too."

"I've been sensing something not right," said Mary, "if that is what you are talking about."

Bull sat up. "Yeah, me too. But if you let that out, if anyone at the mill finds out, I'm toast. Seriously."

"No worries from me," said Arthur.

The rest assured him that this was a closed group, even with the inclusion of Ben.

"If we find that we do indeed have something ancient and evil here, and if we find out how they dealt with it," said Charity, "then we may well need the help of anyone gifted, no matter how small their gift."

"Now," said Dan, "let's see if we can make some headway sorting these diaries. I want to see what's here."

First, they sorted all the documents: diaries, legal papers, journals, ledgers, and miscellany. They all agreed that those documents might help later in constructing both an accurate family tree and a timeline. Ben started going through the journals and legal papers, looking for anything in English that might assist him with the genealogy. Dan and Charity set to work on the diaries, while Jen and the others attempted to make some order in the remaining paperwork. It was tedious, slow work, mostly because of the age of the paperwork. Several times, despite their caution, papers turned to dust or tore. Some had faded to the point of being unreadable. But for the most part, the diaries and larger journals were intact. Nevertheless, at Dan's urging, they began photographing everything before handling it.

The diaries were personal accounts of family history, while the journals tended to be listings of purchases and sales from the wood carving and carpentry business that Maksym, Yuri, Stephan, and Mikhail ran. There were lists of lumber types and sizes, deliveries, and equipment purchases. Many of these, to the frustration of all, were undated. Nevertheless, they placed them in a neat stack to go over later.

Suddenly Dan let out a whoop.

"Jackpot!" he said. "This diary is written by Katerina Molovna. It is dated 1802, and the first entry is *'We have arrived in St. Louis and will soon be traveling north along the Mississippi River to claim our new land. This river is huge. It reminds me of the Volga, which I saw only once. As soon as Maksym and Yuri have purchased a wagon and a team, we will continue onward.'"*

He continued reading aloud, as the others sat transfixed, caught up in the magic of the discovery of a new land. The diary told a story of journey, of peril, of discovery, and of more peril.

CHAPTER TWENTY-SEVEN

Dan put down the diary. He took a long drink of water and then nibbled absently at one of the huge chocolate chip cookies Maggie had brought with her.

"They came here with all their worldly goods and a barrel of water from Ukraine," he said thoughtfully. "And dumped the water into the pond. Methinks they were mighty lucky that the wedding was a peaceful affair."

"Sounds like you have some idea of what they were dealing with," said Arthur.

"Nothing positive," replied Dan. "But there are old folk tales, mythology, about water elementals called *bolotniks*."

"You were right, Charity!" blurted Bridgette. "Stephan and the others were right, too."

"Did the others mention a *bolotnik* also?" queried Dan.

"Yes," said Charity. "In the one diary we found that is written in English, by Stephan. I think there must be more, written by him, because he was so determined that this thing be kept in check. If they discovered anything, any way to keep it asleep or even kill it, I think he would have written about it in one of these diaries, in English, so people would find it and protect themselves."

"I'd like to continue looking for diaries closer to the time of this one I just read," said Dan. "I think we need to know more about the history of this thing, or at least the people who were dealing with it."

"I agree," said Arthur. "For one thing, I want to know if this creature is simply a strange, if vicious, animal, or if we are dealing with a magical being like an elemental."

In short order, they came upon Maria Molovna Harper's diary. Dan again translated aloud: "*Занадто багато тварин пропали без вісті. Too many animals are going missing.*" Dan continued the translation of Maria's diary. It, too, told a story of something fearful residing in the area.

CHAPTER TWENTY-EIGHT

I t was three years since she and Yuri married under the tree by the pond. Jennie, their daughter, was two years old. She and Maria were walking along the path that led from their small house toward the pool.

Early this spring Maria realized they were missing several newborn lambs. When she mentioned it to Yuri, he said it was probably coyotes and bought a dog from their neighbor to guard them. The dog was obsessed with keeping the flock away from the pond, so Yuri built a small corral and a water trough up near the house. There was a lot of water running under their land, and they had only needed to sink a well fifteen feet to get enough water to pump out daily for their needs. Jennie delighted in sitting on her mother's lap watching the ewes and their lambs drink from the trough. The two large rams also gave in to the dog's insistent herding and came to the trough daily.

Today's walk had a purpose. Two days ago, their cow had given birth to a healthy young male calf. Yesterday the cow was mooing in pain with too much milk, and Maria discovered that the calf had gone missing. She milked the cow to relieve her discomfort and watched as she searched all day calling for her calf. Maria milked her again in the evening and again this morning. Now she and Jennie were searching for the calf. They heard quacking as they neared the pond.

"Ducks, Momma. Duckies."

Jennie tried to pull away and run to the pond, but Maria held her tight. The dog was also with them, pushing them back away from the pond, whining the whole the time. Maria insisted that Jennie sit with the dog, promising a treat afterward if she was a good girl. Jennie knew that treats usually meant cookies, which she dearly loved, so she sat quietly with Misha while her mother walked slowly around the pond.

Maria found hoof prints, tiny ones, leading down to the pond. As she knelt to examine them, she heard quacking, but could see no ducks. There was no trace of the bull calf nor any hoofprints leading away from the pond. She reached out to spread the bulrushes apart when she saw something swimming toward her swiftly. She sprang up and ran to Jennie. Snatching her up, she ran to the house, Misha following, where she signaled the dog to bring the flock of sheep into the corral. She closed the gate tightly, told the dog to stay, and with Jennie still in her arms, she ran for her mother's house a quarter mile away.

Katerina Svetlana was old. Her daughter, Maria, was born when Katerina was nearly forty. She and Maksym had given up on having children, so Maria was a complete surprise and an utter joy. Now in her sixties, Katerina's hair was snow-white, and her face was wrinkled and browned by long hours of work in the sun. She adored her granddaughter and lavished treats and attention on her in equal amounts.

By the time Maria and Jennie arrived on her porch, Katerina had a plate of cookies and two glasses of icy cold milk waiting for them. Her welcoming smile turned to concern when she saw her daughter's face.

"What is it? Has something happened to Yuri?"

"No, nothing like that. But worse, I think."

Maria sank into the chair and took a long drink before continuing. She also plucked a cookie from the plate and took a big bite. Oatmeal, with raisins.

"There's something in the pond," she said. "Something evil, horrid, and dangerous."

She described what she had seen to her mother, telling her of the loss of lambs, the disappearance of the new bull calf, and the dog's fierce refusal to let Jennie or any of the sheep go near the pond. When she mentioned she had heard quacking, Katerina's face went white. "Oh, by all the Fates, I fear we have brought a *bolotnik* to America."

"A what?" said Jennie.

"A *bolotnik,* an Old One, and a dangerous one even though not big or terribly powerful like some of the Old Ones. But I do not know what it will do in a strange new place, where the water tastes different, and the animals are different."

She sat quietly, deep in thought.

"We must tell Maksym and Yuri," she finally said. "We must call together as many women who follow the Old Ways as we can find. Will you help in bringing them here?"

"Of course. Jennie will stay with you."

The little girl squealed in delight, unaware of the women's concern. She loved her Babusya.

"Go inside, Jennie. Mowr has had kittens, and you can play with them. Be gentle."

Katerina quickly made up a list of all the women she knew. Some of them would know others. Maria went to the woodshed where Maksym was busy sawing planks for an addition to Maria's tiny house.

"Mama needs you," she said.

He immediately put his tools down, gave her brief hug, and headed toward the house.

"She's out front," called Maria. "Jennie is in the house playing with the kittens."

He waved in acknowledgement and headed for the front porch. Maria consulted her list and decided riding would be best. She quickly saddled up Poppa's new mare, who was the gentlest of the five horses in the paddock next to the woodshed, and probably the quickest.

First, she rode home to find Yuri. She assumed he would be chopping trees in the forest to the south to take to her father for more planks. She was correct. She pulled up as the tree he was working on crashed to the ground. He turned toward her, and his smile grew large as his eyes sparkled. He never ceased to be in awe of her beauty. Yuri loved Maria with an all-encompassing joy. She asked if he could go to her father's home. He immediately shouldered his axe, kissed her gently but deeply, and headed off to hang the tool in the shed and go to his in-laws' cabin.

Maria headed toward the small village that lay upriver two miles. She recognized at least three of the names on her list as women who lived there. As she rode, she tried not to think of what she had seen. She had never heard of a *bolotnik*, but the look of shock and horror on her mother's face was enough to convince her they were in mortal danger. She rode swiftly and pulled up to the large water trough in the center of the village. The mare sank her soft lips into the water and slowly drank.

Midwood was a tidy little village, with a dry goods store, a blacksmith, a school, and a church, all surrounding the center park. There were several small cottages, each with its own neat garden and a small well in the front yard. The blacksmith was also a wainwright, and one of the cottages had a neat little sign in the window offering—in Ukrainian—*New Clothing & Repairs* with a clumsy drawing of a treadle sewing machine. Another cottage had a sign that simply displayed a small quilt with the word занятта. Maria had learned to make quilts from her mother and grandmother but thought she would someday bring Jennie here, since she lacked her mother's patience for teaching.

The quilt teacher's name was first on her list, so she walked up the path and knocked softly on the door. It was opened by the roundest, happiest-looking woman she had ever seen. Natasha Bondar was plump, pink, and covered in flour. It was hard to tell where the grey in her hair ended and the flour began.

"Come in, come in," she said. "Have you come to sign up for classes?"

"My mother has sent me," replied Maria. "Katerina. She said to tell you it's about a *bolotnik*."

Natasha carefully put down the large bowl of bread dough she had picked up. She covered it with a towel, and then moved to the table, motioning Maria to sit also.

"Tell me," she said.

"I don't know much," replied Maria. "Some of our animals have been going missing, but that's to be expected out here in the wilderness. However, last year we lost so many lambs that Yuri, my husband, bought a dog to help guard the sheep. He's a good dog, won't let them go near the pond, and the number of losses went way down. Then, yesterday, our newborn bull calf went missing. Yuri was upset but assumed it was wolves, or perhaps someone stole him. But I found his hoofprints leading to the pond when I went looking. Then I heard quacking, so I reached into the bulrushes to see if there were baby ducks. That was when I saw the eyes coming toward me."

Maria sat back, panting as the terror began rising in her again.

"There was something about them, about ... I don't know. I felt evil heading for me."

"When and where does Katerina want me?" asked Natasha.

"At Mama and Poppa's house. Tonight, please."

"I will be there. Let me see your list of names." She looked it over carefully.

"These four live above the mill, just over the top of the hill. You'll find a small group of cottages in the woods. Please be careful that you aren't seen. They like to keep to themselves."

Maria mounted the mare after wiping her down a bit and once again set out, this time north along the Martin's Way River toward the textile mill. She didn't like the mill, didn't want to encounter any of its owners or supervisors, wanted nothing to do with it. She knew they used Negro slaves as workers. The word Negro had no counterpart in Ukrainian; the closest they came was *nehrytyans'ka sober*. She felt a kinship to these people who labored long, hard hours with their children beside them. In Ukraine they had been treated little better than these slaves by the ethnic Russians, who, like the white slave owners, considered themselves to be superior beings. She wondered if any of the slave women possessed the powers she and her mother and grandmother had so carefully nurtured.

Soon she reached the clearing, about a mile north of the mill. Four cottages sat side by side, with a large well centered in front of them, surrounded by brightly colored flowers. The cottages were all made of stone, each with its own garden. A tall man, skinny but muscular, was working on a vegetable garden in the side yard of the first house. He heard the mare snuffling as she rode up and straightened to greet her.

"You'll be Maria, daughter of Katerina Molovna," he said. "No, no magic involved." He laughed when he saw the look on her face. "You're the spitting image of your mother, and you have her hair, too, or at least what her hair used to look like."

He walked over and offered her a hand down.

"My name's Mikhail Farmington," said the man. "Welcome to our little community."

Maria saw that three people had come out of the other houses without her realizing it and were all gathered, waiting for her to speak.

"Mother wants you all to come to her house," she blurted out.

She started to apologize but was waved into silence.

"With that hair," one of the women said, "you'll be Katerina's daughter, Maria."

"Who are you people?" she blurted out, and then blushed at her rudeness.

They all laughed.

"Don't worry," said a tall, rangy blonde woman. "We tend to do that to people. I'm Katya. This is Mikhail, that woman with the apron who's been making apple pie is Jane, and this long drink of water"—she pointed at the tall young man standing in the back of the group— "is our eldest ..." She paused, searching for the word. "He's the one who *knows* things. His name is Stephan."

The young man dipped his head, while the others smiled as they were introduced.

Stephan stepped forward. "What has you so upset, sister?" he asked.

"Mother says, well, she thinks, that we have a *bolotnik*."

A hissing intake of breath went through all four.

"A *bolotnik*. That's what she said?" asked Mikhail.

"Yes. I've never heard of one. But I can tell you what I saw."

Swiftly she retold the same story she had told Natasha Bondar. They all listened silently and then began to converse amongst themselves. Finally, they once again addressed Maria.

"I'm sure you have tons of questions," said Katya. "And in good time we will answer them. For now, you go home as swiftly as you safely can. Make sure your animals are safely penned, far away from the pond. Keep yourself, your daughter, and your husband at your parents' house. And stay away from any wells. We will meet with Natasha, and be at your parents' house just before sundown. Please tell Katerina that we will bring white candles. Have her gather rosemary from her garden. And flowers, any that you have."

With that they waved her out of the clearing and on her way home. Mikhail went into his house and brought out a large, round slab of wood. Stephan got a hammer and nails. The two men nailed the cover to the well, making certain it was tight and flush. All the while the two women chanted in Ukrainian, circling the well and pouring salt in front of themselves until the well was completely encircled. The men were careful not to step on or smudge the salt as they stepped back.

They were correct. Maria had a bushel of questions, most of

them about who these people were, what were they, why did they keep their existence secret? So many questions. And she doubted she would get many answers, despite Katya's promise. She rode home, oblivious to the beauty of the early spring woods, worried for the safety of her new and precious family.

CHAPTER TWENTY-NINE

Shortly before sunset, as promised, Stephan and four other people rode up in a wagon. He had stopped in the village to pick up Natasha Bondar and three other women. They untied the horse and led it to the back, where Maksym helped wipe down the gelding. They gave him a long drink and an oat bag, after which they secured him in a stall.

They all gathered on the porch, either in rockers or on the steps, and gratefully downed large mugs of homemade beer and slabs of thick brown bread smeared with fresh butter. Little Jennie sat on her mother's lap, smearing butter all over her face.

Stephan spoke first. "Tell me about your trip to America, Yuri, if you don't mind?"

"It was uneventful," he said, "well, except for the death of Mikhail Sloven. He was just eight, went up on deck during a small storm and was swept overboard. And his mother perished from a broken heart before we landed. Nothing else of note happened."

"What about before?" asked Stephan. "Did you bring anything special with you?"

"I don't know as you'd call it special, but I did get an extra-large barrel of water from the family farm to bring along. My folks said having Old Country water would ensure good crops and fertile pastures. Nonsense, of course, but I humored them."

"That's the barrel we emptied into the pond, isn't it?" blurted Maria.

"Yes," replied Yuri.

"I heard something," she said. "At the time I dismissed it as nerves, but now I'm not so sure. I heard what seemed to me an extra splash, and a chuckle."

She shivered as she recalled the menace in that chuckle.

"Well," said Stephan. "I agree we have a *bolotnik* on our hands. I'm sure you've told Maksym and Yuri about what Maria saw and heard today?"

Katerina nodded.

"Other than the usual binding spells, which will only be temporary, does anyone have any ideas on how to proceed?" asked Stephan.

They all shook their heads.

"Do you know how the pond stays filled?" asked Stephan.

"From the underground waterways," responded Yuri. "I checked it when we first arrived to see if we could rely on it to water the herds. We bought two breeding pairs of sheep on our way up from St. Louis where we crossed the big river."

While the discussions continued, Katya and Jane took the flowers and rosemary that Katerina and Maria had picked, with Jennie's enthusiastic help, and began laying them around the base of the well. Then they carefully traced a circle of salt to completely enclose the well. Maria and Katerina went inside and tucked Jennie in, making sure she was sound asleep before leaving Misha the dog beside her and rejoining the others.

Katya and Jane had moved from the well to the pond while the others were inside. While they traced the pond in the same manner as the well, the men secured a lamb, and Stephan swiftly cut its neck while Mikhail made sure to catch the blood in a small bowl.

Katya raised a stick, covered in feathers and symbols, and walked the perimeter of the pond, chanting:

Sleep the sleep
In silence deep
Stay within
In Darkness Dwell
When next comes Spring
You may Awake
But Sleep 'til then

The lamb was pushed out onto the pond where it floated for a minute or two and then was suddenly pulled under, startling everyone on the shore. Quickly Mikhail poured the bowl of blood into the pond and joined Katya in the chant. Over and over, they repeated the words until all was silent in the pond and no movement could be seen.

"We will come in the morning and offer a chicken, if you don't mind sparing another animal," said Stephan.

Yuri, at first inclined to deep skepticism about the whole business, nodded, obviously subdued and a bit frightened.

Beds for the four who had traveled the farthest were made available. Natasha insisted she would be okay traveling home if they could spare the loan of a gentle mare and promised to return the horse in the morning. The others were too tired to resist. Natasha rode off into the night, promising she would do a long and careful search of grimoires, diaries, and other writings from the old country. Natasha further hinted that she might have access to a more permanent solution but would not go into details.

"Later," she said. "Let me do some thinking and searching, but I think I might have a solution."

They finally fell asleep, Katya and Jane at Yuri's home, and Mikhail and Stephan in the barn behind Maksym's home. Despite her weariness, Maria took a long time to fall asleep, nestled in

Yuri's arms, listening to the soft snores of little Jennie in the next room.

The following day, Yuri, Stephan, and Mikhail rode out, planning to visit as many wells as they could find in the area downstream from Yuri's farm. Before they left, they beheaded the chicken Yuri brought them and floated it out on the pond. Nothing happened, which they all found encouraging.

The evening of the third day, the three men rode back up the wagon trail to Maksym's house. Maria was first to see them and ran to greet Yuri with a hug and a kiss. Jennie came pounding down the steps yelling Poppa, Pop Pop Pop. Yuri held them both close while Stephan and Mikhail helped Maksym remove the saddles and bits, rub down the horses, and put them safely in the barn with water, oats, and hay for the evening.

"I do believe we were successful," said Stephan, putting down his empty beer mug and sighing with contentment. He wiped the foam off his lip and continued.

"We listened at every well that anyone knew of or that we could find. We even stopped at ponds, and at a couple of places where the river forms quiet pools along shallow banks."

"I'm afraid we are criminals, though," said Mikhail. "I did not think that a rabbit carcass or two would be enough to attract a *bolotnik*. Against the wishes of these two, I stole a lamb from a flock when we were midway between here and the southern end of the river. I cast an attraction spell on it, slaughtered it in the old way, and threw it down a well where I could hear running water far below. Nothing happened. No noises, no quacking, nothing. I believe we can rest easy for now."

Maksym and Maria had gone to the pond every day, also, and had heard no further quacking. And the dog seemed content not only to drink from the pond himself but to allow the sheep and new lambs to browse around its shore.

Long after the four had left to return to their small homestead, Maria was still mulling over Stephan's last words: "for now."

"Mama," she asked Katerina, "are we going to have to do this every spring?"

"Until or unless someone finds a more permanent solution," her mother replied.

"And when do we start teaching Jennie?" she asked.

"Not until her first moon cycle," replied Katerina. "She will be powerful, more powerful than anyone amongst us. We must keep that power under control until she is ready."

Katerina sat quietly for a long time. Then she sighed and reached out to take her daughter's hands in hers.

"We will find a way. We must. We have brought something here that should not be here. The others do not blame us, and we must not blame ourselves. But it is our duty to fix this. Go, read the old books, study, meditate. And above all, let Jennie play. While she can."

For now, they would have to be alert and ready to put the *bolotnik* back to sleep when it next awoke. Stephan made certain they were prepared, going downriver to St. Louis to obtain wax for candle making and a large quantity of salt. He also remembered to purchase flour, rice, and cloth. He managed to sell most of the carvings he had made the previous winter, and he splurged a bit for his sisters and got deep red cotton and some gold trimming he spotted at the dry goods store.

CHAPTER THIRTY

D an set aside the diary. He took a drink of water and sat back
while they all let the story soak in.

"Obviously, they found something to control it each year, but
did they ever figure out how to keep it under control permanently?" asked Jen.

Charity spoke quietly, a bit of worry showing on her face.
"What if they found a way to kill it?"

"Why would that matter?" asked Maggie.

"Well, we all seem to be assuming, even if we haven't said,
that we still have a *bolotnik*. And I am confident that we do, that it
merely slept, and something woke it. But what if they did find a
way to kill it? What if I am wrong? Then we must face the
prospect that someone, if not Harve, then someone else, right here
in Harper's Landing, is committing horrible murders."

They all sat silently, contemplating the horror of such a possibility. Martin, ever the realist, reminded them that his client was
his first and primary interest. And to that effect, he wanted to get
some rest and dig back into the pile of documents the next
morning.

I wonder what that bolotnik *thought,* mused Charity. *Did he
even know he was being put to sleep every year?*

Arthur and his fellow researchers broke off with the sorting and the reading at dinner time. Since it was Sunday, dinner was at The Rectory. It was a simple meal: bread, cheese, fruit, and salad. All topped off with, of course, apple pie.

They were all mentally and physically drained. The diaries were detailed and painted a picture of people annually at dire risk. There was a feeling of desperation in some of the writings: a recognition that their actions might not be adequate to hold the monster at bay.

None of them wanted to stop reading. However, Bull Harper had to work the following day; Mary had a quilt workshop starting next weekend and still hadn't gotten all the class materials printed or the fabrics chosen. Morey and Maggie had to open the diner. Bridgette asked if she could take her mother's place as waitress. She knew that Jen would be of more help with Charity, Dan, Arthur, and Ben. She also knew that her mother wanted more time with Dan. Bridgette couldn't blame her mother for that. He was handsome, about Jen's age, obviously intelligent, and possessed of a wry sense of humor. She hadn't seen her mother this alive since, well, forever.

They agreed that the work would continue. Sorting and cataloging would be Jen's job; Ben would continue to build the family tree. Arthur would keep them fed, hydrated, and help if arcane material was located.

Everyone had forgotten about Martin Rutledge. He had spent the day alternately listening to the reading and preparing his Motion to Dismiss to be presented to Judge Cramer on July third, two days before Harve's arraignment. He would argue that the State had presented no evidence tying Harve to the crimes. Harve's DNA wasn't found on any of the corpses, nor did it match the tissue found on his truck tailgate. No murder weapon had been found, and none of Harve's edged tools matched the cuts on the bodies where the heads and limbs had been removed. He had a strong case and hoped to speak with the State's attorney before the hearing on the motion. He would try to persuade him to drop the charges, without prejudice, pending further investigation.

They were about to disband for the evening when Jim Burch and Linda Collier made their way into the library. Jim was carrying a bottle of single malt, and Linda had a bag of what turned out to be marvelous chocolate truffles. The two begged the rest to stay for a while longer. They had been out walking, had an early dinner, and were now seeking some conversation.

"This whole month has been a succession of horrors," said Jim. "I need to sit and sip scotch and talk. That is, if you don't mind."

Two more chairs were found, and Arthur brought crystal tumblers from the dining room. The truffles looked amazing and tasted wonderful. They all sipped in silence, enjoying the evening breeze through the open library window. The lilacs were in bloom, and their sweet scent filled the room.

Dan sipped his scotch slowly, savoring the dark peaty flavors. He was delighted to be in this company. There is nothing in the world that can compare to the comfort of good friends who trust and love one another. The silence was companionable, not awkward. No one felt the need to break it. Dan had felt the pull of Harper's Landing as soon as he left the Interstate and headed for Jen's cottage. He knew he belonged here; he was needed. And not just for reading Ukrainian diaries. It was as if the town had tasted him, tasted his soul, and found it pleasing and useful. It wanted him, and he wanted to be here.

He also found himself utterly smitten with Jen. She was five years his senior, which did not bother him in the least. She was obviously intelligent and had a deliciously wicked sense of humor. She was everything their correspondence had suggested, and more. And Bridgette, her teenage daughter, was equally compelling. Both women followed the same Old Ways as he did. He could sense their power, but it was Bridgette who was going to be the most powerful among them. She was growing into it, slowly but surely.

Arthur and Charity were a delightful surprise. Arthur was obviously powerful and well trained. Under his cheerful, avuncular appearance lay a keen intellect and a mighty opponent of whatever darkness was attempting to tear apart this small town. Charity was too old to bear arms against the darkness, but her mental strength and personal power were undeniable.

Bull and Mary Harper both had power, also, but it was untrained and probably more dangerous to themselves than useful against the ancient evil he sensed flowing beneath this peaceful enclave. They would need to be used only in the direst circumstance and then only with much direction and protection. Morey and Maggie Farmington were equally untutored and possessed of different powers. They would be invaluable in providing the physical as opposed to magical sustenance that would be needed in the coming confrontation.

Ben was completely devoid of magical gifts. However, he was intelligent, curious, and possessed talents they would need: his genealogy skills and his talent with growing things.

All in all, Dan realized this would be a good group, mighty warriors against an evil they had yet to fully identify.

He turned his attention to Jim Burch and Linda Collier. Jim was utterly devoid of any magical or occult power. He apparently was what he appeared to be: big, solid, reliable, and a cop. Linda, on the other hand, positively radiated power. It was lusty, sensual, intelligent, and completely untutored. He wondered how she could have lived this long, apparently well into her forties, without something happening to trigger her interest or her awareness or at least attracting someone to her to help master and develop such a trove of power.

"She married young," said a quiet voice at his elbow. He turned in his chair to hear Jen better.

"Her husband was vicious, a drunk and a rapist. He was caught three years after they married raping a twelve-year-old in their bedroom. He was convicted, sent to the state prison in Jefferson City. She divorced him right after the trial. He died in a prison riot two years later. She took her maiden name back and never remarried."

"You know she has power," said Dan.

"Oh, yes, but she shut it down as much as she could when she married Tom. He beat her near to death shortly after the marriage when he found her grimoire, candles, and the like. Said he wasn't going to tolerate a witch in his house. She was terrified of him. After he died, she confided in me that he told her if she ever told anyone about the beating, or if she did any more of her witchy things, he would kill her and her parents."

"That explains the sadness," said Dan. "Can we help her?"

"Perhaps. We can certainly let her know, quietly and subtly, that we are available. But she will have to make the move. Problem is, I think she is sweet on Jim, and while he is the kindest and gentlest man I've met in a long time, he is also as hard-bitten and practical as they come. It would take a great deal to make him open to the idea that something occult was going on right under his nose, let alone that his new girlfriend had magical powers."

Dan gazed at the objects of their conversation for a while, then turned back to Jen.

"We probably should try anyway. I think we are going to need all the help we can get, and power like that? The only other person I've met here with even the potential for it is Bridgette, and she still needs so much training."

"Linda will, too. She hasn't used her power since she was twenty and married Tom. That's twenty years of suppressing the truth. It must take quite a bit of energy to deny something so powerful."

The compassion and pain in Jen's voice prompted him to put an arm around her briefly, giving the slightest hug. He was overjoyed when she leaned into the hug. He held her a little closer.

Loss is a cruel teacher. Whether we lose a child, a spouse, a parent, or something less tangible, like a career choice or simply hope, loss writes its name on us. It is an unwanted tattoo on our soul, and it hurts with every reminder of the day it was inscribed, as if it were being written all over again. Dan looked around the table. He could instantly identify who had submitted to that fateful needle: Jen, Linda, Jim, Ben, Arthur, Charity. He started up with a flash of inspiration. That was what bound them. Even Bridgette, as young as she was, had suffered that indignity, that reduction to a ball of pain: first her father and now her first boyfriend. Surely Martin had lost also, though he seemed less affected than the others. But the inspiration was a light bulb—no, more like a burning sun. It was that experience, that knowledge, by which they could be molded into a working group. Even Jim, the realist; even Linda, who had walled herself off from her true self for so long. He would enlist Arthur's help, and together they would form the required bond.

CHAPTER THIRTY-ONE

On June twenty-fourth, the State Crime Lab completed its analysis of the dismembered corpses and clothing. DNA testing identified the four boys. No other DNA was found on the clothing or on the corpses. The jagged tears at the neck, arms, and legs were devoid of foreign tissue of any kind. DNA testing of the tissue found in the hinge of the truck tailgate did not match any of the victims, nor did it match Harve. It did, however, reveal a familial match to Harve, which would necessitate further interrogation.

The bodies, or what was left of them, were released to the families for burial. At the request of all four families, the remains were wrapped in cotton and placed in plain, untreated pine boxes. This had been the tradition in Harper's Landing for as long as anyone could remember.

The families chose to have one service for all four boys rather than put themselves and the town through four separate burials. Arthur and Ben went to every home in Harper's Landing on the 25th and 26th, asking for flowers to fill the church for the funeral to be held on June 27th. Some families gave them flowers to take with them; others promised to bring flowers early on the 26th.

Harve gave Arthur permission to strip the flower beds at his home to decorate The Rectory dining room. Morey and Maggie Farmington started immediately preparing massive amounts of nourishing but comforting food for after the services. They even closed the diner for the three days, with black bunting around the door.

Everyone in town wanted to participate in some way. Ten men showed up at the cemetery after their shift was done at the mill, wanting to help dig the graves. Arthur showed them where and gave them the dimensions. Several women appeared at the church on the morning of the 26th, and started arranging the flowers, creating wreaths and sprays, quietly and reverently turning the simple, plain chapel into a breathtaking display of love and compassion.

One of the new residents on Jackson Hill was a photographer and had the equipment and means to create large pictures of the boys. He visited as many of the other high school kids as he could and got enough pictures to create wonderful collages of the boys' school days. Mary provided easels for displaying the pictures.

Bridgette Stevens opened the ceremony with a haunting acapella rendition of *"Vichnaja Pamjat,"* an ancient Slavic dirge. As she sang, the sun rose to the right position to send a shaft of light through the upper front windows and illuminate the four coffins. The seven parents had arrived in a limousine, hired by Saul Grossman, and they entered the church as Bridgette sang, each accompanied by two young men from the high school. Suzie Stoneman clung to the arm of Jim Burch, who needed to half carry her to her seat in the front pew.

He seemed quite comfortable in the role of guardian and protector. It was his forte. Although the whole affair brought memories of Beth to the surface, he was in control. In fact, he was in awe of the outpouring of genuine comfort and compassion for these parents. His own experience with loss and grief had been far less communal and supportive.

The parents' families had resided in Harper's Landing for generations. Their ties to the eastern church, though no longer practiced, were nevertheless still present. Arthur had sent a message to an old friend in St. Louis, Bodhan Ponomarenko, who was an Eastern Orthodox priest. Bo had immediately agreed to come. He had arrived on the morning of the 26th, settled in at The Rectory, and then gone to meet with each set of parents individually. He discussed their wishes, prayed with them, blessed and comforted them, and then spent the evening preparing his part in this day's ceremony.

When the knock comes to your door, or your phone rings, or the doctor summons you to the ICU, the realization of death is rarely immediate. Even though the loved one has been kissed, the body has been touched, its waxy stillness increasing as it cools with every passing minute, even then you go home, and you bargain. You pray or hope, depending on your beliefs, that this was all an awful nightmare, that you will awaken, and she will be by your side, that he will be downstairs wolfing down an inadequate breakfast before bounding out the door. You bargain, you plead, you avoid the reality. And then the urn arrives, or the funeral begins, or the casket is lowered into the grave, and the reality hits you like a box truck. You will never see them again, never hear their voice, feel their touch, watch them grow.

Grief overcomes you, robs you of words, of feelings, sometimes even of tears. You sit in disbelief, knowing that your world is forever changed. You could see that on the faces of the seven parents. All their dreams of the future encased in pine boxes, sitting on supports, waiting to be carried outside to the small cemetery and forever locked away.

Father Bodhan spoke first when Bridgette finished the song, and everyone was seated. He spoke of love, of transcendent love, that carries the memory of the lost one into the future and animates the past. He spoke of compassion, of the need to hold one another without words, for no words are adequate to assuage the loss of a child. And he spoke of community, of the gathering together of those who lived and worked together. He spoke of his own feelings: of the great solace he felt upon his arrival in seeing an entire community band together to hold up and protect these parents who had lost so much. And finally, he blessed them all, reciting an ancient prayer:

O God of spirits and of all flesh, Who hast trampled down death and overthrown the Devil, and given life to Thy world, do Thou, the same Lord, give rest to the souls of Thy departed servants in a place of brightness, a place of refreshment, a place of repose, where all sickness, sighing, and sorrow have fled away. Pardon every transgression which they have committed, whether by word or deed or thought. For Thou art a good God and loves mankind. Amen.

Arthur spoke next, inviting any friends of the dead boys to speak if they so wished. Several of the members of the football team, and some of the other kids, stood and spoke of their friendship, their sense of loss. While none of them spoke ill of any of the boys, it was noticeable that Gary Miller was rarely spoken of. Bridgette finally could stand it no longer and sprang to her feet.

"I know that many of you had little regard for Gary. But he was my friend, and as I got to know him, I discovered his sense of humor, his love of jazz, his compassion for animals, and his desire to do good. He wanted to leave a mark on the world, to make his life mean something. He had trials and difficulties that none of you know of, and I will not speak of them here. But despite his problems he never deliberately hurt anyone, never stole anything. He was good and kind and generous to me. And I will miss him every day of my life."

She sat back down, tears flowing, and leaned against her mother's shoulder. There was silence for a couple of minutes, until the organist began playing "Amazing Grace." The congregation sang along, finding comfort in the old, familiar words.

At last, Arthur stood and handed each of the parents a small bag. He then gave them each a small quantity of herbs.

"What you have in your hand is a blend of sage, lavender, and sandalwood. For hundreds of years, people have believed in the healing powers of these herbs. Each of you, please take a pinch of the herbs and place it in the bag I have given you. As you do this, remember your son's laughter." He paused. "Now take another pinch, place it in the bag, and remember your son's face, the way he looked in the morning as he contemplated the day." Again, he paused. "And now, take the remainder and put it in the bag. As you do, remember how you felt the first day you saw him, and the last. Remember a happy time, a trip, a picnic, a school play." Again, he paused. "Now, pull the strings on the little bag and tie it shut. Tuck it away, keep it with you or place it in a special place in your home. This is the tangible expression of the love and memory each of you have for your son."

He then recited a brief prayer:

In this time of darkness, please bring me back to light.
Ease the sorrow and the burden, during these harrowing nights.
My son's time here is done, for with life is given death.
Keep with me the beautiful memories,
Lord of us all, please alleviate the rest.
For only You are eternal, even the sun must disappear.
Gone from body but never from heart, my son is always near.

The service closed with a group recitation of the Lord's Prayer.

The graveside ceremony was blessedly brief: lowering the coffins into the graves, placing flowers and other gifts on top, and leaving while some of the men remained to fill in the graves. Tombstones would be added later. A fund had been established to raise the money to carve them. Everyone then entered The Rectory and found a comfortable place to sit or stand in the dining room. The tables groaned with food, all of it easy to digest and comforting and tasty. Even the parents of the four boys found themselves able to eat a bit and have a drink of tangy lemonade.

Jim stood in a corner, watching. He knew he should go back and be with Harve. The man was a wreck, professing his innocence, and grieving for the loss of four kids he had also known. He had begged to be allowed to come to the funeral, but Arthur had convinced him it would be inappropriate, even if he were later found to be not guilty. He promised he would come to see him as soon as everyone had left. Jim was again struck by how tightly knit this community was. All his life he had lived in big cities, where community meant a defined area. Here it meant its original meaning: a feeling of fellowship, of connection with others. He needed to make more of an effort to establish that connection. *Or perhaps,* he thought, *I just need to be open to it.*

CHAPTER THIRTY-TWO

J ohn Kavanaugh loved to fish. Now in his mid-fifties, he was still fit enough to make his way to even the most inaccessible fishing spots. He would travel almost anywhere in the Midwest to catch bass. He held records for the largest bass caught in twelve different lakes and two rivers. His wife, Susan, loathed fishing. But she loved quilting, or, more specifically, she loved buying quilt fabric. It seemed natural that they would travel north from St. Louis to Harper's Landing when Susan received the brochure for the quilters' retreat. It had arrived in mid-March, and after some research, which included the discovery of Big Bass Pool, John urged her to sign up. They booked a room at The Rectory, registered Susan for every class she could squeeze into the schedule, and John blissfully read up on the Martin's Way River as well as the various types of fish that might be caught there. He had all the appropriate tackle. And he loved bank fishing. This could not have been more perfect.

In late June, Susan handed him a copy of the newspaper as he drank his morning coffee. He looked up, irritated. She knew he did not like to disturb his breakfast with the news. These days it was more likely to cause dyspepsia than information.

"What?" he asked. "Bad news?"

"Maybe," she said. "We are scheduled to arrive in Harper's Landing on July fifth, but I don't know if we should still go."

He took the paper and frowned at the headline.

Four Boys Die In Harper's Landing Pond

"I don't think we have to worry," he said. "They probably drowned while indulging in some horseplay."

"I read the article, and ..."

"Don't. Just don't tell me. I've been looking forward to this vacation since March. And so have you. So don't read this nonsense. Probably mostly made up anyway."

She turned and started making his lunch. She didn't miss his mutter. "Damned women, always making mountains out of mole-hills." Not for the first time, she wondered if she could sneak ex-lax or something equally awful into his chocolate chip cookies. She finished making the tuna salad sandwich, made just like she had for fifteen years. She put it in a seal-tight bag, added two chocolate chip cookies, a box of raisins, and an apple, washed but not cut or peeled. She put it all in the lunch box which fit neatly into his briefcase. For as long as she had known him, when she first started as his receptionist, John had taken lunch at his desk, reading softcore porn novels or the latest best-selling murder mystery. Life with him was so predictable, and so dull.

She was surprised when he had suggested this trip in the first place. He resented her fabric buying, even though they could well afford it. She guessed it was because of the fishing opportunities, the chance to get away from her for a while. Well, what was sauce for the goose. She would be away from him and in the company of women (and maybe a man or two) who would not judge or humiliate her.

On the morning of July fifth, Susan was nearly done packing. They would leave at 11:00 AM and arrive mid-afternoon. She had her sewing machine, her portable iron and pad, all her threads, extra needles, scissors, and cutting mat with a rotary cutter. She also had packed comfortable, lightweight clothing, enough for a week. John was dropping the girls at his parents' house, where they would be spoiled rotten for the week. She added her charger for her cell phone and her tablet and charger to the clothing bag. In the bathroom she packed up toothbrush, deodorant, and lens cleaner. She had decided to go without makeup for the week.

At age forty-eight, Susan Kavanaugh had smooth, unblemished skin. Her hair was still a rich, dark auburn, and her eyes were as green as polished emeralds. She could easily get away with going makeup-free, even though her husband preferred that she wear blush and lipstick at least. She wasn't yet done with pleasing him, but a week without the need would be welcome.

They arrived at The Rectory at 4:30 PM, with just enough time to check in, unpack, and have a quick washup before dinner was served. There were twelve couples seated around the table, with a rotund, jovial man at the head who introduced himself as Arthur Willingham, local parson, and manager of The Rectory.

"Mary asked me to tender her apologies," he said. "She is busy finishing your class materials and preparing fabric choices for those of you who decided to purchase them here rather than bring your own. She will join us for dessert. Please enjoy your meal."

Dinner was bass cooked to perfection, baby potatoes, fresh baked carrots, and obviously homemade sourdough bread with churned butter. Arthur told them everything was made or grown right here in Harper's Landing. They prided themselves on using mostly locally sourced foods at Morey's Diner, the provider of their meal. He told them that Morey and Maggie had closed the diner for the week just to feed the quilters. Of course, there was food for Morey's Regulars, too.

As they were finishing, two petite women came in, bearing baskets filled to the brim with pies. They were obviously mother and daughter, each with deep blue eyes and thick auburn hair. The smell of the freshly baked pies was divine, and even those who had been certain they wouldn't eat another bite couldn't wait to try a piece. There was vanilla ice cream or wedges of sharp cheddar cheese to go with, and Arthur chose both. Several of the other men, including John Kavanaugh, who never ate sweets, chose pie and cheese also. Susan stared at him in shock as he ate not one but two pieces of pie. She had to agree that it was the best apple pie she had ever encountered. She wondered how much time John would spend at the gym up on Jackson Hill in the morning to counter the massive number of calories he had consumed.

As if he had read her mind, John asked, "Is the gym mentioned in the brochure open early in the morning? I'd like to get a workout in before breakfast and still get to the fishing spots early."

By 10:00 AM the following morning, Susan was settled in at her assigned station in The Rectory classroom, seated next to a lovely grey-haired lady named Maria and her husband, Michael, who was also a quilter. She was working on her third cup of coffee and an amazing chocolate chip muffin. She needed to pace herself or she would be waddling out of this week.

She was anxious to get started choosing fabric for the week's projects. Over breakfast John told her she could spend $300 on fabric. That, together with the $400 she had managed to tuck away by spending her grocery budget wisely, would allow her to get some nice pieces. She deeply resented being micromanaged on money like she was a child, but it had been that way since they were first married, and John was unlikely to change. She wondered if she could work out a duplicate receipt deal with Mary that showed deep discounts in case John requested receipts.

CHAPTER THIRTY-THREE

John found Big Bass Pool by 9:30 AM, a little later than he would have liked to start fishing. But it was midsummer, and the weather had been unseasonably cool. The waters were still chilly, and the bass would likely be swimming on the bottom of the pool, digesting their morning meal of midges and water walkers. He had put in a request the night before for a packed lunch and was favorably impressed with the quantity and quality of the food. There was a small thermos of hot coffee, a breakfast muffin, and a plastic container that held a substantial ham sandwich, fresh fruit, and carrot sticks. The bread was rye with an aroma that can only be achieved through home baking. He set the small basket in a shady spot and poured himself a cup of the hot coffee.

He had rigged his line last night, before bed, and now he flipped it into the still, deep waters and settled back on his three-legged camp stool. It was blessedly quiet here. No other fishermen had shown up, there was a slight, pleasant breeze, and the Martin's Way River flowed swiftly around the bend next to the pool. He relaxed, put on his ear buds, and turned on some good, old-fashioned St. Louis jazz.

Over the next few hours, John managed to catch several crappies, two quite respectable bass, and a large catfish that he tossed back as soon as he pulled it ashore. He gutted the crappie and bass and returned the innards to the pool, probably as a late dinner for the catfish. He then stored the fish in the creel he kept especially for the purpose, lined with plastic, and filled with crushed ice he had picked up from Morey's. If he kept the creel out of the sun, the ice should be good for several hours.

As he caught his third and largest bass, a voice startled him, nearly causing him to drop the fish.

"Nice catch there," said a man.

John turned and smiled at the middle-aged potbellied fisherman who had come upon him. Inwardly, he seethed. Now he would have to move.

"Thanks," said John. "Has to be my last for the day. Time for lunch, I'm guessing, and my wife will probably want to eat with me."

"I thought I recognized you. I'm Homer Atkins. Wife and I came up here from Jefferson City for her annual quilters' retreat. Your wife is the beauty with the auburn hair, right?"

John nodded. He set about cleaning the fish, carefully removing all the innards and tossing them into the pool. He then washed his hands in the chilly water, packed up his creel, and secured his line and lure to his pole.

"Nice meeting you. Hope you have as much luck as I did," he said.

"Maybe you could come join me after your lunch with the missus," said Homer. "Mine doesn't like me coming up there until they're done for the day. I think she enjoys being without me now that I'm disabled and home all the time. It's fine with me. I'd just as soon be here fishing."

John shuddered inwardly. The idea of spending any time at all with this unhealthy, blabbing fool made him feel slightly ill.

"I don't know if I can," he responded. "I have papers to review before we return home at the end of the week."

"Oh? Attorney?"

"No, I'm a judge. Got a big case starting next week."

"That wouldn't be the one about those dead boys, would it? Now that was awful; what a horrible thing."

"No," said John.

"I get it," responded Homer. "You probably can't talk about it. Well, have a good day. Maybe I'll see you at some of the other spots. There's a lot of good fishing around here."

John returned to his car, carefully stowed his gear in the trunk, and sat his lunch on the passenger seat. He contemplated where to go next.

Somewhere not popular, he thought. Suddenly he had a macabre idea.

I wonder if there are fish in that pond where the boys died? At any rate, it would be interesting to see the place, purely from a legal point of view of course. John wasn't self-aware enough to admit to any base curiosity of the kind employed by the general population. He had long ago convinced himself of his superiority to his fellow man.

He pulled out the local map he had obtained. His interest in the case had led him to mark the location of Harve's home and the pond, and he saw that he was about five miles away. He would go there, have lunch, and perhaps see if there were any fish in the pond. He knew from the accounts he had read that the pond would no longer be taped off, since all the forensic work had been completed. He also knew that he would be committing trespass, but if it came to that he could claim innocence of the area, especially if there were no fences or signs. He carefully stashed away the map in case he was questioned by the locals. It wouldn't do to have it in sight.

The dirt road to the pond was unmarked and ungated. John recognized the place from some of the photographs in the newspaper articles about the incident. He drove down the drive, pulling over south of the pond.

The place was beautiful. Harve's gardens were full of daylilies, irises, and clematis.

Roses and begonias lined the driveway down to Harve's tiny log house. The brilliant yellow of yarrow grew all around the bottom of the front and side of the house visible from the road. The meadow leading down from the pond to the house was full of grasses and wildflowers. Around the edges of the pond, clumps of bulrushes, some as tall as John, swayed in the slight breeze, their fat brown tops threatening to break the stems.

As he stepped out of his car, he heard the occasional deep-throated croak of bullfrogs and the constant hum of insects. Unlike the water at Big Bass Pool, which had a slight but detectable current, this pond was utterly still, except for the occasional water walker skittering across the surface. He was surprised by the lack of water birds. This time of year, there should have been ducks and geese, eager for the plentiful supply of protein and the relative protection of inland water.

Lunch was as good as it looked. He sat on his camp stool, finishing the last bits of the ham sandwich. He had brought his own bottled water, and took a long, satisfying drink. The fruit was succulent and sweet, and the carrots were crunchy and fresh. He was a snob about food, and this little diner in the middle of nowhere was a real surprise. He would have to stop in and compliment them. Perhaps he could place a standing order for the rest of the week. The retreat cost had included room and food for two, three meals a day. He only hoped he could make special requests at no additional charge. They certainly hadn't seemed to mind today.

He looked at the uneaten breakfast muffin. Unsure what to do with it, he finally peeled off the paper and tossed the muffin into the pond. Whatever lived there would eat it, or it would simply disintegrate into crumbs and disappear. He turned his back just in time to miss the sudden disappearance of the muffin into the depths of the pond.

He put away his lunch things and headed for the car's trunk. He paused, again savoring the beauty of the landscaping, when something caught his attention. He shaded his eyes, peering intently at the cabin. He could have sworn he saw something moving inside. He thought about going up and knocking on the door, but then thought better of it. He knew the owner was in a jail cell. *There's no one there,* he thought. *Just the wind or my imagination.* He pulled his tackle out of the trunk, set it carefully on the ground, and then reached in and pulled out his thigh-high waders. It looked shallow at the edge, and he might need to go in a bit to get a feel for whether there were fish in there or not.

CHAPTER THIRTY-FOUR

He was hungry and lonely. Harve had been gone for almost a week, taken away by men in big trucks. At first, he thought Harve would come back, but nobody came. The men and women, their trucks, their tape, everything, had left. They were gone.

He had finally come out of his cabin and cautiously entered Harve's, using the key Harve gave him years ago. It was the second time ever he had used the key, the first so long ago he didn't quite remember why. But the key still worked, and he entered through the kitchen in the back. It was a mess, and it smelled. The dishes hadn't been washed and put away. Harve's work clothes lay in a basket in front of the washer, smelling of mud and weeds. A thin film of dust had begun to accumulate.

He started by washing the dishes. He decided, after scrubbing a bit, that he would leave them to soak in the hot, soapy water and put the work clothes in the washer. First, he needed gloves. He found a box in the bathroom closet, unopened. *How can anyone clean without gloves?* he wondered. He slipped them on and returned to the washer. Now he could bear to lift the garments. He checked the pockets, where he found a lighter, a few coins, and a large ring of keys, each with a name on them. He did not recognize the names, but assumed they were Harve's clients. These were probably keys to tool sheds. He put the work clothes in the washer and started it.

By the time he had completed these tasks, the dishes were ready to wash. He set about cleaning and rinsing them and placing them in the drying rack that sat next to the double sink. He would let them dry on their own. He then thoroughly dusted the house, stopping only to switch the laundry from the washing machine to the dryer, and to add a second load of towels and other clothing he found in a second basket.

He had finished the dusting and sweeping and was about to head for the bathroom when he noticed movement up at the pond. He pulled the curtain aside slightly and peered out. Someone was parked near the pond and was walking around. He was seized with fear and indignation.

What if the Provider gets mad again? he thought. The last time all those people were up there the Provider didn't call him for three days. And then he had to sneak to the pond in the dark of the night with the sheep he had found and drop it. He had been rewarded with a lovely squirrel specimen, one that when the taxidermy was complete would fetch a good price. But he knew the Provider was angry, and hungry.

He had intended to feed him today, but now here was another intruder. He stopped himself from running out, yelling at him to go away. He hadn't spoken to anyone other than Harve for ten years, not since the last doctor visit when they told him nothing more could be done. He did not want to speak to anyone now.

He went into the bathroom, which was also in the back of the cabin. He would not go into the front part again, not until the man had left.

He carefully cleaned the entire bathroom. In the tiny bedroom he swept the floor, shook the rugs out the back door, and made the bed. He then carefully folded all the laundry and placed it just so in the dresser. He straightened everything on top of the dresser, in the bathroom, and in the kitchen. Harve would now be able to do good work when he came back home. Good work requires good work habits. Mother always told him that.

He removed some milk, fruit, and vegetables from the refrigerator, took frozen meat from the freezer, and rice and cereal from the cupboard. He would not return until Harve was home.

CHAPTER THIRTY-FIVE

Mary's quilters' retreat was held in the large classroom next to the dining hall. When The Rectory was restored, Arthur had instructed the renovators to remove the walls between the three smaller classrooms that had once served as hotel ballrooms. The space was lit with both lots of hanging lights and large windows which let in a great deal of natural light. It was a perfect room for quilters, and fortunately none of the materials in the library had to be put away. Arthur had made sure to lock the door when he left the night before. Now, Arthur, Jen, Charity, and Dan were sitting at the table, enjoying the morning sun, drinking coffee, and finishing their cinnamon rolls from breakfast. The library windows started three feet up from the floor and rose nearly to the ceiling, two stories high. They were three feet wide, and the top of each pane was curved upward to a point, giving them a Gothic feel. Close examination revealed that the windows were in fact constructed in two pieces so that the lower half could be opened. A walkway with two attached roller ladders spanned the entire room, and the shelves, ceiling to floor, were filled with books.

Ben came in, looking as healthy as any of them had ever seen him. Sobriety had done him a world of good. As Arthur had suspected, Ben wasn't an alcoholic. He was, however, a gentle man, easily frightened, and utterly unprepared for what had happened in the pump house. Now that he had told his story, had repeated it several times to Arthur in even greater detail, he felt no further need to drink.

Ben picked up his chalk and turned to some of the land deeds, property tax bills, and other documents in English. Slowly he began to fill in the family trees, showing how they overlapped and separated again and again. Originally, Stephan and his siblings had been utterly unrelated to any of the Harpers or other people from the Molovna line. But over the years, given the rather small pool of prospective spouses, the lines between the families had blurred.

He was especially interested in the birth certificates he found in one of the newer trunks. He unearthed Harve's, which showed he was born at home with the assistance of a midwife on May 14, 1980. He also found a certificate for one Jeremy Sanders, born with the assistance of a midwife on May 14, 1980. The parents on both certificates were Leonard Sanders and Marie Harper Sanders. Harve had a twin! He needed to let Martin know. Heck, everyone should know.

But first, he must call Martin.

Martin arrived shortly.

"Wow," he said. "You guys have made a lot of progress!"

The diaries had all been sorted, first by author and then by date. Fortunately, their ancestors had been careful to date every volume and each entry.

"Have you found anything of interest?" Martin asked.

"Harve has a twin," blurted Ben. "Would that explain the DNA on the truck? The tissue?"

"How do you know about that?" asked Martin.

Ben blushed.

"I was sitting in the corner when you and the state guys went over the evidence," he said. "You started before I had a chance to let you know I was back there. I sat quietly in the dark. I like to come in here in the evening, sit in the dark corner by the stairs, and listen to the silence. It's helping me to learn to be calm."

He blushed again.

"Well, you can't and must not say anything more, not to anyone, about what you heard. That was privileged conversation. You know what that means?"

"Yes, I do. And I'm sorry, Martin. I didn't mean to break any rules."

"Okay. Just remember. No more talking. Now I'm going to go visit Harve and find out about this twin. How did you find out about him?"

Ben showed him the birth certificates. Arthur took them to the back of the library, into his small study, where he made copies of both certificates and gave the copies, three of each certificate, to Martin.

"I don't suppose this is going to help much," Arthur said.

"I think it will. But sorry, I really cannot tell you why," replied Martin.

"I understand. But I do want to ask a favor of you."

"Ask away."

"Harve's dying in there, emotionally and spiritually. You can trust Jim Burch. He's a good man, and I suspect he doesn't think Harve's guilty, either. But he can be trusted to stop Harve if he starts talking about incriminating stuff. Harve needs to talk. I think you should let him talk to Jim. He's not stupid, you know. Tell him what he can and can't talk about, and he'll be careful."

"Let me think on it, on my way over," replied Martin.

Martin left, papers in hand, and headed for the sheriff's office. He was about to have some quality time with Harve.

Jim Burch was sitting at his desk, a large mug of coffee at his left hand, and one of Maggie's huge cinnamon rolls in front of him, half consumed. He was staring out the window, a slight smile on his face. The object of his attention turned and waved. Linda was out watering the flowers in boxes at the front of the paper. It was a pleasing sight.

Martin came in, sat down, and snagged a piece of roll, and joined Jim in contemplation of Linda's charms.

"She's a nice woman," he said. "Smart, self-assured, and generous."

"Yup," said Jim. "We had dinner the other night. She's a wealth of information and history about Harper's Landing."

He sat up a bit taller and put his full attention on Martin.

"What brings you here? And please, take as much as you want of that roll. I swear, Maggie is trying to fatten me up like a hog for market."

"I need to talk to Harve," said Martin, as he snagged more of the roll. "You got any more coffee around here?"

Jim brought him a cup of coffee and pulled another monster roll out of the breakfast basket Maggie had sent over with Jen for him and Harve.

"I'm here for several reasons," said Martin. "First and foremost, I'm giving you permission to talk to Harve. Now mind you, ordinarily I wouldn't do this at all. But Arthur assures me that you will not stray into discussions about the murders, the crime scene, etc. If you can promise me that you won't go there, and that you will stop Harve when he does and remind him about Miranda warnings, if you are comfortable with that then I will give permission for you two to talk. Because he is going bonkers."

Jim thought about it.

"As an officer of the court, I can't tell him not to talk. But without bothering my conscience too much, I can get up and go to the bathroom if he strays into forbidden territory."

"That'll do," said Martin. "Then you two discuss landscaping or the weather, something neutral."

Martin walked back to the holding area. Harve's cell was spacious and clean. He had several books Martin had been allowed to bring him, along with a small portable TV provided by Jen. He had also been allowed to use his laptop after it had been inspected thoroughly by the forensics lab. Martin found him watching an old John Wayne Western.

"I can come back when it's over," he said.

"Nah," replied Harve. "I've seen this a million times. I'd rather talk to you."

He turned off the set. Then he hollered to Jim.

"Can I have this cell door open, please? So we can talk without the damn bars in the way?"

Jim came back, carrying his key ring.

"I'll be right outside," he said. "But if the state guys drive up, you can expect me back here pronto locking you in."

"Fair enough. You're a good man, Jim. Thank you."

Once Jim had left, Martin pulled out one copy each of the two certificates and handed them to Harve.

"Care to explain this?" he asked. "You never mentioned a brother, let alone a twin."

Harve buried his face in his hands. Where to begin? How to explain Jeremy? He was overcome with a deep aching sadness for his lonely, disfigured twin, who was about to get exposed to the world from which he had hidden for so long.

CHAPTER THIRTY-SIX

K avanaugh hated the waders. He only wore them when he had to, and then only if he was alone. He pulled them on and shrugged into the suspenders. He picked up the pole and walked five feet into the pond. It appeared to be approximately thirty feet across, and when he reached the five foot point the bottom began a sharp slope downward toward the middle. He stopped, released the hook and spinner lure from the pole, and cast out near the center of the pond. The weight hit bottom, and the lure began its slow slide up the line. Kavanaugh had put just enough weight on the spinner to keep it turning about five feet from the bottom. He prided himself on his skill in preparing tackle as much as his success in trophy fishing. He would have to stand for a while, but he was fit and standing in water was easy.

The pond was silent, as he had noted earlier, except for the occasional throaty croak of bullfrogs around the edges among the bulrushes. The sun was warm but not yet hot; he had a hat and had remembered to apply ample sunscreen. If there were any fish in this pond, John Kavanaugh would find them. Of that he was certain.

He reeled in the metal lure and again cast toward the center, this time to the north and a bit west. Again, he felt the solid thunk of the weight hitting the pond bottom and the slight pull as the lure ascended five feet. After twenty minutes, he had still not had a tug or any indication of fish in this pond. He knew from the various newspaper accounts he had read that there was a tunnel, for want of a better description, leading downward from the center of the pond to the underground streams that filled this area.

Since most of those streams spilled out into the Martin's Way River, according to the maps he had consulted, he was certain that some fish should have made their way to this quiet, bug-filled pond. Bass would have been attracted to the abundance of water walkers and chiggers, but then there should have been ducks dropping in for meals also. The bullfrogs were undoubtedly well fed. He reeled in again and waded to the south, hoping for luck on the opposite side of the pond.

He was wearing his ear buds, listening to the soulful sounds of Bix Beiderbecke, or he might have heard the splash at the center of the pond. He was looking at where he was placing his feet, or he might have seen the wave headed toward him. He was focusing on where to sink his next cast, or he might have felt the grip on his leg sooner.

CHAPTER THIRTY-SEVEN

J im wandered in and handed Martin the key to the cell.
"I'm heading out, doing a drive around the area," he said.
"I've been sitting in this office for too long. Gonna get callouses on my butt. Promise me if the state boys come in, you'll lock that cell."

Martin promised. He followed Jim out to the main office and watched as he crossed the street and briefly spoke with Linda Collier. She went inside and emerged in a moment wearing a pale pink cardigan. She locked the front door of the *Gazette* and climbed into Jim's car. Martin smiled, and then returned to Harve's cell. Harve still had his head buried in his hands.

"Is it that awful?" Martin asked.

Harve looked up, real pain and anguish in his face.

"No," he said, in answer to Martin's question. "I don't think he's responsible for what is going on. I really don't. But there's going to be a crap ton of people descending on him, and he's not up to that. Hell, he hasn't spoken to anyone but me for the past ten years. Not after that last doctor."

Slowly, Martin drew the story out of him.

Jeremy and Harvey Sanders were born at home on May 14,

1980. Their mother, Marie Harper Sanders, was a tiny woman and the delivery was difficult. Harvey was born first; Jeremy had to be pulled out using forceps. He took a long time to start breathing, and by the time the twins were two months old, it was apparent that Jeremy had cerebral palsy.

The family travelled to St. Louis where they learned how to exercise his muscles and try to avoid the constrictions that would prevent him from walking. They were only partially successful. He gradually learned to walk. He was extremely fortunate in not having any difficulties with his arms. When he was five, they again travelled to St. Louis, where a new set of doctors told them that Jeremy did not have CP. He had suffered a pinched nerve in his spine during delivery, which had affected his legs. They were told that while he would always have some difficulty in walking, he could overcome most of that, in time, with rigorous physical therapy. The family stayed for two weeks, learning how to perform the exercises. They also visited the Gateway Arch, strolled through Forest Park, and visited the St. Louis Zoo. One day while Jeremy and Marie were learning a new set of exercises, Harve's dad took him to the Missouri Botanical Garden. Although he was only five years old, Harve knew from that day on that he wanted to be a landscaper. He was entranced with the many flowers, the trees, and the butterflies. He begged his father to take him again, but they had to leave for home the following day. Harve promised himself he would visit again once he was able to travel alone.

Jeremy and Harve were inseparable. They were identical twins, and only Jeremy's disability kept them from successfully pranking their teachers and parents. Not that they didn't try. They were happy boys: outgoing and personable, possessed of a keen wit and an even keener sense of humor. They loved school. Harve started a garden shortly after they came home from St. Louis, when he was five, and although Jeremy did not share his love of gardening, he was willing to help with planting and weeding. They grew flowers and vegetables, and it was Jeremy who came up with clever devices for keeping deer and rabbits out of the gardens.

When the boys were eighteen and about to graduate from Harper's Landing High School, their parents surprised them with a trip to Washington, DC. They left the day after graduation, drove two days across many states, and arrived late in the evening at their hotel in the capital. The boys were beside themselves with excitement. They wanted to see everything. But with only three days available, they had to limit their activities. After much discussion and looking over tour guides, they all decided that three days at the Smithsonian would be marvelous.

Jeremy was overwhelmed and overjoyed. He had envied Harve's ambition and dedication to his vocation, which he had held onto for so many years. Jeremy had never found anything that captured his imagination. But now he stood in the great hall of the Natural History Museum and knew that he wanted to learn how to preserve animals with the perfection and beauty of these specimens. He asked their guide what you called people who preserved them.

Taxidermists. He called them taxidermists. A search of the guidebooks revealed that the name was a derivative of the word taxonomy, which meant the classification of organisms.

In the gift shop, Jeremy's search was rewarded with a book on basic taxidermy. He spent his graduation gift money on the large volume and insisted on keeping it with him on the way home in the car. Jeremy was utterly absorbed in his book, as was Harve, who had found a book on famous botanical gardens, when the car suddenly swerved. Their father hit the brakes hard, and the tires screeched. Both boys were thrown against the backs of the front seats and onto the floor as the car slammed into the oncoming pickup truck that had jumped the center divider. The impact tore the back door off on Harve's side, and he was tossed into the ditch alongside the center divider. His head hit the fence, and he blacked out.

He learned later how his brother managed to crawl out of the car, how the car had caught fire and Jeremy had tried in vain to pull his parents from the car, and how Jeremy had sustained serious burns to one side of his face and most of his chest. The coroner reported that both parents had died instantly upon impact, but Jeremy could not be convinced. He was certain they had died because of his failure.

Jeremy underwent multiple surgeries to remove the burned skin and later to attempt a reconstruction of the right side of his face and to remove the constricting scars on his chest.

Harve recovered from his concussion swiftly and stayed by Jeremy's side throughout the early stages of his treatment. When he could, he took him home to Harper's Landing, and they travelled to St. Louis multiple times during the next six years for surgeries, physical therapy, and attempts to help heal Jeremy's psyche. Most of the treatments failed. Finally, ten years ago, when the twins were twenty-four, the doctors told them there was physically nothing more they could do for Jeremy. Plastic surgery had failed to remove the disfiguring scars on his face. The attempted repairs on his chest only resulted in more scars which slightly twisted his body.

Despite the horrific damage to his body, the worst damage was to Jeremy's mind. He refused all psychiatric care, and with the passing years retreated further and further from the world. Finally, he moved into his great-great-grandfather's cabin, behind the one he and Harve had shared for so many years and immersed himself in his taxidermy. Harve gave up his dream of going to Washington University to study botany. Instead, he remained at home caring for his brother and took correspondence courses in companion planting, irrigation, garden design, and other courses to increase his skill and knowledge in landscaping. Harve started his business, funding it with his share of the settlement from the accident. Jeremy's share went toward correspondence courses in taxidermy and acquisition of all the books and tools he would need to pursue his dream.

Harve was a skilled and talented landscaper. But it was

Jeremy whose work gained international fame. The collectors who vied to purchase his works of art never knew his real name. At first, Harve would take specimens with him when he went to St. Louis to purchase trees, plants, and other items for his business. He would take the specimens around to shops that did consignment. The specimens sold almost immediately. Three years ago he had taken a half-dozen of Jeremy's best specimens and driven to the Wonders of Wildlife Museum in Springfield. The museum curators were so impressed with the quality of his work that they bought all six specimens and requested more as soon as they were available.

Harve, inspired by the response, shipped off two specimens to the National Museum of Natural History. Those were purchased also, and they, too, requested more specimens. In fact, Jeremy's work had made him wealthy, and Harve managed his money. Jeremy still refused to leave his cabin for other than the occasional visit with Harve. He was, for all intents and purposes, a hermit.

Harve omitted telling Martin about Jeremy's severe OCD, which began shortly after the accident. He also omitted Jeremy's obsession with pleasing his dead mother. He knew Jeremy was seriously mentally ill but was convinced that he was also harmless.

"They won't have to disturb him, will they?" he asked. "He wouldn't be able to bear it at this point. He would ... I don't know, he would hide, I think. He hasn't spoken much since our parents died. I don't want him taken away."

"I'll hold this information for as long as I can," said Martin. "But the group of folks going through the diaries and journals from up at Charity's place were the ones who found the birth certificates. I wouldn't hold your breath if I were you. It'll come out sooner rather than later."

"Please protect him," begged Harve. "He's so fragile, so damaged. And people won't be able to hide their reaction on seeing him for the first time. Even some of the doctors couldn't."

"Don't tell Jim," replied Martin. "I've decided to allow you two to talk. But you must be careful. Okay? Nothing about your brother, nothing about your property, nothing about the murders."

"Okay," said Harve. "But you believe me, don't you? That I'm not guilty? I don't even use bug spray on my gardens. I don't know what killed those boys, but it wasn't me. And I'm damn sure it wasn't Jeremy, either."

CHAPTER THIRTY-EIGHT

J im and Linda drove out along County Road 22, admiring the summer wildflowers and enjoying a beautiful day. He wanted to drive by Harve's place, to make sure all was okay, but Linda begged him not to.

"I can't face it," she said. "Those poor boys. And poor Harve. You don't think he did it, do you, Jim?"

"Not for me to decide," he replied. "I think we all want it not to be Harve. But at this point it's probably going to be up to a judge and jury. There's so much circumstantial evidence to link him to the crime. Let's hope we get an easygoing state attorney instead of some young hotshot trying to make a name for themselves."

"What about Jeremy?" asked Linda. "What's going to happen to him? And why is Harve a suspect and Jeremy not?"

"I didn't know you knew about Jeremy," said Jim.

"Oh, we all do," said Linda. "But he's been isolated for so long, refusing to see anyone other than Harve, that we all forgot him. I feel bad about that. So does Charity."

"Charity knows?" asked Jim.

"Everyone who has lived here for more than a few years

knows about them and the accident. We are all feeling bad about ignoring Jeremy. Though it appears he has been happy to be by himself, away from prying eyes. I know his injuries were horrific."

"The state folk don't know about him yet, but they will soon enough. I suspect they may want to charge him, too, or instead. I can't defend them, Linda. I can only go by the evidence, which at this point is damning."

County Road 22 going north led up to the Grossman Textile Mill, now a protected historical site, though again a working mill. They sat watching the huge waterwheel slowly turning in the rapid currents of the Martin's Way. It was fascinating, how the boards were pushed by the water, turning the wheel, which then turned smaller wheels, which gained speed as they reduced in size until they were small and fast enough to turn the great thread spindles inside.

"We've got two hours until lunch time," said Jim, looking at his watch. "Why don't we go into the museum? I haven't seen it yet, nor have I ever seen the mill at work."

"Sure," said Linda. "That would be wonderful."

The building that once housed the slaves and later the freedmen who worked the mill had been restored and converted into the museum. Grossman had obtained antique mill equipment which was on display in various glassed-in alcoves. Along with each piece of equipment was a sample of the various products produced by the mills. There were cones of thread, bolts of cotton, woven bolts of wool, piles of raw wool and cotton, and various sizes of shuttles, needles, and spindles. A large display in the center of the building featured a video showing how the great looms were warped, as well as several different sizes and types of looms. A door to one side of the exhibit displayed a sign: *COMING SOON—A History of Weaving and Spinning. Anticipated opening in September 2014.*

As they finished watching the video, Bull Harper came into the room through a door marked *Mill Floor—Do Not Enter.*

"Hey, there," he said. "Didn't know you were coming up here. Would you two like a tour of the actual mill?"

They both gave an enthusiastic yes.

"Let me turn in these papers at the office, and I'll show you around."

The mill was noisy. The waterwheel continued to turn, and the smaller cogwheels inside spun freely. The looms stood idle while workers redid the warp. Once it was complete, the large looms would shift the warp threads back and forth in various configurations as the weft, attached to the shuttles, shot back and forth, creating the patterns in the woven cloth. Bull explained that they were about to weave a large quantity of fabric for a tailoring shop in Chicago, specializing in custom suits of lightweight wool. Jim and Linda were disappointed to hear that the looms would not start for another two or three days. They would have to return to see them in action.

Bull told them they would probably know when the looms started turning, since the waterwheel made an awful racket on the first few turns.

"We started the wheel for the first time a month ago, come to think of it, right before Rory went missing. It's a sound you can't miss if you're on the alert for it. Like a whole bunch of planks spanking the water. None of knows what it will sound like when we attach the looms to the wheel and start them turning."

Bull then led them down a long walkway outside to a recently constructed outbuilding. This building housed the large spindles where the thread was made from raw cotton or wool. A second building housed the carding machines that were used to prepare the fibers. The road had been finished, leading from the main highway past the Jenkins Farm pump house and up to the loading dock of this building. Four large trucks were lined up as workers unloaded each. First the raw wool was scoured in a series of alkaline baths containing water, soap, and soda ash. Rollers in the scouring machines squeezed excess water from the fleece, but the fleece wasn't allowed to dry completely.

Next, the fibers were passed through a series of metal teeth that straightened and blended them into slivers. These machines, called carders, also removed dirt and other matter left in the fibers. The carded wool, intended for worsted yarn, was then put through gilling and combing, two procedures that removed short fibers and placed the longer fibers parallel to each other. The carded wool was then placed on a conveyor belt and sent to the thread building for spinning. Workers there were attaching three to four threads per bunch, and continually adding to them. As the thread was spun it was wrapped around a commercial drum. Small trucks, like golf carts, then took the drums to the dye house, where the thread was dyed according to the buyer's specifications.

"We are making a plain weave worsted," said Bull. "There are two types of weave: plain and twill. The twill allows us to make lovely, multicolored fabrics. But this order is going to a tailor who wants plain weave in black, dark blue, and deep brown. We will dye the yarn first, after it is all spun. And then start making the cloth. You come back late next week, say Thursday, and I'll show you the looms in action."

Jim and Linda returned to the car and drove back to Morey's for lunch. It had been a thoroughly pleasant morning, a good diversion from the awfulness of the last few days. They pulled into the back parking lot of the sheriff's office and walked over to Morey's together. It amused them both to think of how many tongues were going to start wagging.

They looked for Arthur, Jen, or Ben. None of the three was there. Morey came out, drying his hands.

"If you're looking for Jen and company, they're having lunch in The Rectory library. I could send you up with yours if you like. They'd probably like to have you. I guess you forgot that we closed for the week to take care of the quilters."

They both agreed, waited for lunch to be packed into the baskets

Morey and Maggie used for the purpose, and set out for The Rectory. The day had warmed considerably, and they were happy the walk was only a few blocks. They entered the cool vestibule and headed for the library. The happy chatter of the quilters could be heard from the dining room, where Maggie undoubtedly was serving up something delectable and homey followed by something chocolate. If there was one thing quilters had in common, it was a love for chocolate.

They opened the door to the library in time to hear Dan sum up what he had been reading in the latest diary.

"It appears that Stephan and Jennie were in agreement that it would be necessary to find a permanent solution to the *bolotnik*."

"To the what?" asked Jim, his eyebrows lifted.

"Oh boy," muttered Arthur. "This is going to be fun."

"You'd better sit down, Jim," said Dan. "You too, Linda. This is going to take some explaining, and I'd rather put it off until after we've finished eating. Ben here is anxious to show you the family tree. Or at least what he's been able to assemble of it."

Arthur poured them each a glass of strawberry lemonade from the big pitcher on the middle of the table. Lunch was thick roast beef sandwiches on slices of homemade whole wheat bread, slathered in house-made mayo and freshly churned butter. There was a green salad with tomatoes and cucumbers, two little tubs of dressing—one blue cheese, the other Thousand Island—and fresh fruit salad.

"My god," said Linda. "Does Maggie think I'm a horse?"

Everyone laughed.

"I don't think she knows how to make small meals," said Jen. "But more likely Morey threw this together for you. She's in there serving up potato salad, hot ham slices in raisin sauce, fresh carrots, and chocolate cake. Those quilters are going to founder before the week is over."

They ate in companionable silence, soft chamber music filling the air, the scent of the summer flowers blowing in through the open windows. As expected, apple pie was the dessert. Jim was surprised to see that both he and Linda had received a substantial wedge of sharp cheddar.

After lunch was completed, Jim was about to ask if there was any coffee when Maggie magically appeared at the door with a large urn.

"Made too much for them," she said. "I am always overestimating the capacity of other people."

She bustled back out of the room, leaving the half-full urn for the seven of them.

"Now," said Jim. "What's a bobolink or whatever that was?"

"A *bolotnik*," said Dan. "It's a Ukrainian mythological creature. However, like most mythological creatures, it likely has some basis in reality. Our ancestors, the ones who wrote these diaries, believe they may have inadvertently brought a *bolotnik* with them from Ukraine at around 1802 or so."

"What's this thing supposed to do?" Jim asked.

"Short answer: drag people and animals underwater and eat them."

There was a long silence. Jim stared at them, first at Dan, then at Arthur. Even Jen looked solemn-faced. They weren't joking. He turned to Linda. The blood had drained from her face. She chewed on a knuckle, shook her head, and finally said, "Are you sure?"

"Now look here," said Jim. "I know that none of you wants to believe that Harve had anything to do with those deaths. Hell, neither do I. But going around making up stories about imaginary water creatures who lay in wait and eat people isn't going to help him."

He was angry, angry at all of them. They should know better. They were intelligent, well-educated people. He took a deep breath and tried to calm himself.

Arthur reached over and pulled a volume from the stack of already read diaries. It was the first one that Charity, Jen, and Bridgette had read together. Stephan had written it in English, and Bridgette had gone home and printed out the Folklorepedia page about *bolotniks*, which now was in the back of the diary.

"Here, Jim. Sit over there, in the sunlight, and read this," said Arthur. "Note the date, and please handle it carefully. The paper is handmade and quite fragile."

Jim gingerly took the diary and sat in one of the wing chairs next to the open window. He began to read and was soon oblivious to everything else. The story the diary told was compelling and persuasive, if more than a bit hard to believe.

Meanwhile, the others returned to the task of sorting and cataloging. Ben was sifting through his trove of documents, filling in the family tree when he stumbled on a new name. It was quickly becoming clear that many of the residents of Harper's Landing were related.

Linda was deeply troubled. She didn't want to be here. This was a part of her life she had cut off, turned off, shut down. And now it was spread all over this table, speaking to her in a thousand little whispers. Calling for her help. She wanted none of it.

"It's painful, isn't it," said the calm, gentle voice at her elbow. She was startled. It was Arthur, Arthur the preacher, Arthur the connoisseur of fine whiskey and good literature. How did he know? She was horrified to discover that tears were running down her cheeks. She turned so Jim could not see her.

"Why don't we go into my study?" asked Arthur, as he gently guided her into the small room at the back of the library.

She chose a large wingback chair by the window, enjoying the warmth of the afternoon sun on her back. The things she had seen and heard had given her a chill.

Arthur asked, "When did you first turn off your power, or try to?"

"How do you know about that?" she asked sharply.

"I can see it," replied Arthur. "I am an ovate Druid, which means I have studied and practice the Druidic way particular to communing with and healing nature. That's a short version. The long version, well, that's for another day. Suffice it to say, I have a great interest in keeping nature balanced, healthy, and in check. You, dear lady, radiate so much personal power. Now mind you, I'm not talking about all that fluffy bunny woo-woo stuff. I'm all about letting people do whatever makes them happy. But with you, as well as with myself, I'm talking about the power that allows us to know when something is wrong, when nature is being messed with, when people are doing bad things, when animals are endangered. And to know how to use the right herbs, the right time of day, the right prayers or spells, to set things straight again."

"He beat me," she whispered. "He said I was evil and needed to be purged. I would have left, but he said he would find me and kill me and my parents. I knew he meant it. Knew in that way you are talking about now. But I also knew I did not dare use my power against him, though I could have. But I didn't. And I had to be careful because my rage and fear were so great."

She stopped. Took a deep breath. Sipped on the small snifter of brandy he handed her.

"I'm babbling."

"No, you are speaking the truth, perhaps for the first time."

"I was so careful. Even after he got arrested, after I divorced him, even then I never allowed myself to wish him ill. But when he was killed in that riot, I was so afraid, afraid that it was me who got him killed."

"I don't think so," said Arthur. "Men like that attract violence. It comes to them like a magnet. But you can't keep this hidden forever. It will come out, and better you should have it under control."

"I need to help them, don't I?"

"We are going to need all the help we can get. If I can win over Jim just a bit, it will make our job easier. With the state boys off our backs, we can focus on learning if there is still a *bolotnik* and how to deal with it."

"But how could it still be here, after all these years?"

"If it is a *bolotnik*, they are basically immortal. Lesser elementals to be sure, but, nevertheless, elementals and therefore not easily dispatched. We are hoping to find references to what they did to render him inactive for so long. Come, help us with the sorting and research. You and I will begin your training another day. That is, if you are willing?"

"Oh yes," Linda said with relief. "Oh my, yes."

CHAPTER THIRTY-NINE

J im was startled from his reading by the sudden burst of chatter and happy laughter in the hallway. The quilters were done for the day and more than ready for dinner. It was meatloaf day, and many of them had been here previous years and knew the wonders of Maggie's Marvelous Meatloaf. Jim and the others put down their books and papers, carefully locked the library door, and joined the happy group in the dining hall.

Morey, Maggie, and Bridgette had outdone themselves. The tables in the dining room had been set up in a U shape. Mary Harper would be presenting a trunk show of her work after dinner. Each of the three tables had two large meatloaves on it, sliced into thick slabs. Bowls of mashed potatoes sat to either side of each platter, and tureens of rich brown gravy were placed beside them. Baskets of hot, steaming rolls were placed on each table, along with crocks of freshly churned butter and squeeze bears of local honey. There were also bowls of buttered carrots, fresh peas, and green tossed salad. The smells were intoxicating. Suddenly, even those who claimed not to have room for any more food found themselves ravenously hungry.

A tall, brunette woman stood to one side, looking nervous and worried.

"Come on now, dear," said Maggie, taking her arm. "Your fellow quilters won't bite."

"No, it's not that," said Susan Kavanaugh. "It's my husband. He's not here. He's not in our room, his car is still not back, and he isn't answering his cell."

Jim overheard her as he entered the room and introduced himself.

"Did he have specific plans for the day?"

"Just fishing. It's why he came along. He wanted to fish Big Bass Pool. It's one of the few places in Missouri he's never fished."

"Oh, here now," said a large, bearded man. "I saw your husband out there about lunch time. He had quite the catch, he did. Said he was going to join you for lunch, and then was going to find another place. I invited him to come back and fish the BBP with me, but he seemed keen on finding other areas."

Susan smiled wryly.

"He took his lunch with him. He's not the most social person. Probably wanted to be alone but not insult you."

"Oh, that's fine. Lots of fishermen prefer fishing alone. Me? Fishing's never been a meditative sport if you know what I mean. I like to share a few beers, tell a few tales, and if you catch a fish, well, that's all the better."

"Homer Atkins, are you going to eat or stand there jawing?" said a tiny little woman with grey hair and sparkling blue eyes. She laughed up at him.

"Well, ma'am," said Jim. "Seems your husband saw this lady's husband out fishing today, and her husband hasn't returned. Maybe he can help us."

"Don't keep him too long. Maggie's meatloaf never lasts long."

"Did you happen to notice which way he went when he left?" asked Jim.

"No, sorry. You know, that drive to Big Bass is treelined and all. Hard to see anything back on the road. And I didn't pay much attention to which way his motor went. Let me think a moment."

He cocked his head and closed his eyes.

"North. I do believe he went north up County Road. Sorry I can't be of more help."

He was eyeing the table and slightly moving toward it.

"Go, eat," said Jim, with a laugh. "Mrs. Kavanaugh, why don't we have something to eat and give him a little more time to get back? It's easy to get lost if you don't know these parts well, and there are areas where there is no cell reception up north along the Martin's Way. If he's still not back in the morning, we'll start looking."

CHAPTER FORTY

W hat shall I do? He's been calling me all day, begging for food. Demanding food. Threatening for food. That car out there. Will someone come back?

And now he is silent. Satisfied. He must have found a deer wandering too close to the edge. Or perhaps a wild turkey or two. I should learn to preserve birds. They are so beautiful. And so difficult. Perhaps Harve will bring me some books. I want Harve. I need Harve. The bad men have not brought him back. I want him back.

He stopped staring at the car, went out the back door and down the path to his own house. It was getting dark. He needed to be inside, to do his work, to clean his house, to sleep. So many things to do. And all must be done correctly, at the proper time and in the proper way. Order was so difficult, especially with all these people. They needed to go away.

He sat at his table, working on the tiny, matched pair of chipmunks. It was an order from the National Museum. Chipmunks were easy to catch. They loved peanut butter. He would put some in a small live trap out by his back door, and they would get caught. He hated killing them. Harve did that for him. And the Provider. The Provider did most of his killing now, and the specimens he left were splendid. As a bonus, the Provider cleaned them out, mostly; the one part of the taxidermist's job he hated.

At 5:00 PM, he rose and prepared his dinner. It was meatloaf in a tray, with mixed vegetables. He put it in the microwave, took out a roll and butter, and set his place at the small table in his kitchen. He put out a plate, a fork and knife, and poured himself a glass of lemonade. Harve needed to get him more frozen lemonade. Where was he? He should have come back from town by now. He set aside thoughts of Harve. It was dinner time. Dinner must be eaten by 5:30 PM, and the kitchen must be cleaned by 6:00 PM. He ate slowly, listening to the sounds of crickets and owls. The sweet scent from Harve's gardens floated through his open window. It was 6:15 PM when he heard scraping and scratching at his back door. It was the Provider, with a gift. He would open the door and get it once he heard the Provider leave. It would not do to see him or be seen. He knew that.

He washed his dishes, put them in the cupboard in their places, put the silver away in the drawer, disposed of the tray, and dried the glass. He made sure it was carefully lined up on the shelf. He decided to leave whatever the Provider had deposited at his back door until the morning. He would not be ready to work on anything new, and it was still cold enough at night that the specimen would be okay overnight.

He went to his worktable, where he resumed working on the chipmunks. This was a special order, and he gave it his entire attention. Fischer Supplies' eyes, as always, were perfect. He trimmed the tiny hairs, replaced some whiskers, fluffed the tails, and carefully inserted the wires that would keep them curved and lifted. Before he realized it, the sun had completely set, and it was getting dark. He lit an oil lamp beside the table and cleaned and sorted his tools. It had been easy to start his day's work, as it would be tomorrow, because everything was where it should be. Good work requires good work habits. Mother always told him that.

CHAPTER FORTY-ONE

The next day, the sixth of July, Jim filed a missing person report on John Kavanaugh. He printed out the picture Susan had on her phone and sent a complete description along with the picture to the State Police in Jefferson City. Harve Sanders' arraignment date, originally set for the fifth, had been postponed by the judge so he could study the motions Martin Rutledge had filed on his behalf. Jim had been looking forward to some quiet time, but he knew that the continued absence of Judge Kavanaugh required his attention.

Jim organized a search party. Homer Atkins volunteered since he knew the area well, and Harry Randle was assigned to ride with him. Jim and Susan would take Jim's car and search north of Big Bass Pool. The other two would go south and check out spots along the river. Mrs. Kavanaugh wasn't in a mood for talking, so they rode in silence, looking out for the Kavanaugh's silver 2014 Mercedes CLA.

They had been on the road only fifteen minutes when Jim's cell rang.

"Jim," Harry said. "We found the car. I think you'd better come quickly."

"Where is it?"

"Parked at Harve's pond."

"Damn," said Jim, disconnecting the call and turning the Explorer around at a wide spot.

"Did they find him?" asked Susan.

"No, but they found the car. Did your husband have any special interest in our recent incident up here?"

"You mean those poor boys who were killed?"

"Yeah. Did he know about it, talk about it?"

"He knew about it. We didn't discuss it. But then he can't talk about things like that, I guess."

"Why's that?"

"As you know, he's a judge. Sits on the county bench in St. Louis, but I know from time to time he gets called to smaller counties like this one. Though I don't think he would have come on this trip if he thought he would be asked to sit for that case. He's careful about conflicts."

"Okay. They've found his car. It's parked by the pond where the boys were found."

"Oh my god. Is he ...?" She couldn't ask.

"No one there or they would have told me. But let's get over there, positively ID the car, and go from there. Don't go worrying before there's reason."

He knew his words were futile, but he had to try anyway. This was one tough woman. She sat up straight, silent, no tears, but obviously shaken. They arrived at the road leading to the pond and drove up next to Homer's car.

There was no sign of John anywhere. Jim got permission from Susan to look inside the car. He found the remnants of a lunch, an empty thermos, and the usual detritus of a family car, but there was nothing suspicious or unusual, and nothing to indicate what had happened to John Kavanaugh.

The trunk was partially full of various kinds of fishing gear. They found the bass and crappie he had caught at Big Bass Pool, carefully packed in dry ice in a cooler. Susan mentioned that his waders were gone, along with one of his poles.

Jim and Harry searched the area for footprints, but other than what appeared to be John's, they found nothing. Jim took several pictures of what they presumed were John's footprints, together with pictures of the car and the surrounding area.

After a long discussion with Harry, Jim grudgingly agreed that they should treat it as a crime scene. While Harry taped off the car and pond area, Jim called Clay Murdoch.

"Hey, there," he said. "I am calling as Sheriff for now, not Coroner. But I guess you and Blake better get up here again with some crime scene guys. Here, let me send you the pics. Got them on my phone."

He sent the pictures and waited for the return call.

"Tape around the entire pond," he said to Harry after he hung up. "And block the entry from the road up there. No one except officials in or out."

A few minutes later, Blake called him.

"You want divers, too? Given as how it's the same pond those boys went missing in. Maybe we'll find his gear, or ..." He let the sentence trail off.

"Yeah, bring a diver," said Jim. "This is going to play hell with Mary's quilters retreat. Town will turn into a gossip factory again."

He hung up and turned to Susan.

"I'm taking you back to The Rectory."

She started to object, but he stopped her.

"It's going to be at least two hours before the crime lab folks and the diver can get here from St. Louis. I don't think they'll find anything. But I don't want you sitting out here stewing while you wait for them. The women at The Rectory will help you keep busy and calm. I'll be there, too. And when the guys from State arrive, I'll go with them. I will call you and keep you posted; I promise."

After he saw Susan safely in the company of her fellow quilters, Jim went to the library and found Arthur with his nose in a book. He helped himself to more coffee. He found the diary where he had left it the night before. He sat in the same wingback chair, ready to resume reading. After a bit, Arthur came over and sat next to him.

"What do you think?" he asked.

"It's compelling," replied Jim, "if unbelievable. I mean, an animal of some sort, transported all the way from Ukraine by ship in 1802? It would starve to death on such a long trip, even if it did eat the Sloven kid. And by the way, if it did eat the Sloven kid, where were the clothes?"

Arthur sat back, steepled his fingers, and thought for a while. This was something he hadn't considered. It certainly argued for the Sloven child having fallen overboard rather than being consumed by some monster trapped in a barrel. However, it didn't mean that there wasn't a *bolotnik* accidentally introduced into the waters of the Harper's Landing region. The question was how to present this to Jim in a way that wouldn't completely turn him off?

"*Bolotniks* were believed to be immortal, lesser water elementals," he said. "Dan could tell you more about them since he specializes in Slavic mythology. It's his area of study for his doctorate in cultural anthropology. I know it's a huge stretch for you, but if there were a *bolotnik* in Harve's pond, swimming in and out through the tunnel at the bottom, it would be as close to immortal as anything you could imagine."

Jim started to protest, but Arthur held up his hand.

"Hear me out," he said. "A Greenland shark was found that was estimated to be 392 years old. Some koi fish have reportedly lived more than two hundred years. Rougheye rockfish live for two hundred years. Orange roughy, also known as deep sea perch, can live up to one hundred forty-nine years. And many of them are known to hibernate. It could be that the *bolotnik* was a rare and long-lived species that consumed any prey that entered its habitat. Myths and folktales have developed for lesser events than a fish with a long life."

Jim sat silent, holding the diary. He took a long sip of coffee.

"But there's more to it, isn't there?" he said. "You're giving me answers that provide rational explanations for something that appears irrational. You're more than a Harvard trained preacher; I'm just not sure what that *more* is."

"I'm an Ovate Druid, trained in all of the paths of Druidry, but specializing in the way of the Shaman. I try to keep nature in balance around me and to protect the people who share that space with me. I'm also a trained Unitarian minister, and no, I don't see a conflict in that. The teachings of Jesus, as presented in the Bible, present no conflict at all with my mission as a healer of the animals, plants, and waters around me. If anything, they enhance the urgency of my mission and provide a path for bringing people into harmony with themselves, with each other, and with the world around them."

Jim was trying to assimilate all this. Ovate Druid? Shaman? He had spent his entire adult life dedicated to protecting people from each other. Sure, he had saved people from drowning, pulled one woman out of a house fire, and killed a guy who was trying to kill two kids. But he hadn't ever felt a whiff of a connection with them. It was his job, his calling. Beth had often told him he was the softest tough guy she knew. He had never understood that. But what Arthur was saying somehow made perfect sense.

For Jim, police work was a calling, a dedication. It was all-consuming. He thought back on how he had come to be the sheriff in Harper's Landing, how the desire to stay and protect them had *called* to him when John Hartley died. Every fiber of his being wanted to deny what he was hearing. It went against everything he believed, everything he served. He was an atheist, a scientist, a realist. And here the man he considered his best friend was telling him there were things that could not be seen, could not be labeled, or catalogued, or photographed, that were every bit as real as hard evidence.

Jim was at a crossroad. He could stay on the side of measurable science, or he could go down the path Arthur was describing. He thought for a while, tried to wrap his mind around his friend being a Druid. Weren't they tree worshippers in a distant past, somewhere in Ireland or something?

Then a thought occurred to him, something he hadn't yet considered.

"Could I walk on both paths?" he asked.

"Which paths?" replied Arthur.

"Well, I'm a realist, a scientist of sorts. And you've tried to explain things in terms you thought I would find more believable. And you're right, they were more believable. But I know, and you know, that you are walking a path I have never stepped on, not even brushed against. A path that is magic, witchcraft some would call it. I'm a cop. I've encountered about everything there is to see, I suspect. And I've met some people who honestly believed that they were seers."

He stopped and thought for a moment.

"There was one woman I'll never forget. We were working a horrible case. Three women murdered and dismembered. Couldn't find a connection among them; no forensic evidence to lead to their killer. Distraught families. And the media and the mayor's office hounding the hell out of us to solve the case. People were afraid because that's what a serial killer does: spreads fear throughout the community."

Jim paused, took another sip of coffee, and resumed his story.

"One day I was sitting at my desk, and this woman walked in, asked for the lead detective on the case. They sent her to me. She was amazing: six feet tall, coal black hair done in a single long braid, dressed in a blue shirt and gray leather pants. Eyes, oh, those eyes; bluest I've ever seen. Like to pierce your soul. She stood at my desk and said, 'He lives in Grant Park, near the fountain. Moves from place to place so he doesn't get caught. He's a bit shorter than I am, dirty blond hair about shoulder length, wears a hoodie and ragged blue jeans. He's getting ready to kill again. I saw him last night in my sleep, following a pretty blonde girl. But he didn't get her. Patrol came through, so he melted back into the bushes. But I feel his need. You must get him now.'"

Arthur shifted in his chair, reached the coffee pot, and poured them both more.

Jim continued, "She left without another word, no name, nothing. I was going to chalk her up as a crackpot, but something about her seemed so authentic. I grabbed a couple of patrol guys and another detective and told them I'd gotten a tip about a guy hiding out in the area. We went there and searched. And we found his hidey hole, among the larger bushes. He kept trophies, their jewelry. We set up a stakeout, and he showed up shortly after dark. Had a woman with him, so drugged she could hardly walk. The other women were roofied, and we figured she was, too."

There was a long silence. Jim was obviously still shaken by the memory of this case.

"Ever since, I've tried to be open, because I have no explanation for her. We searched; we questioned the crap out of him. And we were all convinced he was a loner, no accomplice. I couldn't explain how she knew. Put feelers out to some First Nation I knew, because she looked indigenous, but either no one knew a woman fitting that description or they weren't going to tell me. Either way, I never saw her again, but I believed that she *saw* something. Beth wasn't the least surprised."

"Beth?" asked Arthur.

"My late wife. Lost her to cancer five years ago. Came to Harper's Landing two years later. I miss her. Always will. She was a fine woman, strong and beautiful. And smart, too. Person dies, hope and the future die, too. I know I need to make a new future. Just haven't gotten around to it yet."

"Well, you can't go wrong making it with Linda Collier," said Arthur.

Jim looked at him sharply. "Is it that obvious?"

"Yeah, kinda is. At least to the inner circle. But Harry Randle has been noticing, and probably Martin Rutledge, too."

"At least those two aren't Druids, too. I don't think I could take it if the whole damn town was dancing nekkid in the woods at full moon every month."

Both men laughed.

"Gave that up a long time ago," said Arthur. "Seriously, there's a lot of plain hogwash around about what magic is, and then there's the whoopee witches. Little fluffy bunnies waving their crystals around, smudging the world."

"I'm guessing there's more to it than what you told me," said Jim.

"Oh yes, a lot more. But that's for another day. Now to your question about walking on both paths. The short answer is no. Want the longer answer? Got time?"

"Yeah. Clay and Blake won't be here for at least another thirty minutes, maybe more. They had to find a diver."

"Oh, man, not another one!"

"I hope not, but we have a missing man, and his car is parked at the pond."

"Would that be John Kavanaugh? I met Susan last night and spent time with her. She was worried. I do hope he hasn't come to a bad end of some sort."

"We don't know yet. That's why the guys are coming up here. You were telling me why I couldn't walk both paths. What's the long answer? The short version of the long answer, that is."

They both laughed. Arthur got them some more coffee and leaned back in his chair.

"There is a middle way. Those who walk the middle are one of two kinds: there are those who lean toward the ways of Druidry but make room for science, and those who are grounded in science but have a tolerance, if not an actual respect, for Druidry. I suspect you will be most comfortable on the latter path. I can tell you are open to different ways of approaching problems, but I also know that you have spent a long time and a lot of learning on your approach to real-world problems. I respect that, and I know you respect me."

He gestured at the diaries and journals spread out on the table.

"These people were realists. They worked the land. They carved wood, fished, hunted, tended gardens. But they had a relationship with nature far more like Druidry than modern science. And it's all here in these books."

He pointed to a section of his large library.

"You will find books there that explain in detail much of what I've been telling you. You are always welcome to read them. But I don't think you want or need to try to walk any path other than the one you walk so well. Understanding the other path will help you, but I doubt you will ever walk it."

He stood and stretched.

"I see that our friends from St. Louis have arrived. For now, let's not involve Blake and Clay in this. Frankly, I hope I never have to try to persuade them. Those guys are firmly rooted in police methodology. I can just see their faces if we told them I'm a practicing Druid."

Blake Meadows and Clay Murdoch pulled up in front of The Rectory. They drove a state crime lab van, and a diver and a forensics tech had come with them. It was nearly lunchtime, and Maggie and Jen appeared at the library door as Jim and Arthur were about to leave, carrying two large baskets.

"You are going to want food and drink," said Maggie. "I suspect you are going to be there for a while. There's enough for the two of you, Harry, and those four state folks. Just don't expect pie. Today is cookie day."

They picked up the overflowing baskets and took them to the Explorer. The state crime lab van followed behind as they left for Harve's pond. Susan Kavanaugh stood at the window watching them leave, chewing her lip.

CHAPTER FORTY-TWO

O h, this was too much. Another head! And not an animal head, a specimen for mounting. This was another human skull, no eyes, no brain, just remnants of hair and, of course, all the teeth.

What was he to do? He had made it clear that he did *not* want human heads. At least, he thought he had made it clear. Beside the head was a nice raccoon, gutted just like he asked for and ready for preparation.

But this head? What was he to do? He couldn't dump this head into the pond, the only place close enough to walk. Those people were out there again, disturbing things.

The Provider was going to be upset. He hated noise. He hated his pond being disturbed.

Maybe that was it! Maybe the Provider thought this was all his fault, all the noise and disturbance. Maybe this wasn't a gift but a warning. He shuddered. Harve would know what to do. Harve always knew what to do. But they had taken him away. Perhaps Harve wasn't coming back. How would he sell his specimens? How would he get this order of chipmunks to the National Museum?

He felt the panic rise. He was losing control. He stuffed the head into the burlap bag and thought, *What would Harve do?* After some thought, he realized that Harve would burn them all. He would burn them, then crush them, then bury them. Otherwise, someone might think Harve had done this. Someone might think *he* had done this.

He would crush it. That was it! First, he placed a plastic sheet on his workbench. He picked up a scraping tool and carefully removed all the skin and hair. He cleaned the inside also. He placed the tissue in his small burn box he kept in the workroom for disposing of unwanted animal tissue. He would wait until night when the smoke would not be visible to burn it. He then took the skull and placed it on a second plastic sheet on the floor. He took a small hammer and repeatedly smashed the bone until it was mostly powder. This he placed in a small burlap bag which he sat beside the door. While the tissue was burning, he would go deep into the woods and bury the powder. Then he would also burn the bag.

After dark, when he was sure everyone had left, he carried out his plan. It was successful. No one saw him; no one came knocking at the door. He had buried the powder, and all the rest had been burned. He cleaned out his burn box and buried the ashes out back.

He searched his entire cabin, looking for dust, dirt, for things out of place. He examined the clothes hanging in his closet. They were all neat and tidy, arranged by color like he was taught. His drawers were equally tidy, socks folded just so and arranged by color and weight; underwear folded properly and lined up, each kind in its own drawer. The top of his dresser, his desk, his night table, all were clean and tidy. His kitchen was clean and organized. Good work requires good work habits. Mother told him; Mother taught him. He did good work, he had good work habits.

Why was he being punished? Why had they taken Harve away from him? Why all these heads?

He needed Harve. He fell to his knees beside his worktable, grabbed a rag and began polishing the floor. Good work requires good work habits. Mother always taught him that.

CHAPTER FORTY-THREE

Jim, Arthur, Harry Randle, Clay Murdoch, and Blake Meadows stood beside the empty Mercedes, watching as the diver made his way out toward the center of the pond. The CSI guy was walking around the pond, taking pictures, and looking for footprints. Arthur was worried. He knew the diver was armed with a barbed spear, but it was on his back. If he and the other members of his grove were correct, the diver might not have time to ward off an attack.

Jim was torn between his desire to warn the man and his need to maintain his respectful relationship with the state troopers. There was no way he could explain his concern for the diver's safety without revealing the possibility of a creature, a monster out of children's fairy tales. He would be scorned. Instead, he remained alert and ready to go to the man's assistance at the slightest hint of anything wrong.

The diver disappeared toward the center of the pond. He swam toward the opening at the bottom which led to the tunnel they discovered when they drained the pond earlier. He shone his light across the bottom of the pond, looking for any clothing, fishing equipment, or other items of interest. He saw a reflection right at the opening to the tunnel and swam over to investigate. It was fishing tackle, a spinner caught on the roots at the bottom of the pond. He gently tugged on the line attached to the lure and pulled up a fishing pole. He swam back to the surface and brought the gear to the edge of the pond. The forensic tech took it into the van.

The diver returned to the pond, and again approached the tunnel. He shined his light down the tunnel. About five feet down he noted what appeared to be pieces of clothing. He entered the tunnel slowly and swam toward the objects. It was a fishing jacket, along with a shirt, a belt with torn-off pants still attached, and rubber waders, ripped into long, jagged strips. He gathered all the items and brought them to the lab tech.

On his third trip, the diver spotted something white a bit further down the tunnel from where he had found the clothes. It appeared to be cloth, caught at the juncture of the tunnel and the underground waterway below. He swam down, where he found not just an undershirt but one that contained a torso, missing limbs, with no head. Horrified and a bit frightened, he grabbed the object and swam quickly to the surface, where he yelled for help and went immediately to shore. The diver put the torso on the ground, went ten feet away into some nearby bushes, and lost his lunch.

"I know I should have taken pictures," said the diver on his return to the group. "But I just wanted to get out of there. I'm not going down again. I can describe where I found it, but no way. Not going down there again."

Jim knew these divers were professionals, and this one's fear had him spooked, too. He looked around and saw similar expressions on the faces of the others.

The forensic tech didn't seem the least bit bothered. He was taking pictures from all angles, and finally brought out a body bag and put the dismembered torso inside. He left the shirt on for removal by the docs at the state lab. He bagged the clothing and fishing tackle and put everything in the van. Then he brought a clipboard over to Jim.

"I need you to sign these chain of evidence papers as coroner, if you would, please?" he said. "I'm assuming you want us to take the torso to the state lab, like the others?"

"Yeah," said Jim. "We don't have any facilities here in Harper's Landing. Will it go to St. Louis or Jefferson City?"

"The autopsy will be done in Jefferson City. I would prefer to take all the evidence to one location if that's okay with you."

"Yeah, sure. Better to keep it in one place. By the way, did the jeans still have pockets? If there's a wallet, I'd like to see it before you take it all down south."

The tech opened the bag, checked, and pulled out a wallet. He handed Jim a pair of gloves. Jim opened the wallet, dreading what he would find. Credit cards, other membership cards, and a driver's license, all as he feared with the name of John Kavanaugh. He handed the wallet back after taking pictures of everything on his cell. The tech resealed the bag, and he and Jim initialed the new tape.

Jim turned away, thinking about his next words.

"Clay," he said. "Can you and Blake stay here while these two take the van down to Jefferson City? We can put you up for the night if you stay that long. And either way I can have Harry Randle take you back down to St. Louis. We need to talk to Harve and Martin Rutledge."

"Sure," replied Clay. "I can stay. But Blake here must get back down to Jefferson City. He's got a hearing in court first thing tomorrow morning."

"I reckon Clay can handle it," said Blake. "I don't see how we can continue to hold Harve Sanders, seeing as how he couldn't have had anything to do with this one. I'm going to contact the State's Attorney first thing and ask them to dismiss the charges. And it's like the others. But I'd still like to wait for forensics from the lab before I announce the connection."

"How about I take a couple of vacation days," said Clay. "Jim, you could drive me over to Wally World, couldn't you? Let me pick up some necessaries and a couple of shirts, maybe some jeans. I could use some time off. And I wouldn't mind eating Maggie's food and jawing with Arthur."

It was all settled. Blake would remain with Harry at the car until the tow truck arrived from St. Louis to take it to Jefferson City and the crime lab. Clay would stay at The Rectory. He had been warned about the quilters. And once the forensics were done, unless there were surprises, they would talk with Martin Rutledge about Harve's release.

"We're about the same size," said Jim. "Arthur will have the clothes you're wearing washed and clean for you in the morning; why don't you come by later and borrow some of my clothes instead of spending money. I know Arthur keeps all the rooms stocked with any toiletries you could imagine needing."

Clay happily accepted the offer.

"You know we're going to have to take a closer look at Jeremy," said Jim.

Arthur nodded.

"Who's Jeremy?" asked Clay. He was watching the van departing up the long driveway.

"Harve's twin brother," replied Jim. "We haven't seen or spoken to you since we found out about him. Hell, I don't even know if he's still alive or if he lives around here."

Blake looked around. He spotted the cabin back in the woods that he had seen the first time he was here.

"Who lives there?"

"Don't know if anyone does," replied Jim. "But it isn't on Harve's property, so it wasn't examined when the warrant was executed. Guess maybe we should ask Harve about it if Martin will let us."

"Twin, eh? Considering the familial DNA match we found from the tissue taken from the truck tailgate, I think we need to pursue this vigorously. Let Clay talk to Martin Rutledge, okay?"

Jim grudgingly agreed. Arthur, meanwhile, was thinking he might have his own private talk with Harve, in his capacity as spiritual counselor. The three got into Jim's car and headed back into

town, each lost in his own thoughts. Jim was contemplating something at best extra-legal, if not downright in violation of the law.
While he didn't want to obstruct justice, he also didn't want a man
who was likely mentally fragile being badgered by state troopers.
He decided he was going to do a little jurisdictional muscle
flexing.

When they arrived, Jim got out first and hurried in, pulling
out his phone.

"Martin," he said when the attorney answered. "Can you
make yourself scarce until I can get over to see you? Like, maybe
not answer your phone for anyone named Meadows or
Murdoch?"

"Sure thing, Jim. I'm guessing this has to do with both Harve
and Jeremy."

"We'll talk."

He hung up just as the others came in. Arthur showed Clay to
the one remaining room, at the far end of the building. The room
was sparse since it had been intended only for students and not
guests. Clay assured him it would suit him fine.

"Dinner will be in two hours," said Arthur. "I hope you don't
mind dining with a bunch of quilters. They're interesting, funny,
and talkative."

"It will be a pleasant change. The bachelor life has many
charms but getting to socialize is not one of them. Mind if I take a
quick shower?"

"Not at all. It's down the hall and to the left. There are towels
in that cupboard there, and a robe in the closet if you want one.
And if you need it, I have a safe in my library that locks. Don't
know if you want to keep your weapon on you or lock it away."

"I'll keep it with me. I stow the ammo separately."

"Okay, then. See you at dinner. Just follow the chatter to the
dining hall. I believe tonight is pot roast night, with apple pie for
dessert."

Clay almost drooled.

CHAPTER FORTY-FOUR

J im walked over to Martin Rutledge's office. He knocked and opened the door. Martin was absorbed in a Harlan Coben mystery.

"I knew we were kindred souls," said Jim. "My favorite mystery author, for now."

"He does spin a good tale. It's after 4:00 PM. Join me in a scotch?"

"Don't mind if I do."

Martin poured two glasses neat and moved to the couch along the wall, facing Jim, who sat in the client chair.

"Would I be correct in assuming that this visit is not official?" inquired Martin.

"Anything but," replied Jim.

He tossed a dollar on the table.

"What's this for?"

"Retainer."

Martin laughed, pocketed the bill, and took a sip of his scotch. Jim did the same.

"Damn! That stuff will knock your socks right off!" exclaimed Jim.

"Lagavulin, sixteen-year, single malt. Hard to come by up

here, so I lay in a stock when I go down to St. Louis or Jeff City. I'm a scotch snob."

"I'm gonna have to visit you more often," said Jim. "Next thing you know you'll be offering me a good cigar."

Martin reached into his vest pocket, pulled out a cigar case, and handed Jim a medium-sized dark brown cigar.

"Hand rolled, Cuban, from Havana by way of a grateful client. I've got three humidors full, keeping them fresh. Won't see their like again for a while."

The two men lit up cigars, sipped their scotch, and sat in silence. Finally, Martin spoke.

"You might as well spit it out. Otherwise, you're going to change your mind, want your dollar back, and I'll be back to one client."

"We have another body, out at Harve's pond. And I'm damn sure it got there after Harve was put in jail. Can't prove it yet, but I'm certain the results from St. Louis tomorrow will confirm that it is the body of one John Kavanaugh."

"John Kavanaugh, the judge in St. Louis?" asked Martin incredulously.

"One and the same. He and his wife came up here so she could go to the quilters' retreat and he could go fishing. He went missing yesterday, and when he still wasn't back early this morning, we went looking. Found his car next to the pond."

Jim took another sip of scotch and puffed his cigar.

"And ...?" asked Martin.

"Oh hell," said Jim. "I might as well. The worst they can do is try to take away my badge. We found a mangled torso, just like the others. Thing is, I need to know if Jeremy is still alive and if he lives behind Harve."

Martin sat back, brow wrinkled.

"Why would knowing that get you fired?"

"That's not the part that matters. I want to know before I tell the State guys. I think I want to protect Jeremy. And then there's the whole business of the *bolotnik* to consider."

"The what?"

"Oh geeze, that explanation is going to have to come from Arthur. How much have they told you about themselves? That bunch going through the diaries and stuff?"

"You mean the Druids and the Slavic pagans?"

"Does everybody but me know this stuff?" complained Jim. "Or did you all decide to keep it to yourselves until I had need to know?"

"Well, the latter. But mostly because we didn't think you would take it seriously."

"I'm not sure yet that I do. But how about you? Are you one of them, too?"

"No." Martin laughed. "Not a sensitive bone in my body. But I'm open, because like you I've seen a lot I couldn't explain through rational scientific method. Some things must be taken on faith. I'm taking that group on faith. Because they are good, thoughtful, and intelligent people."

He sat silent for a moment.

"Tell me something, Jim. Did you feel *called* here, or did you just end up here and decide to stay after having some of Maggie Farmington's cooking?"

"I, uh, I came into town and immediately liked it. I decided to stay for a few days, and then John Hartley, the sheriff, died, and suddenly I just knew I wanted to be sheriff here."

"It was the same for me," said Martin. "I was looking for somewhere to fish, stopped here, and then the only lawyer got himself dead, and I suddenly volunteered to take on his caseload."

Martin paused for a moment to take another sip of scotch.

"I think this town finds the people it needs. I know how that sounds," Martin said, "but think about it. Ole JB Harper, the preacher, gets killed in a fishing accident, and Arthur just happens to be in town. John Hartley dies, and you just happen to be here. And then George Paper dies of a heart attack just after I stop in to stay at Bull and Mary's. Coincidences? Perhaps, but that's a hell of a lot of coincidence if you ask me."

"Do you think the town called you, me, and Arthur?" Jim shook his head. He was confused, puzzled, torn. All of this was too much. He couldn't deny the coincidences, and he didn't believe in coincidence. But he couldn't believe in something so ridiculous as a town that *called* people, that knew what it needed. But hadn't he been musing over the same possibility? Best to just let it lie, not try to analyze or understand it.

"Mind if we forego this topic until we have Arthur with us?" asked Jim.

"Sure," said Martin. "For the record, I understand why it's harder for you to accept than me. You cops deal in reality every day. I know that. You are our foundation, Jim. Don't lose that."

Jim suddenly felt deeply saddened. Beth had called him her foundation. Was that how people saw him? Was that such a bad thing? He shook himself out of his morose mood.

"I need to talk to Harve," said Jim. "They aren't going to let him out until the forensics come back. But it's damn conclusive in my opinion. Thing is, and this is where I'm treading on thin ice and may need to invoke privilege, Jeremy is implicated because of the familial match of the DNA. If it is Jeremy's, it is likely they are identical twins. I need to talk to Harve before the state boys do. Can we arrange that?"

"Sure can," replied Martin. "And I don't think you have anything to worry about, legally. This is your jurisdiction. You are the county sheriff. You called in the state boys only because they have the lab and the divers. But the prisoner is yours. And if Jeremy exists and is alive, he is your suspect, not theirs."

"Fair enough," said Jim. "Now how about we go over and have dinner with Arthur in his library? We can pick his brain about why he thinks this town always gets the people it needs. And maybe score leftover apple pie for dessert."

"I wouldn't turn it down for the world. You know, if I didn't know better, I would say that damn pie is magical."

Jim didn't disagree.

✳

Jim had a lot of decisions to make. At the top of the list was when to talk to Harve. The forensics on what were surely John Kavanaugh's remains wouldn't be complete until tomorrow afternoon at the earliest. He would love nothing more than to have dinner with Arthur and Martin and then discuss the esoterica of magic over brandy or scotch. But Clay Murdoch was here, and any conversation of that sort would send Clay to the phones and bring an even larger team up here poking around where no one wanted them.

For the same reason, they couldn't discuss Jeremy or Harve over dinner or after, since Clay would want to go to Harve immediately and demand to know the whereabouts of his twin brother. He might even try to threaten Harve with obstruction. Martin would be there to protect Harve, but the threat would be made, nevertheless.

The only logical solution Jim could think of was to have his and Martin's dinner brought to his office along with Harve's evening meal. He discussed this with Martin, who immediately agreed.

Jim hoped Harve would open up, tell him about Jeremy and what, if anything, his role might be in all of this. Jim would need to persuade both Harve and Martin that his primary intent would be to protect Jeremy while serving the law, rather than serving Jeremy up on a platter to the state police. To that end, he phoned Arthur, told him of his plans, and asked if he could help keep Clay entertained. He then phoned Jen, who was busy in the kitchen, and asked if it would be too much to ask her to bring three dinners to the jailhouse instead of one. As he suspected, it was no problem.

His next call was to Linda. If anyone could charm Clay enough to keep him away from the sheriff's office, at least for a while if not for the entire evening, it would be Linda. She was delighted to be involved in a *wee bit of intrigue*. She hadn't been looking forward to another evening of dining alone. She threw on a sweater and hurried over to The Rectory, hoping to provide assistance in the kitchen and have a chance to talk to Jen. Two women are capable of distracting just about any man when they put their minds to it. Especially two *gifted* women.

CHAPTER FORTY-FIVE

The fax machine in Jim's office rang twice and then began spitting out paper around midday the next day. It had been a late night, and Jim was still trying to clear the cobwebs out of his brain. He was working on his fourth cup of strong black coffee and hoping that another cinnamon roll would provide enough sugar to get things working. He gathered up the fax papers and set them aside, promising himself he would read them later.

Martin had left at around 2:00 AM, long after dinner was finished, and the dishes were sent back up to The Rectory dining hall. Harve was certainly talkative last night. He insisted on starting at the beginning since neither Jim nor Martin had been present for most of the diary readings. They knew next to nothing about the history of Harper's Landing, and Harve was a treasure trove of information. Martin told him about the diaries, deeds, and other documents, and Harve declared that as soon as he got out, he was heading up to the library to see them.

The story he told was the same as what Martin had heard that first day when Dan began translating the diaries. Jim hadn't heard any of this and was fascinated with the tale of the crossing, the lost child at sea, and the mother's subsequent death. He tried to imagine what it must have been like, leaving everything to make a perilous journey across an ocean to a foreign land. And then to sink almost all their savings into wagons to bring themselves and their worldly goods to an area rumored to be peopled by savages and runaway slaves.

It seemed to him that these people, at least by their own stories, were different from the western Europeans who were his ancestors. They seemed more tolerant, more willing to share, and more connected with the land. This last realization was foreign to him. Perhaps it was simply that he had always been a big city guy, born and raised. He had never entertained the idea that he might somehow relate to the natural world, with plants and animals. He had enough problems with the connections he felt with his fellow humans. It was a cop's problem: staying connected and sympathetic enough to get people to trust you while at the same time maintaining enough distance so the evil in the world didn't eat you up.

According to Harve, the property with the cabin, along with the pond and surrounding woods, had been in the family since Yuri and Maria received it from her parents as a wedding gift. He said the woods and cabin behind his was separate property and had been handed down to other descendants of the family starting with Katerina and Maksym Molovna.

Jim was inclined to just let Harve talk. He really wanted to know about Jeremy, but the family history was fascinating, and the more Harve talked the more relaxed he became. Finally, he got to where his parents met and married. Leonard Sanders was a skilled carpenter, who had arrived in Harper's Landing in the early 1970s, seeking work at the mill. His skill in wood turning earned him a job creating and repairing the thread spindles, and he helped to build several of the looms the mill employed for various kinds of fabrics. He taught himself how to build and repair the wooden cog wheels that connected the waterwheel to the inside gears. And eventually he also learned how to repair the paddles on the wheel itself.

He met Maria Harper at a church social. She and Maggie

Morris were fresh out of high school and learning how to cook and bake the pies and other delicacies that Morey's Diner was so famous for serving. That evening, they had brought apple pies to the social, and after one taste Leonard declared that he would marry whoever made it if only she would introduce herself. There was much laughter and giggling at this announcement, but Leonard soon found that he was quite serious. He sought out the girls, hoping to learn which of them had baked such an excellent dessert. The truth was that Maggie had made the pie, but she was sweet on Morey Farmington and determined to get his attention. He was young, ambitious, and had plans to turn the broken-down old diner into a fresh and inviting meeting place. She knew she would love working there. The girls told him Maria had made the pie.

Leonard and Maria were married on April 9, 1976, the Reverend JB Harper, Maria's father, presiding. It was a traditional Christian wedding with all the trappings: bridesmaids, grooms-men, reception, cake, and music. What JB did not know—and never would—was that his daughter hadn't shunned the Old Ways as he had, and in fact had brought Leonard into the group for training. Leonard was quite open to it all and learned quickly. In fact, he had latent talent himself, something he hadn't previously known. The second wedding took place two days later when the moon was full. It was at midnight, in the Grove where Stephan and his siblings built their cottages. Two of the cottages were still home to some of their descendants. The other two held the precious books, diaries, and other papers important to the families, along with the paraphernalia employed by the practitioners. The entire grove was lit with the flames from milky white candles. The scent of rosemary and thyme filled the air, and great bundles of the herbs mixed with lilies and roses hung from trees and circled the great star drawn on the ground with white stones where Leonard and Maria would share their vows in the old tradition.

The couple was happy, in love, and full of ideas on how to make the small cabin they had inherited into the home they wanted forever. Leonard built on an addition during the evenings after work and on weekends, which became his and Maria's bedroom. He enlarged the porch, so it stretched across the entire front of the cabin and created beds for flowers, herbs, and vegetables on the hill leading up to the pond. He also created a large, covered trench to direct any overflow from the pond into the lower pasture to the south, in case of a heavy rainstorm or other incident that might cause the pond to flood. Two years later he added another room to the back part of the cabin as a bedroom for anticipated children.

By the end of the third year, Maria had begun to despair of ever having children. Just as she was preparing to travel to St. Louis for testing, she began to feel ill in the mornings. She checked the calendar, and indeed she was late. She waited to tell Leonard until a second period had been missed and then shared the news. A visit to the local midwife confirmed that she was pregnant, and they began preparing the newest addition to the cabin as a nursery.

On her fourth visit to the obstetrician over in Harwood where the regional clinic was located, just south of Harper's Landing, Maria was informed that she was having twins. The couple could not have been more excited.

"And this is where I begin to ask questions," said Jim. "Harve, you and Jeremy were born when?"

"March 14, 1980. At the cabin, with the midwife. My father later told me that he lost the argument with my mother. He wanted us to be born at the hospital. But Mother wanted us born in the traditional way, and she wanted us to be immediately blessed in the old ways."

"Is Jeremy still alive?" asked Martin.

He already knew the answer. But it seemed better if the question came from him instead of Jim.

"Yes. He lives in the cabin behind mine. Back of mine. He lives alone, never goes out. I take care of him."

Jim thought, considering how to ask the question he needed to ask. "You weren't fraternal twins, were you?" he finally said.

"Yes, we were. But we looked enough alike we could've fooled most people. Except for Jeremy's ... his disabilities."

He told Jim the entire story. How Jeremy had been born crippled but had, with time, learned to walk well. He then told the story, with many pauses and many tears, of the death of their parents and the horrendous injuries Jeremy suffered trying to save them.

"He's horribly disfigured," he said. "His face is scarred over the entire right half, although both of his eyes are fine. But his right ear is missing, and most of his hair never grew back. And the scars on his chest have caused him to twist. He feels like a monster. After the accident, he called himself Jeremonster until I made him stop."

Harve stopped, buried his face in his hands, and then gratefully accepted the sip of bourbon Jim brought him and followed it with a glass of water.

"He doesn't talk. Correction: he talks to me, but that's all. I can understand him. Most people can't. But he's an artist, and he makes a great living from it."

"What kind of art?" asked Jim.

At that point Martin stepped in. "I'm going to have to tell him not to answer that question. Harve, it will come out soon enough, but for now, I'm telling you not to talk further about what Jeremy does."

"Fair enough," said Jim. "Harve, I hope we can let you out of here tomorrow. I'm sorry, but I must wait for the forensics report to come back on this most recent body, and the State will have to drop its charges against you. But unless this most recent body has been there since before we locked you up, I suspect you'll be a free man sometime tomorrow."

"Jim, you've been good to me. Everyone has. And dammit, I didn't do anything. I feel awful about those poor boys, and about Rory. But it wasn't my fault. I had nothing to do with it."

"Okay," said Martin. "Time for sleep. Jim, do you think you could spare a little more of that bourbon for Harve? We've put him through the ringer."

"Sure," said Jim.

As soon as he left, Martin told Harve quietly, "Don't you talk any more. I know you trust Jim, and I like him, too. But he is the law. Don't talk to him, not even when he lets you out. Just thank you, good food, whatever. Chitchat's fine. But no talking. You understand?"

"Okay. Sure. I understand. They aren't going to go bother Jeremy, are they?"

"I'm going to do my best to keep them away until you can be there. But yes, I suspect they are going to want to talk to him," replied Martin.

Harve sighed deeply. He had failed. He had sworn to protect his brother no matter what, and now Jeremy was going to be exposed, to be seen, and to feel humiliated. When Jim brought in the bourbon, he downed it in one swallow, turned his back, and curled up on the jail cot. He knew he wouldn't sleep a wink, but he was out in seconds.

CHAPTER FORTY-SIX

Charity knelt at the pond. The tapes were gone, the car towed away, the detritus of the search removed. It was night. There was a full moon, and soft breezes rustled the bulrushes. It was a midsummer moon, white as white, reflecting off the still waters of the pond, the image disturbed only by the occasional passage of a water walker. Lightning bugs flickered above the water, adding a splash of color to the cold white reflection of the moon. Occasionally, a bullfrog would send out a full-throated croak, and in the distance she heard the hoot of an owl.

She had come, silent and alone, to mourn the dead. Rory was buried on Jackson Hill, as were the four boys, and soon John Kavanaugh would be buried in his family's plot in St. Louis. The final reports hadn't been sent to Jim Burch, and even Susan Kavanaugh hadn't been told her husband was dead. Despite all of that, Charity knew he, too, was gone.

She also knew there were others, ones whose names would never be known. Wanderers in this strange land before cars and phones and lamps and police. Souls lost to the evil below who would never be named, who until now would never be mourned.

She believed in mourning the dead. She held it true as a necessary rite of the passage from this life to the next. She had no fear of death, nor did she take any morbid enjoyment in this mourning. It was her duty, to herself, to the land, to the Old Gods and Goddesses who watched over her from the beginning of time.

This she knew. She knelt at the edge of the pond, lit her candles, laid out the rosemary and sage and violet and ivy from which she would weave a wreath as she chanted the oldest of old prayers for the dead. Her fingers weaved the circle with the deftness of one who had done so many times. Her voice was strong yet quiet, as she sang the song of departure. On this night, she returned to the grief and solace of her childhood.

Glorified and sanctified be God's great name throughout the world which He has created according to His will.

She sang the Kaddish, she sang an ancient Celtic death ballad, she sang of love, of redemption, of passage. She chanted a Slavic dirge, ancient and long forgotten by most. She set the now-finished wreath afloat on the pond, pushing it toward the center. She sat back on her heels, covered her face with her shawl, and silently cried. She cried for Rory, for Billy and Steve and Mike and Gary, and for their parents, for John whom she never knew and Susan, whose coming grief she knew all too well, for Jeremy and Harve's parents, for her dead husband and the child that was never to be. And she cried for Harve and Jeremy and the horrors that were yet to come for them.

She was heard. He heard her and yet could not, would not, approach. She was dangerous. And there was a great sadness about her that touched something incredibly old and ancient in him, from a time when once he was something else. He had forgotten, it had been too long. He swam away, leaving her to her sorrow and tears. There would be other food, other days. Not this day.

Charity was equally aware of his presence, though she could not have said what or who he was. She only knew that something not human, something ancient and evil, had for a moment touched her mind, then left. But it was enough. She knew beyond a shadow of a doubt that she and the rest of the grove would need to read and act swiftly, to learn how their ancestors had dealt with this ancient being. She sensed hunger more than evil, but enough of both to make her shudder and leave as swiftly as possible.

On her way back to her car, she paused and looked toward the cabin back by the woods. She saw what appeared to be the flicker of candlelight. She opened her trunk, pulled out a pie, rolls, and stew she had planned to take to her cottage to sustain her for the week. Instead, she carried them back to the cabin door. She set them on the stoop, knocked on the door, and called out.

"Jeremy, it's Charity. I've left you food here on the doorstep. Please don't worry. Harve will be home soon."

She left, climbed into her car, and drove home. She would get more food tomorrow from Jen at The Rectory. For now, Jeremy's needs were more important than her own. Once home, she fell deeply asleep and dreamed the dreams of eternity.

CHAPTER FORTY-SEVEN

The forensics lab called Jim Burch the following day, around 1:00 PM. They were able to formally identify the remains as those of the Honorable John Michael Kavanaugh. No foreign DNA was found anywhere on the torso, in the wounds, or on what remained of the clothing. They were surprised that no boots or shoes had been found, but Jim told them that Susan had confirmed that John's shoes were in the trunk and that he rarely, if ever, wore anything other than socks when he pulled on his waders. The fax, long since forgotten by Jim, contained all this information, including the scientific details that might be required in court if things went that far.

The lab confirmed that DNA swabs had also identified John's DNA on the shoes. Nothing of interest was found in the vehicle, and it could either be returned to Harper's Landing or claimed at the Jefferson City Lab by next of kin. Jim said he would consult with the widow when she was able to plan and get back to them.

There was an additional report from the state medical examiner, stating the cause of death as asphyxiation by drowning. Kavanaugh's lungs had been full of pond water. The report added that it could find no reason for the dismemberment, which would remain a mystery for now.

Jim steeled himself for the job yet to be done. First, he called Judge Cramer, who had ordered Harve to remain behind bars in the Harper's Landing County Jail prior to formal arraignment. Cramer confirmed that Jim could indeed release him, though he said it would have to wait until he got there, about three hours or so, and that Martin should have a petition for dismissal in hand at that time. The state attorney's office faxed a motion for dismissal, which Jim left on Judge Cramer's desk. Jim called Martin Rutledge, told him the news, and relayed Judge Cramer's instructions. He then called Mary and Jen Harper and told them he would be coming up to The Rectory to see Susan Kavanaugh.

"It's not good news, is it?" asked Jen.

"No, I'm sorry. Mary, can you fill in the other quilters, while Jen and I talk with Mrs. Kavanaugh? I'm afraid something like this cannot be kept quiet. Better they should know. They can probably help with comforting Susan, as if anything could. But she's going to have to make decisions, the first being whether she wants the car brought back up here or to arrange transport to Jefferson City to claim it instead."

"I'll enlist some of the others once you've arrived," replied Mary. "There's good people among this bunch; in fact, all of them are. This is about the best retreat group I've ever hosted. Susan will be in good hands."

"And I'll be there as much for you as for Susan," said Jen.

Jim hated this part of his job. It would never be easy. He started to call Arthur, and then decided against it. He would join him in the library after he had told Susan and handed her off to the capable and kind ministrations of Mary and company. He knew that Charity, Dan, and Bridgette were still pouring over the diaries and other papers with Arthur. And he was fairly sure Ben would be there also, working on his family tree. He would tell them all at the same time, and he would damn well be off the clock, because he was going to need some of that scotch Arthur kept in his office.

The road from his office to The Rectory was lined with

summer flowers. Harve Sanders' handiwork was everywhere in this small community. He maintained the medians on the county road and the sidewalk planters here in town proper. As far as Jim knew, he did it for free. It seemed unfair that Harve had spent any time behind bars. Something was eating at Harve; Jim was sure of that. And it wasn't just worry about his case. If anything, Harve seemed certain he would be cleared. He was worried about something else, probably his brother. And he was right to be worried. Because if someone was responsible for these deaths, right now all signs were pointing squarely at Jeremy Sanders.

Jim put that out of his mind. For now, he had to break the bad news to Susan Kavanaugh.

He couldn't put it off any longer. He picked up his pace and entered the gardens of The Rectory, heading for the front door.

"Over here, Jim," someone called.

He turned and saw Mary Harper sitting with Susan Kavanaugh on one of the carved wood benches that faced the wildflower meadow. Jen Harper was coming out the side door, carrying a pitcher and a tray of glasses. He joined the women and helped Jen set down the tray and pour glasses of cold water all around. It was a hot day, and the drink was welcome.

"He's dead, isn't he," said Susan Kavanaugh, without warning, her voice low and husky.

"Yes, I'm afraid so," responded Jim.

"I knew it. I knew it from the moment I saw his car. I just didn't want to believe it. Was it the same bastard who killed those boys?"

"We don't know. Right now, we don't know who killed the boys. The MO is the same, though."

"What killed him? How did he die?"

"We don't know that for sure," said Jim. "There were no drugs or alcohol in any of the bodies, except for a small amount of marijuana in three of the boys. But no disabling drugs, no poison. The coroner is ruling the deaths as ..."

He paused. He didn't want to say it.

"Go ahead. I'm a judge's wife—well, widow, now. I've heard it all."

"As drowning, with subsequent dismemberment. The cases will remain open, all six of them, for now, because we still don't know how they got dismembered."

"Six?" exclaimed Susan. "Not another!"

"We had a death prior to the four boys," said Jim. "A local fella turned up in the same condition. Took us a while to connect them. It seemed like we had a serial killer."

"I thought you had arrested someone," said Susan.

The other two women found her calm unnerving, but Jim knew all too well that what seemed like calm was denial, and soon the initial shock would wear off. He answered as quickly and succinctly as he could.

"We did, but he was already in jail when your husband went missing, in fact for several days before, so he couldn't have been responsible. But don't worry, if this wasn't an accidental death, we will find who did this, and he will be brought to justice."

Susan suddenly let out a howl of pain and rage. "No," she wailed. "No. No. No."

She leaned into Mary's waiting arms and cried like her heart would break.

"Let's leave the car and other things until later," said Jen.

"Of course," said Jim.

He left Susan in Mary's capable hands and entered the library with Jen. Dan, Arthur, Bridgette, and Ben were chatting amiably, sorting out papers, setting diaries aside for later examination. Charity was sitting at a table in the corner, making notes as she poured over an old and large book.

They all looked up at Jim and Jen's entrance and fell silent. Arthur closed his eyes briefly, and his lips moved silently. Charity gasped. Dan merely sighed and buried his head in his hands.

It was Arthur who broke the silence. "It was John Kavanaugh," he stated.

"Yes," said Jim. "I guess we all knew it would be, but it doesn't make it any easier. I'll take a big shot of the scotch if you still have some."

Arthur hurried into his study and emerged with the bottle and several glasses. He poured Jim a large splash and a smaller amount for everyone else, except Ben. He handed him a bottle of Harve's root beer.

They all raised their glasses in a silent toast to the man whose death so intimately involved them, even though none had met him, not even Arthur.

"I suppose they'll be letting Harve go now," said Charity. "And about time. I'm not mad at you, Jim. You're doing a good job. But really? Harve? He wouldn't hurt a fly."

"But this does put a spotlight on Jeremy, doesn't it?" asked Jen.

"That it does," said Jim. "That it does."

CHAPTER FORTY-EIGHT

On July fifteenth, after all forensic evidence had been entered in the books, after everything had been bagged and tagged, after numerous attempts by the young state attorney who came up from St. Louis to have Harve held until he disclosed information about his brother Jeremy had failed, Harve Sanders was finally released and allowed to return home. He arrived to find his refrigerator full of casseroles and rolls and pies of various kinds, enough to last for a week for the two of them. He also discovered more in his freezer.

His house was as clean as it had ever been. Harve suspected that was the result of Jeremy's work rather than anyone from the town. He was surprised to discover his flower beds had been weeded and watered. When he wandered around to the side of his cabin, he found Ben Jenkins pulling weeds and moving the hose to the freshly weeded herb bed.

"Ben?"

"Oh, hi, Harve. Hope you don't mind my taking care of your plants and such. I've done about all I can with Arthur's garden, except for the weekly maintenance. I didn't want yours to go untended."

"I'm touched. And grateful. Thank you. Let me help there. I need to get my hands into the dirt again."

The two men weeded, trimmed, and deadheaded in silence, enjoying the sun and the sounds of birds and the joy of gardening. Harve went to his tool shed and brought back two pair of clippers. They cut flowers and herbs and carried them into the house.

"Root beer?" asked Harve.

"That would be great. You brew up some truly tremendous stuff."

"It's a family recipe. Not a secret. I can share it with you if you like."

"That would be nice. I presume you grow sassafras. And that you don't grow vanilla." They both laughed, and Harve showed Ben his sassafras bed.

"The leaves aren't much good for anything, but you dry the root and pound it into a powder. It's why they call it root beer."

"I did not know that, but it makes sense. What else is in it?"

"Cherry tree bark, wintergreen, molasses, anise, licorice root, cinnamon, and honey. I have hives around back in the woods, over where the cherry and apple tree orchards are. Bees love those blooms. Cinnamon and vanilla, I get from St. Louis. Everything else I grow myself."

Harve warmed up one of the casseroles Maggie had sent to his cabin. He put rolls, butter, honey, and root beer on the table. Then he set out three plates and sets of silver. And one more glass, with a glass straw.

"Three?" asked Ben. "Someone else coming to dinner?"

"I hope so," said Harve. "But first, you must promise me that no matter what you might feel—no matter what, mind you—you will NOT react. I know you, Ben Jenkins. You have the best poker face in the world. Promise me on all that you care about, no reaction."

Ben promised. Harve left through the back door, leaving Ben puzzled and slightly shaken. He had never seen Harve quite so worked up. Who was coming to dinner? And why the poker face?

When the door opened again, Ben immediately understood. He maintained his best poker face, stood up, and held out his hand.

"Hi, I'm Ben Jenkins. You must be Harve's brother, Jeremy."

Jeremy was stunned. Harve was right. The man did not recoil, nor did he turn away. In fact, he was being friendly. Jeremy extended his left hand since the movement in his right arm was severely limited by the scarring. Ben shook it firmly and sat at the table.

"Damned if it isn't sweet potato and ham casserole, from Maggie, right?" he said. "That woman would turn the whole town into blimps if we let her. Cooking this good doesn't just happen every day. How did we get so lucky?"

Jeremy took a sip of root beer and smiled.

"Good," he said. "Really good."

Ben could barely understand him, but Harve was overjoyed Jeremy had finally spoken to someone else. This was a start, and he hoped it wouldn't end here. But he knew there were hard times coming.

After dinner, the three men cleaned up. Ben quickly discovered that Jeremy was the neatest, tidiest person he had ever seen. He was smart enough to realize that this was a form of control for him, and he stood out of his way while Jeremy put everything in careful alignment once it was dried. They then went out and sat on the porch to enjoy the evening air.

The silence of friends is precious. Even though Ben and Jeremy had just met, even though Ben had nearly lost himself in drink for so long, even though Harve was private to the point of secretive—despite all that and more, they felt like old friends. They felt no need to talk; instead, they sat and rocked and listened to the sounds of the night. It had been so long since any of them had felt safe, comfortable, or secure. It was a blanket of joy that lay light but warm upon them.

The moon rose, waning after last night's fullness, but still bright white, and the meadow leading up to the pond glistened with reflected moonlight. The air twinkled with fireflies, and the croak of the bullfrogs filled the night. It was magical and comforting.

It was Jeremy who broke the silence. Harve had to translate for him at first, but Ben was finding it easier and easier to understand him. Jeremy was hesitant at first, telling them what he had to tell them would sound crazy, even psychotic. But he assured them he was not.

"For some time now, probably close to a year, I've been hearing a voice speaking to me. It's not words—more like suggestions in my head. Sometimes it is images, sometimes it is a feeling."

"A voice speaking, but not really speaking?" asked Harve. "Not sure I understand that."

"Well, it's like I'm experiencing someone else's hunger, someone's need. And he sends me mental images. Usually of things like sheep or deer."

Ben stared at him, speechless. *What the hell?* he thought. But he could see that Jeremy was sincere, and frightened.

"The first time I responded to the image in my head, I went to the woods and shot a deer. I hauled it to the pond because that's where the suggestions, the pleadings, seemed to be coming from. I shoved the deer out there, and it disappeared. The next morning, I found a perfect head specimen on my porch."

"You found a what?" exclaimed Ben, sitting upright in his chair.

"Jeremy's a taxidermist," said Harve. "He is world-famous, though no one knows his real name; that is, the people who buy his stuff don't know. He has specimens on exhibit in some of the world's greatest natural history museums."

"Oh," said Ben. "I see what you mean. What you're saying is this creature that is *calling* to you for food is paying you with specimens you can mount?"

"Yes," replied Jeremy.

"Jeremy was sick for months before your home burned," said

Harve. "I almost took him down to St. Louis. It was a horrible flu that wouldn't go away. It took him forever to get better. Charity brought some of her teas, rubs, and stuff, and it helped him get better. He couldn't have had anything to do with the animals that Zak fella was talking about going missing. I guess you heard about that like everyone else?"

Jeremy was shaking, but stayed, staring at Ben, who finally sighed and sat back in his chair.

"Well, good then," said Ben. "Fair enough. Now, Harve, if I could trouble you for a ride home?" asked Ben. "It's late, and a long walk, and I promised Arthur I would paint the bathrooms tomorrow, now that the quilting folks are gone."

CHAPTER FORTY-NINE

J im hated unsolved cases. He especially despised cases that listed cause of death as *possible* or even *probable*. He liked tangibles, solutions, hard facts. This case was as slippery as an oil slick and twice as nasty. He also hated what he was about to do. But there didn't seem to be any other way.

He sighed and reached for a yellow writing pad and pencil. He spotted Linda, out watering her flowers. He could wait. He wanted to talk to her.

She heard his door close and turned to greet him. He was once again struck by her loveliness. She did not have his Beth's or Jen's earthiness. Hers was a quiet, still grace; a ripple as she walked rather than a skip or a stride. She smiled her small, easy smile.

"Beautiful morning, Jim. Going to be warm though; thought I'd give these a drink early."

"They are beautiful. More of Harve's handiwork I suppose?"

"No. These are all mine. I sent away for the seeds. I wanted heirloom flowers, something that had grown here long ago, so I could harvest the seeds and restore them. Harve did take seeds last year though, and he's planted a lovely bed up by the new recreation center."

She invited him into the shade of the *Gazette*'s awning, where she had placed a stunning wood carved bench.

"When did you get this?" Jim asked. "I don't recall seeing it before."

"Charity and Jen found it in one of the cottages when they were cleaning out places for themselves and Dan. Stephan and Mikhail, their great-great-grandsires, were skilled wood carvers. Arthur restored it for me. I love it."

"It is glorious, and comfortable for sitting. I don't blame you for wanting it."

He stretched out his long legs and sighed deeply.

"That bad, huh?" she asked.

"I like things neat and tidy. And this whole business is anything but. And now I've got to do something that I don't want to do. I'm putting it off, sitting here with a beautiful woman enjoying the day." He blushed. "I'm sorry. I shouldn't have blurted that out. I hope I didn't offend."

"What woman would be offended by being called beautiful?" she replied. "Seriously, it feels good to be called beautiful, to be told a man wants to spend time with me. You know my story. I don't feel safe with men. But you? You are our foundation, and I love that you want to spend time with me."

It was Linda's turn to blush.

Well, thought Jim. *This certainly wasn't going the way I antic-ipated.* He stretched again, feeling joints pop and muscles letting go, as tension eased out of his body.

"It feels like forever since we've had a quiet day here," he said. "Before that day when Rory went missing, everything was so quiet and easy."

"Maybe too easy," said Linda.

"What do you mean?"

"You talked to Arthur, right?"

He nodded his head.

"What he may not have told you is that I'm part of all this, too."

"If by *all this* you mean you folks being related and having powers and stuff, yeah, I kinda guessed that. And the way Dan's been giving you books, taking you off for long talks, hauling you and Bridgette out to the woods, I figured something was going on."

"I didn't know you knew."

"Not much gets past me," said Jim, with a hint of pride. "I can see most of what goes on here in town from my front window. And Harry Randle drives around more than most of you realize."

"What do you think of what Arthur told you, of what Dan is teaching us?"

"I'm keeping an open mind. I've had my share of experiences as a cop to remind me that not everything is as it seems. Generally, I find there's a rational explanation for just about everything, including so-called psychic visions. But what Arthur explained makes a lot more sense than some woman in a darkened room peering into a crystal ball and intoning my dead grandmother's poetry."

Linda laughed, a big belly laugh that made Jim smile and laugh, too.

"I'll have to share that with Arthur and Dan, next lesson. That is, if you don't mind?"

"Oh, not at all. I've even thought about coming to some of those lessons."

He noted her startled look.

"Oh, don't worry. I wasn't being serious. If there is such a thing as a sixth sense, they passed me over when it was being given out and made up for it with rugged good looks."

They laughed again.

"Don't think any of you are going to like me much, though, after what I have to do."

"Can you talk about it?"

Jim thought for a moment. The idea was tempting. It would be good to bounce this off a sympathetic listener. But he already had a second deputy, and he couldn't share this with someone who wasn't official.

"Don't you hold office in this town? Or some county office?"

"Why, yes, I'm the County Recorder. Not that there's been much to record. Although the Camby family up off Main just had a baby. First baby born around here in a long time. I was happy to record his birth certificate. And, of course, I recorded the sale of Jenkins Farm to Grossman Textiles. And Rory's death and those poor children, too."

She was puzzled by his question and waited for him to explain.

Jim sat in thought, then said, "Hold on a moment, okay?"

He took out his phone, walked out of earshot, and dialed Martin Rutledge.

"Hey, Martin. Does that dollar retainer still hold?"

"Sure does, Jim. What can I do for you?"

"If I need to do something that is police business, that might involve an arrest, and I need to talk to someone about it, can that someone be a county officer? Or do I have to talk to a deputy or the DA?"

"Depends. Are you asking for advice on how to proceed or even whether? Or just looking for someone to bounce things off?"

"Mostly the latter," said Jim.

"You'd be safest with me," said Martin.

"Are you still Harve's lawyer?"

"Not really. He's paid me in full. Signed off and everything. But I'll admit it's a gray area. And if this is what I think it is, well, Harve's asked me to represent Jeremy if push comes to shove."

"Then no, I don't think I can talk to you. But can I bounce stuff off someone who's a county officer? Or would I have to deputize her?"

Martin didn't miss the *her*. He also didn't comment on it.

"As your lawyer, not as the sheriff's lawyer, but yours personally, I would advise you to deputize. Safer that way. And if you are worried about deputizing too many people, there's nothing that says you can't deputize the whole damn town if you wanted to. Just not me."

How the hell, thought Jim. *I know he's not one of them. At least, I think Arthur said he wasn't. So how did Martin know that Jeremy was the subject of this problem? And how did Martin know that he had been thinking about deputizing Linda, and rejected it?* He wanted a drink in the worst way, and it was only 10:00 AM.

Instead, he pocketed the cell and returned to the shade of Linda's awning. He sat, took a long drink of water, and then said, "Would you be willing to be one of my deputies? On call when I need you, but authorized at any time you see fit to act in my place for the safety of the public?"

Her mouth dropped open. That was the last thing Linda had expected to hear. She thought about it. It was obvious Jim wanted to unburden to her. Perhaps this was the only way he could do it. Being a deputy, for her, meant taking on a serious obligation. But if Jim thought she was worthy, then so be it.

"Yes, of course."

He swore her in, promised her a badge in a couple of days and told her no, she couldn't carry a gun or a nightstick. She giggled a bit and suggested perhaps a baseball bat. He finally got her to stop, though her joking had cheered him considerably.

"What did you want to tell me, Jim?"

"You can't talk about this, and you can't make phone calls. But hell, you already know that. I'm blathering, because I don't want to do it, and I don't want to talk about it, and I don't think it's fair. Oh shit, I don't know what to do."

He looked at his watch.

"Would you mind terribly if I called Jen and asked if she could bring us lunch over here? You are on the Friday plan, aren't you?"

"Yes, I am. And that would be nice. I wasn't looking forward to a noisy lunch. Early breakfast was bad enough."

He made the call, and Jen said she would send Bridgette over with their lunch as soon as it was ready.

"I always pick up breakfast and take it back to my office. Old habit, I guess, from the City. Beth worked late until she couldn't work anymore. I didn't want to wake her, so I would pick up breakfast on my way to work. Sit at my desk and do paperwork while I ate. And then, when she was too sick to work anymore, I would let her sleep. Ate breakfast at my desk."

"Would you like to have breakfast with me occasionally?" asked Linda. "I could bring mine over, or you could come and see the offices. People tell me I've made the paper cozy. It suits me."

Lunch arrived. It was a good summer lunch: fried chicken, potato salad, fresh melon cut into cubes and mixed with grapes, and strawberry lemonade in a thermos with glasses for them both. As usual, the basket also contained real silverware and ceramic plates. Morey and Maggie had never used paper plates and weren't about to start.

The two ate in companionable silence, enjoying the food and the warmth of summer. Although it was late July, it wasn't unbearably hot nor was the humidity high. That would come later, probably in mid-August.

Once lunch was finished and the dishes packed away in the basket, Jim sipped the last of his lemonade and considered how to present his problem. It wasn't a dilemma. He knew he had to do it. He just didn't want to, at least not until he had talked it out with someone he trusted.

"It's about Jeremy, isn't it?"

Jim nearly dropped his glass. *I wish these people would stop doing that,* he thought.

"Yes, but how did you know? Are you reading my mind now?"

She laughed heartily. He could learn to love that laugh.

"No. It's logical. I mean, you have six murders on your hands. And no viable suspect now that Harve's been cleared. The only thing you have is that DNA, and it clearly points toward a relative of Harve's. Sure, there could be other familial matches. Most of us old-timers are related anyway. But I'm guessing it was a close match. Just putting two and two together."

"Oh, okay. Yeah, you're right. And I have to call Judge Cramer, ask for a search warrant. And I don't want to. I've got enough to get it. But Harve made it quite clear that his brother is fragile, and I don't want to harm him, physically or mentally."

"Why don't you have me and Arthur come along, then, as your part-time deputies? I don't think Harry would be good for the job. And he seems to enjoy driving around town staring at things and being all official."

"That's a good idea. I'm going to go back to my office and make that call. If I keep putting it off, I'll never do it, and Clay and Blake will be up here with that hotshot deputy state attorney they brought in. I've had enough of the state folks all over my turf."

As he predicted, Judge Cramer granted the search warrant. It was past four in the afternoon when the warrant was finally faxed to his office. He decided to wait until the morning to serve it. He would have breakfast with Arthur and Linda, lay out his plans for serving the warrant, and the three of them would drive over, probably around 11:00 AM. He would make sure to let Morey know he would need lunch for four to take with him. Also, he wanted to be sure Harve was away at work when he arrived. He did not want any interference, nor did he want to risk Harve warning Jeremy. That was always a possibility.

After dinner, he contacted Arthur and Linda and arranged to meet them at his office for breakfast. The gang of five, as he had taken to mentally calling Jen, Dan, Ben, Bridgette, and Charity, would be reading and sorting diaries and papers. It was best to keep this business as far away from them as possible. Even though both Arthur and Linda were part of Arthur's Grove—Arthur's name for his group—he trusted them not to gossip with the others.

CHAPTER FIFTY

The following morning, Jim, Arthur, and Linda gathered for breakfast. It was going to be a hot day. There were no clouds, and not a breath of wind stirred anywhere in Harper's Landing. Gnats swarmed here and there, and mayflies could be seen performing their mating dances midair. Jim had brought out spray cans of mosquito repellent in case the pond had attracted the pests. They all wore boots with their pant legs tucked in as protection against ticks.

They were absorbed in their breakfast and the plans for the day. Otherwise, they might have seen Benny Jackson and several of his friends on their bikes, headed out of town toward Harve's property.

The kids didn't like going up to the new recreation center pool. For one thing, there was too much chlorine in the water. And then there were all the little kids, the moms, and the high school lifeguards, lording it over middle schoolers like Benny and his friends. They were going to Harve's on a dare.

They didn't know the four boys who died there in June. Like everyone else in town, they heard about the car and were sure that the boys had just tried to drive the car into the pond. Becky Sloan rode with them, certain they would chicken out at the last moment and not go in the pond. Jim Barton and DeAnna Camby were in on the dare. They were going to wade into the pond, at least. Their reputations, as well as all of Larry Martin's Legos, were on the line. And if they didn't go in, Larry would get all their Legos. Benny had the most Legos of all of them. He knew he had to win, or his dad would have his hide for losing all of his. He was glad that the dare did not include already constructed Lego projects. But he also wanted to win, because getting all of Larry's Legos would boost his collection and let him build some truly monster creations.

The kids were sweaty and thirsty by the time they arrived. Becky and DeAnna had brought water, and they reluctantly shared it with the boys. The four of them stood staring at the pond. Dragonflies danced from bulrush to bulrush, gnats swarmed above the surface, water walkers skittered across the water, and here and there a bullfrog croaked, occasionally shooting out its long tongue and pulling in a snack. Despite the calm and quiet, the four shivered in fear and anticipation. Becky had already decided there was no way she was going near the pond, let alone into the water. She had nothing to lose by refusing. Neither did DeAnna, but she was such a tomboy she would do anything the boys tried. However, it seemed like no one wanted to go first. The boys were daring each other, and DeAnna was egging them both on by threatening to go in before them both.

Becky was already tired of it.

CHAPTER FIFTY-ONE

Jim, Arthur, and Linda set out in Jim's Explorer for the cabin behind Harve's. The plan to execute the search warrant was simple. Arthur would stand guard behind the cabin, since he already knew there was a back door. Jim and Linda would go to the front door, and when Jeremy answered he would be served. Linda would try to get him to go sit on Harve's front porch with her and Arthur, while Jim did a cursory search of the cabin. He had already decided if anything of interest showed up, he would seal off the cabin, take Jeremy into custody, and have the state forensic lab people come up.

Jim turned into the driveway and headed toward Harve's parking area. Suddenly, he saw a youngster running toward them. It was a girl, screaming and waving her arms. One arm appeared to be bloody. He pulled to a stop as Arthur and Linda leaped from the car.

"A monster, a monster!" the girl screamed.

Blood was pouring down her upraised arm, and the three adults could see a jagged gash on her forearm. Jim grabbed the first aid box from the back while Linda embraced the screaming girl and tried to comfort her. Arthur pulled a blanket from the back of the Explorer, and together they managed to get her to sit.

She was still sobbing and screaming. Jim carefully rinsed the gash with clean water from a bottle in his cooler and wrapped the wound.

"That's going to need stitches," he said. "You reckon the nurse at the new recreation center can take care of it?"

"Let me call up there," said Arthur. "Linda, try to get her name."

The girl continued to sob, unable to form any words beyond *monster*.

Jim walked over to the pond, and his heart sank. Four bicycles lay on the ground. Three pair of shoes and socks lay next to them, and footprints led into the pond. *Oh God, no,* he thought, *oh damn, damn, damn.* He returned to the car.

The girl was somewhat calmed down, though still shaking and crying. Linda had managed to learn that her name was Becky Sloan.

"I recognize that name," said Linda. "I think her mom and dad both work at the mill. Arthur, can you call up there and find out?"

He nodded. The nurse had agreed to examine the girl as soon as they could bring her up. She also agreed to arrange transport over to the next town where there was a small medical clinic if further treatment was needed. Arthur looked up the number for the mill office and dialed.

Barry and Helen Sloan both worked at the mill. Arthur told them their daughter had been injured, but not seriously, and gave them directions to Harve's place. Both parents said they were coming immediately. It would take them fifteen minutes at most.

Jim stood in the sun, thinking hard. Should he execute the warrant? Call the State Police? Try to get more out of the girl, now that she was less hysterical? He felt like slapping himself. He was an experienced cop, a big city detective. Had the small-town life cost him his edge?

Becky was clearly calming down, though still terrified and in pain.

"What happened, Becky?" asked Linda. "What do you mean, a monster?"

Becky hiccupped, and suddenly bent over and vomited. The adults all waited, and Arthur carefully moved the blanket away from the mess. When she was done, Linda helped her rinse and wipe her mouth.

"They went in there, all three of them. I told them it was an awful idea. But they said they were only going to wade in a little bit, and I should film them to prove they won the bet, so they could have all of Larry's Legos. Only now they won't, and I dropped my phone in there, and it bit me!"

She started crying again. Linda held her while the adults looked at one other silently.

"What's this about a monster?" Arthur asked gently. "And where are the other three?"

Becky took a deep breath, looked at the pond, and shuddered, backing up toward the SUV. Slowly she managed to tell them about the dare, how the other three had taken off their shoes and socks and waded into the pond, over by where the bikes were.

"Who were the others?" asked Linda.

"Benny Jackson, Jim Barton, and DeAnna Camby. We all go to school together, and we've been friends since forever."

Becky started to cry again.

"I should have stopped them. I knew it was stupid. But Larry Martin called them scaredy-cats and babies, said they were too weak to go in. I told them it was him who was too scared, or he would have come along."

"Is that Billy Martin's brother?" asked Jim.

"Yes, and he knew better than to come down here. And we should have, too. And now they're gone! The monster got them, and it almost got me. It bit me. My arm hurts a lot."

"Alright," said Jim. "We're going to wait for your parents, have them take you to get that arm looked at. I want you to concentrate on breathing and keep yourself calm. I know it's a warm day, but you're shivering right now, probably from shock. Let's put this blanket around your shoulders. I'm going to need to talk to you, probably tomorrow, maybe today. But I would like to have your parents with you."

As he covered her, the Sloan's car came roaring down the driveway, going way too fast and kicking up dust. They pulled to a stop, and Helen came charging out of the car to her daughter. Barry was right behind.

"What the hell happened here?" demanded Barry.

"We don't know yet," replied Jim. "Your daughter's been hurt, not seriously, but still bad enough to need professional attention. And when she has calmed down, we are going to need a complete story from her about what happened. For now, I think you and your wife should take her up to the nurse at the rec center, let her look at that arm. We can talk later."

Helen tugged at Barry's arm. "Your questions will still be there," she said. "For now, let's get Becky taken care of."

She shot Jim a glance. "We will be back, either here or at your office, after we get her taken care of. My sister can watch her."

"I'm going to need to talk to her, Mrs. Sloan. It can be at my office, or you can bring her back here. I would advise my office. If you want, you can have Martin Rutledge come with you."

"Why would she need a lawyer?" Barry said.

"She doesn't. But sometimes people feel more comfortable having one."

"We'll cross that bridge later," said Barry. "We'll call you about where to meet. Can you wait until tomorrow to talk to her?"

Jim thought for a moment.

"Mrs. Sloan, would you mind taking Becky to the clinic in Harwood? I can have Arthur drive your husband up in a while. That way we can get her treated, and I can answer your husband's questions."

"Sure," she replied.

She left with Becky sitting in the front seat, still crying and shaking.

Barry sat on the running board of the Explorer.

"What's going on?" he asked.

"That's what we are going to find out," replied Jim. "Apparently your daughter rode out here with three friends." He consulted his notes. "Benny Jackson, Jim Barton, and DeAnna Camby. I'm guessing those are their bikes over there."

"The purple one is Becky's," said Barry. "I don't see the other kids often enough to say for sure, but those look like their bikes. Those kids are inseparable. So where are Benny, Jim, and DeAnna?"

"We don't know. Becky was too upset to talk about it. She kept saying something about a monster, and that it bit her."

"Oh God, this is where those other boys died, isn't it? And that judge fella who came up to fish? This is the place?"

"Yeah," said Jim. "It is. But your daughter is safe, okay?"

Barry nodded.

"Can I go to her now?" he asked.

"I'd like to have you stay here with me, if you would," said Jim, "until the State Police and crime lab people get here."

Arthur touched Jim's arm.

"Why not let me take Mr. Sloan to his daughter and stay with him? Linda can go, too, and she can bring your vehicle back. I'll stay and make sure they don't question Becky without me there. I am, after all, a sworn deputy."

Jim reluctantly agreed. He watched as they drove away, sighed, and pulled out his cell.

"Clay? I'm gonna have to ask you, the diver, and the forensics guys to come up here again. I think we've got another."

CHAPTER FIFTY-TWO

A fter he finished his call, Jim called Harry Randle and told him to bring the yellow tape. Then he called Linda.

"How fast can you get back here?" he asked.

"Leaving now."

"Good. The state guys are on their way, and I want to serve this warrant first. And if we must hold Jeremy, I want him in my car before Clay and his team get up here."

"I'll get there as fast as I can. I'm leaving Arthur with the parents at the clinic."

Jim realized suddenly that he was ravenous. They had all forgotten about lunch. While he waited for Linda, he opened the large cooler, and pulled out potato salad and some of the fried chicken. Maggie knew he loved the stuff. Her breading was homemade. And the potato salad wasn't commercial either. He was delighted to spot apple pie. Jim got himself a piece of that first. He sat on the floor of the back half of the SUV, the door open, feet resting on the ground.

It was hot, and the humidity was starting to rise. He drank half a bottle of water, ate three pieces of chicken and a large serving of potato salad. He decided to have another piece of apple pie. When she returned, Linda sat next to him and nibbled at a chicken leg, ate a half cup of potato salad, and then dug into the apple pie. She also drank a lot of water.

"How are we going to do this, Jim?" Linda finally asked. "You want me around back, or to be the one to knock?"

"How strong are you?"

"I work out. Why?"

"I think I want you at the back. If he breaks for it, tackle him. By what I know of him, based on Harve's description, he won't put up much of a fight. But if he's armed with anything, you holler for me and get out of there."

"Why don't you give me a gun instead?" she asked. "I've been hunting since I was six, and I know how to handle a gun. I'm betting there's more in here than the one on your hip."

He unlocked the gun safe under the floorboard on the front passenger side and handed her the .357 he kept there just in case. She opened the magazine, checked to make sure it was full and the gun ready to fire. She closed it up again, left the safety off, and carefully tucked it into the back of her belt. He was pleased to see she knew to tuck just the barrel, both for safety and ease of retrieval.

They walked down the drive past Harve's house. Jim looked around the side, toward the cabin at the back. He saw no movement and motioned Linda to move to the bushes that lined the walk toward the back. She kept low and moved quickly to the back of the cabin.

Jim didn't like involving Linda. But he felt like he had no choice. He simply didn't trust Clay and his team to treat this man gently. He knocked on the front door. He heard a chair scrape, and then footsteps move toward the door. He heard a voice, and at first he couldn't understand what was said, other than that it was a man's voice.

"Sheriff Burch here," he said. "Can you please open the door?"

He heard a bolt being thrown, and then the door slowly

opened. Jim couldn't help himself. He gasped, took a step back, then caught himself.

"Jeremy?"

The figure nodded.

Truth was that Jeremy Sanders was the definition of monster. Huge, ropey scars extended from his right shoulder to the top of his head, pulling the right side of his face into a permanent scowl. He had no hair, and scars made the skin on his head shiny. His right eye, a bright, piercing blue like Harve's, was barely visible through the mass of scars and distorted skin. His mouth was twisted in a perpetual grimace. His right arm was pulled up, and Jim suspected his chest was also a mass of scars.

He was wearing a leather apron, which appeared to be wet, boots, also wet, and was carrying large knife. When he saw Jim, and the gun on his hip, he turned and placed the knife carefully on a side table by the door. He then stepped into the doorway. Jim noted blood on his left hand. Jeremy saw his look and wiped his hand on his jeans as he took another step.

Linda came around the corner from the back, caught a glimpse of him, and turned away briefly. When she turned back and approached the porch, she held out her hand and said, "Hello, Jeremy. I'm Linda, and this is Jim Burch, our sheriff."

Jeremy moved as if to close the door, but Jim held it open. Jeremy stopped, but made no move to shake Linda's hand. She dropped it to her side.

"I'm sorry to do this, Jeremy, but I'm going to have to put you under arrest. Linda here is going to call your brother and your attorney to come up here. In the meantime, please come out here onto the porch and sit on that bench. I'm going to handcuff you by your left arm to the arm of the bench. I'm not going to hurt you. Do you understand?"

Jeremy nodded. He looked bewildered and frightened. He sat on the bench and let Jim handcuff him.

"You have the right to remain silent. Anything you say can

and will be used against you in a court of law." Jim continued to read him his Miranda rights while Linda made the call.

When he finished, she said, "Harve is on his way, and so is Martin. And Martin says no questions until he gets here. Harve says Jeremy probably understands his rights as you've told them to him, but maybe not. I'm advising you to err on the side of caution."

"Oh, I agree. But I am going to execute this search warrant."

He handed the document to Jeremy.

"This paper gives me the right to search your house. A judge has signed it. You can show it to your attorney when he and your brother get here. I promise I'm going to be careful inside. Do you have any pets? Large dogs? Snakes?"

Jeremy shook his head no. He said something, but neither Jim nor Linda understood him.

Jim entered the house. He couldn't escape the reality of the situation. He had a terrified teenager with a large cut on her hand, screaming about a monster. He had a man handcuffed to the bench on the porch whom any youngster would see as a monster. And that same man had blood on his hand and water on his shoes and apron. Additionally, there were three kids missing, and Jim was damn sure they were in that pond somewhere.

The house was clean and neat. The daylight shone in through windows that were polished, revealing a wood floor scrubbed and waxed until it glowed. The fireplace was free of ashes, and wood was neatly stacked waiting for winter and the need for heat. The windows were open in the front and back, allowing for a breeze to blow through, though at the moment, the cabin was stifling hot because there was no breeze.

Jim moved on to the kitchen. Everything there was clean also. In fact, the house was preternaturally clean. He was quite sure if he took a straight edge to the row of glasses on the open shelf above the table, he would find they were even. He opened one of the drawers and found the same precise arrangement. The cupboards were the same.

He moved on to the bathroom and bedroom. Here again he found spotless order. Nothing was out of place. It was almost spooky, the level of cleanliness and order. He knew what this was. He had seen obsessive compulsive disorder before, but never to this extreme.

He noted a door to the side of the kitchen. It appeared to lead into an extension to the back of the cabin. He opened it carefully. There was a bright light in the room, fueled by propane. The light was aimed at a table like a draftsman's table, slightly tilted with a tall chair in front. Tools were lined up along the back of the table, on a ledge. Jim glanced around, left the room, closed the door, and went out to the porch.

Harve pulled up as Jim returned to the front porch of Jeremy's cabin. Harve ran back to the porch, but Jim stopped him from going to his brother.

"I'm sorry, Harve, but Jeremy's under arrest. I can't let you go any further."

Martin pulled into the drive next, and he hurried back to the small group. "I'm going to need to talk to my client," he said. "And if I can't understand him, well, I'm going to ask you to allow Harve to help me. They are both my clients now, Jim."

Jim thought for a moment. He knew he had to let Martin talk to the man, but he was sure he didn't want Harve up there, too.

"Harve, can he write?"

"Of course he can."

"Well then, get one of those legal pads you always bring with you, Martin. If you can't understand his answers, have him write them. And when you are done, I need to question him. I understand that you'll be there. But I don't want Harve there. Maybe later. We'll see."

Martin reluctantly agreed. He knew Jim was right, legally. He hoped Jeremy was up to the task. He tried not to cringe when he saw the man. Harve had told him about his injuries and deformities, but nothing could have prepared him for this. Linda left once he had sat next to Jeremy. He held out his hand, and Jeremy tentatively extended his left. They shook.

"Hi, I'm Martin Rutledge. Your brother retained me to represent you. But I need to know from you if that is okay."

Jeremy nodded. Then he spoke. "I can pay you. Harve doesn't have to spend his money."

Martin barely understood him but was certain as they progressed, he would get better at it.

"If I can't understand something you say, I'm going to ask you to write it. Is that okay?"

"Of course," said Jeremy. "I have a special glass inside. It has a straw, so I can drink. I need some water."

Martin got up and went to Jim to convey the request. Jim went into the house and got the glass from the desk where Jeremy said it would be. Jeremy took a long drink, then looked over the papers Martin had pulled from his briefcase. They were a standard retainer agreement and an estimate of hourly costs for representing him. He signed both and handed them back to Martin.

"Is there anything inside that is going to incriminate you?" asked Martin. "I need to know. And what you tell me is privileged, so you can trust that I won't tell Jim or the state folks when they arrive."

"They aren't going to be happy about the heads," replied Jeremy. "None of them."

Martin felt slightly sick inside.

"Yeah," said Jeremy. "I didn't kill them, if that's what you're thinking. It has been leaving them, and I don't know what to do. I kept them. Well, after the first one. That one I got rid of. But it kept leaving them, and I can't make it stop. I had to get rid of them so no one would blame Harve."

Martin had struggled to understand his words. It was getting easier. But this had to be discussed before he let Jim question him.

"I need to know what *it* is. And you can't tell any of this to the police when they start questioning you. Don't volunteer anything, okay?"

"Okay. It is the Provider. I call it that. It brings me specimens for my taxidermy. But only when I feed it. I take it deer, sheep, that sort of thing. And later it brings me specimens, nice ones. But lately it's been bringing human heads. I don't want them! I try to make the Provider stop, but it won't. I got rid of the human heads."

Jeremy's voice was getting louder; he was getting quite agitated. And Jim was taking notice. Martin laid a hand on his arm and gently spoke to him about the necessity of remaining calm.

Jim was getting antsy. He wanted to talk to Jeremy before the state guys arrived. He walked up to the bench, leaned against the porch railing, and addressed them both.

"Jeremy? Martin? There's some things out there in your shop I need to talk to you about."

"Jim," said Martin. "I think I'm going to have to advise my client not to speak for now. I know, that's not what you want to hear. But until we get everything sorted, and by that, I mean all the forensic people done with their stuff, all that stuff gathered and evaluated, I'm advising him not to talk."

Jim sighed. "Then you know I'm going to have to lock him up."

"Yes, I do. And I'll explain to him why. And I'll go along with him to the jail. Are you going to do it?"

"No, I want to stay here for when the state people arrive. There's more to this than this cabin. I would prefer you and your client not be here when they arrive. And not just because I don't want them questioning him yet. I'll have Linda, here, drive you to the jail. Harry Randle will meet you there. I think we can let Jeremy stay in his own clothing, but Harry will have to search him."

"Okay. I'll explain everything, and I'm going with him."

Jim called Harry Randle and told him to meet Martin and Jeremy at the jail, and to send Linda back while he processed Jeremy in as a prisoner.

"Don't forget to lock the cell," said Jim. "And you are going to stay there. Because sure as hell Harve is going to be going there, too. And he can't talk to Jeremy, no matter how much he wants to. You got that?"

Jim walked Jeremy to the Explorer and saw him safely into the back of the car. Martin sat next to him, and Linda got in front and drove away toward town. As she was pulling out of the drive, the state forensic van and a state trooper car pulled in. She ignored them and kept going.

"That woman is a treasure," Jim said aloud to no one in particular.

Clay Murdoch and Blake Meadows got out of the car. The van parked behind it, and a diver got out, followed by a man and woman, each carrying a large case that Jim recognized as the forensic equipment all Missouri forensic technicians now carried.

"Who was in the car?" asked Clay.

"The guy who lives in the cabin out back, his lawyer, and my newest part-time deputy. They're headed for the jail. Harry Randle is going to book him and stay there. And there goes Harve, just like I thought."

They all turned and watched Harve's Econoline he used for work pull out onto the county road and head for town.

"Okay," said Blake. "What do we have this time?"

"Oh, God, where to start?" replied Jim.

Carefully he laid out everything: the girl who had been injured and her three missing friends; the bicycles and shoes with socks laying by the pond; the cabin and what he had found inside that made him step outside until they arrived. He had persuaded Martin to let him keep the search warrant, promising there was a copy at his office that Martin could keep. He had left it on the fax machine.

"The girl is being taken care of medically, over at the clinic in Haywood. Her parents are with her and will bring her back home after her wounds are attended to. We can talk to her once she's calmed down. In the meantime, we need to find out what happened to her friends."

"She didn't say?" asked Clay.

"She couldn't. She was as scared as anyone I've ever seen. All she could say was *monster*, and she said, 'he bit me.' I thought getting her arm fixed right away was more important than trying to question her, hysterical as she was. We don't have an EMT here, you know, just a volunteer fire department."

Jim stopped. He realized he was rattled and talking more than usual or than he wanted. He calmed himself. He was letting Arthur's talk about a creature get to him. Proper police procedure was what was needed here, and once he got into that rhythm, he would be okay.

Blake and Clay stared at Jim. He was usually taciturn. He was obviously shaken, but by what? They waited patiently. Then Clay spoke.

"Jim, this is your turf for now. What do you want from us? Why did you call us up here?"

"Oh, hell, okay. First off, the three kids not here are probably in there." He pointed at the pond.

"Damn," whispered Blake.

"We're gonna need the diver to go check. And then there's this."

He held out the search warrant.

"Judge Cramer felt it was justified, based on the DNA evidence from the truck and Harve's revelation about his twin brother. But when I went in, I saw something in his studio. Something that made me decide the search requires a trained crime scene tech, and, frankly, I'm glad you brought two of them."

"What did you see?" asked Blake.

"I don't know. Lots of animal skulls in there. We need to have the zoological people down in St. Louis check them out, tell us what they are."

Jim sat in one of the rockers on Harve's porch.

"You guys do this however you want. I'm plain wrung out. But that cabin's got to be searched, carefully. And I don't want to think it, but I do think there's three kids, or what's left of them, in that pond."

He carefully avoided any mention of Jeremy's preoccupation with order. They would find that out soon enough. Right now, Jim wanted to sit, have some water, maybe some lunch. He was done for the moment with being a cop. He wanted to be human. He discovered, to his dismay, that he wanted to cry. That was something he would not do in front of these pros. But later, in the privacy of his home, or perhaps on Linda's front porch? Maybe.

The diver put on his wetsuit and got his other gear assembled. He had a large light and a bag for holding any evidence he might find. Jim wanted to tell him to arm himself, to take something to ward off an attack. But that would require an explanation he wasn't quite ready to give. Nevertheless, he called to Clay.

"Please tell that guy to take some protection with him."

"I'll do you one better," Clay replied. "Hey, hold on!" he yelled at the diver.

He headed for the van. Jim was startled to see Clay pull off his clothes and put on a wetsuit and diving gear. He watched as Clay and the diver walked into the pond and then sank below the surface as they approached the center.

They were down there for some time. Meanwhile, the crime scene investigators had gone up to Jeremy's house, carrying evidence bags, tags, and cameras. They donned paper booties over their shoes and put on gloves before they entered. Jim ignored them, instead focusing on the pond. Blake was taking multiple pictures of the four bicycles and the footprints leading into the water. He also walked the edge of the pond, looking for prints and other objects of interest.

As Jim began to worry, the two divers emerged. Their hands were empty, and the bags the one man carried appeared to be empty. Clay pulled off his mask and breathing apparatus and walked over to Jim.

"Nothing down there that we could see. We even went down that tunnel. Damn, that was daunting. Made sure the pond was empty before we entered, but still I didn't like it. Glad to be out."

Linda arrived back at the pond shortly after the diver and

Clay had peeled out of their wetsuits. She told Jim that Becky's parents were with their daughter at the clinic, still getting her arm cared for. They would call as soon as they were back home.

"I hope Martin is up to the task of defending Harve and Jeremy," Linda said. "And I hope that Arthur and Harry will be sufficient for you as deputies. Because I'm handing in my deputy papers, Jim. I'm your friend, and I'm going to be working hard with the folks from the Grove to find a way to put an end to this. I don't think that those things combine well with being an officer of the law. Even if it is just a deputy."

"Arthur is my deputy, too," said Jim. "Doesn't seem to pose a problem for him."

"Perhaps Arthur's friendship is different from what I want." Linda blushed deep red. She handed Jim back the paperwork he had given her earlier.

"I'll give you a written resignation if you require it," she said.

"No," he replied. "This is fine."

Jim felt something he hadn't felt for a long time, a deep sense of *rightness* he had only felt with Beth. Now, he felt that same feeling rising in him toward Linda. He was surprised. He had sworn he would never marry again, never have a romantic connection with another woman. Yet here he was sitting with a beautiful, powerful woman who made him feel happy and safe, in the way only a strong woman can. And he didn't want it to stop.

"Let me drive you back into town. I can leave for a few minutes, and this is going to be an exceptionally long session. Maybe you could bring us out food later? Or ask Morey or Jen to bring some out? I know I'm going to be hungry, and so are these guys."

"Sure, Jim. I'm happy to do that. But why not let me call Jen and have her pick me up? That way you can stay on top of things here."

Again, Jim was impressed by how Linda knew just what he needed. He agreed. She called Jen, who said she would be down in a while. Jen reminded Linda that it was already late in the afternoon, so she might as well bring dinner. She also asked Linda to let Jim know that dinner was being provided for Harry, Harve, Martin, and Jeremy at the jail.

It was going on 6:00 PM when Jen and company arrived at the driveway. Jim drove up to the entry, undid the tape, and motioned them to drive down. Arthur and Morey had come with her. The two of them pulled up next to Jim's car.

The two crime scene investigators were called down to Harve's porch, where they joined Jim, Clay, Blake, and the diver, Mike Call. Mike was new to the force and had never been to Harper's Landing. He had no idea what was in store for him when Morey used Harve's keys to go into the house and bring out a couple of folding tables. Morey then set out thick roast beef sandwiches, homemade dill pickles, potato salad, cheese wedges, and two freshly baked apple pies. Arthur pulled out the basket which contained ten plates, ten sets of knives and forks, cloth napkins, and plastic glasses. Morey apologized for the plastic glasses.

"I wasn't sure what eating situation we'd have and didn't want to break any more glasses."

They all assured him that plastic was fine. There was strawberry lemonade in a large cooler with a spigot dispenser. They all dug in, only just realizing how hungry they were. When it was apple pie time, everyone watched Mike take his first bite. They were not disappointed.

"Holy mother," he blurted. "That is pure food of the gods. Can I get some to take home when I go back? Is it for sale?"

Morey laughed and assured him there would be a nice pie waiting for him to take home to his family.

Arthur then spoke up. "Did you find them?"

The diver and Clay both shook their heads.

"We're going to have to search, go back down there, I guess. But I'm too damn tired tonight to do any more." Clay stretched and yawned. "What about you?" he asked the diver.

"I would not go down there again, not until we've had some sleep. It's not safe."

"Well, then, why don't you plan to come up to The Rectory when you are done for the night?" asked Arthur. "There are plenty of rooms, I have pajamas to fit all of you, and your clothes can be washed and dried while you are sleeping. I imagine you will welcome a hot shower and a nice bed before you get back to this awfulness in the morning."

"Harry can spend the night up here," said Jim. "He'll watch the houses and the pond. No one in town is going to come down here. They'll all be up at the Happy Time speculating on why I'm not in my office. I hope they didn't see Jeremy."

"No," said Arthur. "I was there. Linda and Harry took him in through the back. And Jen here was careful about taking food over. Said Harry was minding the store for you. Harve and Martin stayed in back with Jeremy, so no one saw them there."

Everyone accepted the offer. It was a long drive back to St. Louis for Clay and Blake and even longer for the crime scene techs and the diver, who had come from Jefferson City. Harry Randle arrived shortly, with a couple of members of the high school football team in tow.

"They'll watch up at the road, Boss," said Harry. "They brought a tent and said they'll take turns sleeping. I hope it's okay."

"Of course," said Jim. "This way things will be even more secure. Tell them no matter what, stay the hell away from that pond. By the way, make sure that they stop by my office tomorrow and fill out the temporary hire form so they can get paid for the night. If I'm not there, the forms are in the filing cabinet in the back room."

Harry nodded and went to help the boys set up.

They locked up the forensics van, and everyone piled into the state trooper vehicle and Jim's Explorer. Morey and Jen left with the dishes and leftovers, headed for the diner. The drive back to town was quick and silent.

Jim knew he had a long and painful evening ahead of him. He would get Arthur and Linda to help when they called in the parents of the three kids. And then there was Becky. He would have to talk to her. He hoped he could leave the crime scene investigation to the state people and question her tomorrow. He hoped her parents would take the day off to be with her.

Jim didn't want to terrify the girl, but he did want to take her to the jail and have her see Jeremy. He needed to know if he was the monster she was referring to. He had also asked the nurse to swab Becky's wound or have the doctor at the clinic do it. He needed to have it checked for foreign DNA.

Arthur rode with Morey and Jen and arrived at The Rectory before the rest of the group.

"I have rooms for each of you, complete with robes and personal items, toothbrushes and the like. You will find towels and cloths. I'm afraid you will have to share the shower, but each room has its own sink and water closet. Once you are cleaned up, you are invited to join me in the library if you like, for a drink and conversation."

Jim raised an eyebrow in query. Did Arthur really want this bunch pawing through those precious documents? Arthur drew close and leaned over toward Jim.

"I had them put all the stuff away. We're nearly done sorting anyway, and now it's time to start reading in earnest."

He led the CSIs to their rooms, then showed Mike his room. Blake and Clay had been here many times, so Arthur just pointed to the adjoining rooms at the end of the hall.

"There's a shower up here, next to the ladies' room, and a larger one at the end of the hall next to Blake's room, with two stalls. There's soap, shampoo, and conditioner in the dispensers in each stall. If you need anything, I'll be in the library over there. Oh, and if you want your clothes washed and dried overnight, put them in the bag and hang them on the door. I have a nice young lady who comes in to do all that stuff; she gets here at about 5:00 AM so you should have your clothing back by 7:00 AM at the latest. Don't worry, she doesn't run the vacuum until 8:00 AM at the earliest."

Jim and Arthur went to his study. Arthur poured Jim a double shot of bourbon and chose a brandy for himself. They sat in the wingback chairs by the open window, sipping their drinks in silence. Somewhere a recording of flute music played, filling the room with peace and calm. Jim felt himself begin to unwind.

"God, Arthur. I don't know how much more I can take. And how much the town can take. Those poor kids. And we have to tell their parents. We have to tell them now, and I'm not sure how to do it without that bunch"—pointing vaguely toward the rooms —"swarming all over them."

"I have an idea," said Arthur. "Why not take Linda and go visit each set of parents individually? That way you don't have to worry about the state folks, and I think it's better to see them individually. If they need me, you can call, and I'll get there right away. I can always give this bunch a plausible excuse."

Jim called Linda, reluctantly. He hated this part of his job, and he hated involving someone else in it. But she was willing to accompany him. He didn't even know what to tell them, since all they knew was that the kids were missing. He knew the bodies would turn up eventually, and his biggest fear was that they would be mutilated like the others.

Jim and Linda drove to the Camby home first. Lonnie and Harriet Camby lived on Paper Lane, just off Main Street to the north of town. Their home was a white craftsman surrounded by stone walls and beds of colorful flowers. Jim was again struck by how much the people of Harper's Landing seemed to love flowers. He resolved to plant some around his house next spring.

Lonnie and Harriet had put their new baby to bed and were wondering where DeAnna was. When they saw the sheriff at the door, with Linda at his side, Harriet stuck her fist to her mouth and grabbed Lonnie tight with her other hand.

Jim and Linda asked if they could come in. They entered the large, open living room, with its signature columns on either side, and an open dining area beyond. A door to the left apparently led to a main floor bedroom, and stairs were visible leading to the second story.

"Do you have a nursery monitor?" asked Linda.

"Yes," said Lonnie. "I'm guessing you think I should close this door?"

"That might be best," said Linda.

He closed the door, made sure the monitor was working, and sat on the couch next to his wife. Jim and Linda took chairs opposite the couch.

"This is about DeAnna, isn't it?" asked Harriet.

"Probably," said Jim. "When did she leave this morning?"

"I think it was around 11:00 AM," said Harriet. "She and her three friends were going for a bike ride, and maybe up to the rec center for a swim. Though come to think of it, I don't think she took her bathing suit."

"Do you recall what she was wearing?" asked Jim.

"Sure. Red tennies, always the red tennies. Jean shorts, you know the kind you cut off. I made sure hers were only cut to mid-thigh. And a blue shirt, a sleeveless tank-top style."

"She's dead, isn't she?" Lonnie asked. His hands were shaking, and his eyes were wide.

"We don't know for sure," said Jim. "The four kids were last seen over at Harve's pond. Becky Sloan is being treated for a bad cut on her arm. I'm guessing she's home by now. We haven't found your daughter or the two boys. Becky says they were pulled into the center of the pond."

The parents collapsed in each other's arms. Lonnie worked hard at being stoic. Finally, he asked Jim, "When will you know for sure?"

The baby began to cry. Linda rose, opened the door, and went into the nursery to soothe her. She had lost her pacifier, and Linda returned it to her tiny mouth. After a few moments, the baby was again asleep, and Linda returned to the room. Jim was talking with Lonnie, and Linda sat next to Harriet and put her arms around her.

"I need to go see the Jacksons and the Barton family. Do you want Linda to stay here with you?"

"Why don't you call and have them come here?" asked Harriet wearily. "We might as well all be together now. We will be soon enough, I guess."

Linda nodded at Jim. Obviously, she thought this was a particularly good idea.

"Do they have other kids?" asked Jim.

"Yeah," said Harriet. "They might as well bring them along. I should go get cookies started or something."

Linda got up with her.

"Let's go to the kitchen, see what we can find. We can make tea at least. And maybe Morey and Maggie have cookies already made."

Why do women always turn to food at times like this? Jim wondered. *I guess it's second nature. We drink tea or coffee, we nibble on cookies, we bring each other casseroles. Feed the body, feed the soul? Maybe.* He turned his attention back to Lonnie.

"Do you have their phone numbers?"

"Yeah. We're tight, the four families. Should I call the Sloans, too?"

"No, I don't think so. Becky was traumatized. I think we should let them stay out of this, at least for tonight."

"Okay. Let me call the others."

He first called Ben Jackson.

"You and Lois should probably come here," was the last thing Jim heard him say before hanging up.

"They know something's wrong. They were about to call me to ask if I'd seen Benny. He's Ben, Jr."

Lonnie's phone rang.

"Hello? Oh, hi, Andy. No, I haven't seen Jimmy. But listen, can you and Camille come over here? Ben and Lois are on the way."

He listened for a moment, then sighed. "Yeah, I'm afraid it is.

Barry and Helen are with Becky. Apparently, she's been injured and is badly shaken up. Please, come on over. We need you."

He hung up.

"How do you do it?" asked Lonnie, wringing his hands and shifting from foot to foot.

"Do what?"

"Tell people this stuff. I mean, how do you keep your sanity? You must have had to do it a lot."

"You never get used to it. I thought that it would be different here. And it was, until lately."

"Jim, what the hell is going on?" asked Lonnie.

"I wish I knew. I really do."

When the other two families arrived, Linda helped get the kids situated in the dining room with games and cookies. They had found a box of lemon drop cookies and a bag of Oreos in the kitchen, and there was soda pop for the kids. Tina Jackson was eight, and the Barton twins were ten. They were soon busy giggling, playing Uno, and wolfing down Oreos. The lemon drop cookies were a little less popular.

Meanwhile, the adults sat in the living room trying to talk quietly so as not to upset their kids. Mickie Barton wandered into the room.

"Mom, where's Jimmy? I thought we were going to pick him up here. But he's not here, and he didn't come home."

Camille Barton collapsed in tears, along with Harriet Camby and Lois Jackson. The men sat pale and shaken, trying helplessly to comfort their wives. The other kids came pouring into the room, aware that something was dreadfully wrong.

Linda slipped into the nursery and gently lifted the sleeping baby. She brought her in and placed her in Harriet's arms. Harriet instantly put the baby up over her shoulder and patted her gently. It was the soothing she needed. Linda then pulled out her phone and gave Arthur the directions to the Camby home. He said he would come immediately.

"There's not much chance they're gonna show up, is there?" asked Ben Jackson.

Jim shook his head. He stood and motioned to the other men to follow him. He went out onto the big porch and waited for the others to come. He closed the door and went over to the far corner where he sat on the wide stone wall. The other three men joined him.

"You remember the four boys that went missing at Harve's pond?"

They all nodded.

"Well, it appears your kids were there today, and Becky Sloan was the only one who came back."

"Oh, God," said Andy. "Those boys, they were ripped apart, weren't they?"

Jim nodded. He felt tired to the depths of his soul, like some celestial dog had shaken him and tossed him in a corner.

Lonnie leaned over the wall and threw up. He wiped his mouth on his sleeve, stumbled over to the rocking chair on the porch, and sat down, too shaken even to cry. Andy and Ben sat on the porch floor, their backs against the wall. Ben had tears flowing down his cheeks.

"Dear lord, how are we gonna tell the kids?" asked Ben. "And how do I explain to my wife that the casket has to be closed. And Andy, isn't Camille pregnant again?"

Andy nodded. "Twins again, if you can believe it."

"Jim," said Lonnie, "do you have the bodies?"

"No. The divers didn't find anything. They're going back down tomorrow."

Jen and Mary Harper pulled up in front of Lonnie's house. They were carrying quilts, cookies, and flowers. Other neighbors began to appear carrying casseroles, desserts, and toys for the kids. It seemed news of the missing kids was already spreading throughout Harper's Landing.

This was the power of small towns. They could be unbearably stifling with everyone knowing everyone else's business. But when tragedy or illness or even good fortune struck, they were there to share the sorrow and the joy. Every baby was celebrated, every death was mourned, every wedding rejoiced. This was community, and compassion. This was what he had needed. There were those who had tried to persuade him that the town called him because it needed him. He believed the town had sought him out because of his own need. But now wasn't the time for him to be comforted or to be giving out comfort. He left them to their task and turned to go.

Linda slipped out the front door before he could reach his vehicle.

"Jim," she said. "Can I come see you tonight? After I'm done here?"

"Sure. You want me to wait for you at my office?"

"No, I know where you live."

She slipped back inside. Jim headed for home and the vacuum cleaner.

CHAPTER FIFTY-THREE

The following morning, Jim stopped at Morey's for his usual breakfast. Jen had it ready but stopped as she was about to hand it to him.

"Jim Burch, you look about as rested and bright-eyed as I've seen you in days. I'm glad you were able to get a good night's sleep, seeing what a busy day you had—and have today."

She handed him the bag after slipping an extra cinnamon roll inside.

"I'll bring Jeremy's breakfast over," she said. "Morey stayed with him last night. I think you forgot that someone needed to stay there."

Jim was dumbfounded. She was right. He had completely forgotten, and that was not how he did things. As he stood staring at her, shaking his head, he heard the door behind him open.

"Good morning, Linda," said Jen. "I was going to bring your breakfast over to you."

She looked at Linda, then at Jim. Comprehension dawned on her face. She smiled and winked at them both.

"Why don't I give it to you now? You can take it with you."

She grabbed a bag, put in a plate, some silver, a cinnamon roll, and a dished up a small container of scrambled eggs. She added a bag of cut-up fruit.

"Enough fruit for both of you," she whispered, and winked again.

She turned away as the two quickly left the diner, blushing furiously. Jen was happy for them. Jim had been grieving for far too long, and Linda was lonely. And they were two of her favorite people. But she was also worried. This wasn't going to be an easy day. Not for the first time, she wondered if Linda was up to dealing with all the horror that was coming their way. Dan had similar misgivings, but he also assured Jen that Linda was the most powerful adept he had encountered in some time, and he believed that as she came into her powers, which she was doing rapidly, she would have enough strength to deal with whatever the *bolotnik* could dish out.

Jen prepared Jeremy's breakfast, adding a glass straw for his thermos of iced coffee. She knew he loved the cinnamon rolls and could manage one if he tore it in small pieces. She put one in, along with a generous serving of soft scrambled eggs. The last item was a cup of applesauce with a sprinkle of cinnamon.

She liked Jeremy. At first, she had been unable to understand him, but now it was easy, and he was eager to converse. Jim had allowed it, as long as no one else was there to see them. He didn't think it would go over well with that hotshot state attorney. And while he still didn't care much what the higher-ups thought, he didn't want Jen or Jeremy to get in trouble.

When she arrived, Jim and Linda were finishing their breakfast.

"You'll have to leave it this morning," said Jim. "The Sloans are bringing Becky in for an interview. And they'll have Martin with them."

"Gotcha. And Linda, do you want lunch at the *Gazette* today, or are you going to come in?"

Jim glanced out the window. He leaped out of his seat, his face red with anger. "Who the hell ...?"

He ran out the door, yelling "Don't even think of parking there!" Jen took Jeremy's breakfast to him while Linda joined Jim in front of the sheriff's office. Two news vans, one from a station in St. Louis and one marked CNN were in the middle of the street, while Jim yelled at them to get the hell away from the sheriff's office. She walked out to the idling CNN van. The attractive young blonde in the passenger seat rolled down her window.

"Is he for real?"

"Oh, you betcha," said Linda. "Tell you what, why don't you folks go over on Main Street. That's the one you just turned off. Head south a block and park there. That'll put you right in front of the Happy Time Tavern, and you might get some nice stories once the afternoon shift is over. Or you could go up to the Grossman Textile Mill and Museum for some local color. Because right now, this town is in mourning, and some heavy shit is about to hit the fan here. And you are *not* going to get to film it."

"But we're the press," said the young blonde reporter from CNN.

Linda interrupted her. "And I'm the local press," she said, pointing at her office and the *Gazette*'s clearly marked window. "Right now, that's all you are going to get. Cooperate, and we will find the time to give you interviews with law enforcement. Just not right now. Don't cooperate, and you are going to find yourselves in the biggest stonewall you've ever encountered."

The CNN reporter conferred with her driver and cameraman. Then she got out and went back to talk with the St. Louis station people. She returned to her van.

"Okay," she said. "We're going up to the mill, and we're going to get some local shots. But if we see someone walking, we're going to talk to them. That okay with you?"

Linda could see she was aching for a fight.

"That's fine. And come back here at, say, 3:00 PM this afternoon? I'll make sure the sheriff, at least, is available to you. And if the state folks are here, I'll ask them if they'll talk."

"What's your name?"

"Linda Collier, editor and publisher of the *Harper's Landing Gazette.*"

Linda stood and watched as the vans drove off, turned around in the courthouse driveway, and then turned south on Main Street. She walked to the corner and saw that the St. Louis van was staying in front of the Happy Time, while the CNN van headed south out of town. She wondered how long it would take them to find out that the mill was north of town. She went back into Jim's office, where he had retreated when he saw she was handling the problem.

"They'll be back. But not before 3:00 PM. I told them it was either that or no story at all."

"I just want to kiss you, woman. Thank you."

"Didn't you get enough already?" asked Linda.

She blushed brilliant pink when Jen walked in from the back. She had obviously heard their exchange.

"Hey, I'll keep your secret if you want. But you gotta know that unless you find a way to remove that glow, the whole town's going to know in about six hours, give or take."

"It's alright with me," said Jim. "Been a long time since I felt this way. I like it."

"And so do I," replied Linda. "But we've got business to take care of. I need to print an edition of the paper, and here come the Sloans with Becky, to talk to you."

She headed out with Jen, the two chatting companionably until they parted ways across the street.

CHAPTER FIFTY-FOUR

The Sloan family arrived shortly after the media left. They saw the van in front of the tavern, but Jim assured them that they would not be interviewed or filmed. He brought them inside and lowered the curtain on his front window. Becky was clearly more settled, though still frightened and mourning. She knew about her three friends, and she was obviously going to need time, and probably help, to deal with all of it.

He hated that he was probably going to add to her fears and wondered how he could lessen the blow. He decided to tell her about Jeremy, what had happened to him, why he looked the way he did.

Jim explained to Becky that he needed her to look at someone, tell him if she had ever seen the man before. He told her Jeremy's story. He could see that she was feeling sympathetic toward him.

"I won't lie to you," he said. "He's extremely hard to look at. He scared me when I first saw him. If I had known what you know now, I don't think I would have been frightened at all. But he is, well, monstrous. Do you think you can look at him?"

"I'll try," said Becky. "Why do you need me to see him?"

"He lives up above the pond," said Jim. "You said you were attacked by a monster, and we need to know if it was him."

"Is he in jail?" she asked.

"Yes," said Jim. "If he is the one who attacked you, he cannot get to you. And your parents and I will be with you. Nothing is going to happen to you, I promise."

"I want to see him," she said. "I'm not afraid. Take me back."

Her parents were not so sure, but Jim promised them that if he wasn't the monster she spoke of, they could talk to him and find out what a truly kind and gentle person he was.

They walked into the cell area.

"Jeremy," called Jim. "There are some people here to see you. Are you decent?"

"Yes," said Jeremy in his distorted voice. "Do they have to?"

"I'm afraid so," said Jim.

Jim was startled to see Martin in the cell next to Jeremy. The door was open, and Martin was working on papers and the remains of his breakfast.

"Have you been here all night?" asked Jim.

"Nope. Morey let me in around 6:00 AM. He called, needed to go to the diner, so I came over. You can tell me later where you were."

He went back to work.

Jim led Becky to the front of Jeremy's cell. His back was turned, but it was clear how his body was bent and twisted. He slowly turned around, showing the good left side of his face first. When his entire face came in to view, Becky gasped.

"Oh, you poor man! That must hurt something awful. I am so sorry that happened to you."

Jim was startled by her compassion. That was not something he had expected from a twelve-year-old.

"Is this the person who attacked you?" asked Jim.

"Oh no," the girl said. "The thing was green, scaly. It looked like a shriveled, rotting man. It was evil, and it had a huge mouth and huge teeth. And it was big!"

She suddenly wilted, right there in front of Jeremy.

"It lives in the pond near your house. I should have saved

them. Instead, I got you into trouble, and I don't even know you. I'm so, so sorry. I just want my friends back!" she wailed.

Jeremy moved to the bars.

"You will recover. I promise. And you will remember your friends as they were. I can still hear my mother's voice, and it's been years and years since she was killed. She still tells me what to do, how to take care of myself. You'll be okay."

Jeremy spoke with a clarity that startled them all. Even he seemed a bit surprised. Becky moved closer, shaking off her father's restraining hand. She touched the right side of his face, and Jeremy did not shrink.

"Does it still hurt?" she asked softly.

"Not really. Only when I try to talk or eat, and then just a little."

"Ask for Charity to visit you," she said. And turned and went back out to Jim's office.

Her parents followed.

"Can you please let him go now?" asked Becky. "He's terrified and anxious, and he's not the one."

Jim looked at her, trying to figure out the right answer. He decided on the truth. This girl would not accept less.

"I don't think so. Not yet. There are too many unanswered questions. He has things in his house that must be explained. If we can find the answers, then he can go home."

"Why not put one of those ankle thingies on him?" the girl said. "He's not going to leave anyway, but you could keep track of him that way."

"This isn't television," said Jim. "We don't have ankle tracers here. Maybe they do down at the capital, but not up here."

"Then get someone to stay with him," blurted Becky. "He's scared. He needs to be home, not here. You're going to make him worse until people think he's crazy. He needs to be home."

"How do you know all this, Becky?" asked her mother.

"I don't know. I just do. I touched him, and I *saw* how scared he is and how much he needs to be home."

"Okay," said Jim. "I want you to sit here and write out exactly what happened yesterday, starting with when you left your house. Do you think you can do that for me? You can use the computer if you want, or you can write it out on paper."

"The computer," she said. "I type faster than I write."

Becky opened a text document and started to type as Jim's cell rang.

It was Bull Harper. "Jim," he said. "We need you up at the mill."

"What's up, Bull?" replied Jim. "We're busy here."

"I have a feeling you're going to be a lot busier. We've got bodies—well, body parts—floating in the water south of the waterwheel. They aren't going anywhere because of the grate just beyond. But I figured I'd better leave the retrieval to you."

"We'll be right there. Don't touch anything. But Bull? Please take a video with your cell phone if you don't mind," said Jim.

Bull agreed.

Becky had finished her statement and was printing it out. *This was one tough young lady,* Jim thought. And no doubt Arthur or Dan would tell him she was one of the gifted. Jim didn't know what to think, so he wasted no brain power on the problem. Instead, he read her statement, and then asked her to sign and date it.

"I can't promise we will let Jeremy go home, but I will do what I can to make it happen. I can promise that."

Becky nodded, and left with her anxious parents. She wanted to go home, to take a pain pill, and to cry for her lost friends.

Jim drove out to the mill. He asked Linda to call Clay and have him and his team meet him there. He parked south of the waterwheel, which was still turning. Bull was waiting, along with a group of millworkers who were standing on the walkway, staring at the water. He saw that the media weren't up here. He would have to find and thank whoever had kept them in town. He was sure that hadn't happened by accident.

"Can the wheel be stopped?" asked Jim.

"Damn, I'm sorry I didn't think of that. It'll take about ten minutes. First, we have to stop the looms, and then we can put on the wheel brake. I'll be right back."

Stopping the wheel only took five minutes. During that time, Jim walked up to the railing and stared at the rushing water and the legs, torsos, and arms bobbing against the wire mesh.

"The wire mesh grate goes all the way across the river just south, over by that elm tree," said Bull, pointing to a tree leaning over the water fifteen feet south of where they stood. "It will stop the parts from washing on downriver."

Clay, the diver, and the CSIs arrived and pulled out their gear. The diver went over and looked at the wheel and the currents.

"With the wheel stopped, I think it's safe for me to go in," he said. "Give me one of those nets with the telescoping handle, will you?"

One of the CSIs brought over the net, while the diver put on his wet suit and a snorkel. He grabbed the net and jumped in. He swam south toward the grate, where he found the body parts and torsos. After netting them, he sent them toward the shore, where the CSI placed them in body bags.

It took almost two hours for the diver to retrieve all the body parts. Because of the grating north of the waterwheel, there was little in the way of garbage, tree limbs, or other materials to interfere with the retrieval. One of the torsos was badly ripped; the other two were reasonably intact. The arms and legs were ripped away, as were the heads. All three heads were found, along with three pairs of legs and arms.

"How soon do you think the state lab can let us have the bodies?" Jim asked. "These parents need to bury their kids. And the longer it drags out, the more they'll want to see them. We can't let them."

"I can try to speed it up," said Clay. "I'll send Helen down to Jefferson City along with Mike with the heads and torsos. I didn't tell you, but the conclusion by the autopsy docs down there for those four boys and Kavanaugh was death by drowning. Apparently, the lungs were full of water from the pond. I'm sure it will be the same for these three. I would guess maybe a week at the longest."

"Yeah, I got a copy of the report by fax," said Jim. "Oh, and so you know, St. Louis Post-Dispatch and CNN are both in town."

Clay cursed under his breath.

"I guess it was inevitable. Can you stall them? Tell them we'll hold a joint press conference tomorrow?"

"I can try."

"They had a field day with John Kavanaugh's death in St. Louis. Lots of sensational headlines about a mass murderer wandering the woods up here. I'm surprised you haven't been flooded with lookie-loos."

"We've had our share of tourists coming through, but mostly they end up at the Grossman Mill and Museum. We don't tell them where Harve's pond is, and it isn't marked on any map. They wander around for a while, shop at Mary's, and go home."

Jim watched as the CSIs loaded the remains into body bags. He signed the transfer papers and watched Carolyn and Mike head off in the van. The other guy stayed behind. He said he would be continuing to process Jeremy's house.

"Did you find anything of interest?" asked Jim.

"Nope. This guy is as neat freak as they come. Pathologically so, in my opinion. Not a trace of anything to be found except some animals he evidently stuffed. No tigers or anything."

Jim drove back to Jeremy's house, following Clay and the CSI. He entered the cabin, giving it a closer look this time. He was intrigued by Jeremy's workroom. There was a box of chipmunks, so lifelike Jim half expected them to jump out and run away. A work order in the box indicated they were to be shipped to the Smithsonian National Museum of Natural History.

"You gotta see this," said the tech. The name badge on his uniform said *Brockman*.

"What's your first name?" asked Jim.

"Franklin. Most people just call me Frank. Anyway, come in here. Maybe you can explain this."

He led Jim into the bedroom, where the drawers of a beautiful, aged wood dresser stood open. They were full of women's clothing, all neatly folded, with tissue paper between the folds on the larger pieces.

"Is he a cross-dresser, you think?"

"No," said Jim. "His mother's clothes, more likely. He got scarred up trying to save her."

"Thank God he didn't try to preserve her, too," Brockman laughed.

Jim looked at him. "She was burned to death in a car crash. Jeremy damn near died trying to get her out."

Brockman flushed and apologized.

"Anything else of interest you need to be showing me?" asked Jim.

"No," said Frank, obviously chastened. "Nothing. Like I said, neat as a pin. And no blood or tissue. I wonder what he does with the innards. Maybe tosses them in the pond?"

"I'll be sure to ask," said Jim, and turned and walked out. He wanted nothing to do with this man.

He went out front, where Blake and Clay stood talking by their patrol car.

"Just the man we wanted to see," said Blake. "Our boss wants us to stay up here with you, talk to Harve some more if Martin will let us, maybe talk to Jeremy, too. And be with you for the press conference tomorrow. You're gonna need crowd control, I'm fairly sure. Likely the whole town will be there."

"Yeah, I know. But the townspeople are good folks. I don't

anticipate trouble from them. Can you send Brockman back to St. Louis with the car, or wherever he belongs? I'll drive you both back down when you need to leave."

"We're gonna go down, drop him off, and pick up some fresh clothes and stuff. We'll be back later today, stay the night at The Rectory, and be fresh for the presser. You'll tell the parents?"

Jim nodded.

"Okay, then we'll see you back at about 4:00 PM, maybe 5:00 PM."

"Hold on, Blake," said Jim. "I need to ask you something."

They walked up to Harve's porch and sat for a minute.

"I don't know that I can just let Jeremy go," Jim finally said.

"You like him for this?" asked Blake.

"No, not for the murders. But maybe as an accomplice. I just don't know. Those animal heads in his workroom? Some of them are a match for descriptions given by Zak and their owners to pets that have gone missing. And Jeremy was talking kinda weird and crazy when we first picked him up."

"Crazy? As in upset, or psychotic?"

"A little of both," Jim said. "Linda said he was talking about something he called the Provider. She thinks he meant this person or thing provides him with his specimens. He said it demands food, like a voice in his head, and if he doesn't get it, usually sheep or deer which he puts into the pond, the voice gets louder and more demanding."

"That sounds like we need a psych exam before we let him go."

"My thinking, too. I don't even want to consider it, but I have to."

"What? The psych exam?"

"No. The possibility that Jeremy provided him with more than animals for food. That he had something to do with all these people getting killed. I mean, he couldn't have, could he? He's crippled up. We have a witness for this last group, the last three kids. And she says the monster she saw, the one that bit her, wasn't Jeremy."

"Jim, I think these people drowned, and then their bodies got ripped apart by that waterwheel. I don't think it's anything more than that. Maybe it's wishful thinking on my part that they drowned accidentally. Because if it isn't Harve or Jeremy, then who? Or what? Do you think we should get Becky to sit with a sketch artist? See if we can get a picture of this monster, and maybe somebody can identify it? Maybe there is a gator down there."

"We can try. She's a plucky little thing. Determined to solve the murder of her friends. Mentally strong for a twelve-year-old and smart, too. I'll ask her parents, and if they agree we have a surprisingly good artist in town here."

"Okay. See if you can get that done before the press conference. I'd like to have something to show those news hounds, send them off chasing monsters instead of bugging my people or your people, or the brothers."

"I'll have Linda put together a press packet, too. Pictures of the kids and Rory. I'm guessing they have lots of pictures of the judge. I'll have her throw in some stuff about the town, but no pictures of the pond or Harve and Jeremy's homes. Just information about the victims, and perhaps an address if people want to contribute to the burial and memorial funds."

"Good idea. As to your dilemma about Jeremy, I don't have any solid ideas. I guess you should talk to the state attorney. I know you don't like him. I don't care for him much, either. Come to think of it, though, don't you have a DA up here?"

Jim hit his head with his open hand.

"Damn, forgot completely. We do. He stepped aside when that whippersnapper came up from state for the bail hearing and arraignment. Mark Whitaker, been DA for a while. I forget because like Judge Cramer, he only comes when I call. I'll talk to him about it. You want me to let you know what he decides?"

"Not necessary. Would you please let Arthur know that Clay and I will be staying the night?"

"Sure thing. Travel safe and leave Brockman behind when you come back."

❋

Jim called Mark Whitaker before he left. Whitaker was fishing at the headwaters of the Martin's Way. He promised to finish up and meet Jim at the jail.

"I'm gonna want lunch," said Jim. "Do you want some brought over for you, too?"

"Only if it includes a piece of Maggie's pie." Whitaker laughed. "I think today's meatloaf day, so what could go wrong? I'll meet you there in about an hour."

It turned out lots could go wrong. When Jim turned on to Main Street, he encountered the CNN van, the *St. Louis Post-Dispatch* truck, an AP van, and someone from Reuters. In addition to their news vans, several reporters had driven up in their own cars, and Main Street was a madhouse.

Morey's was packed, with people waiting out front for lunch. Jim showed his badge and waded through the crowd. Once inside. he managed to catch Jen's eye. She hurried over.

"Are you going to be able to deal with all this?" asked Jim.

"With Maggie's secret weapon, you betcha."

"What's that?"

"Well, let's just say, don't eat the pie from the shelves on the counters. She's made her *go away* version, instead of the *stay here* kind you usually get."

Oh god, thought Jim, *in addition to fairy tale monsters in the pond, now we have magical pie? What's next? Leprechauns running the bank?*

"Okay. Make sure to send over some of the *stay here* kind then. Seriously, Mark Whitaker is joining me for lunch, and

Jeremy is still there. I'm going to need lunch for three. Can I send Harry over to pick it up in half an hour?"

"Sure thing, Jim. You don't need lunch for four?" She winked.

"Nothing I'd like better, but Mark and I have business to take care of. Linda and I will have dinner later. With any luck, these vultures will be gone by then. But I'm afraid they'll be back tomorrow, because there isn't going to be any press conference until then."

He made his way through the waiting customers and walked over to his office. Harry Randle had put up NO PARKING signs in front of the office and the courthouse. He also put some in front of the *Gazette* across the street. Jim reversed his steps and entered the newspaper office. Linda was hard at work at her computer, and two teenagers were busy folding large sheets of paper as they came off the two big printers in back.

"Hi, Jim. Meet Mitch and Debra. My new interns from the high school journalism club." Jim waved at the busy teens and then focused on Linda.

"I need a favor if you don't mind. We're having a press conference tomorrow morning. I need packets for the press, names of the kids, ages, pictures. And something nice about Rory. Mary can fill you in on all the details, but I know he had a Purple Heart and a Silver Star. Maybe more, I don't know. I know it's last minute, but if you can, we need probably twenty packets."

"I'll get interns to help out," replied Linda. "We'll get it done. Don't worry. We have most of the information on the kids here already, since they were either graduating from high school or middle school. I have nice pictures of them, and one of the older kids can get additional information from John Grayson."

"Who?"

"Oh, the principal. New this last year. You didn't meet him?"

"Right. I forgot. I feel like my mind is going sixteen ways from breakfast. And to think I moved here for the peace and quiet."

Linda moved closer and spoke quietly.

"Would you like to come over again tonight? It might be nice to have dinner, just the two of us. I do know how to cook, and even though Maggie's serving the *go away* pie along with the *you don't like it here* meatloaf to the unwelcome hordes, there will be a lot of them wanting to stay over. Arthur's already full up."

"Damn," said Jim. "I forgot. I should have called him right away."

"Oh, don't worry. He's holding Clay's and Blake's rooms." Jim stared at her.

"Jim Burke, have I grown an extra eyebrow or something?"

"No, it's just ... how the ... oh, never mind, I'm just going to have to get used to you people and your ability to know everything before I even say anything. And I know you'll tell me it's common sense. And you may be right. But I like being a little mystified. You're all an enigma wrapped in a mystery, as some wise person once said. I'll be at your place around 6:00 PM if that's okay."

"It is. And I found a new toothbrush." She laughed. "But no underwear, so it's BYOB."

Jim hurried across the street. BYOB? Oh, boxers. He blushed bright red and waited for his pulse to slow before entering his office. Mark had already arrived, so Jim sent Harry over to fetch their lunch along with Jeremy's. He sat at the desk, Mark on the other side absorbed in a book. He put it down, leaned back, and regarded Jim intently.

"I wondered when you were going to remember me," he said. "Not that I mind. Shoulda retired a couple of years back, but since Middlewood County is mostly just Harper's Landing, I figured there wouldn't be much work taking me away from fishing. Bob Cramer and I were out on a boat when you called. Bob decided to stay. He figures he'll be called in soon enough; that is, if he's needed."

Jim steepled his fingers, leaned forward, and thought.

"I have a problem. Oh heck, a whole basket of problems. But the one on the table here is whether to let Jeremy in there go. And that's where you come in. We're supposed to be on the same side, you and me. But I admit to a fondness for Jeremy, and my inclination is to believe that he is not involved in this business, at least not in any criminal way. Let me lay it out for you."

Jim told him everything: the twins, the accident, Jeremy's skill with taxidermy, his disfigurement, his extreme OCD, and his current obsession with the Provider.

"I thought he was just rattled, or maybe not quite right in the head," said Jim. "Now, I'm inclined to think there is something or someone providing him with specimens for his taxidermy. The question is: who or what is this Provider he talks about? And is that same entity bringing him specimens for his taxidermy business? And is Jeremy holding back on us, not identifying the Provider? He says he doesn't know what it is, just that he talks to it in his head. We need to get Martin's permission to question Jeremy in detail about this. Everything I know so far has been from other people telling me what Jeremy has said. I want to hear it straight from him."

Mark thought for a while. Harry, meanwhile, arrived with their lunch, which Jim helped spread out on the desktop. Harry took Jeremy's lunch to him. Jim noticed that Harry had lunch for himself and figured he was planning to join Jeremy.

"I think," said Mark, "I'm going to ask Bob for a seventy-two-hour psych hold and evaluation."

Jim started to object, but Mark stopped him.

"Think about it, Jim. Even if you and I and the whole town think Jeremy's perfectly sane, the state attorney is going to raise hell if he finds out about this and discovers we didn't get an evaluation. And there's no one here who can do it. We need to take him to St. Louis and have it done there. I'll talk to Bob, arrange to have Harve go with him if he can. And we'll get Martin to explain it to Jeremy, so he doesn't go all apeshit on us."

Jim knew it was the logical and correct action. He just didn't like it. But it did have the virtue of getting Jeremy out of town and away from the prying eyes of the news vultures.

"Can you get Judge Cramer here quickly?" he asked. "I'll call Martin and Harve and get them to come over. Tell the judge to use the back door to the courthouse. We'll take Jeremy out back and into the back of the courthouse. God help us if any of the press see him."

Mark called Judge Cramer, while Jim contacted Martin. The lawyer said he would be right over. Jim then called Harve and briefly explained the situation. Harve also said he would come right away. Jim cautioned him to come in by First Street, not Main, and go to the back.

Mark, meanwhile, was quickly drafting a motion for a seventy-two hour hold and observation. Jim showed him the computer and turned on the printer.

The hearing took twenty minutes. Martin had explained the situation to Jeremy, who at first was extremely upset and agitated. However, the judge agreed to allow Harve to accompany Jeremy to St. Louis, which calmed the poor man considerably. Harve hastily drove to his house and gathered up clothing for himself and Jeremy, as well as a picture of their mother for Jeremy. Within three hours of Mark and Jim's initial conversation, Mark, Harve, and Jeremy were headed for the St. Louis University Hospital, admission orders in hand. Judge Cramer called ahead and faxed the order for a seventy-two hour hold to the hospital. He told the head of the Mental Health Department that DA Whitaker would provide them with all the details.

It was late afternoon, and Jim was in no mood to face the news folks, or much of anyone else, for that matter. He closed and locked his office, told Harry to take the rest of the day off, and headed for Arthur's. On the way there, he activated his Bluetooth and asked Arthur to call the parents of the missing children and have them meet him at The Rectory library.

CHAPTER FIFTY-FIVE

J im found the gang of five in the library pouring over documents. He saw Arthur in his office, and with a brief nod for the others, he headed back there.

"Scotch or bourbon?" asked Arthur.

"Shows, does it?"

"Oh, yeah. You've been through a ringer, no doubt about it. And I don't think it's going to end anytime soon. Or at least not as soon as we'd like."

"I'll take bourbon," said Jim. "And quiet. No disrespect intended. I don't want to talk for a while. Let those birds out there do the talking."

The windows were open; the birds chattered and chirped in the trees and bushes. Several small ones were gathered at the large feeder Arthur had mounted outside his study window. Four or five hummingbirds vied for spots at the three feeders. It was peaceful and calming. Jim slowly began to unwind. He had a second bourbon, poured by Arthur without even asking.

Reluctantly, he told the five researchers to put away their things and go home for the day.

"We have some parents coming. In fact, they are pulling into the drive now. It isn't going to be pretty."

To his great surprise, they all wanted to stay. He realized this was the community activating again, as it had when the four boys died. He accepted their offer, knowing the parents would need comfort. He dreaded what he had to tell them.

When all three sets of parents were seated, Jim faced them, wondering how to start. He knew he couldn't tell them about the scene at the mill. At least he could spare them that horror.

"We believe we have found your children," he said. "I would like each of you to write down what they were wearing when they left home."

"They're dead, aren't they?" asked Lonnie Camby.

"Nothing is official until the State Medical Examiner has done his work," said Jim, "but yes, I think so."

All six parents collapsed in various states of grief or disbelief. Finally, Lonnie spoke up again.

"Were they murdered? Assaulted?"

"I suspect they drowned," replied Jim. "Like the other kids and that judge. I'm so sorry. I wish I could say something definitive, but honestly, we won't know for several days. I will let you know as soon as we have answers. But right now, I don't think it was murder."

The parents all had questions, most of which Jim could not answer. He was surprised none of them were angry. He was angry with himself, for not having thought to fence off that damned pond. Or post a guard. Or something.

Gradually, the parents calmed enough to be able to drive home. Lonnie invited them all to his house, where there was still plenty of food from that first night after their kids had gone missing. The other parents agreed.

Jim wanted nothing more than another drink. But he needed to drive. He glanced at his watch and realized he had just enough time to get to Linda's home by six. He thanked Arthur and headed out the door. He was looking forward to a quiet evening of conversation, good food, and other intimacies.

Linda had a small, two-bedroom cottage three blocks from the

Gazette offices. It featured a large, screened porch, beautiful flower gardens presently filled with roses and begonias, and boxwoods around the skirting.

The house smelled amazing when he arrived. She had prepared a leg of lamb, along with baby potatoes, freshly picked peas from her small garden, and a green salad. The pie was obviously from Maggie, but that was fine with him. Linda provided a lovely white wine which she admitted to making herself from the pear orchard up by Charity's cottage. It was more mead than wine, and Jim knew he would have to go easy on it in case he was called out on an emergency. He was strongly tempted to turn off his cell phone, but with all the people in town, including the news folks who insisted on sleeping in their production vans, he erred on the side of availability.

After dinner, they moved into her comfortable front room. Linda showed him the press packets she and her interns had prepared. They were remarkably professional-looking, with pictures of each victim, along with their age, their activities, honors, etc. They had even included John Kavanaugh. Survivors were also listed. A map of the area was provided, and Jim was pleased to note that although Big Bass Pool was marked on it, Harve's pond was not. The Grossman Textile Mill and Museum was featured prominently, as was Mary Harper's quilt shop, as co-sponsors of the memorial fund for the victims' families. The address for the fund as well as the bank's routing number and the account number for the fund were included. They had prepared twenty-five packets, which would likely be enough.

"Would you mind if I give you a bit of a trim?" asked Linda. "I went to beauty school before I got married, and you're looking a little shaggy around the edges. You should look professional for tomorrow's press conference."

Jim readily consented. Beth used to trim his hair, in between barber shop visits, and Jim found he still enjoyed the intimacy of getting a trim from a beautiful woman. He promised himself he would shave in the morning as soon as he got to his office.

As if she had read his mind, Linda said, "I have an unopened razor in the bathroom closet. I couldn't bring myself to throw it away after ..." She let the sentence trail off.

In anticipation of many more happy evenings, Jim had dropped off a small bag of deodorant and other personal items earlier in the day, which he now retrieved from her back stoop.

"Do you mind if I stay again?" he asked.

"I thought you'd never ask," she replied.

CHAPTER FIFTY-SIX

The next morning, Jim arrived at his office early and found Jen waiting with breakfast.

He realized to his chagrin he hadn't told her or Morey about Jeremy and the others going to St. Louis. She had a grin on her face.

"Might as well call her and tell her to come over here for her breakfast," she said. "Thanks to you, there's plenty available."

"I'm sorry," said Jim. "Too much going on. I'll make it up to you."

"Oh, stop it," said Jen. "You get Linda over here, and I'll call Dan, and we'll have some social time before the shenanigans start."

Breakfast was a noisy affair, with lots of laughter. It was the perfect antidote to the horror of the last few days. They cleared their dishes and packed up the basket. Dan and Jen headed for the diner to drop it off. They were looking forward to a day of reading and research at The Rectory. Jim and Linda picked up the press packets and walked next door to the courthouse.

Blake Meadows and Clay Murdoch were there already, along with the state public information officer. Lonnie Camby usually handled A/V stuff for the city, but today Morey had left the diner as soon as breakfast was done and set up the microphone and dais himself. The CNN guys had set up cameras and their own sound equipment. The AP reporter had a still photographer with him, and the *St. Louis Post-Dispatch* reporter was taking his own pictures.

It looked like the whole town had turned out for the press conference. Jim decided to take charge, strode to the dais, and tapped on the microphone.

"Good morning," he said. "We are going to make this short. I'll be making a statement, then the state folks here can fill you in on what they've learned at their labs. We'll take questions after that, so please hold your horses until we're done." He paused.

"On June sixteenth, Rory O'Connor went missing after doing some work at the Jenkins Farm. His remains were found a few days later, by Big Bass Pool on the Martin's Way River. DNA testing has confirmed that the remains were Rory's. As you will see from the press packets Ms. Collier and her interns are handing out, Rory was a highly decorated Afghan war veteran. He will be greatly missed.

"On or about June twenty-third, Gary Miller, Billy Martin, Steve Blinder, and Mike Stoneman went missing after they went swimming in a private pond. To protect the owners, we are not providing the name or location of the pond. A few days later, the remains of all four boys were found. Again, DNA testing at the state lab in Jefferson City confirmed their identities.

"On July sixth, Judge John Kavanaugh, who was here on vacation with his wife, Susan, went fishing first at Big Bass Pool and then at another location. He also went missing, and his remains were found the following day."

The crowd began to murmur. Many of the townsfolk, especially those who lived up on Jackson Hill, hadn't known there were so many victims. Linda's interns were scribbling furiously, trying to keep up with all the information.

"Two days ago, DeAnna Camby, Benny Jackson, Jim Barton, and Becky Sloan went to the location where the four high school boys drowned. Three of them also went missing, with Becky Sloan being the only survivor. The other three bodies were recovered and have been identified via DNA testing.

"Although there are as yet no official results for the last three victims, it has been determined that the others died of drowning. It is presumed the last three also drowned. At this time, it has not been determined if the drownings were accidental. The state information officer will address that issue in her comments.

"While I can confirm that all the bodies were mutilated, we do know that for the previous victims, the mutilations were post-mortem. We presume this will also be the case with the last three; however, in deference to the families and close friends of the victims, we will not be going into detail on the nature of the mutilations.

"At present, we do not have a suspect in custody. This is an ongoing investigation, so we will not be providing details on locations where bodies were recovered, or, for that matter, where they went missing. Now, I'm going to turn things over to the state public information officer."

Jim left the dais. He was emotionally and physically drained. He did not want to answer questions. He did not want to listen to the details of the lab findings all over again. He wanted to go sit in Linda's office, eat pie, and drink coffee, and give in to the deep, painful pool of mourning that had been forming in his chest for the past three days.

"Blake? Can you and Clay handle this? I need to do something."

Blake looked at Jim closely. It was apparent the man was stretched thin.

"Go. I'll answer their questions. And don't worry. Nobody's going to tell them about Harve or Jeremy."

Jim almost hugged him in relief. He slipped away from the crowd and ducked into the *Gazette*. Linda was waiting.

"Come on," she said. "The kids will keep things open. You and I are going out the back and up to The Rectory. No one will see us."

The late morning sun had warmed the room nicely. It wasn't yet unpleasant, though it would be later when the full force of the western sun hit the windows. For now, they could leave them open, enjoying the sounds of the birds and the scent of the flowers.

Ben was hard at work transferring his findings from the chalkboard to paper. Jim was surprised to see that he had been able to complete the family tree for both Yuri's and Maria's families, finding where they overlapped and where they split again. It was obvious that most of the long-term residents of Harper's Landing were related to one another.

Dan, Charity, and Bridgette were reading diaries. Dan was writing down information from the Ukrainian ones, while Bridgette and Charity were making notes from the English diaries. Occasionally, they would compare their findings. It was apparent from the snatches of conversation Jim overheard that they were focused on finding a way to deal with the *bolotnik*.

Arthur was absorbed in a large leather-bound book covered with ornate drawings and symbols. Jim and Linda were content to sit in the sun and sip coffee. It was good to be quiet.

Jim felt overwhelmed. It wasn't just that he thought he had left murder and mayhem behind when he left the big city. He was enough of a realist to know that bad people are everywhere, and some of the worst dwelt in the tranquil byways of the country. It was his reawakened libido, accompanied by an unavoidable sense of rightness about himself and Linda. He thought he should feel a sense of betrayal. Hadn't his vows to Beth been forever? He wondered what Beth would think of Linda.

"She would like her," said Arthur quietly.

Jim nearly jumped out of his chair. He looked around wildly. Linda had left the room. Arthur was looking at him with a small, quiet smile on his lips. He moved over to the chair Linda had abandoned.

"Beth would want you to be happy," he said. "And you, of all people, deserve it. You are a good and decent man, and a caring one. You cannot carry the world alone on those shoulders, no matter how broad. That is what a good partner does: shares the burden."

"Aw, hell," said Jim. "I won't even ask how you knew what I was thinking. I'll just agree. You're right; it's what she would have wanted, and I think they would have liked each other a lot. And yet they're not anything alike."

"You've moved on, grown, since Beth's death. Your grief has changed you in a thousand little ways. Mourning does that. Linda is what you are ready for now, and the universe made sure you'd meet."

"You really believe that don't you?"

"Yes, I really believe that."

"So do I," said Linda's warm, lovely voice behind him. "When this is all over, Jim, and it will be, we will have all the time in the world to talk this out. For now, let me help you carry the burden. We have children to bury and families to comfort."

Jim decided to take the path of least resistance. He needed a break, a recharge, and he would take all the help he could get.

"Can we have lunch up here? I don't think I can face that bunch. I like the media, and they do a good, professional job most of the time. I know that Clay and Blake and that PR lady will give them all the meat they can, and I'm confident they'll protect the families and Harve's property. I can't guarantee they won't tell them about the twins, but I can hope."

Arthur made a quick phone call. An hour later, Jen popped her head into the library. Jim hadn't even realized she had left.

"Lunch is served in the dining room. Everyone, come eat."

Platters of fruit, cheese, and fresh baked bread lined the long table. There was freshly churned butter, homemade jam, and squeeze bottles of honey, as well as a large roast beef with a knife for carving. Freshly cut tomato slices were piled up on separate plates, along with leaves of lettuce still wet from washing. There was also pie, but Jim was surprised to see that it was cherry rather than apple.

"Maggie used up all the apples for the *go away* pies," said Jen, noticing his look. "This is her *we love you* cherry pie. It's for special occasions, like weddings and funerals. She's making hand pies of it for next Monday."

Once lunch was completed, the conversation turned to Monday's funeral. Linda had gone to her office and then to Jim's office, where she found the fax from the State Medical Examiner's office. The fax stated that the cause of death was drowning, and that the dismemberment was post-mortem, consistent with the damage one might expect from a waterwheel. The medical examiner promised to release the bodies for transport to Harper's Landing by Friday, three days from now. Linda showed the faxes to Jim as soon as she returned to The Rectory. He read them to the group after lunch.

The parents had opted for one service for all three youngsters. As they had done with Rory's and the service for the boys, the town would supply the flowers. Arthur predicted the church would be filled to overflowing with wreaths and bouquets. Jim hadn't asked before, but now inquired who built the pine boxes.

"Several of the men from the mill," said Charity. "We have a large stack of pine boards up at the Grove for the purpose. We are going to have to renew the stack soon."

"I will order some when I go down to St. Louis to pack up my office," said Dan.

At Jim's inquiring look, Dan said, "There's no need for me to stay there to finish my doctorate. I'm ABD, so I don't need to teach classes anymore."

"ABD?"

"All but dissertation. Many never get beyond that point. It's easy to get caught up in teaching and other things, and never complete the degree. But I must. I want to, also. But part of my visa requirement is that I finish my Ph.D."

"Will you have to leave when that's done?"

"If I stay and teach, I can get a permanent green card when my student visa is up, and I've just been told the high school history teacher is going to leave after this next school year is finished. If I can finish the dissertation by then, and if the Harper's Landing School Board will have me, then I can get permanent resident status."

"And there may be other reasons for staying here, too," said Jen. She smiled shyly at him, a slight tinge of red touching her cheeks.

"Well, yes, there is that."

Jim wondered if Maggie added something else to the pies, other than *please stay*?

"Arthur," said Charity. "Have the parents said what service they want?"

"Traditional Christian," he replied. "But without the hellfire and brimstone that ole JB used to deliver. I'm going to stick with the tried and true: Lord is My Shepherd, singing 'Amazing Grace.' Comforting, no promises made you can't keep, and focus on community and love."

Jim looked around the table. *What good fortune had brought him to this place?* he wondered. Arthur, fine and gentle and intelligent; Jen, earthy like her mother and full of humor and grace; Ben, now that he was sober, generous with his time and labor; Charity, a puzzle to him but always cheerful and a good steward for the orchards.

Then there was Linda. He had never thought to find love again, and yet there it was, staring him in the face. And Dan apparently was finding love here, also. Come to think of it, he had yet to meet a single person in this town who wasn't basically good and kind, with the exception of Gary's father. It was for that reason he was leaning more and more toward the mutated animal idea and less toward the mass murderer option.

But how to prove it? Or solve the murders? That was the big question, and for now he had no answers. It was Thursday, and there were three children who needed burying in just four days. He needed to ask Blake and Clay to bring up the remains by Monday morning. He picked up his cell.

CHAPTER FIFTY-SEVEN

S aul Grossman closed the mill for the day on Monday, as he had for the funeral for the boys earlier in the month. He also provided a generous donation to the memorial fund for the families, as did Mary and Bull Harper. All the stores were again closed, and Morey's Diner closed immediately after breakfast. Maggie and Jen had worked until late in the night making food for after the service. The two of them changed clothes and joined the rest of the town in the ancient church.

The sun shone brightly on the large stained-glass windows, lending a soft glow to the entire interior. Arthur chose not to turn on any lights, instead lighting two large banks of white candles on either side of the small altar. Three white pine caskets sat on biers in the front. Soft flute music filled the sanctuary. It was so much better than organ music. Once everyone was seated, from high up in the balcony a lone piper played "Amazing Grace." After he finished one verse, the congregation joined in singing the ancient and powerful song.

Arthur rose when they were done and read Psalm 23.

"The Lord is my shepherd; I shall not want."

Again, the congregation joined in.

At the parents' request, no one spoke at this rite. Instead,

Arthur invited them to sit in silence as the lone flute played, recalling these three lovely children and the joy their brief lives had brought to the community. Shortly into the silent period, Becky Sloan left quietly by a side door. Unable to control her tears, she sat under a tree and sobbed. She knew she couldn't have saved them, but she was still wracked with guilt and sorrow. And her arm hurt terribly. Charity slipped out and sat next to her. She pulled a small tin from her bag, unwrapped the girl's arm, and gently covered the healing wound with some of the salve in the tin. She replaced the wrapping, and the two sat quietly, Becky's head on Charity's shoulder.

The three caskets were borne by several men who worked at the mill with the children's parents. They were laid in the newly dug graves up behind the church. Several friends and relatives dropped flowers, candy, and other mementos into the graves. The parents of each child put the first shovel of dirt in and then stood and watched as the congregants filled the graves, shovel by shovel.

As he had at the funeral for the boys, Arthur gave each pair of parents a small bag of herbs, speaking with them privately.

Jim stood at the edge of the gathering, wondering how much loss this community could bear. He knew he couldn't stand any more. He wanted hope, future, a tomorrow. The sound of each shovel of dirt was a silenced bell, a thud of finality rather than a gong of welcome. Each death had been a reminder of Beth, of his loss. He wanted no more of it. He vowed then and there that they would do whatever it would take to rid this town of the evil that had come here. It would not be made to leave; it would not be made unwelcome. No, he and Arthur and the others would destroy it. This he vowed, an unspoken promise to the living and the dead. Whether it was human, a serial killer yet unfound, or something more sinister, it would be destroyed forever.

CHAPTER FIFTY-EIGHT

Two weeks had passed since the funeral. The news vans were gone. The state police no longer swarmed over Harve's and Jeremy's homes and land. Jeremy had been released after his seventy-two-hour hold. Harve and the doctors had tried to persuade him to voluntarily stay, to get some help with his overwhelming guilt that drove him deeper and deeper into the clutches of OCD. But he refused. He returned to his little cabin and sent off the chipmunks just in time to fulfill the order.

Ben had been taking care of Harve's clients and his gardens around his house. Harve hired Ben full-time upon his return, and they were busy making plans for a garden at the school. Ben had also drawn up plans for a much larger vegetable garden for Morey and Maggie. They had approved, and the two men would prepare the beds and mulch them for the winter sometime in September.

August arrived with a blast of heat, and harvest time would soon start. Charity's apple orchard was nearly ready to pick, and Maggie and Morey had hired a team of men from Harwood to come over and enlarge the fruit cellar. Maggie and Jen drove to St. Louis and picked up all the supplies and ingredients for canning applesauce. They would also freeze a considerable quantity of apples and cherries for year-round pie making.

Despite the unsolved deaths of eight of their residents and one visitor, Harper's Landing was settling back into its quiet, friendly pace. Even Jim had relaxed. He and Linda were having dinner together regularly, and someone declared they had spotted Jim in the jewelry section of Wally World over in Harwood a week ago. When questioned at Morey's, Jim neither confirmed nor denied.

Early on the morning of August fourth, Jim's cell rang. He answered and was dismayed to hear Harve's anxious voice.

"Jim, can you please come out here as soon as possible?"

"Please tell me it's not more dead bodies."

"Oh, no. Sorry. Nothing like that. But I'm worried about Jeremy, and myself. I can't explain it. I want to see if you feel it, too."

"Okay if I bring Linda and Arthur? We were going to have breakfast. And can it wait until we do, or do I need to come now?"

"Have breakfast for sure and bring them. Bring the whole bunch if you want. You know who I mean."

Jim did. He rolled out of bed, shook Linda gently, and padded into the loo. He then went to the kitchen and started the coffee. They were both partial to an early cup before breakfast. She appeared in the doorway, wrapped in a robe, still sleepy-eyed.

"You promised we were going to sleep in," she teased. "Who was on the phone?"

"Harve. He wants us to come out there right after breakfast."

"Oh, no. Not another."

"He says not. Says he's worried about Jeremy, and himself, whatever that means. Guess we'll find out soon enough."

They ate breakfast at Morey's, enjoying the company of their friends and neighbors, as well as the relative calm after so many days of chaos. Arthur and Dan came to the diner, too, and Jim filled them in on his early morning wake-up call.

"Why don't you and Linda go in your car?" asked Dan. "Charity, Arthur, and I will ride in mine. Jen has chores to do here, I'm told."

"She'd better, if she wants to keep her job," yelled Maggie

from the kitchen. She followed it with a wink and a quick hug for
Jen. As they got up to leave, Maggie came out with a bag of
cinnamon rolls. "Jeremy loves them; so does Harve. Treat's
on me."

Harve's work truck was still parked in his drive when they arrived.
He, Jeremy, and Ben all stood twenty feet from the pond, staring
at the water. Harve and Ben were scratching their heads vigorously. Jeremy had his hands clapped over his ears and was slightly
bent over. When Jim stepped out of his car, a buzzing sound
flared inside of his head, followed by the sensation of ants
crawling in his brain. He resisted the urge to scratch. Linda, on
the other hand, appeared to be in pain. Like Jeremy, she had her
hands over her ears and finally got back into the Explorer and
closed the doors and windows.

Arthur, Charity, and Dan arrived next, and their reaction was
like Linda's. Arthur stepped forward, shouted a few foreign
words, and again covered his ears. Dan was next, and when he
shouted words which Jim recognized as completely different from
Arthur's, the buzzing and itching in his head went away. He noted
that Jeremy took his hands away and stood up. Arthur and Dan
looked relieved, and Linda tentatively stuck her head out the
window and then got out of the car.

"What in the seven Hells was that?" asked Linda.

"The Provider," said Jeremy. "It is angry and hungry."

"Yes, Jim," said Dan, seeing Jim's sidelong look. "The
Provider, as Jeremy calls him, is real. You experienced its commu-
nication as discomfort, probably like something crawling in your
head?"

"Like a gazillion ants on my brain," said Jim. "It will be way
too soon if I ever feel that again. How did you make it stop?"

"I told it, in its native language, that we would feed it."

"*What?* Over my dead body you will."

"Whoa, Jim," said Arthur. "It prefers sheep or deer. One of my congregants dropped off a roadkill deer. I'll go get it, bring it back. You all wait here."

Arthur left before Jim could say anything more. Instead, he looked at Jeremy. He seemed different, somehow. He was more relaxed, which could be expected after a hospital stay with good food and better drugs. But there was something else. Then it dawned on him. Jeremy's face looked better. The scars on the right side of his face were less shiny and seemed looser. But how could that be? He hadn't been treated for his physical deformities in St. Louis. He remembered that Becky Sloan had touched him right at the spot where he seemed improved. *No,* he thought, *I'm imagining things.*

Harve was standing to one side, and Jim realized he was trying to get his attention. He walked over and sat on a stone bench next to him. Harve was alternately eyeing Jim and staring at Jeremy.

"He's better," he finally said. "Not just in the head, though that, too. But look at his face."

"Did they did treat him there?"

"No. He wouldn't let them. And he refused mental health care, too. First thing after he got home, he asked me to get Charity to come see him. She's been coming here every day, bringing him salve. And he's getting better."

Jim remembered Becky's last words to Jeremy: "Get Charity to come see you." He vowed to examine this further, but Arthur had returned with the deer, and it was time to see if they could find out just what this Provider was.

Arthur and Dan carried the deer to the edge of the pond, while Jim held his pistol cocked and ready, pointed at the pond. Linda had her video recorder running on her cell phone, and Ben, Harve, Charity, and Jeremy stood back twenty feet, away from possible trouble. Dan pushed the deer out toward the center of the pond, and again he spoke loudly in Ukrainian. He explained later that he had invited the *bolotnik* to come to dinner.

Suddenly bubbles appeared at the center of the pond, waves

rippled out toward the edges, and a large, vaguely humanoid figure appeared, swimming toward them. It was greyish-green, scaly, and hideous. It seized the deer, and as quickly as it had appeared it was gone, leaving only a few ripples behind. Jim realized it fit Becky Sloan's description. He stared, open-mouthed. Linda gasped and stepped back even further, as did Ben. Harve and Jeremy looked relieved. Arthur, Charity, and Dan all said *Bolotnik!* the moment they saw it.

"That will keep him quiet for a while," said Dan.

"Have you folks found any answers about containing or eliminating him?" asked Arthur.

"Nothing," replied Dan. "Everything our ancestors tried merely put him to sleep for a year or so. And that not reliably."

"Hold on," said Jim. "I'm not denying that those folks thought they brought something over with them. But what if they didn't? What if this is a mutation? I mean, there's that nuclear plant over between St. Louis and Jefferson City. What if stuff got into the underground water and affected one of the critters that live under there?"

"That's possible," said Arthur. "But from all I know of Slavic elementals, plus what Dan has told us, that was definitely a *bolotnik.*"

"Then let me put it differently," responded Jim. "If you guys haven't come up with something that is effective against this thing, we're going to have to have help. We can't have a murdering thing, whatever it is, slithering around in the waters, ponds, and wells of this area. And it's going to be hard enough persuading the state authorities that we have a mutation. I couldn't even begin to persuade them it's an ancient Slavic elemental."

"He's got a point," was all Dan said.

Linda called Jeremy, Ben, and Harve over. "Jeremy," she said, "was that your Provider?"

"I don't know. I've never seen it. But I think so. It sounded like him."

"Why do you call it the Provider?"

"Because when it first started calling me, asking for food, I would push animals into the pond and the next day he would bring me really nice specimens for my taxidermy. It's hard for me to catch my own. I'm not good at trapping, can't shoot well, and don't go far from my cabin. It hurts to walk. I was grateful. Until the heads, that is."

"If we come back up here tomorrow morning, before you go out back, and we look on your back porch, are we going to find a gift?" asked Jim.

"I don't know," said Jeremy, "but I hope so. Because that will mean I'm not crazy, that it really is the Provider. And maybe if we can kill it or something, no one else will have to die. I will find other ways to get specimens. I have good work habits. Good work requires good work habits. Mother always told me that."

He started to cry.

"It wasn't my fault. I know it wasn't my fault. But I still hear her; I can still smell her. If I follow her rules, if I keep things clean and neat and tidy, and always have good work habits, she will always be with me."

Arthur put an arm around the man, and he and Charity led him back to his house. The two of them went inside, and Arthur firmly closed the door.

The rest stood in an awkward silence, not looking at each other. Harve finally broke the silence.

"You know, parents try hard not to have favorites. But me and Jeremy always knew I was Dad's favorite, and he was Mom's. They had a special bond. He was always an artist, and so was Mom. Dad wanted him to be like me, to like the dirt and hunting and fishing. But he had soul, and Mom saw that. I thought he was going to die that first year, not just because he was hurt so bad, but because I thought his heart would break.

"And then, when I discovered he had kept Mom's things, I didn't stop him. I kept a couple of Dad's things: his rifle, his fishing stuff. But Jeremy kept, well, you know, you went through his house. I thought it would help him.

"Then he started being so neat. That's not me. I'm not a slob, but he was, you know. I moved him out back, after we got great-grandfather's cabin cleaned up. And he's been there ever since. He's world-famous, even if no one knows his name."

"Perhaps it is time to change that," said Linda. "Maybe you should start selling his artworks under his own name. He may never be able to appear in person, or have his picture taken, but he should start getting credit."

"I'll talk to him about it," said Harve. "I think you're right."

Jim had been standing on the porch, staring at the pond. "I think we should come back tomorrow morning," he said. "And if we find the specimens, and I think we will, then I think we should bring the state police up to help."

He held up his hand as the others started to protest.

"Not to get these guys into any more trouble. To show the state folks that we have a mutation up here, a killer in the waters that must be trapped and probably killed."

"How do you propose we show them?" asked Dan.

"Same way you showed us today. We wait a day or two, until it's hungry, and feed it, with them all here. We show them the video Linda took, and then we show them the real thing."

"That would work for me," said Ben. "I don't need no more convincing."

"One thing I gotta ask," said Jim, "and I can't believe I'm asking this. If this is a *bolotnik*, didn't you say that they were elementals?"

"Yes," replied Dan. "Minor elementals, but this one has grown huge, probably because of being out of its usual habitat."

"Does that mean it's immortal? Or can we kill it?"

"Any magical creature can be killed. Some just take more than others. This one is so distorted from what it used to be; I suspect it might be more vulnerable. I could be wrong, though. It could be stronger. There is no way to tell."

"And there's nothing in any of your books about destroying or getting rid of a *bolotnik?*"

"Not really. They're amphibious if I'm reading the descriptions correctly. But a lot of the Slavic folk history is oral history. Which means much of it is lost with modernization or suppressed by the Church and governments. That's why these diaries and papers we found at Charity's place are so valuable. They tell the history of the Ukrainians who settled this area, but they also talk about the rituals, practices, and beliefs of non-Christian Ukrainians who came here to escape religious persecution."

"But not how to rid ourselves of a monster," said Charity. She had left Jeremy's house and stood with the rest of them, staring at the pond.

"Let's go back to the library," she said. "Arthur will be along shortly. Harve? I think you should go be with your brother. Once he's settled, can you get us a deer? Or should I send a couple of the men out to get me one?"

Harve said he would go hunting, but not until the next day, and only if there were gifts on Jeremy's porch in the morning.

The rest of the day was spent in the library. Linda stopped at the *Gazette* long enough to hand out assignments to her eager interns and to read their latest articles. She found them refreshing and thorough. Because they wrote so well and so much, she decided to start printing the *Gazette* daily and had one of the older interns drive over to Harwood to see if the Wally World would carry it in their newspaper racks. The manager was happy, almost eager, to do so.

Linda was delighted with the work the kids had done. *I wonder if we could set up a fund to provide scholarships for kids like these,* she wondered. *We need to support these young people, more than we have in the past. I want them to stay; to come back here after they get an education. We will need them when we grow. Harper's Landing will not always be this small.*

Linda wanted to get her hands on some of the legal documents: wills, deeds, etc., that were found along with the diaries. Now that Ben had completed his family trees and was absorbed in transferring the information to his laptop and to paper, she wanted to use her training in documentation to figure out who owned what land and how it had been passed down from family to family. But first, she wanted to get someone to help her with the boxes of old town records, currently stored in the basement of the *Gazette* offices. She left a note for the interns who would come in the following morning, asking them to bring the boxes upstairs. She would come later in the day and help sort through them.

Jen finished her work at the diner and joined the others at The Rectory library. Dan was absorbed in reading the diaries written in Ukrainian, while Bridgette and Charity were making copious notes about the other diaries. Linda began sorting the birth and death certificates, marriage licenses, deeds, and wills by date. Arthur sat in his study, writing Sunday's sermon, while Jim was content to sit in a wingback chair by the window, absorbed in a new Harlan Coben novel.

It was a necessary respite from the nightmares of the past couple of months. Harper's Landing had enjoyed years of quiet, removed from the busy life of the city, rarely invaded by tourists except when Mary Harper held one of her famous quilter retreats or an avid fisherman heard about the great fishing. And even then, the people who came were easygoing and comfortable. It seemed unimaginable that something ancient and evil had been lurking beneath them, apparently awakened when the mill owners restored operations with the waterwheel.

Jim could not turn off his mind, not even with a good book. He kept rehashing events, going over the timeline, mentally cataloguing the evidence: the heads, the torsos, the clothing. Tomorrow they would know if there was a Provider. Jim had seen the thing in the water. He had reviewed Linda's video over and over. It was human-sized, swam like a human, was humanoid in every way he could see. The cop in him screamed *costume*, that it wasn't a monster but a person playing games with them. But that didn't explain the buzzing in his head, or the itching.

He set aside the book. He realized he had read five pages without registering a single word. Perhaps a walk would help. He wandered out into the garden. The green beans needed picking. He found an empty bucket and started filling it. He was looking forward to a dinner with squeaky beans, as his mother called them. He smelled Linda's perfume before she said a word. She had come out to join him, and together they stripped the vines. They moved on to the carrot patch, where they pulled up the ones peeking above ground. Linda added onions to the bucket, and they found a patch of garlic with a few cloves ready to pull out of the soil.

They sat on the grass, enjoying the smell of the flowers and chives, watching the bees and butterflies flicking about. Linda held out her hand and a large dragonfly lit on her palm. After a moment it flew away, only to be replaced by a monarch butterfly, seeking nectar. Finding none, it, too, left. She leaned into Jim's embrace.

After a long comfortable silence, Jim reached into his pocket. Now was as good a time as any, he figured. He pulled out a small, blue velvet box, not yet opening it, and turned on his stomach, leaning on his elbow, and looked up at her. Should he be old-fashioned? Nah, that wasn't either of them. He sat up, took her hand in his, and looked at her.

"I've got a question for you," he finally said. He found himself flustered and sweaty. He felt like a teenager on his first date. "Linda Collier," he blurted out. "Will you marry me?"

"Yes, oh, yes, yes, yes," she said. And kissed him passionately.

They heard cheering from the library, as Jim slipped the ring on her finger. It was a blue amethyst surrounded by tiny little diamonds. The group inside had set aside their books and were standing at the open windows, openly crying, and smiling and clapping. Jim simply held her tight; he never wanted to let her go. He looked up at the happy group inside and smiled. Joy bubbled up from inside.

CHAPTER FIFTY-NINE

All was quiet once again in Harper's Landing. It was a subtle feeling, as if a great cloud had moved on, letting the sun shine clear and bright once again. The press had gone back to the city; the state forensic lab declared its work completed.

Dr. Brett Michaels was stumped. In all the years he had been a pathologist, he had never failed to find a cause of death. He knew that all nine victims had died from drowning. What he couldn't explain was how they had been decapitated, or why the limbs had been ripped away. He had searched rigorously but found no foreign DNA in any of the wounds. This was especially exasperating, since it would have been easy to declare that someone had let a pet alligator or the like loose in the waters under Harper's Landing and all of Middlewood County, an alligator which had munched on the victims. But he knew from sad experience that at least some of the victims would have DNA left in their wounds from a predator of that sort. These wounds resembled the wounds he saw from industrial accidents where body parts were forcefully torn away.

Dr. Michaels called Jim Burch. He hoped the sheriff might have some answers for him. He was especially interested in the possibility of something mechanical having caused the dismemberment and decapitation, along with deep scratches he found on three of the torsos.

Jim told him about the mill with its large waterwheel. He intentionally did not tell him about the "thing in the pond," as he had taken to thinking of it. Jim wasn't sure when or if he would tell any of the state officials about what he had seen.

"Do you think it's possible the waterwheel or some other mechanical part of the mill might have done this?" asked Michaels.

"Maybe," replied Jim. "According to the locals, all these underground waterways up here are interconnected and connect with the Martin's Way River. You know anyone who might be interested in exploring them?"

"The divers are spooked," replied Michaels. "They refuse to go into those caves again. But I have a crazy idea that won't risk anyone. There's a fella down here who does telemetry on migrating animals. With your permission, I'll ask him if we can use the rubber ducky solution to scope out your waterways."

"The *what*?"

Brett laughed. "He's been tracking some underground waters we have down here in Jefferson City. He puts sensor devices on large rubber duckies, weights them down just a bit so they'll sink but still get washed along in the currents, and then tracks them. It's been successful in tracking where waterways are so new developments don't get built over them."

"Now that's one for the books," said Jim. "Underground rubber duckies with tracking devices. Sure, why not?"

"Would next Monday work for you?" asked Michaels. "We could come up late Sunday, if there's a place to stay overnight, and get started early in the morning. That will give you time to find out if the waterwheel could have done this. Any information you can get from the mill would be helpful."

"I'll let Arthur Willingham know that you will be staying at The Rectory."

"Be sure to let the mill owners know that the victims died of drowning. That's official. I would hate to see them deny you information out of a mistaken belief they had any liability in the deaths of those poor people. See you next Sunday?"

"Alright," said Jim.

Jim called Arthur to inform him of two guests arriving late Sunday. On a whim, he asked if Arthur would like to accompany him to the mill. He wanted to tell Arthur all about the rubber duckies. This had to be shared with someone. Arthur was happy to get out for fresh air and a field trip. He had been in the library for far too long.

The drive to the mill office was short but pleasant. On the way, Jim told Arthur about the duck telemetry. As anticipated, Arthur shared his amusement over the idea of tracking yellow rubber duckies through the underground waterways of Middlewood County.

"Do you suppose they'll let us watch the screen with them?"

"I'd like to see them try to stop us," replied Jim. "I suppose it will just be a blip on a screen. Too bad we can't see the ducks."

Saul Grossman was in his office at the back of the new museum. Once Jim was able to convince him that the mill had no liability for the deaths, Saul relaxed and began describing the restoration process.

When the engineers first inspected the waterwheel, they found that considerable damage had been done to the wooden paddles. The wheel was hoisted out of the water. The first repairs involved riveting steel plates to each paddle, which would retain the original structure while preventing further damage.

To ensure that the wheel would be protected, divers were sent into the Martin's Way River above and below the wheel, where they installed steel mesh grates across the narrowest places in the riverbed to prevent fish from swimming upstream and branches or other debris from similarly impacting the wheel coming downstream. No mention had been made of any connecting tunnels from underground waterways in the region, but they hadn't been looking for them.

When the wheel was lowered back into the river and the brake removed, the engineers noted whirlpools forming on either side of the wheel. They assumed it was the result of the combination of the grates and the increased pull of the steel plates that extended beyond the paddles. Since the pools did not impact the function of the wheel or the mill, they did not think they would ever be a problem.

"What happened when the wheel was first started up again, when it once again powered the mill operation?" asked Arthur.

"I'm not sure what you mean," answered Saul.

"I'm sorry. That wasn't particularly clear. Did anything unexpected happen?"

"That wheel starting up again was noisy as hell. It creaked and groaned so much, I was afraid it was going to break. But apparently that's normal for a wood waterwheel. The engineers tightened up everything, put in some new braces, replaced some of the spokes. It was impressive, watching it. They installed new cog wheels inside to turn the looms, and with the increased power provided by the steel paddles, they were able to add two looms."

"Linda and I were up here a while back," said Jim, "and the looms weren't turning. Sounds like they are going now. Can I call her up here and can the three of us get a tour of the operation?"

"Sure," said Saul. "You give her a call, and I'll let Bull Harper know you want to see the mill in action."

Linda said she would be there in fifteen minutes. Meanwhile, Jim and Arthur strolled outside along the walkway that had been installed on the side of the mill next to the river. They watched the water flowing past the mill, turning the great wheel. Arthur looked around to make sure no one was watching and pulled a large carrot from his pocket. He tossed it into the stream, and they both watched it get pulled into the wheel.

The walkway curved around the mill and stopped just beyond the other side of the wheel. They hurried past the wheel and watched to see if they could spot the carrot. What they saw instead were pieces of carrot bobbing along downstream.

"Well," said Arthur, "I guess that answers part of the question. Something going in there is going to come out less than whole."

Linda arrived a few minutes later, and the three of them followed Bull Harper onto the mill floor. He handed them all headphones to protect their ears from the noise. Four large looms were at work, the shuttles flying back and forth as the large metal shafts flew up and down, powered by treadles at the bottom. Bull led them to the small, soundproofed computer room where all the looms were controlled. Once inside, they were able to remove the headphones.

Bull told them how when the mill was reconditioned and started again, Saul Grossman had decided to put in four new computer-operated looms. He kept the four original looms, now fully restored, operated by human workers. These four were powered by the waterwheel and cog system. The human operators would set the treadles into the slots on long boards which were then lowered or lifted by the cog wheels attached to the waterwheel. It was a complex operation. Grossman had the intricate patterns ordered by his customers made on the human-operated looms. The automated looms wove the solid cloth.

Jim and Linda returned to Morey's for lunch. Arthur was having his brought to him at The Rectory library, where he was preparing Sunday's sermon. The diner was packed for a Friday lunch hour. A tour bus sat out front, and some of the diners were outside at the picnic tables in back that Morey had recently purchased from Charity. They had been found in one of the cottages and restored by Arthur to their original sheen.

Jim and Linda took a small table by the front window, farthest away from the door. They had ordered lunch when a tourist, apparently from a group of seniors up for a tour of the mill, spotted his badge.

"Hey, Sheriff," he said loudly. "Did you ever catch that mass murderer?"

The diner suddenly went silent.

"Wasn't a mass murderer," replied Jim.

"But what about all those dead people?" the man persisted. "I read there were fifteen or twenty people killed up here."

His wife was attempting to shush him, without success.

"It was nine," said Jim, "and they drowned."

"Well, nine's a lot of people, and the papers down south said murdered."

"Sir, you have your facts wrong," said Linda. "And you didn't get that from the papers down south; you got it from some conspiracy site on the internet."

He flushed. "Who are you," he said, "and what makes you think you know everything?"

Jim started to rise, but Linda put her hand on his arm.

"I'm the publisher and editor of the newspaper here, and good friends with most of the publishers down south. The deaths were ruled accidental drownings by the state laboratory at Jefferson City. Now, how about you let us and all these other nice people enjoy their lunch?"

The man flung his napkin on the table, stuck a couple of tens under his coffee cup, and stomped out of the diner. His wife followed him, stopping only to apologize to all and sundry.

"Poor woman," said Jim. "How long do you suppose she's had to put up with that crap?"

"Probably years," replied Linda. "But don't go feeling too sorry for her. She's probably got crap of her own that he has to put up with. I'm guessing they deserve each other."

"You got that right," said the woman at the table next to them. "I've known Joan and Pete for years, and they feed each other like piranhas at a banquet. She'll probably make his life miserable for the rest of the trip. Trouble is that the rest of us will have to put up with it, too."

"I'm sorry about all those young people you folks lost," said the man sitting next to her. "That's gotta hurt, small town like this, where everyone knows everyone else. Please extend our condolences to the parents."

Lunch was split pea soup with ham. Maggie had baked pumpernickel bread early in the morning, and the rich, deep taste was a delightful companion to the thick, filling soup. Jim realized with a start that although it was only the beginning of September, there was a slight nip in the air. Fall would soon arrive.

CHAPTER SIXTY

D r. Brett Michaels and Jenson Olsen, a state geologist, arrived Sunday afternoon and settled into The Rectory. Olsen brought in a blue plastic tub filled with bright yellow rubber ducks, each about six inches in height. Jim had never seen such large versions of the bathtub toy.

"I get them made especially for me," said Jenson. "You should have seen their faces at the plastic mold place in St. Louis when I first asked if they could make them for me. I'm sure to this day they think I'm some pervert."

He was a tall man with a robust laugh and a keen mind. He identified many of the esoteric volumes in Arthur's library as books he had read. Brett Michaels was surprised.

"You've read this mythology stuff?"

"Oh, sure," replied Jenson. "There are blue catfish and flat-head catfish in Missouri that have weighed in at one hundred and seventeen pounds. That one was caught in 1964. And there's a story of a one hundred-fifty-pound catfish being sold at a market in St. Louis in the mid-1800s. These mythologies are almost always based on real critters, so it pays to be familiar with them. I know some divers who refuse to go down near waterwheels or dams in parts of the state because of legends about man-eating catfish."

"Will these ducks show us the underground waterways and where things might float in them?" asked Jim.

"Not the ducks, but the sensor collars we are going to attach to them will let us track them. It's like banding live ducks, only these guys are bigger, so we put the collars around their necks. We have small weights in them, so they sink below the surface but still float in the current. We can watch their progress on the screen."

"I'm wondering how I'm going to write a report explaining how we used rubber duckies to prove how those poor souls got ripped apart," said Brett. "It's serious business, but it's also damned hard not to giggle."

Since Morey's was closed, Arthur had cooked dinner. It was served in The Rectory's dining hall, and Jim was struck at still another skill this man had. The steak was cooked to perfection, the mashed potatoes were fluffy, and the vegetables were fresh. Somehow, he had managed to get an apple pie from Maggie, and Jim and Arthur had the pleasure of watching Brett and Jenson taste it for the first time.

Linda was due back from a visit with her sister in an hour, and Jim was looking forward to spending the rest of the evening and night with her. He planned to invite her along for the ducky tracking the next day. He left shortly after dinner, with plans in place to meet up with the other three in the morning at Morey's for breakfast. They would go to the Jenkins Farm pump house first, and later to Harve's pond.

The others sat at the table, laughing as they fastened sensor collars around the necks of the duckies. Arthur thought they should have names, and the other two agreed. Huey and Louie would be dropped in the Jenkins Farm well; Dewey and Daisy would go into Harve's pond.

"How do you like being a pathologist?" asked Arthur, watching Brett closely.

"Not as much as I thought I would," Brett replied. "I've been at it now for ten years. I went into it because I like a good mystery. But most deaths are no mystery. This is the first real challenge I've had in a long time, and even this is not about how those poor folks died. They all drowned. Well, except for the first one, the one with just the head and foot. That will remain forever a mystery. But all we're going to find out tomorrow is how they were mangled if we're lucky."

"Do you like dealing with people?" asked Arthur. "Or would you rather stick with the silent dead?"

"After ten years, I could stand to have live patients. I'm done with the dead. Do you need a doctor up here?"

Arthur kept his amusement to himself. The town was working its magic again.

"We could use one. People have to go to Harwood to the clinic or hospital, and it's thirty minutes away on a good day. That poor girl who survived the last set of drownings cut her arm on something getting out of the pond, and it would have been nice if she hadn't suffered so long. If we had a clinic here in town, we could take care of people faster."

"What about you?" Brett asked Jenson. "You ever think about maybe teaching or working for a private company?"

"Not up here. I like the big city. We'd miss you, Doc, but you've been getting antsy for the last couple of years. So why not make the move?"

"It would be expensive, equipping a proper clinic and all," said Brett.

"Oh, I imagine the folks around here would help with that," said Arthur. "We're good at fundraising, and the local credit union is quite flexible about making loans."

"I'll think on it," said Brett, already making mental plans for resigning, finding a home up here, and getting a practice started.

Monday morning was sunny, but cool. The duck herders gathered at Morey's for breakfast. Ben came along since he would be going to the waterwheel to be their spotter in case the ducks came out there. Brett and Jenson demanded that Maggie pack up a box of cinnamon rolls for them to take home later, each of them giving her a generous tip. Jen wasn't at work, but Bridgette was scurrying about pouring coffee and taking orders. Jim grinned. Apparently, Cupid had come to Harper's Landing. After breakfast, they piled into Jim's Explorer and headed for the Jenkins Farm. The pump house was still standing, but not for long. Bulldozers had widened the road and were about to take it down as they extended the road to the mill.

Jim called Saul Grossman and asked him to delay the destruction for a few hours.

"We need to see where that well goes to, if it connects with one of the underground waterways," he explained. "If it does, it won't take us more than two hours, I should think."

Grossman called the foreman and told him to work on the other side of the pump house. They could connect the two ends of the road later.

Jenson set up his telemetry equipment, and Huey and Louie were dropped into the well.

Their sensors immediately showed up on the screen, as they floated southwest toward the mill.

At one point, the pair turned west and then northwest for a bit, still progressing toward the mill. Suddenly, the telemetry went dark for both ducks.

Jim took out his cell and called Ben.

"Anything?"

"Oh yeah, great pieces of yellow rubber ducky floating in the whirlpools between the waterwheel and where Mr. Grossman says the southern grating was installed. I had my video going and filmed the ducks as they entered the river. You could barely see the yellow under the surface, and suddenly, they were flying everywhere getting chopped to pieces. I got it all on my phone, Jim."

"Good work," said Jim. "Now, start a new video when I call you. South of the waterwheel this time. We're headed for Harve's pond."

Dewey and Daisy were released into Harve's pond. Jim called Ben and told him to start the video. The duckies sank slowly. On screen it looked as if they were staying in one place. Suddenly, they started moving rapidly to the west and a little south. This pair moved faster than the first two and suddenly disappeared.

Ben called. He reported that the two ducks appeared from the east side of the river, bounced up on one of the whirlpools, started to head south but got caught by another whirlpool and pulled underwater again. He said the ducks were ripped to shreds, with pieces thrown to the south of the wheel.

Brett and Jenson packed up their equipment and prepared for the drive back to Jefferson City. Brett was convinced from what he had seen on the screen, coupled with earlier reports of body parts having been fished out of the northern portion where Dewey and Daisy had met their demise. He would prepare an official report of death by accidental drowning, with postmortem mutilation due to transport of the remains through the underground waterways to the waterwheel. He promised to send Jim a copy of the report, which would initially go to the State Forensics Lab in Jefferson City. Clay Murdoch and Blake Meadows would also get copies of the report.

Brett was certain this would end all further investigation into the area and its residents. He was also certain that he would be one of those residents within the next couple of months. There was no shortage of young doctors who had completed their residency in pathology and would welcome a position in the Missouri State Medical Examiner's Office. Brett would be happy to be done with it.

CHAPTER SIXTY-ONE

The next morning, Jim, Linda, and Arthur left early for Jeremy's cabin. The drive out was short. Jim munched on a cinnamon roll and sipped coffee, letting Arthur do the driving this time. He could not recall how long it had been since he felt this relaxed, this complete.

They pulled up in front of Harve's and slowly walked back to Jeremy's cabin. The lights were on, and Jeremy stood in the open front door.

"I haven't looked," he said. "Like I promised. But I fed it last night, a nice young pig that I was able to shoot from my back porch. Can we go look now, please?"

"Of course," said Jim. "Come with us. Let's do this from outside."

"Wait," said Arthur. "You can shoot now?"

"Yes," replied Jeremy. "I am getting better. I don't know how, but I am."

They walked around back. There on Jeremy's stoop was a woodchuck pelt. It had been gutted, skinned, and cleaned. The feet and head were still attached. The eyes and brain had been removed. It was perfectly prepared for a taxidermist's work.

Jim was upset. He had hoped that the explanation provided

by their telemetry testing would be the real and only explanation. But here was proof, or at least that is what Jeremy would have him believe, that there really was a Provider, namely the *bolotnik*.

Arthur sighed. He looked and sounded sad.

"Spill it, Arthur," said Jim. "What's bothering you?"

"I don't like killing. At least not wanton killing. But this thing? I think it must be killed. Be it a *bolotnik* or a mutation, it needs to be gone, permanently. It would be nice if we could just bring it a deer or a sheep or a pig or whatever on a regular basis. But it has tasted human flesh and bone, and I believe found it desirable above all other prey."

"What are we going to tell Blake and Clay?" asked Harve. "I don't think they would respond well to tales of the *bolotnik* and other Slavic folktales."

They all laughed.

"I think not saying anything is best," said Jim. "And I think you damn well better come up with a solution that involves destroying the beast. Because I don't want them taking *bolotnik* flesh, if that is what it is, down to the state lab. That would be inviting a mob of biologists, anthropologists, and conspiracy nuts to hold a convention at the same time. I don't think The Rectory would survive. I sure as hell don't think the Harwood Best Western could, either."

It was Jeremy who came up with what seemed to be the best solution yet.

"Let's catch it ourselves," he said. "We can get Charity to whip up one of her sleepy time potions. Trust me, that stuff in the right quantity would put an elephant to sleep. And we lace a pig or something equally tasty with it. And then we catch it and burn it."

"That's a good idea," said Jim. "Except for one thing. Where does it go when it pulls them under?"

"I have a variation on Jeremy's suggestion," said Arthur. "Since we know it leaves gifts in exchange for food, why not set up outside Jeremy's back door and dart it when it comes with the gift."

"I like that idea," said Harve. "Then we dispatch it humanely and burn the corpse."

"You do realize no matter how you do it, we cannot tell the state guys," said Jim. "The state forensic lab, together with the state medical examiner, have called the deaths *accidental drownings with coincidental dismemberment due to environmental conditions*. Say that fast three times."

Jim was struck by how composed Jeremy seemed to be every time he saw him. And he was certain his face was looking less scarred and distorted. He returned to the subject at hand.

"Okay," he said. "I can't be part of it. I won't stop you, and I won't arrest you if you tell me you did it. Though I would prefer you keep it to yourselves. You need to get the group together, without me, and discuss it. And you didn't hear this from me, but if you do decide to go ahead, Linda, you need to lose your cell phone. Not just delete the information on it. You need to lose the whole phone."

He went over to the car, got in on the passenger side, and waited for Arthur and Linda to drive back. He was so conflicted. What he had done wasn't strictly illegal, but it sure as hell was extra-legal. This whole damn business had been pushing him right to the edge. He hated it, but he loved these people. He adored and loved Linda. And he wanted the killing to end.

He wanted to get a brandy, make love all afternoon, and pretend that none of this ever happened. He would get his first and last wish if he wanted, but the middle one would have to wait until night. Linda was going to be involved in whatever discussions they had at The Rectory.

Arthur dropped Jim off at his office. He and Linda went on to The Rectory, where they found Charity and Dan hard at work. They briefly told them what had been found. Arthur took out his cell and started working his way down the list, calling people who he knew possessed the gift. He asked them to stay by their phones and be ready if they were needed. Charity and Dan left for Charity's cottage, where they would make the sleeping potion.

Before he left, Dan called in Ben from the back gardens and asked if he would go hunting for them. They wanted something fat and juicy and appealing. If Ben could find someone willing to donate an animal, all the better. But he couldn't tell them why, just that it was to help The Rectory and the families of the victims.

Ben said he knew of a place where a wild boar had recently farrowed. Her babes would be long gone by now, but she might have stayed in the region, given the abundance of food and water.

Ben went to Morey's house, where he borrowed a rifle and ammunition. He called Bull Harper and asked if the big man would help. It would require both of them to lift the sow into and out of the truck. Bull joined him an hour later, and the two set out in search of the sow.

Charity and Dan spent the afternoon preparing the strongest potion they could think of, an attraction potion, something that would cause the *bolotnik* to want more than anything else to come eat the pig. Then they went to work on a liquid potion that could be put into a tranquilizer dart. They had no intention of simply putting the *bolotnik* to sleep. The two agreed that the best course would be a fast-acting paralytic that would kill it within minutes of paralysis setting in. They donned gloves, aprons, and masks, being careful not to splash anything on their clothing. Once it was made, they reluctantly tried a small amount on a family of squirrels out behind Dan's cottage. The one squirrel who was brave enough to nibble the breadcrumbs Dan placed on the ground toppled over within seconds and died a minute or two later.

Fortunately, the veterinarian in Harper's Landing was possessed of a minor gift and had been included from time to time in seasonal rites such as Ostara and Samhain. He was also a regular customer of Charity's since her potions healed most of the common animal ailments faster than modern medicines. He appreciated that she would tell him immediately if a condition was something her remedies would not treat. She called him.

"Gene? I need something from you. It's a huge favor, but I can't ask anyone else."

"Ask away," replied Gene Harcourt. "For you, anything."

"Not on the phone. Can you come up and see me when your day is done?"

"It's done now. No other patients scheduled, nobody in-house, and I've got my cell if there's an emergency. I'll be right up. Your place, right?"

"And Gene? Bring your tranquilizer gun please."

Gene Harcourt had been a vet for nearly twenty years, most of it in Harper's Landing. The area was rural enough to provide him with enough large animal patients to supplement the income from small animal care. He had been drawn to Harper's Landing because of its wonderful fishing and quiet way of life. Shortly after he arrived, the woman who had been the veterinarian for the entirety of Middlewood County and much of Harwood had died in a car accident. Gene and his wife liked the area, and she agreed that he should move his practice from St. Louis to Harper's Landing as soon as possible.

He arrived at Charity's cottage approximately forty minutes after her phone call. He brought a tranquilizer gun and a rifle, along with several traps of varying sizes.

"The traps won't be needed," said Charity, "but we definitely will need the rifle. Does it hold more than one dart? And are they the darts that release a solution into the target?"

"What the hell are you trying to catch?" asked Gene. "A rhinoceros? Or did a triceratops survive the Triassic?"

"I'll explain fully once we get settled," said Charity. "By the way, I don't think you've met Dan, have you?"

"Hi," the young man said, extending a hand. "I'm Dan Balanchuk. Just moved up here from St. Louis."

"Uh, are you ...?" Gene left the question hanging, not knowing quite how to phrase it.

"Yup, I'm a Ukrainian version of Arthur. Not that we have any Ovate Druids in the Slavic tradition. But close enough. Here, let me help you with that stuff."

He took the rifle and carried it into the cottage. Gene and Charity followed him, Gene carrying a case full of various kinds of tranquilizer darts.

"These contain a hypodermic that injects the contents when you shoot the animal," said Gene. "Sometimes I have to tranquilize a bull, and once there was a cougar hunting sheep. There are only seventy-two cougars left in Missouri, so I took it down with a tranquilizer dart full of ketamine, and then we transported him way back into the wilds."

"Does this gun hold darts that have something like hypodermics in them?"

"Exactly. Now tell me what we are doing."

First, they showed him Linda's video. He was shocked.

"Is that what killed those kids and that judge?"

"We believe so," said Dan. "And it's an elemental, a minor one, but an elemental, nevertheless. We can take the time to tell you the whole story, or we can talk about how we plan to take him down and give you the details later."

"Details later, if at all," replied Gene. "Somehow, I get the feeling the less I know, the better for me and the town."

"You are correct."

Charity told him the plan. She showed him the two potions and described their contents. "I don't know anything about those herbs in that *come here* potion," he said. "But those in that other one? They'll kill a horse in those concentrations. You and I had better be damn careful handling it. I think we should fill four darts, two for the rifle, and two for the handgun, if you don't mind. Dan, can you handle a pistol?"

"Yes. I hate them, but all Ukrainian kids must attend weapons training now. Or at least they did before I left. That was pre-Putin. I don't know about now. But yeah, I can handle it."

"Good. Better to have lots of backup. Now, for tissue disposal, we're going to need a hot fire. As you probably know, crematoriums are really hot, and they still have to pulverize the bone after. I think we are going to want to do the same and spread it in separate locations. And I do not think we should put any of the remains in water. He looks like he lives in the water."

Gene glanced at the video and shuddered. He did not want to see that again.

"I think we are going to play it safe and have an exorcism spell ready also, along with a ritual of binding. We will bind each bundle of ash that we bury to that location, and we will spread them as far as we can."

Charity gave him a long, penetrating stare. *He knows far more than he ever let on. How did I miss that?* she wondered. *I need to keep this in mind. I have a feeling we may need him again.*

The three of them prepared the four hypodermics for the darts and fit them carefully into the rifle and the handgun. They then stored them in a locked case, which Dan put in the trunk of his car.

"Where is all this happening?" asked Gene. "And when?"

"Sooner the better," said Charity, "before he gets too hungry. Up at Harve Sanders' pond."

"Harve!" exclaimed Gene. "Is it true what they say? He has a crazy twin brother?"

"Jeremy. And he is not crazy, but he is deformed as the result of a horrible accident."

"Their parents," said Gene. "I heard about that. I'm guessing you have someone fetching a corpse for the *come here* potion?"

"Yeah, we do. We thought we would try tonight just after sunset before it gets dark. If it doesn't respond to the potion, we'll give it the pig and come back tomorrow morning to see if it brought Jeremy a gift."

"Oh man," said Gene. "I definitely do not want to know what

that's about. Just assure me that Jeremy had nothing to do with the murders."

"Of that, we are certain," said Dan. "And Jim is, too."

"The sheriff is in on this?" asked Gene incredulously. "He doesn't strike me as the kind to accept these kinds of mysteries."

"He isn't, not really. He's trying, poor man, but mostly I think he's just open to whatever will stop the killing."

"Which is why you can never talk about this to anyone," said Charity. "Not even your wife."

"Oh, yeah, I can understand that. The media would have a field day with it, not to mention what the state folk would do to Jim, and probably us."

Comprehension suddenly flooded his face. "That's why you want to burn it. No DNA tests. But won't that leave it unsolved?"

"We're working on that. But yes, it probably will. The state pathology lab has ruled all the deaths, even Rory's, as accidental drowning. But you know those two detectives aren't going to let go of the rest so easily."

"What rest?"

"Missing heads. Rory's was the only one ever found. And the less you know about that, the better. Just in case. There's so much to tell you. Is there any way you can stick with us tonight? We're going to need you, probably all night, because I have a hunch that *bolotnik* isn't going to be affected by this *come here* potion, even as strong as I made it. I think we're going to be out behind Jeremy's cabin for most of the night, waiting for it to deliver a gift."

"You're in luck. Kathy is visiting her sister. Baby's about to pop, and Kathy will be there for a few days to help settle them in."

"I know you have lots of question," continued Charity. "As I said earlier, the less you know the better. Just that this thing *talks* to Jeremy and any gifted folks, in their heads. And it's been bringing Jeremy gifts like Rory O'Connor's head and foot. You might want to wear earplugs, unless you want to take your chances on what you might hear."

"This thing isn't going to be easy to kill, is it?" asked Gene.

"I hope so, by all that is holy and good. I hope so," was all Charity said.

⊛

Ben and Bull arrived at Charity's grove at 6:00 PM. They had a large, dead wild sow in the back of Harve's blue pickup truck. By agreement, everyone had gathered at the grove to plan how they would handle the demise of the *bolotnik*. As desperately as she wanted to be a part of dealing with the problem, Linda felt it would be best for her to stay with Jim, in part to ensure that he stayed away, and in part for her protection. The fewer people who knew the details, the better. Bridgette was deemed too young and vulnerable to participate, so she was designated to stay at Morey's.

Jeremy and Harve were insistent on participating, especially with the feeding. Jeremy was certain that if the Provider could not be enticed out of the pond to get the pig, it would not deliver a gift unless Jeremy was the one giving him the pig. No one disputed him.

By 8:00 PM, with approximately an hour of daylight left, Arthur, Ben, Charity, Jen, Bull, Gene, and Dan were ready to make the twenty-minute drive to Harve's pond. The pig had been injected with a full quart of Charity's attraction potion, and all of them were having an extremely hard time avoiding hugging the dead sow and stroking her silken ears.

Bull and Ben drove the pickup truck with the sow; Arthur drove the others in the church van. They took the roundabout route up to County Road 22 and then down to Harve's to avoid driving through downtown. When they arrived, Jeremy and Harve were standing fifteen feet from the edge of the pond closest to the drive.

"This is where I always leave its food," said Jeremy, "unless it *tells* me to shove it into the pond."

Suddenly, they all heard the *bolotnik*'s demand for food. It was like a snarl in their heads, coupled with a strong hunger. It kept getting louder. Ben and Bull hastily opened the tailgate and pulled the sow out. They rolled her to the edge of the pond. Gene and Dan stood ready with rifle and handgun. Charity was the first to spot the bubbles at the center of the pond, and then they all saw the waves rippling toward shore as a grey-green, slimy-looking head approached. When it was close enough to stand up and walk toward shore, they all let out a collective gasp. It ignored them, focused on the fat, juicy sow. Just as it reached her, Arthur yelled "Now!" and Gene shot the *bolotnik* with a dart.

Instead of falling to the ground, paralyzed, it raised up to its full height, six and a half feet, and let out a terrifying howl of rage. As it turned toward them, both Dan and Gene fired again. They were acutely aware there was only one dart left. With any luck, they would not need it.

The *bolotnik* was biting and pulling at the darts. It managed to remove two, but the one from Dan's pistol had lodged in its back where it could not reach. It continued to move out of the pond, heading for the group of people. They were backing up hastily as the monster approached when suddenly it stopped, looked around frantically, and then fell. It no longer moved.

Gene was the first to approach the creature. He had read about *bolotniks* while waiting for the others to arrive. This monster appeared to match the descriptions. Vaguely manlike, it had long, multi-jointed fingers and webbed toes. Its skin was tough and rubbery. The genitalia were male, and what Gene thought were weeds was green hair growing all over its face and head.

"It could be a mutation," said Arthur. "Though it would have most certainly been a human male if it is. And radiation exposure wouldn't do this to a human. You would see open sores, growths, that sort of thing. I wouldn't want to have to testify to this in open court, but I'm ninety percent certain what we have here is a genuine *bolotnik*. And it's not dead."

"How can that be?" asked Charity. "It's been shot full of enough paralytic and poison to kill an elephant."

"It is a full-grown, ancient elemental. It was never going to be easy. And we need to do something soon because it wants to get at me. Apparently *bolotniks* are not particularly fond of shamans."

Harve turned and ran to the back of his cabin. He came back carrying a large axe. He handed it to Bull.

"I think you have more strength than I. Let's see how long it can survive without its head."

"Arthur, are you going to be okay with this?" asked Charity.

"Yes. This creature, whatever it might have been at one time, is pure evil. I'm not even sure how much it eats anymore. It seems to thrive on killing. Even now, paralyzed as it is, I can feel its desire to kill us radiating from its mind. It is ... terrible."

Bull raised the axe, but Harve stopped him before he could swing.

"Put something under the neck," he said. "Like one of those log cuts over there that I use for pathways; stepping logs I call them."

Gene was keeping a close watch on the *bolotnik*, ready to pump the last dart into it if necessary. Dan fetched one of the thick tree rounds from the pile Harve had pointed to, and he and Bull lifted the *bolotnik*'s head by its hair. It was slimy and gross, and both men looked like they wanted to hurl. Harve shoved the wood underneath its neck. Bull again raised the axe and forcefully brought it down. The head flew across the drive as green ichor poured out of the wound. The stench was horrid, and they all gagged and vomited.

Jeremy and Harve had prepared a bonfire behind Jeremy's cabin. They had cleared out the brush and laid a bed of kindling mixed with dried tree bark. They then made a stack of larger logs three feet high. They left it open in the center, so the monster could be thrown in.

Arthur wanted the head kept as far away from the body as possible. He supervised as Charity and Dan pulled on gloves, put the head in a large canvas bag, and tied it shut. Bull and Harve chopped the arms and legs off, and after putting on gloves and making sure their sleeves were tucked inside them, they picked up the pieces and put them in several buckets Jeremy had brought out. The torso was last, placed on a tarp and pulled back to the bonfire by Harve and Gene. For good measure, Gene fired the fourth and final dart into the torso.

They burned the head first. The canvas bag caught fire and then a bright green flame shot up through the stack of logs they had carefully laid in a triangle, zigzag fashion. The stench of burning flesh was blessedly wafted into the woods by an early evening easterly breeze. Once they were sure it had thoroughly burned, Jeremy used a small, long-handled shovel to pull the skull out of the pyre. Arthur carried it far away from the others to a cement slab where Harve and Jeremy stacked their firewood. He placed the surprisingly small skull on the concrete and repeatedly bashed it with a sledgehammer he found leaning up against the house.

While that was going on, the others burned the rest of the body, piece by piece. Once Arthur had swept up the remains of the skull, the other bones were brought to the slab and broken up by Dan and Bull. Arthur and Charity took the bag holding the skull's bone powder deep into the woods. They dug a hole three feet deep and dropped the powder in. After they had partially covered it with dirt, Arthur found a large fern nearby. They carefully dug it up and planted it in what was left of the hole.

It took approximately two hours to burn, pulverize, and bury the rest of the *bolotnik*. After the bag used to carry the bone fragments and powder had burned, they let the fire burn itself out and carefully removed all the remaining ashes and buried them deep in the woods, far away from the skull. They returned to find that Jeremy and Harve had stacked wood and kindling and set it alight. However, this fire was at the edge of the pond, and they could see that the two men were wisely burning all of the blood shed during the dismembering. Arthur and Dan joined them in digging up the bloodied soil and throwing it on the blazing fire. They would check again in daylight to be sure it had all been disposed of. Each of them pulled off their soiled clothing and threw it into the fire.

They had all brought clean clothing, in case they got soiled. There was no sense in taking any chances. Once they were dressed, they got chairs or logs to sit on. They all sat in silence, staring into the flames. Harve went inside his house and returned with root beer for everyone. Arthur cleared his throat.

"We have destroyed something evil, tonight. But we must not forget that it may not have always been evil. The legends tell us, which Dan has confirmed, that *bolotniks* were once men who dwelt among us like other men. They suffered great loss; loss so strong that they turned their sorrow and grief on the path of revenge. What we saw tonight wasn't just the result of a *bolotnik* brought to a place so foreign to him that it changed him. It was also the result of generations of revenge, of killing, and of sorrow. Please join me in remembering who he once was. The Great Ones will remember, and so should we."

Mother of the East
Father of the West
Brother of the North
Sister of the South

We call upon you to take into your company the soul of this one, so lost to evil, so riddled by pain, so poisoned by sorrow and hate. Cleanse him, Great Ones, and welcome him into the company of the immortals if it be Your will.

Great Guardians of us all, we ask that you cleanse us and forgive us for our part in his sending. We hereby vow that the deeds done this night were done in our role as guardians and protectors. Cleanse from us all anger, all desire for revenge, and accept our humble gratitude for the blessings you send us daily.

This do we swear, by blood and by tears.

Arthur pricked his thumb and let a drop of blood sizzle in the fire. Tears streamed down his cheeks. Each of the others did the same, each repeating as they added their drop of blood to the fire, "This do I swear, by blood and by tears."

Charity went last. As her words ended, the clouds parted and a brilliant full moon shone down on them. They sat in the moonlight, silently watching the fire slowly burn until it was completely extinguished. They returned to their homes in silence.

CHAPTER SIXTY-TWO

J im and Linda's official engagement party was held in mid-September. Charity and Jen had brought out all the tables they could find, picked every summer flower still blooming, and badgered Morey and Maggie for pies and cakes and cookies. Dan brought out his computer and set up a music channel, and Lonnie Camby hooked up speakers.

The good people of Harper's Landing were ready for some fun. Even the parents of the seven dead children were there, if a bit more subdued than the other partygoers.

There were games for the children, a dance area for the teenagers, a liquor table watched over with an eagle eye by Ben Jenkins, and enough fried chicken to keep roosters all over the county busy replenishing the coops for weeks to come.

As the sun set and people began to don sweaters or light jackets against the evening chill, Arthur stood and proposed a toast.

"First, let us drink to absent friends. Their memories will live on for all our days, and their presence among us, no matter how long or short, brings joy to us all."

"Hear, hear," said the crowd.

"Next, TO JIM AND LINDA! May you have a long and

happy life together—that is, if you two ever get around to setting a date."

There was laughter all around, and cheers. Jim and Linda both blushed, and then Jim stood. Everyone grew silent.

"The luckiest day of my life was the day I drove in to Harper's Landing," he said. "Little did I know how much my life would change. I'm a big city boy, born and bred. If someone had told me ten years ago that I would be living in a small town and loving it, I would have said they were crazy. Yet here I am. You have all taught me the meaning of community, of compassion, of caring, and of love. This has been a tough summer, yet here you all are, ready to celebrate love. And that is a precious gift. One we must never lose.

"Linda and I have an announcement, but first, Dan and Jen have one of their own."

Dan and Jen stood. Bridgette's eyes grew big. *They're going to do it,* she thought. *I know they're going to do it.*

Jen held up her left hand, back toward the crowd. There was a gasp as people saw her ring, and then cheers erupted. Jim lifted his glass in a toast to them, and everyone drank and cheered.

"We've decided we'd like to do a double wedding," said Linda. "The four of us have set a date for June eighth, when all these lovely trees will be in full bloom. Maggie will be doing the cake—and yes, it will be cake, not pie. But don't worry," she said.

"Everyone in town is invited," said Jen, taking up the conversational thread. "Including all the kids, *especially* all the kids. And Arthur will be presiding. And since school has just started, the high school choir will have plenty of time to practice whatever music they want to surprise us with."

"As long as it's not 'Need a Little Sugar in My Bowl,'" muttered Jim.

Linda deftly elbowed him in the ribs. The high school choir was grinning and cheering, and from the looks on some of their faces Jim had been right to voice a bit of concern.

The party lasted until late in the night. Parents took their weary children home to bed, while the older teens and adults with no kids sat and chatted, ate pie, drank Harve's root beer, and relaxed. Finally, it was time for everyone to leave. Charity and Jen promised Maggie they would bring the dishes down first thing in the morning.

Jim and Linda drove home to Linda's house. Jim realized it was probably time to settle where they would live, move in, and sell the other house. But that would be tomorrow's discussion. He had other ideas for the rest of the night.

Jen and Dan sat in the quiet clearing, watching the leaves slowly drop off the trees. Winter was coming soon. They would continue to read the diaries so that Dan could incorporate the history and observations of the immigrants into his doctoral thesis. Jen planned to sew dresses for herself, Linda, and all the attendants. Charity was looking forward to long hours in front of her fireplace with books she had put off reading.

As Jen and Dan stood to go into the cottage they now shared, Jen thought she saw movement out of the corner of her eye. It looked like a man, dressed in brown and green, with long limbs, moving away from the edge of the orchard nearest the clearing. She looked again, closer, but saw nothing.

She shrugged. *Probably a trick of the lights,* she thought.

They turned off the lights in the clearing, brought the computer inside, and happily snuggled under the quilt they had unearthed a month ago and restored to its glorious beauty.

All was quiet in Harper's Landing, for now.

THE END

ABOUT THE AUTHOR

A reclusive author and a teacher of 20 years, Shoshana Edwards lives in the Pacific Northwest with her husband, books, massive garden, and multiple cats. She is a lifelong lover of the mysterious, unknown, and fantasy hidden in everyday life.

OTHER TITLES FROM THE PRINCE OF CATS LITERARY PRODUCTIONS

If you liked *Deathly Waters*, you might also enjoy:

MacGyver:
Meltdown
Eric Kelley & Lee Zlotoff

Or Even Eagle Flew
Harry Turtledove

Seventh Age:
Dawn
Rick Heinz

White Fang Law:
This Case is Gonna Kill Me, Book 1
by Melinda M. Snodgrass

Made in the USA
Middletown, DE
09 October 2021